GRAND HOTEL

'A fine and even brilliant novel . . . un-usually exciting and most vividly told. After reading the book, indeed, you feel you must recently have been spending the last week or two at the Grand Hotel, Berlin, and keeping your eyes wide open.' —*Sunday Times*.

'Reading, we know what all the charac-ters looked like. We know their minds as well as their clothes. We know how they appear to themselves and how they appear to one another . . .'—*News Chronicle*.

'. . . done with acid and relentless per-ception and with a quite extraordinary tenderness of heart.'—*The Observer*.

GRAND HOTEL

VICKI BAUM

UNABRIDGED

PAN BOOKS LTD : LONDON

First published 1930 by Geoffrey Bles Ltd.
This edition published 1948 by Pan Books Ltd.,
33 Tothill Street, London, S.W.1

ISBN 0 330 02895 2

2nd Printing (Re-set) 1962
3rd Printing 1972

Translated from the German
by BASIL CREIGHTON

Printed in Great Britain by
Richard Clay (The Chaucer Press), Ltd., Bungay, Suffolk

THE HALL Porter was a little white about the gills as he came out of No 7 box. He went for his cap which he had left on the radiator.

"What was it?" asked the operator at the switchboard, earphones over his head and the red and green stops between his fingers.

"They've taken my wife to the hospital all of a sudden. I don't know at all what that means. She says it's beginning. But, good heavens! it can't have got that far."

The operator was only half listening. He had a call to put through. "Well, don't worry, Herr Senf," he said. "You'll have a fine boy first thing in the morning——"

"Thank you, anyway, for calling me to the phone here. I can't go shouting about my private affairs over there at my desk. Duty is duty."

"Just so. And when the baby's there I'll ring through," said the operator absentmindedly and carried on with his calls. The porter took his cap and went off on tiptoe. He did this unconsciously because his wife had been brought to bed and was about to have a child. As he crossed the passage, where the silent reading- and writing-rooms had half their lights switched off, he let out a deep breath and ran his fingers through his hair. He was surprised to find them wet, but there was no time to wash his hands. After all, the routine of the hotel could not be upset because Hall Porter Senf's wife was expecting a baby.

The music from the tea room in the new building beat in syncopation from mirror to mirror along the walls. It was dinner-time and a smell of cooking was in the air, but behind the closed doors of the large dining-room there was still silence and vacancy. The Chef, Mattoni, was setting out his cold buffet in the small white room. The porter felt a strange weakness in his knees and he stopped for a moment in the doorway, arrested by the bright gleams of the coloured lights behind the

5

blocks of ice. In the corridor an electrician was kneeling on the floor, busied over some repair to the wires. Ever since they had had those powerful lights to illuminate the hotel frontage there had always been something going wrong with the overworked installation of the hotel. The porter pulled himself together and went back to his post. Little Georgi meanwhile had taken charge. Georgi was the son of the proprietor of a large hotel business who wanted to see his son work his way up from the ranks. Senf, feeling somewhat oppressed, made his way straight across the Lounge, where there was now a throng of movement. Here the jazz band from the tea room encountered the violins from the Winter Garden, while mingled with them came the thin murmur of the illuminated fountain as it fell into its imitation Venetian basin, the ring of glasses on tables, the creaking of wicker chairs and, lastly, a soft rustle of the furs and silks in which women were moving to and fro. A cool March air came in gusts through the revolving doors whenever the pageboy passed guests in or out.

"All right," said little Georgi in English as Senf finally dropped anchor at the porter's desk. "Here's the seven o'clock post. 68 has been making a row because her chauffeur wasn't there on the tick. Rather a hysterical lady, eh?"

"68—that's Grusinskaya," said the Hall Porter, and began to sort the letters with his right hand. "That's the dancer. We know her—for eighteen years past. She gets a fit of nerves every night before she goes on the stage, and then she makes a row."

A tall gentleman in the Lounge got up stiffly out of an easy chair and came with bent head towards the porter's desk. He loitered for a bit round the Lounge before approaching the entrance hall. The impression he made was emphatically one of listlessness and boredom as he glanced at the magazines displayed on the little bookstall and lit a cigarette. Finally, however, he fetched up beside the porter and asked casually, "Any letters for me?"

The porter knew his cue in this little comedy. He looked in pigeonhole No 218 before he replied: "Not this time, Herr Doktor." Whereupon the tall gentleman slowly set himself in

6

motion again. After coasting round to his chair he sank down into it stiff-legged, and then stared blindly out into the Lounge. His face, it must be said, consisted of one half only, in which the sharp and ascetic profile of a Jesuit was completed by an unusually well-shaped ear beneath the sparse grey hair on his temples. The other half of his face was not there. In place of it was a confused medley of seams and scars, crossing and over-lapping, and among them was set a glass eye. "A Souvenir from Flanders," Doctor Otternschlag was accustomed to call it when talking to himself.

He sat there for a while surveying the gilded stucco capitals of the marble pillars, a sight he was heartily sick of, and star-ing his fill with unseeing eyes into the Lounge, which was now emptying fairly quickly as the theatres opened. Then he got up once more and stumped across with his marionette gait to the porter's desk, where Herr Senf, putting aside his private affairs, was now officiating with zeal.

"No one asked for me?" Doctor Otternschlag inquired as he glanced at the glazed mahogany board where the porter put notes and messages.

"No one, Herr Doktor."

"Telegram?" asked Doctor Otternschlag after a moment. Herr Senf obligingly looked once more in pigeonhole 218, though he knew very well there was nothing in it.

"Not today, Herr Doktor," and added, with a touch of human kindness, "Perhaps Herr Doktor would like to go to the theatre. I have a stall for Grusinskaya—at the Theater des Westens."

"Grusinskaya? No thanks!" said Doctor Otternschlag and wandered off through the entrance hall and back round the Lounge to his chair. So Grusinskaya doesn't sell out any more, he thought meanwhile. Not surprised. Know *I'll* never go to see her again. He settled down miserably in his chair.

"That man's enough to drive one silly," said the porter to little Georgi. "Everlastingly asking for letters. Every year for ten years he's spent a month or two here, and not a letter has he ever had, and not even a dog has ever asked for him. And there he sits about just the same and waits . . ."

7

"Who's waiting?" asked Rohna, the head reception clerk, from the bureau near by, sticking up his bright red head over the low glass partition. But the porter did not reply. He thought he had just heard his wife cry out and he strained his ears. Then he had to dismiss his private cares again, and help little Georgi unravel some complicated train connections in Spanish for the Mexican gentleman in Room No 117. Pageboy No 24, with red cheeks and well-plastered hair, shot across from the lift and called out excitedly—too loud for the dignity of the Lounge—"Baron Gaigern's chauffeur!" Rohna raised an admonitory and repressive hand like a conductor. The porter passed on the order for the chauffeur by telephone. Georgi opened eyes of boyish expectation. There was a smell of lavender and expensive cigarettes, immediately followed by a man whose appearance was so striking that many heads were turned to look at him. He was unusually tall and extremely well dressed and his step was as elastic as a cat's or a tennis champion's. He wore a dark blue trenchcoat over his dinner-jacket and this was scarcely correct perhaps, but it gave an attractively negligent air to his appearance. He patted Pageboy No 24 on his sleek head, stretched out his arm, without looking, over the porter's table for a handful of letters which he put straight into his pocket, taking out at the same time a pair of buckskin gloves. With a friendly nod to the head reception clerk he put on his dark felt hat, took out his cigarette case and put a cigarette between his lips. The next moment he removed his hat and stood aside to allow two ladies to pass before him through the revolving door. It was Grusinskaya, a small slim figure in a fur coat followed by a vague and self-effacing being with two cases in her hands. When the commissionaire at the entrance had stowed these two in their car the engaging gentleman in the blue raincoat lit his cigarette, put his hand in his pocket for a coin to give Pageboy No 11 who was working the revolving door, and disappeared through its whirligig of reflected lights with the blissful air of a young fellow going out on the spree.

As soon as this charming Baron Gaigern had forsaken the Lounge it suddenly became still, and the illuminated fountain

8

could be heard falling into its Venetian basin with a cool and gentle murmur. The reason was that the Lounge was now empty, the jazz band in the tea room had stopped, the music in the dining-room had not begun and the Viennese Trio in the Winter Garden was having a pause. The sudden stillness was broken only by the agitated and persistent hooting of cars as they passed the hotel entrance and were lost again in the night life of the town. Within, however, the Lounge was as still as if Baron Gaigern had taken the music, the noise and the murmur of voices away with him.

Little Georgi jerked his head towards the revolving door and said: "He's all right. Nothing wrong with him." The Hall Porter shrugged his shoulders with the air of a man who knows his fellow men. "Whether he's all right remains to be seen. He's a bit—I don't know. He's too much of the fine fellow for me. The side he puts on and the tips he gives. It seems a bit queer to me. And whoever travels nowadays to throw his money about, unless he's a swindler? If I were Pilzheim I'd keep my eyes open."

Rohna, the head reception clerk, whose ears were always on the alert, looked up again over the glass partition. The blue-white skin of his head gleamed beneath his thin reddish hair. "That will do, Senf," he said. "Gaigern's all right. I know him. He was at school with my brother in Feldkirch. There's no need to put Pilzheim on to *him*." (Pilzheim was the detective employed by the Grand Hotel.)

Senf saluted and was respectfully silent. Rohna knew what he was talking about. Rohna was a count himself, one of the Silesian Rohnas, an ex-officer, and a good fellow. Senf saluted once again, and Rohna's greyhound face was withdrawn. It was now to be detected only as a shadow behind the frosted glass.

Doctor Otternschlag behind in his corner had sat almost erect as long as the Baron was to be seen in the Lounge. Now he was hunched together again, more forlorn than before. He raised his elbow to empty half a glass of cognac without even a glance at it as he did so. His thin tobacco-stained hands hung down between his parted knees as though they were encased in

9

lead. He looked between his long patent-leather shoes at the carpet that everywhere covered the stairs, passages and corridors of the Grand Hotel; he was sick of its straggling pattern of yellow pineapples mingled with brown foliage on a raspberry-red ground. Everything was so dead. The Lounge was dead. Everyone had gone out to his business or pleasures or vices, and had left him to sit there alone. The woman attendant in the cloakroom suddenly came into view across the deserted Lounge. She stood behind the empty racks in the entrance hall and combed back the thin hair on her old head with a black comb. The porter left his compartment and shot straight across with unseemly haste to the telephone-room. He appeared to have something on his mind—this porter. Doctor Otternschlag looked for his cognac and found it gone. "Shall we go up and lie down for a bit?" he asked himself. A light flush came into his cheeks and disappeared again as though he had betrayed a little secret of his own. "Yes," he replied to his own question, but he did not get up. Even for this he was too listless. He merely raised one yellow-stained finger. Rohna from the far side of the Lounge observed it and with a scarcely visible nod wafted a pageboy to the doctor.

"Cigarettes, newspapers," Otternschlag said dully. The pageboy darted across to the cataleptic lady at the bookstall (Rohna looked with disfavour at this lively exhibition of youthful exuberance), and then Otternschlag took the papers and cigarettes that the pageboy had selected for him. When he paid he put the money on the plate, not into the boy's hand. He always set a distance between himself and others, though he was not aware of it. The half of his mouth that was still intact even smiled after a fashion as he unfolded the papers and began to read. He expected something of them that never came, just as no letter, telegram or caller ever came; he was dismally alone, empty, cut off from life. Sometimes when he was alone he confided this fact to himself aloud. It's a ghastly business, he often muttered, gazing on the stretches of raspberry-red carpet and shuddering at himself. It's ghastly. This is no life. No life at all. But where is there any life? Nothing happens. Nothing goes on. Boring. Old. Dead. Ghastly. Every object around him was a sham. Whatever he took up turned to dust. The world was a crumbling affair not to be grasped or held. You fell from vacancy to vacancy. You carried about a sack of darkness inside you. Doctor Otternschlag lived in the most utter loneliness—although the earth is full of people like him. . . .

He found nothing in the papers to satisfy him. A typhoon, an earthquake, some petty war between blacks and whites. Arson, murder, political strife. Nothing. Too little. Scandals, panic on the Bourse, colossal fortunes lost. What did it matter to him? How could it affect him? Ocean flights, speed records, sensational headlines. Each page screamed louder than the last till finally you heard none of them. The noise and bustle nowadays made you blind and dead and deadened all sensation. Pictures of nude women, of legs, breasts, hands, teeth, surged up before him. Doctor Otternschlag had had women in his earlier days. He still remembered it; but without emotion; the memory occasioned only a faint creeping chill in his spine. He let the papers fall in disorder from his tobacco-stained fingers on to the pineapple carpet—so boring and utterly meaningless were they. No, nothing happens, nothing at all, he muttered. He had once possessed a little Persian cat, called Gurba. Ever since she forsook him for a common street tom he had been obliged to carry on his dialogues with himself.

Just as he was steering a roundabout course for the porter's desk to get the key of his room, the revolving door discharged an extraordinary individual into the entrance hall.

"Heaven help us, here he comes again!" the Hall Porter said to little Georgi and turned his best NCO's gaze upon the new arrival. He was certainly not the sort of person you would expect to see in the hall of the Grand Hotel. He wore a cheap new bowler hat that was too large for him and only prevented by his projecting ears from coming even farther down over his face. His face was yellowish, and he had a thin and timid nose which was retrieved by an aggressive moustache. He was clothed in a tight, much-worn and sadly unfashionable overcoat of a grey-green shade, blacked boots that looked too large for his small stature and showed too much of their tops below

11

his short black trousers. He wore grey cotton gloves and grasped a suitcase. It was much too heavy for him and he held it against his stomach with both hands. Besides this he had a bulky brown-paper parcel clapped under one arm. His whole appearance was comic and pitiful, and he was clearly in the last stages of exhaustion. Pageboy No 24 certainly made an attempt to relieve him of his imitation leather suitcase, but the man would not give it up and his embarrassment seemed to be increased by this officious attention. He did not put his case down till he had reached Herr Senf's box, and then after pausing to get his breath he made a sort of bow and said in a high-pitched, rather pleasant voice: "My name is Kringelein. I've been here twice already. I want to inquire again."

"Will you please inquire over there; but I don't think there is a room free," said the porter and pointed towards Rohna. "The gentleman has been waiting two days for a room here," he said in explanation over the glass partition. Rohna, who had taken in the whole situation without a glance, made a polite and fleeting pretence of looking through the pages of his register, and then said: "Unfortunately we are full for the moment. Extremely sorry——"

"Still full? I see. Well, where am I to find a room, then?"

"You might look round near the Friedrichstrasse Station. There are a number of hotels there. . . ."

"No, no, thanks." He took a pocket handkerchief and wiped the moisture from his brow. "I went to one of those on arriving. That's not what I want. I want a really first-class hotel." He took a damp umbrella from under his left arm and at this the bulky parcel slipped from the grasp of his right and disclosed a few dry and crumbling pieces of bread and butter. Count Rohna suppressed a smile. Georgi turned away and gazed at the keys hanging from the board. Pageboy No 17 gathered up the parched fragments with irreproachable composure, and with trembling fingers the man stuffed them into his pocket. He took off his hat and put it down in front of Rohna on the office counter. His forehead was high and wrinkled and his temples pinched and blue. For a moment he

12

blinked with very clear blue eyes behind the pince-nez that looked as though they would slip off his thin nose. "I want a room here. There must be rooms free here sometimes. Will you please reserve me the first one that's vacant? This is the third time I have come, and you will agree that that is not very pleasant. You can't always be full up."

Rohna shrugged his shoulders with an air of regret. For a moment there was silence. The music could be heard in the red dining-room; also the jazz band, now performing in the yellow pavilion. A few of the guests had reassembled in the Lounge and some of them looked across at this strange personage with a mixture of amusement and surprise.

"Do you know Herr Generaldirektor Preysing? He always stops here when he comes to Berlin. Well, I want to stop here too. I have something important—an important conference with—with Preysing. I was to meet him here as a matter of fact. He particularly recommended me to take a room here. I was to refer you to him. I refer you to Herr Generaldirektor Preysing. So now please, when will there be a room vacant?"

"Preysing? Generaldirektor Preysing?" asked Rohna, looking across to Senf.

"From Fredersdorf. Of the Saxonia Cotton Company. I'm from Fredersdorf too," the man put in.

"Why, yes," said the porter, consulting his memory, "there is a Herr Preysing who's been here once or twice."

"I believe he has a room booked for tomorrow or the day after," Georgi whispered officiously.

"Perhaps you would be good enough to look in again tomorrow, when Herr Preysing is here. He arrives tonight," said Rohna after he had turned the pages of his register and come upon the reservation of the room.

Very surprisingly this news seemed to fill the man with some consternation.

'Arrives today?" he exclaimed as though in alarm, and his voice grew a little shriller. "Good. Then he comes tonight. Good. And there's a room for him. Then there are rooms to be had. Yes, and why should Herr Generaldirektor have a room and not I? What does that mean? I shall not put up with it!

13

What's that? Reserved in advance you say? Well, so did I. This is the third time I have been here. The third time, if you please, I have lugged this heavy bag along here. It's raining. Every bus overcrowded. I am not in good health, I may tell you. And how many more times am I to make this journey? What's that? That's no way to talk. Is this the best hotel in Berlin? Yes? Well, then I want to stop in the best hotel in Berlin. Is it forbidden?" he looked from one to another. "I'm tired," he added. "I am tired out." His fatigue was obvious, and so was his ridiculous effort to express himself in correct style.

Suddenly Doctor Otternschlag intervened in the discussion. He had been standing nearby all this while, with the key of his room in his hand, resting his sharp elbows on the edge of the porter's desk.

"The gentleman can have my room if it's a matter of such importance," said Otternschlag. "It is utterly indifferent to me where I stay. Send his things up. I can move out. My boxes are packed. They're always packed. Do as I say, please. You can see the man's deadbeat and ill," he added, to forestall an objection which Count Rohna was about to bring forward with the eloquently gesticulating hands of a conductor.

"But, Herr Doktor," said Rohna quickly, "there can be no question of your giving up your room. Let me have another look. Let me see—— If the gentleman will be so good as to enter his name. Thank you—No 216, then," he said to the Hall Porter.

The Hall Porter gave Pageboy No 11 the key of No 216. The newcomer took the pen which was handed to him and in a curiously flowing handwriting wrote his name in the visitors' book.

"Otto Kringelein, Book-keeper. Fredersdorf, Saxony, born at Fredersdorf, 14-7-1882."

"There we are then," he said with a sigh of relief as he turned and blinked with wide-open eyes into the Lounge.

So there he stood in the Lounge of the Grand Hotel—Otto Kringelein, book-keeper, born at Fredersdorf and residing in Fredersdorf. He stood there in his old overcoat, and the glasses

14

of his pince-nez eagerly devoured it all. He was as deadbeat as
the winner of a race when he breasts the tape, but he saw the
marble pillars with stucco ornament, the illuminated fountain,
the easy chairs. He saw men in dress coats and dinner jackets,
smart cosmopolitan men. Women with bare arms, in wonderful
clothes, with jewellery and furs, beautiful, well-dressed women.
He heard music in the distance. He smelt coffee, cigarettes,
scent, whiffs of asparagus from the dining-room and the
flowers that were displayed for sale on the flower stall. He felt
the thick red carpet beneath his black leather boots and this
perhaps impressed him most of all. Kringelein slid the sole of
his boot gingerly over its pile and blinked. The Lounge was
brilliantly illuminated and the light was delightfully golden;
also there were bright red-shaded lights against the walls and
the jets of the fountain in the Venetian basin shone green. A
waiter flitted by carrying a silver tray on which were wide
shallow glasses with a little dark-gold cognac in each, and in
the cognac ice was floating; but why in Berlin's best hotel were
the glasses not filled to the brim?

One of the porters carrying the wretched suitcase woke
Kringelein from his trance. Pageboy No 11 conducted him
to the morose one-armed man who worked the lift, and he was
conveyed upwards.

Rooms No 216 and No 218 were the worst in the hotel.
Doctor Otternschlag occupied Room No 218 partly because he
was staying *en pension*, partly because his means were moder-
ate, chiefly, however, because he was too apathetic to demand
a better. Room No 216 was at right angles to it, and the two
rooms were wedged in between the service lift on the back
stairs and the bathroom of the third floor. The waterpipes
sucked and bubbled in the wall. Kringelein, after being led past
groups of palms in pots, bronze chandeliers and pictures of
dead game into ever drearier recesses of the hotel, slowly and
dejectedly entered the room that an old and ugly chambermaid unlocked. "No 216," said the pageboy as he set the case
down and waited for a tip. Receiving none, he abandoned the
speechless Kringelein. Kringelein sat on the edge of the bed
and surveyed the room.

15

The room was long and narrow. It had one window. It smelt of stale cigar smoke and damp cupboards. The carpet was thin and worn. The furniture—Kringelein ran his fingers over it—was just polished nut-wood. There was furniture like that in Fredersdorf. A portrait of Bismarck hung over the bed. He had nothing against Bismarck, but he too was on the walls at home. He had expected other pictures over the beds in the Grand Hotel—gay, luxurious, something out of the common, something cheerful. He went to the window and looked out. There was a blaze of light below, for the glass roof of the Winter Garden spanned the court. Opposite a blank wall shut off the sky. A lukewarm and distressing smell of cooking steamed up. Kringelein felt a sudden nausea and supported himself on both hands over the washstand. The fact is, I'm not quite well, he thought sadly.

He sat down again on the faded bed cover and his sense of oppression increased with every moment. I shall not stay here, he thought. No, I shall not stay here in any case. This is not what I came for. It would not be worth while doing all I've done for this. This is no way to begin. I should be wasting my time in a room like this. They are deceiving me. They have plenty of better rooms than this in their hotel. Preysing does not have a room like this. Preysing would not stand it. He would make a row and they'd soon sit up. Fancy giving Preysing a room like this. No, I shall not stay here. Kringelein broke off his reflections and collected himself. He waited a few minutes. Then he rang for the chambermaid and made a row.

When it is considered that this was the first time in his life he had ever made a row, it must be admitted that he did not do so badly. The white-aproned chambermaid, in alarm, brought on to the scene a superior with no apron. The floor valet stood by in the offing and a bedroom waiter, balancing a tray of cold food on the palm of his hand, listened at the door. Rohna was consulted by telephone and requested Herr Kringelein's presence in the office. A director, one of the four directors, had to be summoned. Kringelein, obstinate now he had run amok, insisted that he required a superior and beautiful and expensive room, at the very least a room like Preysing's.

He seemed to think the name of Preysing was a name to conjure with. He had not yet taken off his overcoat. His trembling hands clutched the old crumbling Fredersdorf provisions, while he blinked his eyes and demanded an expensive room. He was exhausted and ill and ready to cry. For some weeks past he had begun to cry very easily for physical reasons connected with his health. Suddenly, just as he was about to give in, he won the day. He was given Room No 70, a first-floor suite with sitting-room and bath, fifty marks a day. "Good," he said, "with a bathroom? Does that mean that I can have a bath whenever I like?" Count Rohna without a tremor said that that was so. Kringelein moved in for the second time.

Room No 70 was the right thing. It had mahogany furniture, a cheval glass, silk upholstery, a carved writing-table, lace curtains and a picture of pheasants on the wall. Also a silk down quilt on the bed. Kringelein incredulously felt its lightness, its smoothness and its warmth three times in succession. On the writing-table stood a most superior bronze inkstand in the form of an eagle whose jagged outstretched wings sheltered two empty inkpots.

Outside the window there was a chill March rain, a smell of petrol and the sound of motor traffic. Opposite, an electric sign in red, blue and white letters occupied the whole façade. As soon as it had run along to the end it began again at the beginning. Kringelein watched it for six minutes. Down below in the street there was a medley of black umbrellas, light-coloured stockings, yellow buses and arc lights. There was even a tree that spread its branches not far from the hotel, but its branches were very different from those in Fredersdorf. This Berlin tree had a little island of soil in the midst of the asphalt and round the plot of soil there was a railing as though it needed some protection against the town. Kringelein, surrounded by so much that was strange and overwhelming, found something friendly in this tree. Next he stood for a while in perplexity over the unfamiliar mechanism of the nickel bath taps, but suddenly it began to work and warm water shot out over his hands. He got undressed. He found it rather disconcerting to bare his delicate wasted body in the full light of

17

the brightly tiled room. But finally he lay for over a quarter of an hour in the water and felt no more pain. The pains that had pursued him for weeks past had suddenly left him; and he certainly wanted no more of them during the time that lay ahead. . . .

At about ten o'clock in the evening Kringelein was strolling round the Lounge, resplendent in a black coat, tall stiff collar and a readymade black tie. He was not at all tired now. On the contrary he was possessed by a feverish excitement and impatience. Now it's beginning, he kept thinking to himself, while his slender shoulders twitched like those of a restless dog. He bought a flower and stuck it in his buttonhole, slid his feet blissfully over the raspberry-coloured carpet and complained to the porter that there was no ink in his room. A pageboy conducted him to the writing-room. Kringelein was no sooner confronted by the rows of vacant writing-tables, discreetly lighted by green-shaded electric lamps, than his confident bearing deserted him. He took his hands from his trouser pockets and looked rather forlorn. From force of habit he pushed his white cuffs up into the sleeves of his coat before he sat down and began to write in the flowing copper-plate handwriting of a clerk.

To the Management of the Saxonia Cotton Company, Fredersdorf.

Sirs, The undersigned begs leave to say that in conformity with the enclosed medical certificate (enclosure A) he is unfit for duty for the ensuing four weeks. The undersigned requests that his salary for March due on the last of the month may in conformity with his written authority (enclosure B) be paid to Frau Anna Kringelein, 4 Station Road. Should it be impossible for the undersigned to return to duty at the end of four weeks, a further communication will follow. Your obedient and respectful servant,

Otto Kringelein.

To Frau Anna Kringelein, 4 Station Road, Fredersdorf, Saxony [Kringelein wrote next, and he wrote the A with a large and rounded flourish].

Dear Anna, I have to tell you that the result of Professor Salzmann's examination was not very hopeful. I am to go direct from here to a sanatorium, costs to be borne by the sick fund, for which there are a few formalities still to be seen to. For the moment, am putting up very reasonably here at the recommendation of Herr Generaldirektor Preysing. Sending further news in the course of a day or two, as must be X-rayed again before anything definite can be said.—Yours, Otto.

Herr Kampmann, Solicitor, Villa Rosenheim, Mauerstrasse, Fredersdorf, Saxony.

My Dear Friend [Kringelein wrote thirdly], You will be surprised to receive a lengthy letter from Berlin, but I have important developments to communicate and count on you to understand and to maintain a professional silence. It is not easy, unfortunately, for me to express myself in writing. However, I hope that your superior education and knowledge of the world will enable you to put the right construction on my letter. As you know I have never been myself since my operation last summer and have not great confidence in our hospital and doctor. Hence I have availed myself of the inheritance from my father to come here so as to be examined and know what is wrong. Unfortunately, my dear friend, there is something seriously wrong, and, in the specialist's opinion, I have not long to live.

Kringelein paused after this for perhaps a minute with his pen in the air. He forgot to put a full stop at the end of the sentence. His moustache, that absurdly large moustache, trembled slightly, but he bravely resumed.

Naturally such a piece of news as that makes one think and I have not slept for several nights, but only kept thinking things over. The result is that I have come to the conclusion not to return to Fredersdorf, but to enjoy life a little during the few weeks I have to live. It is not very nice to go to one's grave at forty-six without having lived at all and only been harassed and starved and bullied by Herr P. at the works and by the wife at home. It seems all wrong that this should be the end of it all when one has never had a single real pleasure. Unfortunately, dear friend, I cannot express myself properly. So I can only add that the will I

19

made in the summer before my operation remains in force though the conditions have now altered. I have, for example, had all my savings transferred here from the bank, also I have borrowed a considerable sum on my life policy, also I have brought the legacy from my father of 3500 marks with me in cash. In this way I can live for a few weeks as a rich man and such is my intention. Why should only the Prey-sings get anything out of life while fools like us do nothing but pinch and save? In all I have taken 8540 marks. Anna can have what is left over, and in my opinion I don't owe her any more. She has given me a wretched life of it with that tongue of hers and no child either. I will keep you apprised of how I go on, but I must request your profes-sional secrecy. Berlin is a fine town and greatly increased in size, when one has not been here for years. I think of a trip to Paris, too, as I know French pretty well from business correspondence. As you see I am keeping the flag flying and feel better than for a long time past.

Hearty greetings from your moribundus

Otto Kringelein.

PS—Tell our friends at the Musical Society that I have gone to a sanatorium.

Kringelein read the letters through. He had composed them in the course of two sleepless nights. He was not quite satisfied. It seemed to him that something essential was left unsaid in the one to the solicitor, but he could not find out where the omission lay. Kringelein, though he was of a diffident and modest nature, was not actually stupid. He had idealism and aspirations. For example, he called himself 'moribundus' as a joke and this expression was one he had encountered in a book from the lending library, which he had read with some trouble and often discussed with the solicitor. Kringelein had lived from childhood the ordinary life of a small provincial town, the rather dreary, uninspired and pointless life of a petty clerk. Early in life and without any strong impulse he had married Fräulein Anna Sauerkatz, the daughter of Sauerkatz, the grocer. During the time between their engagement and marri-age she seemed to him attractive, but soon after the marriage he found her hateful. She was disagreeable and parsimonious and obsessed by petty cares. Kringelein had a fixed salary with a small rise every five years, and, as his health was not robust, his wife and her family pinned him from the first day to a rigid economy in the vague prospect of his becoming a charge on them later on. For example, he was denied the piano that he had longed for all his life. Also he had to sell his little dog, Zipfel, as soon as a tax was put upon dogs. He always had a sore place on his neck from the frayed edges of the old collars he was forced to wear. Now and then it occurred to him that something was not quite right with his life, but what it was he did not know. Often at the meetings of the musical society, when the high tremolo of his tenor voice climbed above the other voices, he had a soaring, blissful feeling as though he himself escaped on wings. Often in the evening he went out along the road to Mickenau, and then leaving the road, and climbing across the wet ditches, he wandered into the country along the balks dividing field from field. There was a soft murmur between the stalks of the corn and when the ears stroked his hand he felt a strange pleasure. He had also had some remarkable and happy experiences under chloroform in the hospital, though he had forgotten them. It was only in little things that Otto Kringelein, the book-keeper, differed from his fellows. But these little things, combined perhaps with the bewildering dose of death in his veins, had brought this 'moribundus' to Berlin's most expensive hotel, and set him down before those sheets of notepaper to which he had confined his strange resolve and its pitiful causes.

Kringelein rose rather unsteadily to his feet and as he went with his three letters through the reading-room he met Doctor Otternschlag. He had a violent shock when he found the mangled side of the Doctor's face turned inquiringly towards him.

"Well? Settled in?" Otternschlag asked listlessly. He wore a dinner jacket and looked down at the toes of his patent-leather shoes.

"Yes, rather. First-class," Kringelein answered with embarrassment. "Thanks. Indeed it is you I have to thank, sir. You were so extremely kind——"

21

"Kind? I? Not at all. Oh, about the room? Not a bit. Y'see, I've been wanting to move on for a long time, only I'm too lazy. Miserable pub, this hotel. If you'd taken my room, I'd have been in the wagon-lits train now for Milan or somewhere. Been very nice. Well, it's all one. Beastly weather everywhere in March. Same wherever you stick it out. May just as well stay here."

"You travel a great deal, sir, no doubt?" Kringelein asked shyly. He was ready to attribute immense wealth or high birth to every visitor in the hotel. He made a bow of the utmost Fredersdorfian elegance as he went on to say timidly: "Allow me to introduce myself—Kringelein. You have seen a lot of the world, sir."

Otternschlag turned aside the 'souvenir from Flanders'.

"Oh, pretty well," he said. "Been everywhere everyone else goes—India and a few places besides." He smiled faintly at the inordinate hunger for such experiences that shone in the blue glint behind Kringelein's glasses.

"It is my intention to travel too," said Kringelein. "The head of our firm, Preysing, for example, goes abroad every year. A short time ago he was at St Moritz. Last Easter he took his whole family to Capri. That sort of thing must be wonderful."

"Have you any family?" asked Doctor Otternschlag, laying aside his paper. Kringelein took five seconds to consider the matter and then replied:

"No."

"No," returned Otternschlag, and in his mouth the word had something irrevocable about it.

"First I should like to go to Paris," said Kringelein. "Paris must be a beautiful city?"

Doctor Otternschlag, who up to now had shown a glimmer of warmth and interest, seemed to be falling asleep. He frequently had such moments of enervation in the course of the day, and the only resource he had against them was of a secret and vicious kind. "You must go to Paris in May," he murmured.

"I shan't have time for that," Kringelein said quickly.

Doctor Otternschlag got up abruptly and left him. "I'm going up to my room to lie down a bit," he said more to himself than to Kringelein, who was left standing with his three letters in the reading-room. The newspaper that Otternschlag had been glancing through fell to the ground. It was pencilled over with scribbles of little men and over each little man was a thick cross. Kringelein, slightly dashed, left the reading-room too, and timidly went in search of the dining-room. Sounds of music issued from it, insistent though subdued, and the alternating drag and beat echoed all through the big hotel.

THE CURTAIN came down. It met the stage with the dull thud of heavy iron. Grusinskaya, who but a moment before circled as light as a flower among her troupe of girls, crept panting into the nearest wing. Utterly dazed, she grasped the brawny arm of a scene-shifter. Her hand shook and she gasped for breath like a wounded animal. Sweat ran along the wrinkles below her eyes. The clapping made no more noise than distant rain and then it came suddenly near—a sign that the curtain had gone up. A man in the wings opposite was laboriously winding it up with great swings of the crank handle. Grusinskaya adjusted her smile like a cardboard mask and danced forward to make her curtsey before the footlights.

Gaigern, whose boredom had been immeasurable, clapped feebly three times merely from good nature and left the stalls for one of the crowded exits. In the front rows and in the gallery a few stalwarts shouted and clapped. Farther back there was a general stampede for the cloakrooms. To Grusinskaya on the stage it looked like a rout, a panic. All the white shirt fronts and dress-coated backs and theatre cloaks streamed on in one direction. She smiled. She threw up her head on her long thin neck. She made a skip to the right, then to the left. She flung out her arms in greeting to the public that was now in full retreat. The curtain came down, rose again. The ballet stood its ground rigidly posed and disciplined. "Curtain! Curtain up!" shouted Pimenov the ballet-master hysterically. He took charge of the curtain. Slowly it went up while the man at the crank worked like mad. One or two people in the stalls, who were just leaving, stopped and turned round, smiling vacantly and clapping. There was some applause too from a box. Grusinskaya pointed to the girls in gauze, who were grouped around her. Modestly she diverted the meagre applause from herself to these unimportant young creatures. And now a few more came back with their coats and cloaks on and

24

surveyed the scene with an air of amusement. Witte, the old German conductor, down below in the orchestra, was exerting his authority with frantic gestures—for the musicians were already packing up. "No one is to go," he whispered nervously. He too was trembling and perspiring. "No one is to go, gentlemen, please. Perhaps the Spring waltz will have to be repeated."

"No bally fear," said a bassoon. "No encores today. Finished for today. There, what did I say?"

In truth the applause died down. Grusinskaya caught sight of the laughing musician's cavernous black mouth just as the curtain separated her from the house. The applause abruptly terminated and the sudden silence on the other side of the curtain gaped ominously. In the silence the tips of the ballet girls' silk shoes could be heard scraping the stage.

"May we go off?" whispered Lucille Lafitte, the *première danseuse*, in French, to Grusinskaya's trembling powdered back.

"Yes, off. Everyone off. Go to the devil!" Grusinskaya answered in Russian. She meant to shout it, but it died in her throat like a sob. All the gauze rustled off in a scare. The footlights went out and Grusinskaya stood alone for a moment on the stage freezing in the grey light as though at a rehearsal.

Suddenly a sound was heard like the snapping of a branch or the ring of a horse's hoofs. It was unmistakable. One man was clapping by himself in the empty house. Not that there was anything extraordinary in this. It was only the impresario, Meyerheim, making a desperate and courageous attempt to retrieve the day. He struck his resounding palms together with all his might as though in frantic enthusiasm and at the same time threw up an angry glance at the seats that an undutiful *claque* had too quickly deserted. Baron Gaigern was the first to hear this solitary outburst. He came back to see what was going on and to join in the fun, and hurriedly pulling off his gloves swelled the applause. He even stamped his feet like an excited student, as some of the *claque* and a few more inquisitive persons came in again from the cloakrooms. They were

25

joined delightedly by others. It grew to a small spontaneous ovation and at last there were about sixty people, all clapping and calling for Grusinskaya.

"Curtain! Curtain!" shouted Pimenov at the top of his voice. Grusinskaya danced hysterically on to the stage and off again. "Michael! Where is Michael? Michael must come on too," she cried laughing. Blue paint, perspiration and tears were mingled round her eyes. Witte pushed the dancer Michael on from the wings. Without looking Grusinskaya took his hand. It was so moist and slippery that she could scarcely grasp it. Then, standing just in front of the prompter's box, they made their bows with the beautiful harmonious grace of bodies trained to match each other. No sooner had the curtain fallen than Grusinskaya gave vent to her excitement by making a scene. "You bungled everything. It was all your fault. You went to pieces in the third arabesque! Such a thing would never have happened to me with Pimenov."

"For mercy's sake—I? But, Gru!" Michael whispered despairingly in his comical Baltic speech. Witte quickly drew him away behind the third wing and put his aged hand on his lips. "For God's sake, don't answer her back. Leave her alone," he whispered. Grusinskaya took the curtain alone. In between, while the curtain was down, her rage broke out. She cursed them all unmercifully. She called them swine, hounds, rotten slackers, one and all. She accused Michael of drunkenness and Pimenov of worse. She threatened the departed ballet with dismissal and accused Witte, the conductor, who was still there, sad and silent, of driving her to suicide by his murder of the *tempo*. All the while her heart fluttered in her breast like a lost and weary bird and tears streamed down over her waxen painted smile. At last the man in charge of the lighting made an end by turning off the light. The theatre was in darkness and an impatient attendant spread grey cloths over the rows of seats. The curtain remained down and the man who worked the crank went home.

"How many 'curtains', Suzette?" Grusinskaya asked the elderly woman who threw a worn old-fashioned woollen cloak over her shoulders before opening the iron door that led off the

26

stage. "Seven? I counted eight. Seven you say? Even so that was not bad. But was it a success?"

She listened with impatience to Suzette's protestations, according to which the success had been immense, almost as immense as at Brussels three years before. Madame remembered? Madame did remember. As though one forgot a great success! Madame sat in the little dressing-room, staring at the electric bulb that hung in a wire cage over the looking-glass, and consulted her memory. No, she thought gloomily, it was not such a success as at Brussels. She was tired to death. She stretched out her moist limbs. She sat there, like a boxer who lies in his corner after a hard round, and let Suzette rub her down and chafe her and remove the paint. The dressing-room was overheated, dirty and small. It smelt of old dresses, of glue, of paint, of a hundred exhausted bodies.

Perhaps Grusinskaya fell asleep for seconds, for she saw herself in the stone-paved entrance hall of her Villa on Lake Como, but in a moment she was back again with Suzette and her gnawing and feverish dissatisfaction over the performance. It had not been a great success. No, it had not been a great success. And what a wretched, incomprehensible world to deprive a Grusinskaya of a great success.

No one knew how old Grusinskaya was. There were old Russian aristocrats in exile, living in furnished rooms in Wilmersdorf, who asserted that they had known Grusinskaya for forty years. This assuredly was an exaggeration. But there was none in putting twenty years as an international celebrity to her credit, and twenty years of celebrity and success are an age. Sometimes Grusinskaya said to old Witte, who had been her friend and accompanist since the beginning of her career: "Witte, it is my fate to support a weight far too heavy for me, on and on, all my life long." And Witte answered earnestly: "Please let no one observe it, Elisaveta Alexandrovna. Do not speak of heaviness. The world has grown heavy. It is your mission, Elisaveta, if you will allow me to say so, to be lightness. Please do not alter. That would be the world's misfortune. . . ."

Grusinskaya did not alter. She had weighed ninety-six

27

pounds since the age of eighteen and in this lay part of her success and her capabilities. Her partners, once accustomed to this lightness, could not dance with anyone else afterwards. Her neck, her figure that seemed to be all joints, the beautiful oval of her face, never changed. Her arms obeyed her will like wings. The smile that shone out beneath her long eyelashes was in itself a work of art. Grusinskaya bent all her force to one aim, to be as she had been. And she did not observe that it was exactly this of which the world began to tire.

Perhaps the world would have loved her as she really was, as she looked now, for example, sitting in her dressing-room— a poor, delicate, tired old woman with worn-out eyes, and a small care-worn human face. When Grusinskaya did not have a success—and this sometimes happened nowadays—she shrank into herself and became very aged in an instant, seventy years old, a hundred years old, older even than that. Suzette in the background muttered her complaints in French as she stood over the grimy washhand basin and the hot water would not flow properly. Finally, however, she succeeded in producing the steaming compresses and Grusinskaya resigned her face to the tingling heat, while Suzette loosed her pearls from her neck, those world-famed almost fabulously beautiful pearls that came from the days of her Grand Duke.

"You can put the pearls away. I shall not wear them any more today," said Grusinskaya, catching sight of their rosy shimmer from beneath her half-closed eyelids.

"Not the pearls? But Madame ought to look her best for the banquet."

"No. There, that's enough. Make the best of me without the pearls, Suzette," Grusinskaya said, and gave herself up with a resigned air to the fingertips and the compresses and the rouge of her self-effacing factotum. She had to go to a supper given in her honour by the Stage Society and for this she must be painted in as deadly earnest as an Aztec warrior before he went to meet his enemies.

Witte walked to and fro in the passage outside the dressing-room as patiently as a sentry. He tapped the case of his watch which he wore in old-fashioned style in the pocket of his white waistcoat. His old musician's face betrayed anxiety and sadness. After a while, Pimenov, the ballet-master, joined him, and then finally Michael came along. His eyelashes shone with vaseline and he was heavily powdered.

"Are we waiting for Gru?" he asked cheerfully. "Are we all going together?"

"I would advise you to vanish, my boy," said Witte, "however little you may have gone to pieces."

"But I didn't go to pieces. Pimenov, did I go to pieces?" he exclaimed almost in tears. Pimenov merely shrugged his shoulders. He too was an old man. He had a large nose that was full of character, and he loved to wear the old-fashioned cravats of the time of Edward VII. He did not dance any longer but only conducted the rehearsals and composed Grusinskaya's *divertissements*, in the severe style of classical choreography, full of birds and flowers and allegories, danced on the point of the toe. "Go to bed, don't face Gru tonight. Lucille has disappeared already," he said sagely.

Michael's youthful face rose in revolt, and he knocked on the dressing-room door. "Goodnight, Madame," he called out. "I am not coming with you. What time is the rehearsal tomorrow morning?"

"Of course you're coming. You must sit next to me," Grusinskaya called back. "Don't make me so unhappy, *chéri*. We can talk about the rehearsal later. Wait for me. I'm just ready."

"*Tiens*—she's had her cry out," Witte whispered with the air of a conspirator.

"*Larmes, oh, douces larmes*," Pimenov declaimed, with his chin sunk in his collar.

"I wouldn't condemn my worst enemy to dance a *pas de deux* with Gru—if you'll pardon me, my dear fellow," Michael affirmed in his comical Baltic German.

On the other side of the door Grusinskaya was dabbing powder behind the lobes of her ears in the brilliantly lighted mirror of the dressing-room. "Michael must be there," she thought, "I always have old people about me—Pimenov, Witte, Lucille, Suzette." She had a sudden spasm of hatred for the

29

worn out hat that Suzette behind her was putting over her grey hair. She pushed her aside with an abrupt movement and went out into the passage carrying her cloak of black and gold and ermine over her arm. She turned her shoulders to Michael to have her cloak put on. He did this with feminine delicacy, as he did everything. It was a little ceremony of reconciliation. But it was something more. It was an outspoken pleading on Grusinskaya's part for the freemasonry of youth. Michael was young! for Grusinskaya frequently changed her dancer. She was susceptible and exacting when it came to her partner. The rest had grown old with her in her service.

Now, at any rate, she looked dazzling. She was beautiful, distinguished, flower-like, resilient. "Elisaveta looks . . . enchanting," said Witte, with a bow from a past century. He had accustomed himself to the use of studied expressions, firstly in order to conceal his love for Gru, to whom he had been devoted since his youth, and secondly, from the necessity of translating his speeches now into Russian, now into French. Grusinskaya herself slipped continually from one language into another, from the Russian 'thou' into the French and English 'you'. She could speak German too. She was as fluent in the one as the other, however abusive or however amiable it was necessary to be. It was not always easy to follow her. For example, she was no sooner in her motor car than she asked: "Do you think, Witte, it was the fault of the pearls?"

"In what sense the pearls? And the fault for what?" asked Witte in dismay—for the second of his questions arose from pure sensibility. He knew well enough what Grusinskaya meant. *"Mon Dieu,* how do you mean—the pearls?" Pimenov asked too.

"Certainly I mean the pearls. They bring me bad luck, those pearls," she said with childish insistence. Witte folded one old-fashioned glacé kid glove in the other. "But, my dear." He was disconcerted.

"What!" exclaimed Pimenov. "Why, the pearls have brought you luck all your life. They were your mascot, your talisman. And are you going to say now that they bring bad luck? What an idea, Gru!"

30

"They do bring bad luck all the same. I see it," Gru said with a self-willed frown between her artificially emphasized eyebrows. "I cannot explain it, but I have been thinking over it a great deal. They brought me luck as long as the Grand Duke Sergei was alive. *Voilà!* Ever since he was murdered nothing but bad luck have they brought me. In London last year there was the sinew I broke in my ankle. At Nice—a deficit. And altogether nothing but bad luck. I shall not dance in them any more. So now you know."

"Not dance in them! But, dear, dearest Gru, you cannot possibly go on without your pearls. All your life long it has been your firm belief that you could not go on without the pearls, and now suddenly——"

"Yes," Grusinskaya said, "it was just a superstition."

Witte began to laugh. "Lisa," he cried, "my dove, my dear little one, why, you're a child!"

"You don't understand me. You don't understand me in the least, Witte. The pearls are no longer suitable. I shall not wear them any more. In the old days, in Petersburg, in Paris, jewels were *de rigueur*. A dancer had to possess jewels and display them. But now—who wears real pearls today? I am a woman. I have a sense of these things, I have the flair. Michael, are you asleep? Say something."

Michael, without moving his graceful limbs, said in clumsy French: "If you wish to know, Madame; you ought to give your pearls away for poor children and cripples, to give them away for charity, Madame."

"What do you say? Give them away, my pearls?" Grusinskaya cried out in Russian and the word *pozertwowatj* rang out like a song.

"Here we are," Pimenov said as the brake was suddenly applied.

"*En avant*," Grusinskaya commanded. "We must be beautiful—and enjoy ourselves!"

The door of the house was thrown open. Witte, as he went up the steps behind the dancer, remarked: "Elisaveta Alexandrovna has only one fault. She is in love with the categorical imperative."

31

Grusinskaya began to smile and to beam like a light suddenly turned on, and thus beaming and smiling she entered the club where thirty gentlemen in evening dress stood awaiting her entry.

Baron Gaigern was the very last to stop clapping; but, as soon as he was sure that the curtain would not go up any more, he left the theatre with the set face of a man in a hurry. The rain had stopped. White and yellow lights were reflected in the wet surface of the Kantstrasse; policemen were regulating the traffic; the destitute were eagerly opening the doors of motor cars for those in fur coats to step in. Gaigern threaded the crowd, disregarding traffic regulations at the risk of his life, and hurried into the comparative obscurity of the Fasanenstrasse, where his car—an unobtrusive four-seater—was parked. The chauffeur was smoking a cigarette.

"Well?" asked Gaigern with his hands in the pockets of his blue coat.

"She's changed her chauffeur again," said the chauffeur. "It's an Englishman this time. She picked him up at Nice. His employer went bankrupt and left him stranded there. I've had a meal with him, but I can't get anything out of him."

"I've told you a hundred times not to smoke when I'm speaking to you," Gaigern said.

"Right," said the chauffeur and threw away his cigarette. "He's driven round to the theatre now to take her to the Stage Society. He doesn't know yet when he has to take her back."

"He doesn't know?" Gaigern replied and struck the palm of his hand reflectively with his gloves. "Right. Then I'll go across there again. Bring the car round to the theatre and wait there."

Gaigern returned to the front of the theatre with the same set expression of a man intent on business. He found it dreary and deserted. The electric signs were dark and the placards looked as if they had nothing further to say. The stage door did not open on to the street, but into a courtyard where blank walls gleamed with wet ivy. Gaigern wedged himself among the little crowd of loungers who were waiting for Grusinskaya

32

to emerge. Their eyes were fixed on the frosted-glass panels of the door through which a light was shining. First a detachment of the fire brigade marched out. Next came the scene-shifters —brawny fellows with pipes in their mouths. Then there was a pause before the door opened once more and out came the ballet in twos and threes. Their slim figures were concealed in cheap fur coats, scraps of French, Russian and English eddied around them as they went. Gaigern looked after them and smiled. He had known several of them in Nice and Paris. His upper lip shortened when he laughed, like a little child's. It was charming. Many women at least found it so.

My God, what a time it's going to be—as usual, he thought impatiently, as the courtyard fell asleep again. Nearly a quarter of an hour went by. Then the chauffeur in Grusinskaya's motor car stirred like a dog in its sleep and started up the engine. Gaigern had been waiting for this signal. He pressed into the shadow against the wall. When Grusinskaya finally appeared he was invisible. She turned back into the doorway. "Wait here, Suzette," she said. "I'll send Berkeley straight back and he will take you to the hotel." She was cloaked above the chin in an extremely decorative evening wrap of gold and black and ermine and looked every bit as beautiful at this moment as her photographs in the world's illustrated papers. Gaigern fixed her with his eyes from his hiding place in the shadow. As she put her silver foot on the running-board she opened her ermine collar and Gaigern could see the world-famed long white neck. It looked peculiarly naked and flower-like this evening. Gaigern drew his breath through his teeth in a spasm of delight. He had desired nothing more eagerly than to see this bared neck. . . .

She had scarcely driven off when Suzette appeared in the dark and deserted courtyard. The porter followed and shut the stage door behind him. Suzette always looked like an old and faded copy of her mistress, and the reason was that she wore Grusinskaya's old clothes and hats when they had long ceased to be the fashion. On this occasion she shuffled across the courtyard in a long bell-shaped skirt over which she wore a buttoned-up cloak with a kind of Byronic collar. Both her

33

hands were laden. In the left she carried a fair-sized flat suit-case, and in the right a small one of black patent leather. Thus encumbered she made her way slowly as far as the iron gate-way that parted the theatre yard from the street, and there she strolled to and fro in the full light of the arc lamps. Wild thoughts sprang to the surface of Gaigern's mind during these seconds. He stood in his shadowed corner on the tiptoe of suspense, as though making ready for a jump or to start for-ward at the pistol shot. But he attempted nothing, for at that moment that damned fellow Berkeley drew up at the curb on a masterly turn. Suzette got into the grey car just as it struck half past twelve from the Gedächtniskirche, and Gaigern, who for the space of a minute had forgotten to breathe, took in a deep breath. He whistled. His little four-seater came up. "Straight after them to the hotel." He jumped up beside the chauffeur.

"Well, any hopes today?" asked the chauffeur. Again he had a cigarette between his lips as he spoke.

"Wait," Gaigern replied.

"Another whole night to stand by with the car, eh? All the same to you if I ever get another night's sleep or not, I sup-pose?"

Gaigern pointed his finger at the grey car, which was taking the little bend round the traffic sign at the Hitzigbrücke Bridge. "Overtake it," was all he said. The chauffeur accelerated. There was no policeman now on point duty at the bridge. The night life of Berlin thronged the streets beneath a red vault, where not a star showed in the cloudless spring sky.

"It's enough to feed one up," the chauffeur went on. "The game's not worth the candle. The end will be that we'll go bust."

"If you don't like it, you know what to do," the Baron answered amiably, and his upper lip curled. "If you're not pleased you can take your pay and go."

"I mean no harm," said the chauffeur.

"Nor I," said the Baron.

There was silence till they reached the hotel.

"Park at Entrance No VI," said Gaigern as he jumped out.

In the revolving door that led from the small entrance lobby into the hall of the hotel, he came upon a comical gentleman. It was Kringelein who had got stuck there owing to the mistake he made in trying to revolve the door in the opposite direction. Gaigern gave it an impatient kick and sent the glass whirligig, together with its contents, round in the right direction. "That's the way round," he said to Kringelein.

"Thank you. Thank you very much," replied Kringelein, who had wanted to go out and now found himself shot inside the hotel again. Gaigern went quickly for his key, and as quickly to the lift. Arrived at the first floor he told the one-armed lift attendant to wait a moment. He would be back in one second. He ran along the passage to his room, No 69, threw down his hat and coat, snatched up a fine orchid spray from a vase and ran along the passage again. "Tell the lift attendant, please, that I shan't need him," he said to the chambermaid, who, half asleep, sidled along past door after door. She gave the message and the man grumbling took the lift down again. When he reached the ground floor, Suzette was there waiting with her two cases to be taken up. And this was precisely what Gaigern had intended. . . .

When Suzette arrived at the door of Room No 68, the room occupied by Grusinskaya, she saw a charming young man standing behind a palm. His bashful and ingratiating features seemed not unfamiliar to her.

"Good evening, Mademoiselle. Permit me to say one word," he said in his charming and rather old-world French, the French that is taught in a Jesuit seminary. "Only one word. Madame is not in her room?"

"I do not know, sir," replied the well-trained Suzette.

"It is only—forgive the presumption—that I should like so much to lay a little flower for Madame in her room. I have so great a veneration for Madame. I was at the theatre tonight. I never miss an evening when Madame dances. I have read in the papers, you see, that Madame loves these Cattleyas—is it true?"

"Yes," said Suzette, "she loves orchids. We have started the cultivation of orchids in our hot-houses at Tremezzo."

35

"Ah! Then may I give you my spray and ask you to leave it in Madame's room?"

"We have had a lot of flowers today. The French Ambassador sent a whole basketful," said Suzette, who was still smarting from the evening's doubtful success. She looked at the bashful young man with considerable friendliness. But she could not take the spray because she had both her hands full. It was difficult even to get the key into her right hand in order to open the door of Room No 68. Gaigern, who saw her embarrassment, went quickly up to her. "Allow me," he said and put out his hands to take the two cases. Suzette surrendered the larger one, but she drew back instinctively as she maintained her grasp of the smaller one. So the famous pearls are in that one, Gaigern thought, though he kept his thoughts to himself. He opened the door for her and the inner one as well, and with shy and at the same time enraptured steps crossed the threshold of the room where Grusinskaya slept.

The room had the same banal and tawdry elegance as all the others. The cool air inside smelt of a curious aromatic scent as well as of the bouquets of flowers, and the window on to the small balcony stood open. The bed was turned down, and a pair of little bedroom slippers were by the bed. They were rather trodden down and shabby—the slippers of a woman who is accustomed to sleep by herself. Gaigern, as he stood by the door, felt a fleeting tenderness of pity at the sight of these little tokens of resignation on the part of a famous and beautiful woman. He stood in the door holding out his orchids as though beseeching the acceptance of them. Suzette put down the smaller suitcase on the dressing-table between the three mirrors and at last took the flowers.

"Thank you, Monsieur," she said, "what name shall I say?"

"What an idea! I am not so presumptuous," said Gaigern. He looked observantly at Suzette's wrinkled face and saw a strange resemblance to the face of her mistress. "You are tired," he said, "and no doubt Madame will be late. Have you to wait up for Madame?"

"Oh, no, Madame is good. Madame says every night, 'You can go to bed, Suzette.' But Madame needs me all the same.

36

So I wait up for her. Madame is never later than two o'clock because she has to start work every morning at nine. And how she works, Monsieur. Oh, *mon Dieu!* No, Madame is very good."

"She must be an angel," said Gaigern ecstatically. (So there is only a bathroom without a window between 68 and 69, he thought, as he said it.) His wandering gaze returned to Suzette's cavernous yawn.

"Goodnight and a thousand thanks, Mademoiselle," he said politely, and with a smile disappeared.

Suzette shut both doors behind him and after putting the orchids in a glass of water, sank, a little shivering heap, into an armchair—to wait.

Before one o'clock at night there are very few pairs of shoes to be seen in front of the bedroom doors of the Grand Hotel. Everyone is out and about, eagerly savouring the hectic pleasures of the great city in its blaze of electric light. At the end of each passage on every floor a dead-tired chambermaid, faded and virtuous, yawns in her little office. The pageboys come on night shift at ten, but they too, under their jaunty flat-topped caps, have the feverishly bright eyes of children who ought to have been put to bed long before. The ill-tempered one-armed man at the light was relieved at midnight by another equally ill-tempered one-armed man. The Hall Porter Senf, too, was relieved by the night porter at about eleven, and went off half dazed to the hospital, in such a state of anxiety that his teeth chattered. On arriving there he was sent back home by an unamiable night nurse, who told him that it would be twenty-four hours till the baby was born, but this, of course, was his own affair and did not concern the hotel. The hotel, meanwhile, was in all its glory. There was dancing in the yellow pavilion and great inroads had been made on Mattoni's cold buffet. Mattoni's nigger-like eyes were smiling as he shaved off slices of cold beef, or mixed maraschino in iced fruit-salads. The electric fans whirred and spewed out the bad air into the courtyards of the hotel, and down below in the servants' quarters the chauffeurs sat and talked scandal about their masters. (They are an irritable lot, these chauffeurs, because they are not allowed to drink.) In the Lounge, visitors up from the provinces sat in amazement and mild vexation over the Berlin men who wore their hats on the backs of their heads and waved their hands, and over the Berlin ladies with their painted faces. Rohna, spruce and re-freshed by a *friction* of toilet vinegar, as he crossed the Lounge was thinking: It is true that our night-time *clientèle* is not of the first order. But—*que voulez-vous?* nowadays only a vulgar *clientèle* puts money in the till.

Just before one o'clock Herr Kringelein landed in the Bar. He was tired, and he sank down at a small table and surveyed the world about him with watery eyes. To tell the truth, this Kringelein was utterly tired out, but he had the obstinacy of children on their birthdays—he simply would not go to bed. Moreover he felt that he was asleep already, for everything entered his brain like a confused and feverish dream and the noise, the perpetual movement, the voices and the music, seemed at one moment quite close and at the next moment very far away and entirely unreal. The world hummed most strangely about his ears and everything combined to produce in him a mysterious state of intoxication. Once, when he was ten years old, Kringelein had played truant from school. In a panic at the thought of a dictation lesson, he had gone out into the warm morning mist along the road to Mickenau. Then he had left the road and lain down in the heat of the day and slept with his head on a cushion of clover. Later he had got into a grassy hollow by the river and feasted on the raspberries that grew there in immense profusion. All his life he had never forgotten the buzzing of the great gnats that had fastened on his bare legs and his red juice-stained fingers as he pressed in among thorns and nettles to gather handful after handful of raspberries. He felt again, here in the Bar of Berlin's most expensive hotel, the same intoxicated feeling, a sense of exuberant plenty as well as of anxiety and alarm, the faint threat haunting the wicked joy of wrongdoing, the excitement of an escapade. It all came back to him as he sat there between one and two in the morning. The stinging gnats were there,

38

too, in a sense. They had taken on the likeness of figures that tormented his brain, the brain of a book-keeper who had kept accounts all his life long and now could not stop.

Caviare, for example, cost nine marks. Caviare was a delusion, Kringelein decided. It tasted like herring and cost nine marks. Kringelein had gone hot and cold under the supercilious gaze of three waiters while he stared at the wagon of hors-d'œuvres which had come to a stop in front of him. He had had to miss out the *prix fixe* supper—at twenty-two marks —out of consideration for his ailing stomach. Burgundy was a heavy, sour wine that lay in a kind of cradle, like a baby. The rich had odd tastes, it seemed. Kringelein was by no means stupid; he was very willing to learn; and it had not taken him long to see that he had been badly brought up and did not know how to make proper use of the array of knives and forks before him. During the whole evening he could not rid himself of a horrible nervous tremor. Embarrassment over tips, and wrong doors and puzzled inquiries kept him in a constant state of painful confusion. But this first evening as a man of wealth had its great moments. The shop windows, for example. In Berlin, the shop windows are lighted up at night, and the riches of the whole world are displayed there. I can buy what I like, is a novel and enchanting thought for a man like Kringelein. Then again he had been to the cinema. In Berlin you can go to the cinema as late as half past nine. He had treated himself to one of the best seats. There is a cinema in Fredersdorf too. You went three times a week to Zickenmeier's Rooms, where the music club also held its rehearsals. Kringelein had been two or three times with his stingy Anna in the cheapest seats, right in front among the factory hands, and there he had sat with his head screwed back staring straight up at the gigantic and distorted figures on the screen. It was one of the revelations of the evening to find that the film, when seen from an expensive seat, had a totally different appearance. If you could only pay enough, it became as living as life itself. Incidentally, this film of St Moritz opened up a wonderful and scarcely believable world. Kringelein decided then and there that he would go to St Moritz. Those mountains and lakes and valleys were not put there only for the Preysings, he thought to himself, and at the thought, as it recurred again and again, his heart beat. There is a sweet, a bitter, and triumphant sense of freedom in those for whom death is decreed. Kringelein could find no word for it; but, whenever it came over him, he was forced to catch his breath in a heavy sigh.

"Excuse me——" said Doctor Otternschlag, in the midst of these whirling thoughts, as he pushed his bony knees under Kringelein's table. "There is not another seat left in this cursed Bar. Rotten accommodation. Louisiana flip," he said to the waiter and laid his skeleton fingers on the table between himself and Kringelein, like ten cold, heavy metal bars.

"Delighted," Kringelein said in his politest manner. "I am delighted to meet you again. You were so very kind to me, sir —believe me, I don't forget it. No, indeed."

Otternschlag, who had never, over a stretch of untold dreary years, heard anyone describe him as kind, and who for ten years had scarcely spoken to a living soul, felt a slight scorn mixed with a certain gratification at this repeated expression of thanks on the part of the gentleman from Fredersdorf. "Well, here's the best," he said and tossed down his flip. Kringelein, who had ordered something at random that he now scarcely dared to drink, took a sip of the copper-coloured fluid in the shallow metal cup.

"The life here is a little confusing at first," he said timidly.

"Hm," replied Doctor Otternschlag. "At first, yes. Doesn't improve on acquaintance either, when you live here as I do. No. Bring me another Louisiana flip."

"It is not at all as one imagined it," Kringelein said. His strong cocktail was making him reflective. "Nowadays, even in the provinces one is not out of the world. There are the newspapers. There are the cinemas. There are the pictures in the illustrated papers. But even so the real thing looks quite different. I knew for example that bar stools were high. But they are not so very high, I see. And the nigger behind the Bar is the mixer, of course. But there's nothing very wonderful about him at close quarters. As a matter of fact it's the first time I ever saw a nigger in my life. But he doesn't seem at all

40

strange. He even speaks German and you might think he was only blacked."

"No, he's genuine enough. Not much use though. You've got your work cut out to get tight here."

Kringelein listened to the maze of voices, to the clatter and hum, and the loud laughter of the women at the Bar in front. "They are not real *demi-mondaines*, are they?" he asked.

Otternschlag turned the undisfigured side of his face to him. "You'd like something rather more alluring?" he said. "No, they're not the real thing. This is a solid respectable sort of place. No women admitted unless accompanied by men. They're not *demi-mondaines*, nor real ladies, either. Do you want to get to know a girl?"

Kringelein gave a little cough. "Thank you, not in the least. As a matter of fact I could have got to know a girl this evening. Yes, I assure you. A young lady invited me to dance with her."

"Indeed? You? Where was that?" asked Doctor Otternschlag, and the half of his mouth showed a wry smile.

"I was in a place, Casino something or other it was called, not far from the Potsdammer Platz," said Kringelein, trying to copy the staccato speech of the man of the world as he heard it on Otternschlag's lips. "Fine, fine, I tell you. The lighting. Positively fairy-like." He tried to find a more expressive word but gave it up. "Fairy-like. Little fountains with variegated lights changing all the time. Dear, of course. Champagne only. They rook you twenty-five marks a bottle. Unfortunately I can only stand a little. Not in the best of health, you see."

"So I see. I know all about that. When a man's collar is nearly an inch too wide for him, I don't need to be told any more."

"Are you a doctor?" asked Kringelein in a cold sweat. Involuntarily he put two fingers inside his collar. Yes, it had got too large.

"Have been. Been everything one time or another. I was in the medical service in South-west Africa. Filthy climate. Taken prisoner in September '14. Prison camp in Nairobi, British East Africa. Sent home on parole. Went through the whole rotten business as an army doctor till the finish. Shell in the face. Diphtheria germs messing about in the wound till 1920. Two years isolation hospital. There, that's enough. Full stop. Been everything pretty well. Who cares?"

Kringelein gazed in horror at this ruin of a man whose fingers lay cold and lifeless on the table between them. The Bar provided a running accompaniment of assorted sounds and a Charleston could just be heard from the yellow pavilion. Kringelein had caught extremely little of Otternschlag's telegraphic communications; nevertheless tears started to his eyes. His tears came with ignominious ease ever since his operation, which had not cured him.

"And have you no one then, who—I mean—are you quite alone?" he asked in embarrassment, and Otternschlag noticed for the first time what a high-pitched, charming voice he had, a human, resonant, inquiring, diffident voice. He put out his cold fingers in front of him on the table, and withdrew them again immediately. Kringelein looked reflectively at the numerous white stitches and scars in Otternschlag's face and a sudden resolution unloosed his lips.

Alone, he knew what that meant—this was more or less what he said—he too was alone in Berlin, absolutely alone. He had cut the threads. He had severed various ties (such were the choice phrases he used) and now he was alone in Berlin. After spending all his life in Fredersdorf he felt stupid of course in a great city, but not so stupid that he could not see his own stupidity. He knew little of life, but now he wanted to get to know it. He wanted to know life as it really was. That was why he was here. "But," he went on, "where is real life? I have not come on it yet. I have been to a Casino, and here I am sitting in the most expensive hotel, but all the time I know it isn't the real thing. All the time, I have a suspicion that real, genuine actual life is going on somewhere else and is something quite different. When you don't belong to it it's not at all so easy to get into it, if you see what I mean?"

"Yes, but what's your notion of life?" replied Doctor Otternschlag. "Does life exist at all as you imagine it? The real thing is always going on somewhere else. When you're young you think it will come later. Later on you think it was earlier. When you are here, you think it is there—in India, in America, on Popacatepetl or somewhere. But when you get there, you find that life has doubled back and is quietly waiting here, here in the very place you ran away from. It is the same with life as it is with the butterfly collector and the swallow tail. As you see it flying away, it is wonderful. But as soon as it is caught, the colours are gone and the wings bashed."

These were the first consecutive remarks that Kringelein had heard Doctor Otternschlag utter, and he was impressed; but he was not convinced. "I don't believe that," he said modestly.

"Take it from me, it is so. It is the bar stool over again," Otternschlag replied; his elbows were propped on his knees and his hands trembled faintly.

"What bar stool?" asked Kringelein.

"The bar stool you spoke of a moment ago. Bar stools are not so very high, you said. You imagined they would be higher, eh? Didn't you say so? Well, then, one imagines everything higher than it is, till one sees it. You come on your travels from your little provincial town with false ideas about life. Grand hotel, you think. Most expensive hotel, you think. God knows what marvels you expect from an hotel like this. You'll soon know all about it. The whole hotel is only a rotten pub. It is exactly the same with the whole of life. The whole of life is a rotten pub, Herr Kringelein. You arrive, stay for a while and go on again. Passing through. Isn't that it? For a short stay, what? What do you do in a big hotel? Eat, sleep, lounge about, do business, flirt a little, dance a little, eh? Well and what do you do in life? A hundred doors in one corridor and nobody knows a thing about his next-door neighbours. When you leave another arrives and takes your bed. *Finito.* Sit for an hour or two in the Lounge and keep your eyes open. You'll see that the people there have no individuality. They're dummies, all of 'em. Dead, all the lot and don't know it. Charming pub, a big hotel like this. Grand hotel della Vita, eh? Well, the main thing is—have your bags ready packed."

Kringelein took a considerable time for reflection. Then it

seemed to him that he had grasped the meaning of Otternschlag's discourse. "Yes, to be sure," he agreed. He put almost too much emphasis on the words.

Otternschlag, who was on the point of dozing off, woke up again.

"Did you want me to do anything for you? Do you want me to introduce you to Life? You've made a fine choice I must say. I am always at your service, Herr Kringelein."

"I had no wish to be a nuisance to you, sir," Kringelein said with a sad little air of humility. He went on thinking. The polished phrases he had prepared found no utterance. Since he had come to the Grand Hotel he felt that he was in a foreign land. He spoke his native tongue like a foreign language that he had learnt from books and newspapers. "You were so extremely kind," he said. "I was hoping—but, of course, for you everything has another aspect than it has for me. You have it all behind you. You have had your fill. I have it all in front of me. That makes one impatient. Please forgive me."

Otternschlag looked so hard at Kringelein that even the stitched-up eyelid above his glass eye seemed to be focusing on him. He saw Kringelein clearly and completely. He saw his wasted figure in the workaday suit of stout grey worsted, rather shiny in places. He saw the sad and yearning expression round his bloodless lips and beneath that absurd moustache. He saw the wasted neck inside the wide, frayed collar, the clerk's hands and untended nails; he even saw the blacked boots, turned slightly in, on the thick carpet under the table. And finally he saw Kringelein's eyes, the blue human eyes behind the pince-nez, eyes in which was so much yearning expectation, wonder and curiosity. In them was hunger for life, and knowledge of death.

God knows whether some warmth from those eyes penetrated the frigid being of Doctor Otternschlag. Perhaps it was pure boredom that made him say: "True. Quite true. You're right. Right every time. I have it behind me. Yes, I have had my fill. It's all behind me now down to the last unimportant formality. And you say, then, that for you it is all in front. You've the appetite, eh? Of the soul, I mean. Now what's your notion? The usual men's paradise—Champagne? Women? Races? Gambling? Drink? *Tiens!* And so you tumbled for it the very first evening, eh? An acquaintance right off?" Otternschlag said impassively, thankful though he was for the warmth in Kringelein's eyes.

"Yes, quite early on. A lady positively wanted to dance with me. A very pretty girl. Perhaps not quite—I mean something of a bird of paradise" (he took 'bird of paradise' from the *Mickenauer Journal*). "But most elegant. Well educated, too."

"Well educated, too! Well—there! And how did you get on?" Otternschlag murmured.

"Unfortunately I can't dance. One must dance. Apparently, it is very important," said Kringelein. His cocktail made him feverishly enterprising and at the same time sad.

"Very important. Very. Important above all things," replied Doctor Otternschlag in a surprisingly alert tone of voice. "One must know how to dance. The mutual embrace in time with the music, the dizzy turning and twirling of two in one, eh? One ought not to give any lady the go-by. One must know how to dance. Oh, how right you are, Herr Kringelein. Learn quickly, as soon as ever you can find time. Then you will never have to say no to a lady again, Herr Kringelein—your name is Kringelein, isn't it?"

Kringelein looked questioningly and uneasily through his glasses into Otternschlag's face. "Why do you ask that?" he asked, and felt that he was being made a fool of. But Otternschlag went on seriously. "Believe me," he said, "believe me, Kringelein, when I say: He who does not move with the times is a dead man. Waiter, the bill."

Kringelein paid too after this abrupt conclusion and stood up embarrassed. He followed Doctor Otternschlag, whose dinner jacket was stretched tightly over his thin shoulder blades, out of the Bar and stumbling over to the porter got his key.

"Any letters for me?" Otternschlag asked the night porter. He seemed of a sudden to have forgotten Kringelein utterly.

"No," the porter said, without so much as looking, for one porter is not like another and sensibility of soul is not put on

45

with a porter's cap. "Madame's key was taken upstairs by Mademoiselle," he said in French to a lady immediately after. Kringelein could almost understand it, thanks to his practice in foreign correspondence.

As the lady passed him there was a breath of delicate bitter-sweet scent from her golden evening cloak, open at the neck. Kringelein stared at her, for his manners were lost in boundless amazement. Her hair was black and smooth and she wore a diadem in it. Her drooping eyelids were painted blue-black. Her cheeks, temples and chin were ivory white and the veins were blue. Her mouth was carmine, almost purple, and it was rouged in such long curves that the corners seemed to stretch upwards to her nostrils in a fixed smile. Her hair was drawn down over her cheeks in two smooth black wings and where cheeks and hair met there was an ocre shadow laid on with extreme art. She looked tall, though she was scarcely of medium height, and this (as even Kringelein could tell) was due to the perfect proportions of her body and to the lightness of her carriage. She was accompanied by a little old gentleman with a top hat in his hand who looked like a musician. "Could you be at the theatre at half past eight, my dear?" the lady asked, just as she passed Kringelein. "I should like half an hour's work before the rehearsal."

Kringelein, who had never seen such a work of art as this lady, showed his amazement and delight in his face. He pulled Otternschlag by the sleeve and whispered in an undertone: "Who can that be?"

"Don't you know, my dear fellow? It's Grusinskaya," Otternschlag said impatiently and stalked over to the lift. Kringelein stood rooted to the spot. Grusinskaya! Good heavens! Grusinskaya, he thought. For Grusinskaya's fame was such that it had even reached Fredersdorf. So she really exists! That's what she looks like. She's not only to be read of in the newspapers. She's actually on earth. I've stood beside her, brushed against her, and the whole place is scented with her when she goes by. I must write to Kampmann about this.

He set off with speed in order to see her once more and to take a good look at her. At this very moment a little comedy of

46

good manners was proceeding in front of the lift. An exceptionally well set up, elegant and handsome fellow stepped ostentatiously back two paces from the lift, and made way for Grusinskaya with an easy and at the same time chivalrous gesture, as though it were not merely a question of giving her precedence into the lift, but of laying the conquest of an empire at the feet of a queen. Otternschlag, who stood by himself against the wall on the other side of the corridor, muttered, "Sir Walter Raleigh!" Kringelein, on the other hand, now in full career, shot past him and pressed into the lift on the heels of the chivalrous young man. Thus it was that his recently acquired friend remained alone below, since only four could go up at once. They stood somewhat crowded in the little cage of wood and glass. The handsome young man in particular squeezed himself into a corner.

"Ah! So you too are in Berlin, Baron?" Witte, the old conductor, asked, and Baron Gaigern answered:

"Yes, to be sure. I am here too."

Kringelein listened with awe to this talk between fine people. The one-armed man turned the handle, the lift stopped at the first floor, and they all marched off along the raspberry-red carpet to their rooms, Grusinskaya leading, then Witte, then the Baron, then Otto Kringelein. The doors of Rooms Nos 68 and 69 and 70 were opened. It was two o'clock and an old grandfather clock at the turning of the passage struck officiously. The sound of music could be heard faintly from the yellow pavilion, where they were playing the last dance.

Grusinskaya paused a moment between the double doors of her room. "Well, goodnight, my dear," she said to Witte. She spoke German to him when she was in a good humour. "Thank you again for this evening. It really went well, don't you think? Eight curtains. Tell me, by the way. Who was that young man? Haven't we seen him before somewhere? At Nice, was it?"

"Yes, at Nice, Lisa. He introduced himself to me one day. We played bridge together once or twice. He appears to have a great admiration for Elisaveta."

"Ah," Grusinskaya replied shortly. She put her hand under her cloak and absentmindedly stroked Witte's sleeve. "We are

47

tired out. Goodnight, my dear. He's the handsomest man I've ever seen in my life—this Baron," she added in Russian. Her voice as she said it sounded as cold as if she spoke of some object displayed for sale in a saleroom.

Kringelein, lingering at his door and thirsting for Life, listened eagerly to the foreign speech. He had a confused notion that the world was vaster and more exciting and quite otherwise than he had ever imagined it in Fredersdorf.

Then the doors closed throughout the hotel. Everyone locked himself in behind double doors and was left alone with himself and his secrets.

THERE IS not the faintest sign of fashionable life on the ground floor of a big hotel between eight and ten in the morning. No lights, no music, not a single woman to be seen—unless a charwoman in a blue apron, sweeping out the Lounge with damp sawdust, were taken to represent her sex. This, however, did not occur to Count Rohna, who was already at his post, efficient and diligent and calm as ever. He was freshly shaved and a corner of his silk pocket handkerchief made an unobtrusive triangle above the pocket of his coat. It was not at all the right thing in his opinion that the daily cleaning of the hotel should go on under the eyes of the guests. Not done in the best hotels. Unfortunately, however, it was out of his province. It concerned the head housekeeper. In any case the guests paid no attention, for such as are to be seen in a big hotel during the morning are all solid and industrious business men. They sit in the Lounge and conduct their business in all languages, selling stocks and shares, cotton, lubricating oil, patents, films and real estate—and also plans, ideas, energy and even life itself. They make a heavy breakfast and leave the breakfast room full of cigar smoke in spite of a modest notice on the yellow damask wallpaper requesting those who wish to smoke to do so in the grey saloon next door. Newspapers are strewn on every table, every telephone box is not only occupied but beleaguered. The Hall Porter, Senf, has not the slightest hope of getting news from the hospital before one o'clock. On the fifth floor in the corridor just behind the laundry the pageboys are subjected to a kind of parade before going on duty. And the entrance hall of the Grand Hotel is not very different from a Bourse.

Take, for example, Herr Generaldirektor Preysing of the Saxonia Cotton Company. Let us take this excellent and thoroughly average business man as a pattern, and then we shall see what men of his class are about between eight and ten in the Grand Hotel.

General Director Preysing, a large heavy man, rather too stout, arrived at the hotel at the impossible hour of 6.20 am, and the reason was that express trains do not stop at the unfortunate Fredersdorf. In spite of his utmost endeavours he had not so far succeeded in getting a fast train service for the town, though the factory had been granted a siding for loading its goods. This, however, only by the way. Preysing, then, arrived in a somewhat exhausted and shattered state, and he grumbled to himself when he found that the room engaged for him was one of the most expensive. First floor, with sitting-room and bath, No 71, price 75 marks. Preysing was a careful man. For example, the real reason why he did not come to Berlin in his car was that he wished to save the expense of putting up his chauffeur. However, as he had an expensive room with a bath to pay for, the first thing he did was to enjoy a long and luxurious immersion in hot water. (In this he closely resembled the other gentleman from Fredersdorf, Herr Kringelein.) After that he lay in bed for a while, but he could not shake off the fatigue and discomfort of a cold night journey. So he got up again and dressed. Then he unpacked his bag with meticulous care and hung his coats over the coat hangers that he had brought with him. Each shoe, each set of under-clothing, everything, indeed, was enclosed in a clean linen bag, and on each bag the initials K P were neatly marked in red cross-stitch.

While he tied his tie, Preysing looked absentmindedly out on to the street. A morning mist obscured it. It was still early. Street sweepers were brushing the asphalt and yellow buses came like ships through the half light of morning. Preysing looked down, but he saw nothing of all this. He had a heavy day before him. He must collect himself and have everything well thought out. He rang for the valet and gave him his shoes to clean. He had even brought his own polish with him, a brown one and a white. The room was full already of the indefinable smell of a hurried business journey—trunk leather, Odol, eau-de-Cologne, turpentine, cigar smoke. Preysing took out his notecase with the deliberate and fastidious movements that were characteristic of him and counted his money. In the

50

inner pocket was a thick wedge of 1000-mark notes. You could never say in business matters when ready money might not come in useful. Preysing wet his thumb and forefinger as he counted the notes—the sign of a small man who has made his own way. He put the notecase back in the inner breast pocket of his grey worsted suit and fastened up the pocket with a safety pin. For a while he strolled to and fro in red leather bedroom slippers, conducting mute dialogues with the people from the Chemnitz Manufacturing Company. He looked in vain for an ashtray. He disliked having to knock off his cigar ash on the inkstand. Here, too, there was a bronze eagle, like the one that had enchanted Kringelein in Room No 70. The General Director drummed with fingers for a moment or two upon its outspread wings. Then the valet brought his shoes, and at ten minutes to eight Preysing was able to leave his room and arrive second at the hotel barber's. In spite of his cares he looked plump and prosperous enough and in excellent humour, as, freshly shaved, he sat down to breakfast. And there Herr Rothenburger found him when he came by appointment at eight-thirty. Herr Rothenburger was entirely bald. He had not even eyebrows or eyelashes, and this gave him an air of perpetual astonishment that agreed very ill with his cynical pursuits. He was an intermediary between stockjobbers and bankers; now and then he took up agencies besides; and he also sat as director on the board of some small enterprise or other. He knew everything, repeated everything, and had a finger in everything. It was he who was the first to retail the latest stock-brokers' joke and to start those ugly rumours that bring down the price of shares. Take him all in all, Herr Rothenburger was a comical, dangerous and useful man.

"Morning, Rothenburger," said Preysing, and stuck out two fingers with a cigar between them.

"Morning, Preysing," said Rothenburger, and shoved his hat back on to his neck. Then he sat down and put his port-folio on the table. "Back in Berlin again?"

"Yes," said Preysing. "Glad to see you. What'll you have? Tea, cognac, ham and eggs?"

"Cognac for me. All well at home? Your wife and daughters? Quite well, I hope?"

"Thanks, quite well. Good of you to send congratulations on our silver wedding."

"Well, of course. And how did the firm signalize the event?"

"Good heavens! What's the firm got to do with it? I planted them with my old car and took a new one for it."

"Yes, of course. *L'état c'est moi.* I am the firm, a Preysing may say. And how is your father-in-law?"

"Thanks, he's fine. Still enjoys his cigar."

"Lord, the years I've known him now. When I think how he began with six Jacquard looms, in a little bit of a place—and now! Marvellous!"

"Yes, work tells," said Preysing, meaningly.

"Everyone talks of it. I hear you've built yourself a magnificent country house, regular castle, park and all."

"Well, yes. It's come to be quite a nice place. My wife's mad on it. She is a wonderful manager, you know. Quite taken up with her house. Yes, we have a charming place now at Fredersdorf. You must come and see us."

"Thanks. Thanks. Very good of you. Perhaps I may have a business trip to put through—with expenses paid."

After disposing thus of the conventional amiabilities, they got down to the matter in hand.

"A bit unsteady on the Bourse yesterday, wasn't it?" Preysing asked.

"Unsteady? I should say so. Bedlam is nothing in comparison. But since the boom in Bega the whole world has been crazed. Everybody thinks he can do business without security, but yesterday it broke. A thirty per cent drop, I tell you—forty per cent. There are lots who are dead and don't know it. Whoever is holding on to Bega—have you any Bega?"

"Had. Sold it out at the right moment," said Preysing—lying of course in the usual and traditional style customary in business; and Rothenburger knew it.

"Well, don't worry. They'll recover again," he said consolingly, exactly as though Preysing's no had been yes. "What on earth can you rely on when a bank like Küsel in Düsseldorf closes its doors? A house like that! The Saxonia Company is among the sufferers, isn't it?"

"We? Not a penny. What put that into your head?"

"No? I thought it was. One hears all sorts of rumours—but if the Küsel smash hasn't touched you, I can't understand why Saxonia shares have fallen as they have."

"Nor I. I don't understand it either. Twenty-eight per cent is no laughing matter. Other textiles have kept steady that are far worse than ours."

"Yes. Chemnitz Manufacturing Company shares are steady enough," replied Rothenburger to this, without beating about the bush. Preysing looked at him. Eddies of blue smoke curled up between their two faces.

"Let's have it in plain words," said Preysing after a short pause.

"It's for you to put it in plain words. I have no secrets, Preysing. You commissioned me to buy Saxonia Cotton for all I was worth. And so I did—Saxonia shares for the Saxonia Company. Good. We put them up to a very reasonable figure. 184 was really a very respectable figure. They said you were bringing off a big deal with England. The price went up. They said you were amalgamating with the Chemnitz Manufacturing Company. The price went up. Suddenly the Chemnitz people threw all their Saxonia holding on the market. Naturally the price fell. It fell out of all reason. The Bourse is always irrational. The Bourse is a hysterical woman. I can tell you that, Preysing, after being married to her for forty years. You lost money in the Küsel bankruptcy. *Bon!* The English deal has come to nothing. Good again—but all the same a drop of twenty-eight per cent in one day is too much. There's something more behind it."

"To be sure! But what is behind it?" asked Preysing, and a long ash from his cigar fell into his cold coffee. Preysing was no diplomat. His question was foolish and clumsy.

"You know as well as I do. The Chemnitz people are calling the deal off. You've come here by forced marches to rescue what can still be rescued. But what advice can I possibly give you? You can't force the Chemnitz people to love you. If they chuck all the shares they hold in your concern on the market, it's as good as saying: 'No, thank you. We have no further interest in the Saxonia Company.' The question remains—how to make the best of an unpleasant situation. Do you want to buy up any more of your own shares? You can get 'em cheap enough."

Preysing made no reply for the moment. He tried to think and this was no easy matter for him. General Director Preysing was an excellent fellow, correct, straightforward, of irreproachable character. But he was not a business genius. He lacked imagination, persuasiveness and push. Whenever he was asked to come to any important decision, he floundered on slippery ice. He could not even tell a lie with any power of conviction in it. He produced only little feeble abortions of business lies. He soon began to stammer and beads of sweat appeared on his upper lip beneath his moustache.

"If the Chemnitz people don't want the amalgamation, it's their business after all. They have more need of us than we of them. But for this new dyeing process they've got hold of, we should take no interest in the matter whatever," he said finally, and thought he had got out of it very cleverly. Rothenburger raised his ten thick fingers in the air and let them fall again on to the table just beside the saucer of honey. "But they *have* got the dyeing process and therefore the Saxonia *has* an interest in the matter," he said amiably.

Preysing had ten answers at once on the tip of his tongue. 'We lost nothing in the Küsel affair,' he wanted to say, and 'the English deal has by no means fallen through,' and 'the Chemnitz people have brought our shares down precisely because they do want to amalgamate—they'll make a better deal that way.' But finally, he said none of these things, but only blurted out: "Well, we shall see. I'm having a talk with the Chemnitz people the day after tomorrow."

Rothenburger puffed smoke from his throat. "A talk? Which of them are coming? Schweimann? Gerstenkorn? Smart fellows. You'll need your wits about you. That's a job for your father-in-law, if you don't mind my saying so. Well, while there's life there's hope. I must let that be known on the

Bourse. If it does no good it can't do any harm. Well, and how do we stand? Do you commission me to go on buying cotton shares? If there's no one there today to hold the market we shall see a regular collapse. You can take that from me. Well?" And Herr Rothenburger snapped open his portfolio and took out an order form.

A flush had appeared between Preysing's eyebrows when Rothenburger made that tactless allusion to his father-in-law. It was just a fleck of red that came and went again over the bridge of his nose. He took his fountain pen from his pocket and after no more than a momentary hesitation he signed the paper. "Up to 40,000 with a limit of 170," he said coolly. To soothe his vanity he made a thick stroke under his signature. He showed thereby that he would stand no nonsense from his father-in-law, or from Herr Rothenburger either.

Preysing stayed behind in the breakfast room and he felt depressed. There was a faint singing in his ears, for his blood-pressure was not quite right; and an oppressive sensation in the back of his head often bothered him just when he had important interviews on hand. During the last year he had more than once had reverses and now again things were not looking exactly pleasant. It was not an enviable task to have to bring the Chemnitz people up to scratch if they wanted to drop the amalgamation. And at home the old man would sit in his wheeled chair and feel the sly malicious pleasure of old age whenever his son-in-law was in a tight corner. The negotiations with the State Railways about the express train service had led to nothing. That new dyeing process by which cheap fabrics could be given tints that hitherto only better qualities would take had been snapped up under his nose by the Chemnitz Manufacturing Company. That important deal with England had been hanging fire for months. Preysing had been to Manchester twice, and each time the negotiations had gone worse after his return. And now the old man had started interfering in the affair with the Chemnitz Company. He had conducted crafty preliminary negotiations, and old Gerstenkorn had come to Fredersdorf to look into matters and they had argued it all inside out. The famous commercial lawyer, Doctor Zinnowitz, had drawn up a draft contract, which, indeed, had not yet been signed, on the basis that two Chemnitz shares were to be given for one Saxonia. It was good business for the Saxonia—and, when all was said, not bad business for the Chemnitz either. The Bourse knew all about it, so did the whole world (the world of the textile industry), Then of a sudden the Chemnitz people took it into their heads to sing another tune. And now, if you please, when the fat was in the fire the old man had sent him, poor old Preysing, to put things right again. Inadvertently he took a sip of his cold coffee with the cigar ash in it and got up with an exclamation of disgust. His back ached after his journey in that slow train; he yawned spasmodically and his eyes watered. He felt weary and in need of comfort; so he went to the telephone room and asked for an urgent call—Fredersdorf 48.

Fredersdorf 48 was not the factory but his home. It was not long before the call came through, and Preysing settled his elbows on the ledge for a soothing talk with his wife.

"Morning, Mulle," he said. "Yes, it's me. Still sleeping, Mulle? Still in bed?"

"What do you think?" the telephone answered in a distant but amiable voice—a voice that was very dear to the faithful and devoted Generaldirektor. "It is half past nine. I have had breakfast and watered my flowers. And you?"

"*Très bien!*" Preysing said a little too brightly. "I'm having a talk with Zinnowitz presently. Is it sunny with you?"

"Yes," said the telephone; it prattled on faintly in an intimate and homely way. "It is a beautiful day. Just think, all the blue crocuses have come out since yesterday."

Preysing could see the crocuses through the telephone, and the breakfast room with its wicker chairs, the bast-covered coffee pot, the table laid and the knitted cosies over the egg-cups. He saw Mulle too. She was wearing her blue dressing gown and her bedroom slippers and in her hand was a watering-can with a thin spout for the cactuses.

"You know, Mulle, I don't like it here," he said. "You ought to have come with me. You ought really."

"Oh, nonsense——" the telephone said in flattered tones and laughed Mulle's kindly laugh.

"I'm so accustomed to you—and another thing, do you know I forgot my razor and now I must go every morning to the barber."

"So I saw," the telephone replied. "You left it in the bathroom. But I tell you what—buy another. You can get them very cheap at any of the stores. It won't cost more than being shaved every day, and it won't be so tiresome for you."

"Yes. That's true. You're right," Preysing said gratefully. "Where are the children? I'd like to say good morning to them."

The telephone mumbled unintelligible noises from the background and then it called out in a clear voice: "Morning, Pops!"

"Morning, Popsy," Preysing called back joyfully. "How are you?"

"Very well. How are you?"

"I'm very well. Is Babs there too?"

Yes, Babs was there too, and she too asked in her seventeen-year-old voice how he was, and whether it was a fine day and whether Pops was bringing them anything from Berlin, and the crocuses were out and Mulle would not let them play tennis and it was quite warm and might Schmidt get the lawn ready. And then Mulle joined in, and then Popsy, till at last the telephone shouted and laughed with three voices at once, and the telephone girl intervened and Preysing ended the conversation. He stood for a moment in the box afterwards and, though he could not have put it into words, he felt that he held in his hands the warm sun outside the window and the blue crocuses.

He felt in better spirits when he left the box. There were people who called General Director Preysing a regular family man and they were not altogether mistaken. Next, he got another call put through and spoke with his bank. He spoke rather feverishly, for it was a question of cover for the 40,000 for the reckless and even desperate commission he had given Rothenburger on his own responsibility. During these unpleasant ten minutes that the General Director spent in Box No 4, Kringelein walked down the stairs enjoying at each step the raspberry-red carpet that made his downward progress such a splendid and unusual experience, and finally arrived at the Hall Porter's desk. Once more he had a flower in his buttonhole. It was the one of the evening before and after spending the night in his bedroom tumbler it was still moderately fresh. A white carnation. Kringelein felt that its spicy perfume put the last indispensable touch to his elegance.

"The gentleman you were asking for yesterday has arrived," the Hall Porter announced.

"What gentleman?" Kringelein asked in surprise. The Hall Porter looked in the book, "Preysing, General Director Preysing of Fredersdorf," he said, and gave Kringelein's peaky, unpretending face a sharp look. Kringelein breathed in so hard that it was almost a gasp.

"Oh, yes, of course. He's come? That's good. Thank you. And where is he?" he asked with blanched lips.

"In the breakfast room probably."

Kringelein walked away and pulled himself forcibly together. He braced himself up till the small of his back was hollowed. Good day, Herr Preysing, was what he would say. Having a good breakfast? Yes, I am staying in the Grand Hotel too. Certainly. Have you any objections? Is it not allowed perhaps for a man like me? Oh, no. People like us can live as they please, just like others.

Immediately afterwards he was thinking. Why this fear of Preysing? He can do nothing to me. I shall be dead very soon. No one can do anything to me. It was the same not unmixed feeling of freedom that he had felt long ago in Mickenauer forest among the wild raspberries. Swelled out with courage, he entered the breakfast room. He moved now with a certain confidence in these smart surroundings. He looked for Preysing. It was actually his intention to speak to him. He wanted to be even with him. That was precisely why he had come to the Grand Hotel.

Good morning, Herr Preysing, he would say. . . .

But Preysing was not in the breakfast room. Kringelein

strolled along the corridor. He looked into the reading- and writing-rooms, and sought him at the paper stall. He even went so far as to ask Pageboy No 14 where Herr Preysing was to be found. Nobody knew. All heads were shaken. Kringelein was now warmed up. He chafed at these paltry hindrances and wished to be done with it. Arriving at the threshold of a room he did not know, he asked the telephonist, "Excuse me, do you know Herr Preysing of Fredersdorf?" The man merely nodded. His head was too full of figures to reply. He pointed with his thumb over his shoulder. Kringelein went red, then white. For at that moment Preysing, lost in thought, came out of Box No 4.

At once Kringelein collapsed. His neck broke, as it were, at the nape and his head fell forward. His hollowed back relaxed. His toes turned in. His coat collar went up his neck. His knees gave, and his trousers bagged in wrinkles over his sorry shanks. Within a second the prosperous and distinguished Herr Kringelein turned into the poor insignificant book-keeper. It was a subordinate who stood there. He had forgotten, apparently, that he had only a few weeks to live and therefore had all the advantage over Herr Preysing, for whom there were still years of tribulation in store. Kringelein, the book-keeper, stepped to one side and, with his back squeezed against the door of Box No 2, he made his bow and murmured with bent head just as though he were at the factory, "I wish you good morning, Herr Generaldirektor."

"Morning," said Preysing, and passed on without even seeing him. Kringelein stood there for a full minute flattened against the wall and tasted the bitterness of his humiliation. He felt his pains, too, suddenly coming back; excruciating pains in that sick and moribund stomach that was secretly of itself preparing the toxins of a lingering death.

Meanwhile, Preysing went on into the Lounge, where the well-known commercial lawyer, Doctor Zinnowitz, already awaited him.

For two hours Doctor Zinnowitz and General Director Preysing sat with their heads bent over papers in a quiet corner of the Winter Garden, which till midday was little frequented. Preysing's portfolio had emptied out its entire contents, his ashtray was full of cigar ends and the backs of his hands were moist with sweat, as they always were under the stress of exacting business discussions. Doctor Zinnowitz, a short elderly gentleman, with the face of a Chinese sorcerer, gave a little cough, as though he were about to make a speech in court, and tapping the bundles of papers in front of him with an authoritative air, spoke as follows:

"My dear Preysing, it comes to this, we enter the conference tomorrow at a substantial disadvantage. Our shares are in a bad way, both on paper and in fact." (Here he tapped the list of quotations in the midday edition of the *Berliner Zeitung*, which a pageboy had just brought in. It showed a further fall of seven per cent in Saxonia shares.) "Our shares are in a bad way and the psychological moment, if I may so express myself, for this critical interview has been ill-chosen. You know yourself, if the Chemnitz people say 'No' tomorrow, it is all over with the amalgamation. The question can never be raised again. And it is very possible that they will say 'No', as things are now. I don't say it is certain, but it is possible. It is even probable."

Preysing listened with impatience. He was in a nervous state. The lawyer's studied phrases irritated him. Zinnowitz always spoke as though he were at a board meeting, even if he were quite alone. When he rested his knuckles on the flimsy wicker table of the Winter Garden it became at once the fateful green baize-covered table of a board room.

"Should we cry off?" asked Preysing.

"To cry off is impossible without inviting the worst constructions," observed Zinnowitz. "There is the further question, too, whether even putting it off would be a gain or a loss. There are always chances that might be irretrievably lost by a postponement."

"What chances?" asked Preysing. He could not free himself of the foolish habit of asking things that he knew without asking. Hence any discussion in which he took part always strayed from the point and became something at once pedantic and confused.

"You know the chances as well as I do," said Doctor Zinnowitz, and his words sounded like a reproof. "It comes back of course to the situation with regard to the English affair. Manchester, Burleigh & Son of Manchester—that in my opinion is the salient point. The Chemnitz Company is after the English market for their readymade goods. Burleigh & Son have this market to a great extent in their pockets. They have large and constant demands for finished cotton goods, but they themselves produce only the yarn, and they are eager to export their yarn to Germany and to import the finished articles in exchange. They have a great interest in coming to terms with the Chemnitz concern. As to why they do not simply go to them direct, that, my dear Preysing, you know as well as I do. The Chemnitz enterprise is not solid enough for these Englishmen. Its capital is too small. They hang back because they think the basis is not sound. It would be another matter if the Saxonia Company amalgamates with the Chemnitz concern. Burleigh & Son would then find the situation a promising one. The idea seems to be that in that case, if you'll forgive me saying so, your somnolent business would be freshened up and the somewhat too enterprising Chemnitz concern sobered down. It comes to this, then, that Burleigh & Son are interested in the Saxonia Company only if it is amalgamated with the Chemnitz Company, and the latter will only amalgamate if you have the deal with Burleigh & Son, and consequently the English market, in your pocket. Nothing can be done till the agreement between you and the other side is completed. If I may give you my frank opinion, the negotiations must have been incompetently conducted, otherwise we could not have got into such a blind alley. Who has been negotiating with Manchester?"

"My father-in-law," Preysing replied quickly. That was not the fact, and Zinnowitz knew it was not the fact, for he was pretty well informed about the struggle for power in the Saxonia Cotton Company. He swept his hand over the table as though he brushed Preysing's reply on one side.

"I have been," he went on, "in close touch all this while

with the enemy's position" (he liked to bring in the military expressions which he had learnt as a Captain in the reserve), "and I can tell you exactly how they feel about it. Schweimann has dropped all idea of the amalgamation and Gerstenkorn has begun to waver. Why? The big SIR combine is putting out feelers to ascertain whether the Chemnitz people can be bought out—not amalgamated, but bought right out. Of course, Schweimann and Gerstenkorn would remain as directors and be given salaried posts in addition, whereas now they are saddled with all the risks. On the other hand, if the affair with Burleigh's were in black and white, then—such at least is my humble opinion—they would turn down the offer from the SIR and amalgamate with you. That's their position. But what yours is with Manchester, there I am not quite so clear. I have a somewhat guarded letter from your father-in-law——"

Once again, Preysing interrupted the lawyer's clear exposition with a stupid question. "Is this offer of the SIR definite or only talk? How much have they offered?" he asked.

"That is beside the point," said Zinnowitz, who did not know. Preysing pushed forward his underlip and his cigar with it. It was not at all beside the point, he thought. But he could not explain why.

"The affair with Burleigh's isn't exactly in a bad way," he said hesitatingly.

"Not exactly in a good way either, it seems to me," the lawyer replied promptly.

Preysing stretched out a hand towards his portfolio, drew back and then finally took hold of it. He took his cigar out of his mouth, its end was chewed to pieces, and at last, at the third attempt, he pulled out a blue folder in which were filed letters and copies of the replies.

"Here is the correspondence with Manchester up to date," he said quickly and held out the file of letters. He had no sooner done so than he regretted it. The backs of his hands were once more in a sweat. He began to play with a ring on his finger, a habit of his, but it got him no farther. "In the strictest confidence, please remember," he requested urgently. Zinnowitz replied only by a glance out of the corners of his eyes as he read the letters. Preysing was silent. A gentle rattle could now be heard from the large dining-room where the tables were being laid. There was a savoury smell in the air, as there is in every hotel in the world just before lunch, a smell that makes you hungry before the meal and is intolerable afterwards. Preysing was hungry. He gave a fleeting thought to Mulle at home. She would just be sitting down to lunch with the children.   .

"Yes——" said Doctor Zinnowitz as he put the letters aside and looked thoughtfully and at the same time absentmindedly at the bridge of Preysing's nose.

"Yes?" asked Preysing.

"And now," said Doctor Zinnowitz, proceeding after a moment's silence to his pronouncement, "I come back once more to the starting-point. The negotiations with Burleigh & Son are still going on. Consequently we still have this trump card to play in our efforts to bring pressure on the Chemnitz people. If we postpone a meeting with them and Burleigh's refuse to come to terms, as seems very possible from their last letter of February 27th, then we hold this trump card no longer. Then we shall have no card to play whatever. We shall fall between two stools, instead of sitting on them."

A dark red flush suddenly sprang to Preysing's forehead, the skin beneath its wrinkles was suffused with blood and his veins swelled. He had now and then such crises of anger, of blood-pressure and passionate vehemence.

"All this has no sense in it. We simply must have the amalgamation, and there's an end of it," he shouted and brought his fist down on the table.

Doctor Zinnowitz said nothing for a moment.

"I imagine the Saxonia Company won't be bankrupt, even failing the amalgamation," he said.

"No, certainly not. There is no question of bankruptcy," Preysing said heatedly. "But we should have to retrench. We should have to pay off some of the hands in the spinning mills. We should have—but what's the good of talking? I have got to put the amalgamation through. That's what I'm here for. I have got to put it through, and there's an end of it. It's not only—there are other reasons. There is the question of the effect on the management of the business. You understand what I mean. After all, it is I who have made the factory. It is all my organization. That being so I want to have the credit for it. The old man is getting on. And I don't hit it off with my young brother-in-law. I tell you that quite frankly. You know him, of course—well, we don't hit it off. He has brought new-fangled ideas with him from Lyons that don't agree with my notions of business. I am not for bluff. I don't care for sharp practice. I make my decisions on a solid basis. I don't build houses of cards. As long as I am there I intend to be reckoned with, and what I say is——"

Doctor Zinnowitz looked with keen interest at the heated General Director, who was beginning to talk irresponsibly. "You are well known in the trade as a model of business propriety," he remarked politely, and there was a hint of patronage in the tone of his voice. Preysing broke off. He took the blue folder and stuffed it back into his portfolio with trembling hands.

"We agree, then," said Zinnowitz. "The conference will take place tomorrow and we will do all in our power to get the draft agreement signed. If only I knew——"

"Listen," he continued after a moment's silent reflection. "Will you allow me to take one or two of the letters away with me? Some of the more promising ones, you understand me, dating from the earlier stages of the negotiations? I am seeing Schweimann and Gerstenkorn this afternoon. It would do no harm if—of course, I wouldn't show them the whole correspondence, only some of it——"

"Impossible," said Preysing. "We have promised Burleigh & Son to regard the matter as strictly confidential."

Zinnowitz smiled at this. "Why, it's common knowledge in any case," he said. "However, as you think best. It is your responsibility. Now is the time to show your mettle. Everything might turn on a skilful use of the negotiations with the Manchester people. It is the one issue on which we stand a chance of straightening out this somewhat involved affair with the Chemnitz concern. The thing would be to let one or two of the letters fall into Schweimann's hands, quite by the way, quite by accident. A selection, needless to say. A few copies. But—as you please. It is your responsibility."

Once more Preysing was faced with a responsibility. The advance of forty thousand for Rothenburger's purchase of shares still lay heavy on him. He positively had a twinge of heartburn from nervous agitation and his temples throbbed feverishly.

"I don't like it. It isn't straight," he said. "The negotiations with Chemnitz began long before the affair with Burleigh's, nor was there a word said about it between us and Gerstenkorn. Now of a sudden everything is made to turn on it. If the Chemnitz people are willing to accept us only as a catspaw for the deal with England—and that is what it looks like—we are not going to the length of letting them look through our correspondence. I wouldn't hear of it——"

As stubborn as a mule, thought Doctor Zinnowitz, and he snapped the lock of his portfolio. "As you please," he said, and his lips tightened as he got up to go.

Suddenly Preysing gave in.

"Have you anyone who could make copies of a few of the letters? I might let you have a few carbon copies. The original letters must on no account pass out of my hands," he said in a loud and imperative voice as though he had to shout someone down. "It would have to be somebody whose discretion could be relied upon. I have some notes to dictate too, that I shall need for the conference. I don't care to employ the typists supplied by the hotel. You always have the feeling that they give away business secrets to the Hall Porter. It would have to be soon after lunch."

"No one in my office would have time, I am afraid," Zinnowitz said coolly and rather surprised. "We have several big affairs on hand and they have been working overtime in the office for weeks past. But wait a bit—you could have Flämmchen. Flämmchen would do. I'll have her rung up."

"Who—did you say?" asked Preysing, on whom the name made an unpleasant impression.

"Flämmchen. Flamm the Second. Sister of Flamm the

First. You know her, don't you? She's been twenty years with me. Flamm the Second often helps us out when we have more typing on hand than the office can manage. I have taken her with me when I have had to go away on business and Flamm the First could not be spared. She is very quick and intelligent. I should have to have the copies by five o'clock. Then I'll manage it quite unofficially, as I am having dinner with the Chemnitz gentlemen. Flämmchen can bring me the copies direct to the office. I'll telephone at once to Flamm the First to tell her to send her sister here. What time have you engaged the conference room for tomorrow?"

Doctor Zinnowitz and General Director Preysing had quite the right air as they left the Winter Garden with their well-worn portfolios under their arms and crossed the corridor and passed by the Hall Porter's desk to reach the Lounge. Here there were many other men like them, all with the same kind of portfolios and all carrying on the same kind of discussion. But now a few women too had made their appearance, fresh from their baths and scented after their morning toilet. Their lips were neatly painted and they pulled on their gloves with careless ease before passing through the revolving door to the street whose surface was bathed in yellow sunshine.

Just as they were crossing the Lounge to the telephone room, Preysing heard his name called. Pageboy No 18 was going along the passage calling out at regular intervals, in his clear, careless, boyish voice: "Herr Direktor Preysing! Herr Direktor Preysing of Fredersdorf! Herr Direktor Preysing!"

"Here," called out Preysing and put out his hand for a telegram. "Excuse me," he said and read it as he walked beside Doctor Zinnowitz through the Lounge. He went cold to the roots of his hair as he read it.

The telegram ran: 'Negotiations with Burleigh and Son finally broken off. Brösemann.'

That's finished it. You need not send for the typist, Herr Doktor. It's finished. Manchester is done with, thought Preysing while he drew nearer all the time to the telephone room. He stuck the telegram into his coat pocket and gripped it there spasmodically between his thumb and forefinger. Finished.

There's no need to have any copies made, he thought, and intended to say it aloud. But he did not say it. He cleared his throat which was still husky after his night journey. "It has turned out quite a fine day," was what he said.

"Yes. We're at the end of March now," answered Zinnowitz, who had put off his business manner and become a private person with an eye for the ladies' silk stockings. "Box No 2 will be free in a moment," said the operator, with his fingers on the red and green stops.

Preysing leant against the padded door of the box and stared mechanically through the glass panel at a broad back. Zinnowitz was saying something, but he paid no attention. He was obsessed by immeasurable fury against Brösemann, this blockhead of a managing clerk who let loose telegrams like this on him just when he needed a stiff back to pull off a troublesome deal. No doubt the old man was behind it with his senile spite. Now you're in the soup and let's see what you make of it, he would be saying with a malicious joy. The poor General Director could have cried. His nerves were in a pitiful state after his sleepless night. He was worried to death and his upright principles were no match for all these wretched and baffling complications. He tried to get his thoughts straight, but they twisted and turned in his brain. By his side Doctor Zinnowitz was talking in the tone of a man-about-town about a new Revue all in silver, entirely in silver. Then he felt the door of the telephone box against which he leant for support being gently but firmly pushed open and a large and strikingly handsome fellow in a blue coat forced his way out with a friendly air; indeed, instead of taking it amiss, he politely apologized. Preysing absentmindedly stared him straight in the face. He saw it with a strange distinctness at very close quarters, and he too muttered a conventional apology. Zinnowitz was already in the box. He was engaging the services of Flamm the Second, some competent female who was to make copies of letters, and it was now all utterly pointless. Preysing knew well enough that he ought to put a stop to it, but he could not collect the energy to do it.

"I've fixed it up," said Doctor Zinnowitz as he came out of

the box. "Flämmchen will be here at three. There are plenty of typewriters in the hotel. I shall have the letters by five. I'll speak to you on the phone before the conference. We'll bring it off yet. Au revoir."

"Au revoir," said Preysing to the whirling reflections of the revolving door as it ejected the lawyer into the street. Outside the sun was shining. Outside a small destitute man was selling violets. Outside no one was worried by amalgamations and troublesome contracts. Until Doctor Zinnowitz finally disappeared in a taxi, Preysing kept the telegram tightly gripped in his right-hand coat pocket. He now took it out and holding it in his left hand went to a table in the Lounge. There he carefully smoothed it out and folded it neatly together, and then he put it in the breast pocket of his neat dark grey suit.

At five minutes past three the telephone roused Herr Preysing from his afternoon nap. He jumped up from the couch on which he had lain down after taking off his shoes and collar and coat. He had that comfortless and disagreeable feeling which is the usual result of snatching a few minutes' sleep in an hotel. The heavy yellow curtains were drawn. The room was full of the dry hot air of the central heating. His right cheek was marked by the impress of his travelling cushion. The telephone rang on insistently. A lady was waiting for Herr Direktor in the Lounge, the Hall Porter announced. "Send her up," said Preysing and began hastily to make himself tidy. Unexpected difficulties, however, were made in the most polite manner through the telephone. The hotel had its rules and regulations. Rohna, the reception clerk, himself communicated them to Herr Preysing with many apologetic regrets and the smile of a man of the world. It was not allowed to receive ladies in one's bedroom and unfortunately no exceptions could be made. "But, good heavens! this is no visit from a lady. It's my secretary, as you can see for yourself, and I have some work for her," Preysing said impatiently. The smile of the reception clerk became only the more audible. The director was requested to be so good as to take the lady to the room specially provided for such purposes. Preysing rang off, replacing the receiver with a violent jerk as he did so. He felt that he was being submitted to the most shocking inconvenience. He washed his hands, gargled with a mouthwash, wrestled with his collar stud and tie, and hurried down to the Lounge.

In the Lounge sat Flämmchen, Fräulein Flamm the Second, the sister of Fräulein Flamm the First. Two sisters less alike could scarcely be imagined. Preysing had a vague recollection of Flamm the First as a most reliable person with colourless hair, a detachable sleeve on her right arm and a paper cuff on her left, who, with an uncompromising air, barred the way to undesired callers in Doctor Zinnowitz's outer office. Flamm the Second, Flämmchen, on the other hand, had not a trace of this stolid demeanour. She was leaning back in an armchair as though she was quite at home in such surroundings; she swung one foot in a neat shoe of light blue leather, and looked as if she was out to have a jolly good time. She was, as her whole appearance testified, at the utmost twenty years old.

"Doctor Zinnowitz sent me to make the copies. I am Flämmchen whom he said he would send along, I ought to explain," she said without ceremony. She had a dab of red paint in the centre of her lips, dabbed on quite casually, merely because it was the fashion. When she stood up she showed that she was taller than the General Director. Her legs were long and her figure from head to foot was magnificent. She wore a tight leather belt round her remarkably slender waist. Preysing was furious with Zinnowitz for putting him in such an idiotic situation. The scruples of the reception clerk were now very intelligible. She was scented too. He wanted to send her home. "We had better be quick, hadn't we?" she said in a deep and slightly husky voice that young girls often have. Popsy, his elder daughter, had had a voice like that as a child.

"So you are Fräulein Flamm's sister? I know Fräulein Flamm," he said. There was more rudeness than surprise in his voice. Flamm the Second put out her underlip and blew away a lock of hair that hung over her forehead beneath her small felt hat. The little golden curl rose in the air and fell back slowly on to her forehead again. Preysing did not wish to look, but looked all the same. "Step-sister," said Flämmchen. "I am the daughter of my father's second wife. But we get on quite well."

"I see," said Preysing and looked at her with troubled eyes. So now she was to make copies of letters from a correspondence that was finished with, that was utterly senseless, utterly unreal. For months he had been counting on the agreement with Burleigh & Son, reckoning on it in all his plans, and he could not readjust himself all at once. It was simply beyond him to wipe out this affair utterly from his mind. Finally broken off. Brösemann. Finally. There was a letter to Brösemann to dictate as well, a stinger. To the old man, too, about the forty thousand. If the Chemnitz affair fell through tomorrow, the forty thousand for steadying the market had been thrown to the winds.

"Right. Come along to the writing-room, then," said Preysing, and filled with gloom he preceded her along the corridor. Flämmchen with a smile of amusement kept her eyes on the roll of flesh at the back of his neck as she followed him.

Already the typewriters could be heard in the distance like faint machine-gun fire, with their bells ringing at regular intervals. When Preysing opened the door volumes of cigar smoke came eddying out in huge coils. "Fine room for hearing in," said Flämmchen and gave a little sniff. Inside the room a man was walking to and fro with his hands behind his back and his hat on the back of his head, dictating in a nasal American voice. He was the manager of a film company. He looked Flämmchen up and down with the rapid glance of a connoisseur and went on dictating.

"This won't do," said Preysing and slammed the door again. "I must have the room to myself. There's annoyance at every turn in this hotel."

This time he walked behind Flämmchen along the corridor. He was in a rage now, and in the midst of his rage the swaying of Flämmchen's hips warmed and pricked his senses. In the Lounge Flämmchen once more attracted all eyes. She was a magnificent example of the female form—of that there seemed no possible doubt. Preysing found it extremely unpleasant to be making his way across the Lounge in the company of so striking a creature, and left her to stand where she was while he arranged with Rohna for the undisturbed possession of the typewriting-room. Flämmchen, entirely unmoved by the looks that were fixed upon her from all sides (she was used enough to them, Heaven knows), carelessly powdered her nose, and then, without moving from where she stood, took a cigarette case from the pocket of her coat with a free and easy air and began to smoke. Preysing approached her as if she was a thicket of nettles.

"We shall have to wait for ten minutes," he said.

"*Bon!*" said Flämmchen. "But after that we must be quick."

"Are you so punctual as all that?" asked Preysing unamiably.

"Rather!" answered Flämmchen, and laughed roguishly in a way that made her nose quite short like a baby's while her light brown eyes darted a sidelong glance.

"Well, take a seat till then," said Preysing. "And have something. Waiter, give the lady something," he said tactlessly and made his retreat.

Flämmchen ordered a Pêche Melba and nodded her head quite happily. Also she blew again at her lock of hair, but without success. She was as beautifully made as a racehorse and as natural in her movements as a puppy.

Baron Gaigern, who had been wandering about the Lounge for a few minutes, looked at her from the distance with unaffected admiration. After a moment he went up to her and said in a low voice: "May I take a seat beside you? But surely you have not forgotten me? Didn't I dance with you at Baden-Baden?"

"Impossible. I've never been to Baden-Baden," said Flämmchen and took a good look at him.

"A thousand apologies. I see now, I must have made an error and mistaken you for someone else," cried the Baron hypocritically. Flämmchen laughed at this. "You don't get over me with that old story," she said drily. Gaigern laughed too.

"Well, let's drop that nonsense. I may sit here, may I? You

are quite right. You could not be mistaken for anyone else. A girl like you is only seen once. Are you staying here? Are you going to dance this evening? Please—I should so much like to dance with you. Will you?"

He put his hands on the table. Flämmchen's were there already. There was a little space in between his fingers and hers and the air in it began to vibrate. They looked at each other and the mutual attraction and sympathy was instantly complete between these two young and charming people. "Good lord, you've got a way with you," said Flämmchen, enchanted.

And Gaigern answered equally enchanted, "You promise then? You'll dance this evening?"

"I can't. I've work to do. But I'm free tonight."

"But bother it, I'm not. What about tomorrow? Or the day after tomorrow at five o'clock? Here in the yellow pavilion? That's settled then?"

Flämmchen licked her spoon clean, and said nothing.

What was there to say in any case? You picked up acquaintances as you lit a cigarette. You took a few puffs just as you felt inclined and then you trod it out.

"What is your name?" Gaigern asked meanwhile.

"Flämmchen," she said promptly. Immediately upon this Preysing came up to the table with a proprietary air, and Gaigern politely made way for him by getting up and standing behind his chair.

"We can get along now," said Preysing irritably.

Flämmchen extended a gloved hand to Gaigern while Preysing looked on with displeasure. He recognized Gaigern as the man who had come out of the telephone box and once again he saw his face so distinctly that every pore and every little line in it was revealed.

"Who is that?" he asked as he crossed the Lounge at Flämmchen's side.

"Oh, an acquaintance," she replied.

"Indeed. You have a number of acquaintances, no doubt?"

"I don't complain. It doesn't do to make yourself too cheap. Besides, I haven't always the time."

For some obscure reason this reply was comforting to the General Director.

"Have you got a permanent job?" he asked.

"Not at the moment. I am looking out for one. Well, something will turn up. Something always turns up," said Flämmchen philosophically. "I should like best of all to get on to the films, but it isn't easy to make the start. If I could only make a start I should soon get on. But it's so horribly difficult to make a start." She looked with a troubled and comical expression into Preysing's face. She was now like a young cat. All the charm of an animal appeared to meet in the changing expressions of her face. Preysing, who was far from such perceptions, opened the door of the typewriting-room, asking as he did so: "Why the films particularly? You are all film mad." Among the 'all' was included his fifteen-year-old daughter, Babs, who adored the films. "Oh, as to that, I have no illusions about it. But I photograph well. Everybody says so," said Flämmchen and took off her coat. "Shorthand, or straight on to the typewriter?"

"Type it, please," said Preysing. He was now more lively and in better humour. He had rid his mind of the fact that Manchester had fallen through, and as he took the first and still so very promising letters of this correspondence from his portfolio he felt positively happy. Flämmchen was still taken up with her own affairs.

"I am often photographed for the newspapers and so on. Advertisements for soaps are made from me, too. How do I get on to that, you ask? Well, one photographer tells another. I'm very good in the nude, you see. But it's wretchedly paid. Ten marks a photo. Just imagine that. No, the best thing would be if someone would take me travelling as his secretary this spring. Last year I went with a gentleman to Florence. He was working at a book—a professor—charming man he was. Oh well, something else will turn up this year too," she said and put the machine in order. It was evident she had her cares and as evident that those cares weighed on her as little as the lock of hair which from time to time she blew into the air off her forehead. Preysing, who could not reconcile the casual

73

allusion to the nude with any scheme of things to which he was accustomed, wished to say something businesslike. Instead of that he said, gazing meanwhile at Flämmchen's hands as she adjusted the paper: "How brown your hands are. Where did you find enough sun for that?"

Flämmchen inspected her hands and then she drew her sleeve up a little way and looked earnestly at her brown skin. "That's the snow. I went ski-ing at Vorarlberg. A friend of mine took me with him. It was glorious. You should have seen me when I got back. Shall we make a start, then?"

Preysing took a turn through the room, which was thick with cigar smoke, and began to dictate from the farthest corner.

"Date—you've got the date? Dear Herr Brösemann, Bröse —got that? Referring to your telegram of this morning, I have to inform——"

Flämmchen carried on with her right hand while with her left she removed her hat, which she appeared to find in her way. The room looked on to a dark ventilation shaft and was lighted by green-shaded electric lights. In the midst of these business matters Preysing could not help thinking of a chest of drawers, an old chest of drawers of birch wood in the entrance hall at Fredersdorf.

It came back to him at night when he woke up after dreaming of Flämmchen. Her hair had the colour, the flame-like sheen of old birch wood, and the lights and shadows of its grain. This hair of hers was clearly before his eyes as he lay in bed at night, breathing the dry air of the hotel bedroom, while the lights of the electric sign flitted across the drawn curtains. The portfolio on the table in the darkness got on his nerves. He got up and put it in his trunk, rinsed his mouth once more with Odol and once more washed his hands. His suite annoyed him. It was dear and uncomfortable. It consisted of a minute room with a sofa, a table and chairs, and a small bedroom with a bathroom beside it. The bath tap dripped and the drip, drip, drip pursued him till he fell asleep. Once again he got out of bed and set an alarm clock. He had forgotten to buy the razor and would have to be early at the barber's. He fell asleep and again dreamed of the typist and her birch-wood hair. He awoke once more. The electric sign was still passing to and fro across the curtains and the hours of night in the strange bed seemed to him disagreeable and confused. He was in a panic at the thought of the meeting with Schweimann and Gerstenkorn, and his heart thumped in his chest. He had been in a strange confusion of mind ever since he handed over the letters from England and he had a persistent feeling that his hands were not clean. Last of all, just as he was falling into a doze, he heard someone come along the carpeted passage, whistling softly. It was the occupant of Room No 69, who put a pair of patent-leather shoes outside his door as though life were a matter for enjoyment.

Kringelein, too, in Room No 70, heard it and woke up. He had been dreaming of Grusinskaya. She had come to him in the counting-house and put before him some unpaid accounts. He was beginning to feel at home, this Otto Kringelein, this book-keeper from Fredersdorf, this sufferer from claustrophobia, who wanted to seize one hour of crowded life before he died. His hunger was infinite, but he could not stand very much. His weakness of body many a time got the better of him during these days and forced him to retreat from the scenes of dissipation to his bedroom. Kringelein began to hate his ailments, though without them he would never have made his escape from Fredersdorf. He had bought himself some medicine—Hundt's Elixir. From time to time he took a sip and hoped for the best. It had a bitter taste of cinnamon, and he gulped it down and even felt the better for it.

He held out his cold fingers in the darkness and began on a calculation. His fingers always went dead while he was asleep, as though they were making a beginning, and this was unpleasant. He seemed to see numerals with bent heads prowling round his room, till at last he raised himself and turned on the light. Unfortunately, this lifelong habit of the impecunious Kringelein would not desert him now he was a man of wealth. He could not help reckoning up figures. Figures were always pursuing their antics in his head. They formed themselves in columns one below the other and added and subtracted themselves whether he would or no. Kringelein had a little notebook bound in shiny black cloth, which he had brought with him from Fredersdorf, and he sat at it for hours together. He entered his expenses in it, the reckless expenses of a man who was learning to enjoy life and spending a month's salary in two days. Sometimes he was so dizzy that all the four walls with their wallpaper of tulips seemed to fall in upon him. Sometimes he was happy, not entirely happy nor as he imagined the rich being happy, but all the same, happy. Sometimes, again, he sat on the edge of his bed and thought of his approaching death. He thought of it hard and with horror, while his ears went cold and he blinked in anguish of heart. In spite of all, he could make nothing of it. He hoped that it would be much the same as going under chloroform, except that you came to again after chloroform and found yourself in a bad way and in agonizing pain—blue pain Kringelein had called it in his own mind—and also that all those familiar tortures were now to be borne beforehand, not afterwards. When he had thought as far as this, he began to shudder. Yes, Kringelein actually shuddered at the thought of death, although he could form no idea of it.

There were a good many behind the locked double doors of the sleeping hotel who could not sleep. Doctor Otternschlag, indeed, about this time of the night laid a little hypodermic syringe down on his washhand-stand and, throwing himself on his bed, floated away on the light clouds of a morphine trance. Witte, the conductor, who had Room No 221 in the left wing, could not sleep either. Old people sleep so little. His room was the counterpart of Doctor Otternschlag's. There, too, the water gurgled in the wall and the lift rumbled up and down. It was little better than a servant's room. He was sitting at his window, pressing his forehead against the window-pane and staring at the blank wall opposite. Fragments of a Beethoven symphony were going through his head. He had never conducted it. He heard Bach—the tremendous 'Crucify Him' from the Matthew Passion. I have wasted all my life, thought old Witte, and all the never-sung music of his life made a lump in his throat and he gulped it down. There was the rehearsal for the ballet at half past eight in the morning. He would sit at the piano and play the same old march to the convolutions of the Ballet, always the Spring Waltz and Mazurka and Bacchanal. He ought to have left Elisaveta while there was still time, he thought. Now it was too late. Elisaveta had become an old woman and he could not leave her now. They would have to see it through with her for the few years that remained. . . .

Elisaveta Alexandrovna Grusinskaya could not sleep either. In the depth of night she heard the swift and never-ceasing flight of time. There was a two-fold ticking in the dark room —from a bronze clock on the writing-table and from her wrist watch on the bedside table. Each told the flight of seconds, and yet one ticked faster than the other. It made her heart beat to listen to them. She turned on the light and got out of bed, put her feet into her trodden-down slippers and went to the look-ing-glass. The passage of time met her there—there most of all. It met her too in her press notices, in the shocking rudeness of the newspapers, in the success of the ugly and clumsy dancers that were now in fashion, in the losses on her tours, in the feeble applause, in the vulgar way her manager, Meyer-heim, talked—everywhere, everywhere, she saw the passage of time. The years she had danced away were in her tired ankles, in the shortness of breath that came over her after thirty-two tours of classical dances and in her blood, too, that now often pulsed in her neck and flushed her cheeks. It was hot in her room, though the French window on to the balcony was wide open. Outside the motor cars hooted all night long. Grusin-skaya took her pearls out of the small suitcase, two handfuls of cool pearls, and put her face down to them. In vain. Her eye-lids were still hot and still smarted from the paint and the footlights; her thoughts still troubled her, and the clock and the watch still raced on. Grusinskaya wore a rubber bandage under her chin, her hands and lips were steeped in ointment. The sight of herself in the looking-glass was so hateful that she quickly turned out the light. In the darkness she swallowed a veronal tablet and began to weep the hot tears of a lonely and passionate woman; then the drug took hold of her and at last she fell asleep.

Just outside someone got out of the light. It might be the

young man from Nice. Grusinskaya took him with her into her veronal dream. He was in Room No 69 and he was the handsomest man she had ever seen. . . .

He whistled softly on his way to his room, not unpleasantly, and merely because he was happy. He was careful in his room to make no noise and when he was in his pyjamas and smart blue leather slippers he was more silent than ever. There was something of the wild cat in this handsome young man. Whenever he passed through the Lounge it was as if a window of sunshine were opened in a cold room. He was a marvellous dancer, cool, and yet passionate. There were always flowers in his room. He loved them and their scent. When he was alone he stroked and even licked their petals—like an animal. He was quick to follow girls in the street. Sometimes he would merely look at them with pleasure, sometimes he would speak to them, and sometimes he would go home with them or take them to a second-rate hotel. Next morning the Hall Porter would smile, when with a feline and innocent air he made his appearance in the elegant and more or less irreproachable Lounge of the Grand Hotel and asked for his key. Sometimes too he got drunk, but in so amiable and high-spirited a fashion that no one could take it amiss. In the mornings it was not very pleasant to have the room beneath his, for then he went through his physical exercises, and soft thuds came at regular intervals through the ceiling. He wore smart bow ties and low-cut waistcoats. His clothes sat as easily on his muscular body as the hide on a pedigree animal. Sometimes he went off in his little four-seater and nothing more was seen of him for a couple of days. For hours together he pottered about in automobile showrooms, sticking his head under the bonnets of motor cars, breathing in petrol, lubricating oil and the smell of the warmed-up engine, tapping the chassis, stroking the enamel, the leather and the upholstery, blue, red or beige. If he was left alone, perhaps he would lick this too with his tongue. He bought laces from street vendors, cigarette lighters that would not light, little birds of india-rubber and countless boxes of matches. Suddenly a longing for horses would come over him. He got up at six, went by bus to the Riding School and inhaled with delight the scent of sawdust, saddlery, stable manure and sweat. Then if an animal took his fancy he rode in the Tiergarten, breathing his fill of the grey early mist of a March morning among the trees, and returned well satisfied to the hotel. He had been found before now in the kitchen court-yard behind the service stairs standing beside a gutter full of slops and refuse and staring up to the top of the five storeys where the aerials hung beneath the colourless sky. Possibly he had designs on the one pretty chambermaid in the hotel. Her morals were questionable and she had already been given notice. He made many friends in the hotel, for he was always ready to oblige with a postage-stamp, to give advice about long-distance flights, to take an old lady out in his car, or to make a fourth at bridge, and he was well informed as to the resources of the hotel cellar. He wore a signet ring of lapis lazuli on his forefinger with the Gaigern crest, a falcon over wavy lines. At night as he lay in bed he would speak in Bavarian dialect to his pillow. "Good evening, old friend," he would say. "Yes, you are good. You are my dear old bed. You are fine!" He was never long in falling asleep and never dis-turbed his neighbours by snoring, gargling or throwing his boots about. His chauffeur said, down in the servants' quar-ters, that the Baron was quite a good fellow, but a bit simple. But even a Baron Gaigern sleeps behind double doors and even he, too, has his secrets and hidden motives. . . .

"No other news then?" he asked his chauffeur. He was sit-ting naked on the carpet in the middle of his room and massag-ing his legs. He had a magnificent body, and the almost ex-cessively developed chest of a boxer. The skin of his shoulders and legs was a bright tan. The only part of him that was not tanned was the part between his thighs and his trunk which was covered in summer by his shorts. "Is that all you have to say?"

"Quite enough, too," replied the chauffeur. He was reclin-ing on the couch with its imitation Kelim rug, a cigarette hung from his underlip and he was smoking. "Do you suppose they will wait on and on in Amsterdam for the business? Schalhorn

79

has paid out five thousand already. Do you suppose that's going on for ever? Emmy's been lying low at Springe for the last month, ready to take over the goods. In Paris it was a washout. At Nice it was a washout. And if you don't bring it off today it will be a washout here too. If Schalhorn is planted with the five thousand, he'll——"

"Is Schalhorn boss?" asked the Baron, sprinkling eau-de-Cologne into the palms of his hands.

"A boss should be able to do the job. That's what I say," grumbled the chauffeur.

"When the time comes, certainly. It doesn't suit me to work the way you and Schalhorn do. The two of you are always messing things up. I've never yet messed a thing up and Schalhorn has never yet been let down. If Emmy is getting nervous at Springe, she's no use to me, and so I told her last time. If she can't keep quiet in her art workshop and let Möhl get on with his copies of antique settings——"

"We don't care a curse for your copies of antiques. Get hold of the pearls first. Then you can get on with your antiques. All that's only one of your notions. It looked all right at first. The pearls are worth 500,000. True enough. And after reckoning two months' expenses there'll still be something left. It may be true that we could get rid of them better in antique settings. Good. Granted. Meanwhile Möhl stays at Springe making copies of your grandmother's jewellery, Emmy's getting mad and Schalhorn's getting mad. Only don't trust the woman, I tell you. If she loses patience she might play you a dirty trick. So what's to be done? When are you going to leave off amusing yourself and get down to business again?"

"You're getting hungry again, are you? You've forgotten the twenty-two thousand you had from Nice and now you are turning nasty, are you," said the Baron, still in tolerably good humour; he had now put on the black silk socks with white silk sock suspenders and the smart patent-leather shoes which he wore to dance in. Otherwise he was still naked.

There was something about this easy, careless nakedness that irritated the chauffeur. Perhaps it was the loose fall of the shoulders or the supple play of the ribs beneath the skin as they distended in breathing. He spat the end of his cigarette into the middle of the room and stood up.

"I don't mind telling you," he said leaning over the table, "we're fed up with you. You can't take anything in earnest, I tell you. It isn't in you and no good will ever come out of you. Whether it's cards or betting or relieving an old dame of two and twenty thousand or collaring pearls worth five hundred thousand—it's bloody well all one to you. But there's a difference all the same, and a man who doesn't know when it's time to be in earnest isn't fit to be boss. And if you won't get on with it of your own accord, then you'll be made to. See?"

"Lie down," said Gaigern amiably, and he quietly put the chauffeur's fist aside with a little ju-jitsu grip. "I don't need your help to get on with it. All you have to do is to see to our alibi tonight. Then you can start for Springe at 12.28 with the pearls. At 8.16 tomorrow morning you'll be back again. I'll ring for you at nine—at which time you'll be in your bed. Then we'll invite someone to come for a drive. If you move an eyelid over the scene there'll be in the hotel tomorrow morning, I'll have you arrested. I've asked you once before if you had any further news?"

The chauffeur put his hand back in his pocket. There was a red mark round the wrist. It looked as if he was not going to answer, but he answered all the same. "She starts for the theatre every evening now at half past six, because she's nervous," he grumbled out, subdued in spite of himself. "After the performance there's a farewell supper at the French Embassy. It'll be over by two o'clock. Tomorrow at 11 she leaves for Prague, two days there and then Vienna. What I'd like to know is how you're going to get the pearls off her today between the performance and the supper, if it's all to go right. You couldn't ask for better than that unlighted hole of a theatre courtyard," he added with an attempt to assert himself, but he did not look at the Baron who meanwhile was putting on his evening clothes.

"She's not wearing the pearls any longer. She just leaves them in the hotel," said Gaigern as he tied his black tie. "She

81

said so in fact to some idiot of an interviewer. You can see it in the newspapers."

"What? She just leaves them, she hasn't even handed them over to be kept in the hotel safe? What? You can just go into her room and take them?"

"Pretty well," said Baron Gaigern. "Now I want to rest a bit," he said to his gaping accomplice. He saw the gaping mouth with its black and decayed teeth and a sudden fit of rage came over him at the thought of the kind of men he was mixed up with. The muscles of his neck contracted.

"Out," was all he said. "Be at the main entrance with the car at eight."

The chauffeur looked at Gaigern's face and retreated meekly. He could not utter a word of all he had on the tip of his tongue. He even picked up the blue pyjamas from the floor with the servility of a valet, and concluded his report in a whisper. "The man in No 70 is harmless. A wealthy eccentric who has come into a fortune and is chucking his money about."

The Baron paid no further attention. The chauffeur passed between the two doors and superstitiously spat three times over his shoulder. Then he silently shut the door behind him.

Just before eight that evening the Baron made his appearance in the Lounge. He was in excellent form. He was wearing his blue raincoat over his dinner jacket and it never entered the head of Pilzheim, the hotel detective, that this engaging Apollo was industriously preparing an alibi.

Doctor Otternschlag, who was sitting in the Lounge with the exhausted Kringelein over coffee before going to see Grusinskaya together, raised one stiff finger and pointed it straight at the Baron. "Look, Kringelein, there's the sort of fellow one ought to be," he said with envious mockery.

The Baron put a coin into the hand of Pageboy No 18. "My kind regards to your girl," he said and stepped to the Hall Porter's desk. Senf looked at him with alert though sleepless eyes. (It was now the third night and still he had to keep his anxiety to himself.)

"You've got my seat for the theatre? Fifteen marks? Fine,"

he said. "If anyone inquires for me, say I'm at the theatre and after that, at the West End Club," he said and turned to Count Rohna.

"Imagine whom I came across there: Rutzov, that tall fellow, Rutzov! Wasn't he with you and my brother in the 74th Uhlans? He's in the motor trade now. You're all of you such competent fellows. It's only I who am good for nothing, a lily of the field, eh? My chauffeur there yet, Senf?"

He took an atmosphere of warmth with him through the revolving door, and in the Lounge all eyes followed him with an indulgent smile. He got into his little four-seater and went off after his alibi. At half past ten he even rang up the hotel from the club.

"Baron Gaigern speaking. Has anybody been to inquire for me? I'm speaking from the West End Club. I shall not come in before two, or even later. My chauffeur can go to bed."

At the very moment that this voice on the telephone was establishing a gentlemanly and unpremeditated alibi Gaigern himself was clinging to the front façade of the Grand Hotel between two blocks of imitation sandstone. His position was not exactly a comfortable one, yet he enjoyed it. It filled him to overflowing with the joy of the hunter, the fighter and the rock-climber. He had light-heartedly kept on his blue pyjamas for the undertaking, and on his feet he had light chrome leather shoes such as·boxers wear. Over these, in case of accidents, were woollen socks, a pair that he used for winter sports. They were a precaution against leaving undesired footprints. Gaigern was on his way from his own window to Grusinskaya's room. He had just short of seven metres to go in all and he was now half way. The sham sandstone of the Grand Hotel was copied from the rough hewn blocks of the Palazzo Pitti. It looked magnificent, and, as long as it did not break away, all was well. Gaigern carefully embedded his toes in the recesses between the blocks. He had gloves on and he was finding them a thorough nuisance. Nor could he pull them off while he crawled like a beetle along the wall of the second storey. "Damn," he said as mortar and moulding broke off and fell a floor lower on to the zinc roof of a balcony. He felt his throat getting dry and he husbanded his breath like a runner on a cinder track. Once more he came to a halt, supported himself for a moment at the risk of his life on the toe of one foot and then got the rear leg half a metre farther on. He whistled softly. He was wrought up to a high pitch now and so he whistled and kept a cool head. As to the pearls, for the sake of which he was there, no thought of them entered his head. After all he could have got hold of them in several other ways. He could have given Suzette a blow on the head when she left the theatre at night with the suitcase. He could have broken into Grusinskaya's room at night. Or finally, four steps along the passage, a skeleton key, and an innocent air if he were discovered in the wrong bedroom. But that was not his way. It was not his way at all. "Everyone must do as his nature bids," as Gaigern had tried to explain to his confederates, that little band of crooks whom for two and a half years he had kept balanced on the verge of mutiny. "I don't catch game in snares. I don't go up mountains by the funicular. What I can't take with my own hands I'll do without."

Obviously talk of this kind opened up whole realms of misunderstanding between him and his accomplices. They made little account of courage, though they all had an adequate share of it. Emmy—with her trim auburn hair—had attempted an explanation. "He makes a sport of it," she said. She knew Gaigern well and probably she was right. Now, at any rate, at twenty minutes past ten, as he clung to the façade of the Grand Hotel, he was like a rock-climber in a difficult chimney or the leader of a raid about to attack a dangerous position.

The chief danger lay in the projecting bay behind which lay Grusinskaya's bathroom. Here the architect's fancy had chosen smooth surfaces. Also there were no window ledges, for the bathroom was tucked away behind and looked out upon the courtyard where the Baron had been observed staring up at the aerials. On the other side, however, of this smooth space, two and a half metres in extent, was the iron railing of the balcony of Room No 68. Panting slightly and whistling and cursing by turns, Gaigern paused before making the final spring across this even surface that held him up. The muscles of his thighs quivered and his ankles felt the hot vibrating pulse-beat of extreme exertion. For the rest, he was very well satisfied with his situation and the circumstances, gone over a hundred times in his mind, answered to his expectations.

For instance, against observation from the street, which from above looked like a track swarming with ants, Gaigern was completely protected by the powerful lights recently fixed up on the hotel façade. Anyone who looked up would be blinded by the rays of white light. It would be quite impossible to see the small dark blue figure making his way along the black shadow behind these aggressive rays. Gaigern had picked up this trick by watching a conjurer at a variety show who had in the same fashion dazzled the eyes of the audience while he executed his hocus-pocus against a velvet hanging. He had sawed women in two and made skeletons hover above the stage. Gaigern looked down on the street while he took a rest behind the second arc lamp. At his unusually sharp angle the world had a distorted and flattened appearance. The wall descending sheer from his feet looked perilous and threatening. He leaned his head forward and looked down, without venturing to breathe or wink an eyelid. He had not a trace of dizziness—only in his pulse the sweet and tingling sensation that climbers know well. The round tower of the Gaigern castle at Ried was higher than this. And in the college at Feldkirch when you broke bounds at night you had to descend the whole length of the lightning conductor. The Three Pinnacles in the Dolomites was no joke either. The two and a half metres to the balcony were not easy going, but he had been in worse places. Gaigern ceased looking down and looked upwards over the way. There was an electric sign opposite on the roof. The bubbles of a glass of champagne burst upwards in a spray of electric light. There was no sky. The city ended abruptly just above the roofs and wires and aerials. Gaigern moved his fingers inside his glove. They stuck, and probably they were bleeding. He tried his wind and found it in order again. Collecting his strength and bracing himself for the jump he took a blind leap into vacancy. The air rushed past his ears and then he found himself hanging on by the railings of the balcony, with the corners of the iron pressing deeply into his fingers. He let himself hang there for a second with his heart thumping, then he drew himself up like an acrobat on a trapeze, got over the railing, and let go. Yes, he lay now on the balcony with the door open into Grusinskaya's room.

"There we are," he said with satisfaction, and for the moment lay where he was on the narrow cement-floored balcony and recovered his breath. Far overhead he heard the engine of an aeroplane and then he saw straight above his eyes the gleam of its lighted cabin moving across the lurid haze that hung over the city. The street below sent up its loud confused roar. For a few minutes Gaigern lay as though on an island of exhaustion and semi-consciousness, while beneath him motor cars hooted impatiently to reach the entrance, for the League of Humanity was giving a banquet in the Little Salon and women in opera cloaks were creeping like coloured beetles out of closed motor cars and ascending the three steps into the second entrance of the hotel. Lord, what wouldn't I give for a cigarette, thought Gaigern, but this relief to his exhausted nerves was out of the question. He pulled the glove off his right hand and sucked the cut on his forefinger. A bleeding paw would never do for the job he was on. The thin metallic taste vexed him. He felt the welcome coolness of the cement against his moist back. The return journey would be more difficult, he reflected, and looking through the railing of the balcony he measured the distance with his eyes. He had a rope with him. He would have to attach it to the balcony and swing himself across. "Congratulations," he said to himself in the smart officer's voice of his army days. He pulled on his glove again as though he was about to pay a ceremonious call and getting up stepped from the balcony into Grusinskaya's bedroom.

The French window did not stir, only the curtain swayed gently in the air. The parquet floor, too, was pleasingly silent. Two clocks ticked in the dark room, one nearly twice as fast as the other. There was a surprising scent, suggestive of a funeral or a cremation. From the electric sign over the way a triangle of yellow light fell on the floor and extended as far as the edge of the carpet. Gaigern took out his pocket torch, an ordinary cylindrical torch. With this he proceeded cautiously to look round the room. Thanks to his brief dialogue with Suzette on the threshold he had its shape and furniture in his head. He was prepared to counter every artful dodge and to bring the pearls to light wherever they might be concealed, to force trunks, break open cupboards and to unravel the secret of any lock. But when he had followed the circular light of the torch round the room and encountered his own face three times in the dressing-table mirror, he had an almost comic surprise.

On the dressing-table by the mirror lay the suitcase quite peacefully, innocently reflecting the light of the torch from its leather surface. Steady, thought Gaigern, pulling himself together, for the excitement of the chase began to rush to his head. First he put his right hand into his right pocket for safe custody, for it was still bleeding and there it would have to remain to prevent it making mischief and leaving traces behind. He held the torch between his teeth. With his gloved left hand he carefully laid hold of the suitcase. Yes, there it was. His fingers rested on the smooth and polished leather. He turned out the torch and put it down, and then paused for reflection. There was an oppressive funereal smell suggestive of the interment of a deceased grandfather and a funeral oration. Gaigern began to laugh in the darkness when he hit on the explanation. "Laurels," he remembered, recalling Suzette's voice. "Madame has had laurels sent her, Monsieur. The French Ambassador sent a whole basketful." He knelt down in front of the dressing-table—now the floor creaked ominously as if it were alive—and grasped the case with his left hand in the darkness. No, no, he thought and let it go again. Such things brought bad luck. Pocketbooks, cases, purses—they were all sinister things. They had a tendency to refuse to be burnt, to emerge again from the rivers into which they were thrown, to be discovered in drains by sewer men and finally laid most disconcertingly on the table during criminal proceedings. Also, it was not very pleasant to face two and a half metres across a surface as smooth as ice with a suitcase weighing about four pounds between one's teeth. Gaigern drew back his hand and thought again. He turned on the torch and gazed at the two locks of the little case in deep absorption. God alone knows what secret mechanism kept Grusinskaya's treasure safely shut up there. As an experiment Gaigern took out a tool and pressed on the round brass disc of the lock.

The lock sprang up.

The case was not locked at all!

Gaigern started at the snap of the spring. It was so utterly unexpected that his face for the moment looked perfectly blank. "Well, that's good," he said to himself three or four times. "Well, that's good." He raised the lid and opened the jewel case. Yes, there lay Grusinskaya's pearls.

They were no more after all than a little heap of baubles, very little, if you think of it, compared with all the tales that had been spread abroad about this gift of a murdered grand-duke for the adornment of a dancer's neck. An old-fashioned and charming *sautoir* and a rope of medium-sized but perfectly matched pearls, three rings, two earrings with incredibly round and large pearls—there they lay idly in their little bed of velvet while the torch waked their slumbering reflections. Taking every precaution Gaigern removed them from their case with his left hand and put them in his pocket. It struck him as so ridiculous to have come upon these pearls lying open and unprotected that he felt a reaction almost of sobering disappointment. He was exhausted after tremendous exertions, which after all were superfluous. For a moment he even wondered whether he might not simply regain his room along the passage. Perhaps they have left the bedroom door open as well, he thought, with the incredulity which since his first sight of the pearls had kept his upper teeth exposed in a foolish and childish smile.

The door, however, was locked. In the corridor the lift could be heard ascending at irregular intervals and the gate closing with a click, for Room No 68 was very nearly opposite it. Gaigern sat for a few moments in an armchair in the dark and collected his strength for the return journey. His longing for a cigarette was maddening. But he did not dare smoke in case the smell left a clue. He was as cautious as a savage who guards himself against a taboo. He thought of many things at once and, most clearly of all, of his father's gun cupboard. At the top of the cupboard the tin boxes containing the Balkan tobacco were always kept and in each box the old Baron put every three days a small slice of carrot. Gaigern's thoughts were wafted to his home and this sweet sharp scent; he was running down the worn steps at Ried and he lost count of time while he fancied himself in the nook where as a seventeen-year-old cadet he used to lie hidden and smoke. He came back with a jolt to the job in hand. "Look alive, Flix," he said to himself. "Don't go to sleep, but get on with it." He gave himself nicknames now and then, encouraged himself, treated himself tenderly and praised or scolded his own limbs. "You swine," he said reproachfully to his cut finger, which went on bleeding and sticking to his glove. "You swine, can't you leave me in peace." And he clapped his thighs as if they were horses and praised them. "You're fine fellows. Fine, good beasts. Look alive, Flix."

Leaving the scent of laurel in Room No 68 behind, he put his nose out on to the balcony and sniffed. There was that indefinable smell of Berlin in March, petrol mingled with the dampness, of the Tiergarten, and as he pushed past the gently swelling curtain he had already observed that something was not as it should be. It took a few seconds before he realized what it was—his face and body were lighted up in a way they had not been before. He saw the silken reflections on the sleeves of his pyjamas and shrank back with the rapidity of instinct into the darkness of the room, like a beast which, after scenting the breeze at the edge of a clearing, glides back into the darkness of the forest. And there he stood, breathing quickly and straining every nerve. The ticking of the two clocks came to him with an extreme clearness and then from some distant part of the great city the hour struck faintly from a church tower—eleven o'clock. The walls of the houses across the street were bright and dark by turns as the electric signs winked on and off again. "Damn the luck," Gaigern muttered and went out on to the balcony. This time he gave rein to his exasperation as fully and freely as if Room No 68 had been his own room.

The big electric lamps on the front of the hotel had gone out. The new installation had gone wrong again. In the little banqueting-room the League of Humanity sat in darkness, and in the cellar electricians were busy with the switches without avail. Below in the street a small crowd stood and stared with delight at the hotel front, where the four arc lights went spasmodically on and off. Among them was a policeman. Traffic was held up and motor cars were loudly showing their impatience. The electric signs opposite were in full play, proclaiming brands of champagne and doing their utmost to illuminate the hotel front. Finally two men in blue overalls crept out of a window of the storey below, established themselves on the glass roof over the main entrance, and began to investigate the faulty wires. Now that the hotel front was a centre of interests the way back across those seven metres of it was finally blocked.

Congratulations, thought Gaigern again and laughed angrily. Here I am and if I want to get out I shall have to break open the door.

He took out his tools and torch and began, with all due precaution, to fiddle about with the keyhole; but without success. A dressing gown hanging near the door fell to the ground. It touched his face softly as it fell and the fright it gave him was beyond all bounds. He felt the arteries of his neck pulsing like machines. The corridor, too, outside was in a stir. Footsteps went to and fro, people coughed, the lift-gate clicked as the lift went up and down, a chambermaid called out and ran past and another one called back. Gaigern gave up the refractory door and stole out again on to the balcony. Three metres below the two electricians straddled about on the glass roof with wires in their mouths. They were being watched with great interest from the street. Gaigern committed one of his characteristic audacities. Leaning over the railings he called out: "What's up with the light?"

"Short circuit," said one of the men.

"How long will it be?" asked Gaigern. A shrug of the shoulders was the only reply. Idiots, thought Gaigern savagely. The pompous self-importance of these two bunglers on the glass roof annoyed him intensely. Anyway, in ten minutes they'll leave off, he thought, and after looking down at them for a short while he retired again into the room. Suddenly the sense of danger came over him, but it lasted only for a second and then died away. And there he stood in the middle of the room in his socks. At least they would leave no footprints to betray him.

Well, at all events, I mustn't go to sleep, he thought. To cheer himself up he felt for the pearls in his pocket. They were warm from his body. He took off his gloves so as to feel their smoothness and to realize how precious they were. The touch of them delighted him. At the same moment, it occurred to him that his chauffeur would not now catch the train for Springe and that a new timetable would have to be made. Nothing went according to plan. The pearls instead of giving any trouble had been left in an unlocked case, and now, in revenge, all was up with his little climb.

A thought that made him laugh interrupted his reflections. What a woman, he thought. What a very odd sort of woman to leave her pearls lying about like that. He shook his head in astonishment and laughed louder. He knew plenty of women. He found them pleasing enough, but nothing wonderful, and he thought it wonderful that a woman should go out and leave all she possessed in front of a window opening on to a balcony, for anyone to take who chose. She must be a regular happy-go-lucky gipsy, he thought. Or else she must have a great heart, he answered himself. And now in spite of all he felt sleepy. He went in the darkness to the door and picked up the dressing gown which had fallen to the ground a few minutes before and smelt it inquisitively. An unfamiliar bitter-sweet scent came from it, but it did not at all suggest the woman in a muslin ballet costume at whose performances Gaigern had been bored on innumerable occasions. In any case, he wished Grusinskaya nothing but good. He found her quite sympathetic. He hung the dressing gown up carelessly, leaving ten casual fingerprints on the silk, and strolled out on to the balcony again to kill time. The two blue bats were still flapping about over their short circuit. Gaigern wished himself a pleasant time of it and then took up his station between the lace hangings and the door curtain, as erect and alert as a sentry in a sentry-box, to await further developments.

KRINGELEIN BLINKED at the stage through his glasses. A lot
of puzzling things were happening over there and it was all
going much too fast. He would have liked very much to see
one of the girls more clearly, a short dark one in the second
row who was always smiling. But there was no chance. There
were no pauses in Grusinskaya's ballet. It was a perpetual
shimmer as they kept flitting in and out and round one another.
Sometimes the girls formed up in lines on either side of the
stage, touching the edge of their skirts with downward curving
hands, and left room for Grusinskaya herself.

Then she came pirouetting to the front on her toes. Her face
and arms were white as wax, and her toes as rigid and steady
on the floor of the stage as if they were screwed tightly into it.
At last it was impossible to see her face any longer. She became nothing but a whirl of white with silver stripes and
Kringelein felt a little seasick before the dance was over.
"Marvellous," he said with astonishment. "Splendid. What
suppleness of leg. That's first-class. You can only marvel at
that." And he marvelled gladly, though he felt far from
well.

"Do you really enjoy it?" asked Doctor Otternschlag
gloomily. He sat in the box and turned the damaged side of
his face to the stage. It looked ghastly in the yellow stage
lighting which extended far enough to illuminate it. It was
difficult for Kringelein to answer this 'really'. Actually ever
since he had moved into Room No 70 nothing was real to
him any longer. Everything was like a fevered dream. Everything went much too fast. Nothing stayed long enough to be
enjoyed. At his urgent request for instruction and companion-
ship, Otternschlag had taken him round the usual sights—a
drive round Berlin, the Museum, Potsdam, and finally even up
the wireless tower, the Funkturm, where the wind blew a hurri-
cane and Berlin lay below under a pall of smoke pricked out

with lights. Kringelein would not have been surprised if he
had woken out of the deep trance of an anæsthetic to find himself in his hospital bed again. His feet were cold, his hands
cramped and his jaws clenched. His head was like a burning
cauldron and all the thousand and one things thrown into it
began to sizzle and melt.

"Well, are you content? Are you happy now? Are you
getting to know life?" Otternschlag asked from time to time.
And Kringelein stoutly and obediently answered, "Yes,
rather!"

On this evening, the fifth of Grusinskaya's appearance, the
theatre was poorly patronized. It was positively empty. The
stalls were so scantily occupied that they looked ragged and
moth-eaten, and the one or two people in the front row felt
isolated and self-conscious amid so many empty seats. Kringelein felt the same. Except for the stage box, which he had
taken at Otternschlag's advice—Kringelein wished from now
onwards always to have the best seats, at the cinema far back,
at the theatre well in front and for the ballet the front row—
except for their box, which had cost him forty marks, only one
other was occupied and this by the impresario, Meyerheim.
Meyerheim had dispensed with the *claque* for this performance. It no longer justified itself and the deficit was already
big enough. There was a slight outburst of applause before the
interval. Pimenov quickly rang up the curtain, and Grusinskaya came to the front of the stage and smiled. She smiled to
a silent house, for the feeble applause had forthwith expired
and everyone trooped out to the buffet. Something, too, expired in Grusinskaya's face as she stood there to acknowledge
an ovation which after all was denied her. Her skin went cold
beneath the sweat and the paint. Witte threw down his baton
and rushed on to the stage up the iron steps. He was anxious
about Elisaveta. He found Pimenov standing there as though
at a funeral, while scene-shifters dumped down bits of scenery
right against his lean old bowed back in its old dress coat. He
was always in full dress for every evening performance, as
though any evening the Grand Duke Sergei might summon
him to his box. Michael, with a leopard skin of spotted plush

over his left shoulder and bare powdered legs, was waiting with a despondent air near the stage manager. They were all in trembling anticipation of an outbreak from Grusinskaya. They were trembling actually and literally—knees, hands, shoulders, teeth.

"Forgive me, Madame," Michael said in a whisper. "*Pardonnez-moi*. It was my fault, I put you out——"

Grusinskaya came with an absentminded air through the dust and noise made by the shifting of the scenery, trailing her old woollen cloak, and when she stood still and looked at Michael there was a meekness in her face that frightened every one of them.

"You? Oh no, my dear," she said gently, when she had mastered the breaking of her voice and collected her breath, which the last exacting dance had exhausted. "You were very good. You are in very good form today. So am I. We were all good——"

She turned abruptly and walked quickly away, taking her unfinished sentence with her into the darkness at the back of the stage. Witte did not venture to follow her. Grusinskaya sat down on a step of gilt wood that lay at the back among a lot more stage lumber and there she sat during the whole time the scene was being changed. At first she clasped her hands round her right calf in the silk fleshings. Mechanically she re-tied the crossed string of the ballet shoe. For a few minutes she stroked this tired, silken and slightly soiled leg as though it were an animal—with unthinking compassion. A little while after she took her hands from there and put them round her bare neck. She missed the pearls keenly. Often and often it had calmed her to let them slip through her fingers like a rosary. What more! What more do you want, she thought deeply within herself. I have never danced so well as now. Not when I was young, not in the Petersburg days, not in Paris, not in America. I was stupid in those days and not very industrious. Now—oh, now I work. Now I know. Now I can dance. What more do you want of me? More still? More I have not got. Must I give the pearls away. Surrender them? Well, I'm ready to. Oh, leave me alone—all of you. I am tired.

95

"Michael," she whispered. She recognized his shadowy form as it glided past the back of the drop scene.

"Madame," answered Michael with cautious reserve. He had changed his costume and now wore a brown velvet doublet and carried a bow and arrow in his hand, for he was dancing his Archer Dance after the interval.

"Aren't you going to get ready, Gru?" he asked, carefully avoiding a sympathetic tone, when he saw how small and crumpled she looked as she sat huddled up amidst the lumber. The manager's bells rang from eight places at once.

"Michael, I am tired," said Grusinskaya, "I want to go home. Lucille can dance my numbers. It won't matter to anyone. They don't care whether it is I who dance or someone else."

Michael started so violently that he stiffened in every muscle. Grusinskaya, sitting on the step with his knee close to her face, saw the magnificent muscle of his thighs distend and this involuntary movement in a body she knew so well comforted her a little. Michael had gone pale under his paint. "Nonsense," he said. He was rude from dismay.

Grusinskaya smiled tenderly. She put out a finger and tapped Michael on the leg.

"How often have I to tell you to dance in tights?" she said with unusual tenderness in her voice. "You will never really warm up, never be really supple without tights. Believe me when I tell you that, you—revolutionary." She let her hand rest for a few seconds on the warm powdered and youthful skin beneath which his fine muscles stood out. But no, the touch communicated no strength. The bell sounded for the third time. On the other side of the drop scene, with its painting of a little temple, the ballet shoes of the dancers were already scraping over the floor of the stage. Suzette was running up and down the dressing-room passage in an agony like a strayed hen, because Madame sat there instead of changing her costume. Witte, standing at the conductor's desk, took his baton with trembling hand and waited with a set face for the red light which ought before this to have signalled the commencement of the next dance.

"What are you thinking of?" asked Doctor Otternschlag in the box above. Kringelein just at that moment was thinking of Fredersdorf and of the patch of sunlight which on summer afternoons fell on the shabby green wall of the dingy general office. But he came back at once, and very gladly, to Berlin and the Theater des Westens, to the tinsel and glamour of life and his red plush box at forty marks.

"Homesick?" asked Otternschlag.

"No question of that," replied Kringelein with all the callousness of a man of the world.

Witte below raised his baton and the music began.

"Rotten orchestra," said Otternschlag, who was getting heartily sick of his rôle of an amiable mentor and finding the ballet more and more depressing. But this time Kringelein refused to be distracted. The music was just what he wanted. He sank into it as he did into his hot bath at the hotel. He had a chill and heavy feeling in his stomach like a lump of lead. It was a bad symptom, the doctor had said. It did not hurt in the least. It kept to that unpleasant state when a pain is expected but does not come. That was all. That was the only sign death made him. And then came the music to console him a little with its pianissimo on the flutes above the tremolo of the violas. Kringelein's spirits rose, and he floated away on the music, right away into a blue moonlit landscape where a temple was painted on a sea-coast, which was painted too.

The programme proceeded. Michael as an archer appeared with his snow-white calves and brown velvet doublet. He braced his youthful body and shot with a leap across the stage. He sprang high into the air as though on wires. His gestures made it clear that he wished to shoot a bird, a dove that belonged to the temple. After a prodigal display of leaps and spins he finally vanished into the wings after his arrow.

Applause. *Pizzicato* on the orchestra. Grusinskaya made her appearance on the stage. After all in breathless haste she had put on the costume of the wounded dove. A large ruby red drop of blood trembled on her white silk bodice. She is utterly tired out but as light as air, and her arms move in rapid and tremulous wing-beats while she gradually glides towards her

97

piteous death. Three times she rallies but she can fly no longer. At last her long delicate neck falls forward, she lays her head on her knees and dies, a poor dove shot through the heart. A shaft of limelight through a disc of blue glass is directed upon her wound.

Curtain and applause. There was even fairly vigorous applause considering how empty the theatre was and how few there were to clap. "Encore?" asked Grusinskaya without stirring from her pose. "No," whispered Pimenov in a loud and desperate whisper from the wings. The applause was over. It was over. Grusinskaya still lay where she was for a few minutes like a flake of foam, just as she had died in her dance and with the dust of the stage on her hands and arms and temples. For the first time in her life there was no encore for this dance. I can do no more, she thought. No, I have done enough. I can do no more.

"Clear the stage for the next dance," shouted the stage manager. Grusinskaya had no wish to get up. She wished to lie there in the middle of the stage and to fall asleep—to sleep and forget it all. At last Michael came and raised her to her feet. "*Spassibo*—thank you," she said in Russian and walked stiffly away to the ladies' dressing-rooms. Michael took the nearest way through the wings to the left and made himself ready for the *pas de deux*.

Grusinskaya stole away to her dressing-room and pushed the door open with the toe of her ballet shoe. Sinking into a chair in front of the looking-glass she fixed her eyes on the shoe's dusty and somewhat worn silk. Her feet were weary, unutterably weary. They were heavy and they had had their fill and more than their fill of dancing. In the mirror beneath the glare of the electric light she saw Suzette's old and careworn face. The costume for the *pas de deux* rustled in her hands.

"Leave me alone," Grusinskaya whispered hoarsely. "I am not well. I can't go on again. Leave me alone, everyone. Give me something to drink," she added, however. She wanted to strike Suzette on her worn and helpless face because she suddenly saw in it an indefinable likeness to her own. "*Fiches-moi la paix,*" she said imperiously. Suzette vanished. Grusinskaya sat listlessly where she was for a few minutes, and then she suddenly tore the silk shoes from her feet. Enough, she thought, enough, enough!

Still in tights and wearing her costume of the dove, Grusinskaya took to flight. She had only kicked off her ballet shoes and put on some others and thrown her old cloak round her, and thus oppressed and wretched she deserted from the theatre. Suzette when she hurried back from the bar with a glass of port found the dressing-room empty. A note was stuck in the looking-glass. 'I can do no more. Lucille must dance in my place.' Suzette stumbled on to the stage with it and for ten minutes after the theatre was in confusion; after that, however, the curtain went up and the programme proceeded as on any other evening, with Russian national dances, the *pas de deux* and the Bacchanal. Pimenov and Witte saw the evening through like two old generals whose king has fled the field and who have to cover the retreat after a defeat.

But while on the stage the ballet dancers as Bacchantes twirled and whirled muslin veils and strewed the stage with four hundred paper roses, and while Michael executed his leaps as a fawn and Suzette talked helplessly with Berkeley on the telephone in the manager's office—all this while Grusinskaya stumbled in blind despairing flight along the Tauentzien-strasse.

Berlin was brilliantly lighted, noisy and very full. Passers-by looked with curiosity and amusement at her painted, distraught and half unconscious face. Berlin was a cruel town. Grusinskaya, as she crossed the street to the less-frequented side, cursed it. A fit of shivers took possession of her, though the air was mild and damp on this March evening and her woollen cloak steamed. Grusinskaya tried to utter her grief in words which became sobs and stuck in her throat and hurt her. She felt she might cry, but she did not. Her blue painted eyelids only become hotter and drier.

Never again, she thought, never again. She stumbled on as though haunted by this thought. There was no grace left in her movements. She had no control over her body and it drooped forward at every step. A florist's window threw a glare of white light at her feet. She stopped and looked in. There were great bowls with bunches of magnolia. There were cactuses and spiral glasses with orchids growing out of them. But she found not the faintest comfort in all the delicate beauty of the flowers. Her hands were cold, as she now felt for the first time, and she began to search for gloves in the pockets of her old cloak. This was quite absurd, because for eight years past she had only worn this cloak behind the scenes as a protection against the draughts that blow through every theatre in the world. In her mind's eye she saw stage machinery and iron doors with red lamps above them, and the smooth slant of the stage sloping away at her feet. Never again, she thought, never again. The old-fashioned cloak was long. It hid her costume, but it hindered her movements. She pulled it up higher after leaving the window of the flower shop and turned aimlessly into quieter streets. She saw a Buddha in a shop window as she passed by. His quiet gilded bronze hands seemed as though they wished to bring calm to her crumbling world. Never to dance again. Never, never again. She tried to gain comfort from consoling words, but they came in sobs from her throat. Sergei, she cried, Gabriel, Gaston. She called on the names of her few lovers. Anastasia, too, her daughter, and finally even Ponpon, her little grandson in Paris, whom she had never seen. But she was still alone with no one to console her. Suddenly she stopped with a start. What am I doing, she thought. I have run away from the theatre, I can't have done that. It isn't possible. I must go back. A church clock struck eleven slowly and clearly close at hand, though no church tower was to be seen. Grusinskaya took her hands from the pockets of her cloak and let them fall in front of her. The gesture recalled the death of the wounded dove. Too late, the gesture said. The performance must be just ending. Grusinskaya threw back her head and looked at the street she was in, and found that she did not know where she was. She saw a small entrance framed in blue and yellow electric lights and over it the words: 'Russian Bar.' She went across and stood at the door. She blew her nose like a child while she made up her mind. Russian Bar,

100

she thought. Suppose I go in? They would recognize me, and the red-shirted orchestra would play the Grusinskaya waltz. What a sensation.

No sensation whatever, she thought wretchedly a moment later. I can't go in looking as I do. And perhaps I shouldn't be recognized any longer. Besides if they did recognize me—looking as I do now—*tant pis, tant pis.*

She signalled to an old rattletrap of a taxi and, with a face that was suddenly fixed and cold, had herself driven to the hotel.

Gaigern stood like a sentry between the curtains and the lace hangings in Room No 68 and waited for the men in blue overalls down below to finish their job. But instead of this they went on crawling to and fro on the window ledges of the first story. They had been for wire and pincers and they called out to each other with much zeal, but still the lights did not go on. Consequently the whole front of the hotel was all the better illuminated by the arc lights in the street, by the lighting of its five entrances and by the electric signs opposite which advertised now a brand of champagne, now a variety of chocolate. Moreover Gaigern had not been standing there waiting more than twenty minutes before the door of Room No 68 opened. The light was turned on by the very modest illumination peculiar to hotel bedrooms, he saw Grusinskaya enter the room.

This from Gaigern's point of view was a thoroughly rotten business. The shock of it went through him like cold steel. What on earth was the woman doing in the hotel at twenty minutes past eleven? What could you do when you could not even count on the length of a theatre performance? His luck was out, he thought with clenched teeth. Gaigern had a dread of bad luck. And now what but bad luck could account for these cursed complications in which he seemed to be trapped? The light from the room penetrated the lace curtain behind which he stood and imprinted the shadow of its openwork pattern on the balcony. There was nothing for it but to calm himself and keep his heart up. The string of pearls in his pocket had taken the warmth of his body. They ran like peas through his fingers. For a moment it seemed to him idiotic and absurd that this handful of pearl-coloured grains should be worth a fortune. Four months of lying in wait, seven metres at the risk of his life, and no sooner was one risk over than a new one took its place. One danger after another. His life was nothing but a string of dangers. And the life of this Grusinskaya was a string of pearls. Gaigern shook his head and laughed in spite of the fix he was in. Gaigern was no thinker. Life often made him laugh with astonished amazement, almost simple-mindedly, for it was somewhat beyond his comprehension. Now, at any rate, he pulled himself together and, turning towards the room behind the lace curtains, he proceeded to wait.

First Grusinskaya stood motionless for nearly a minute in the middle of the room just below the glass-shaded hanging light and it seemed from her face that she had lost herself. She stood there till her cloak fell of its own weight from her drooping arms, and then she stepped over it to the telephone on the table. It was a minute or so before she got through to the theatre and again a minute or two before she got Pimenov, but she was too utterly weary to be impatient.

"Hallo, Pimenov. Yes, it's Grusinskaya. I am in the hotel. You must forgive me. Yes, I was unwell suddenly. My heart, you know. I could scarcely breathe. Yes, like that time in Scheveningen. No, I'm better now. It must have put you in a fix, I know. How did Lucille get on? What? Oh, fair. And the audience? What's that? No, I am not upset. You can tell me if there was a scene. No? No scene at all? Went off quietly? Not much applause? A different programme you think? Good. We'll talk it over. No, I'm going to bed. No, no doctor, please. Nor Witte either. No, no, no, I want nobody. Not Suzette either. I only want to be left in peace. You will drive, please, to the French Embassy and make my excuses. Thank you. Goodnight, my dear. Goodnight, Pimenov! Listen, Pimenov, my greetings to Witte and to Michael too and all the rest as well. No, don't worry about me. I shall be all right tomorrow. Goodnight."

She replaced the receiver on its hook. "Goodnight, my

dear," she said softly after she had done so, standing alone in the hotel bedroom.

So it was her heart, thought Gaigern. She was unwell. It had needed all his attention to follow the rapid French words. So that was why she had turned up at this worst of all possible moments. She looked wretched certainly. All to the good, for she would go to sleep and then there would be a hope of taking his leave of her. The great thing was to keep calm. He moved cautiously to the edge of the balcony and looked over. The two idiots in blue were sitting there in consultation. They had hung up two fine dark lanterns and looked as if they were prepared to put in the entire night on overtime. Gaigern's craving for a cigarette reached the pitch of disease. He opened his mouth wide and took in a gulp of damp petrol-laden air. Inside the room, meanwhile, Grusinskaya had come up to the cheval glass with its two wings. The plundered suitcase lay in front of it. Gaigern's heart suddenly thumped in his chest. However, she pushed the leather case aside without a glance at it, and turning on the light over the centre of the mirror she grasped its frame with both hands and pressed her face close up to the glass, as though she meant to plunge right into it. The attention with which she then studied her face had something probing, greedy and gruesome about it. Odd creatures, women, thought Gaigern behind the curtain. Strange animals. What can she see in the glass to make such a frightful face over?

He himself saw her as a beautiful woman, undeniably beautiful, even though the paint on her cheeks began to run. Her neck, above all, reflected twice over in the side mirrors, was incomparably delicate and flexible. Grusinskaya fixed her eyes on her face as though on the face of an enemy. With horror she saw the telltale years, the wrinkles, the flabbiness, the fatigue, the withering; her temples were smooth no longer, the corners of her mouth were disfigured, her eyelids, under the blue paint, were as creased as crumpled tissue paper. Another fit of shuddering, more violent than the previous one in the street, came over her while she looked at herself. She tried to bandage her lips but could not succeed. She hurried across the room

103

and hastily turned out the uncompromising light suspended from the ceiling and turned on the table lamp, but even this did not lend any warmth. With a few impatient movements she tore off her costume and went naked, but for the tights that covered her as far as her hips, to the radiator and leant her breast against the grey-coloured pipes. She scarcely thought at all as she did so. She only desired warmth. Enough, she thought, enough. Never again. Finished. Enough. She whispered her irrevocable decision in every language, her teeth chattering all the while. She went into the bathroom and undressed completely. She held her hands under the hot tap and let the warmth flow over her arteries till it began to hurt. She took a friction brush and rubbed her shoulders with it. Then, suddenly, she left off in a fit of disgust and came back naked and shivering and went straight across the room to the telephone. She had to put her lips twice to the telephone before she could speak.

"Tea," she said. "A lot of tea and a lot of sugar."

Then, still naked, she went to the looking-glass and looked in it with gloomy intensity. Her body, however, was of unique and faultless beauty. It was the body of a sixteen-year-old ballet pupil, which the severe and disciplined work of a lifetime had preserved unaltered. Suddenly the hatred she felt for herself changed into tenderness. She clasped her shoulders and stroked their smooth sheen. She kissed the hollow of her right arm and hollowed her hands like shells to receive her small and perfect breasts. She stroked the delicate upward curve of her stomach and her slender shadowed hips. She bent her head down and kissed her poor slim sinewy knees as though they were sick children whom she loved. "*Biednaia, malenkaia,*" she murmured to them. It was an endearment of her early days. Poor little one, it meant.

Unconsciously Gaigern, between the curtains, showed pity and admiration in his face. He was embarrassed by what he saw. He knew many women, but he had never seen one whose body was so delicately and perfectly formed. Yet this was really a secondary consideration. It was helplessness, the lost and tremulous despair of this pitiful Grusinskaya as she stood before the looking-glass that impressed him most. It inspired a sweet and painful sympathy and made him flush to his ears. Though he was a crook, ready to carry off stolen pearls worth 500,000 marks in his pocket, Gaigern was far from being inhuman. He let go of the pearls and took his hands out of his pockets. He felt in his hands and in his arms a compelling desire to support this poor lonely woman, to take her away and console and warm her—to do anything to put a stop to her terrible shuddering and her whispering of an almost crazed despair.

The waiter knocked at the outer door. Grusinskaya put on her dressing gown—the same one that had startled Gaigern in the darkness—and went to the door in her worn slippers. The tea was discreetly handed in and Grusinskaya locked the door behind the retreating waiter. It had come to this, she thought. She poured out a cup of tea and took a packet of veronal from the bedside table. She swallowed a tablet, drank some tea, and then took a second. She got up and began to walk rapidly to and fro across the room, four paces this way, four paces that.

What is the use of it all? she thought. What is the use of living? What is there to wait for? Why endure the torture? Oh, I am tired. You don't know, any of you, how tired I am. I promised myself to leave off when the time came. *Tiens*, the time has come. Am I to wait till I am hissed off the stage? It is time, *malenkaia*—poor little one. Gru is not going to go to Vienna tomorrow. Gru gives up. Gru is going to sleep. You don't know how cold it is to be famous. Not a soul to care for me, not one. They all live on me. Nobody lives for me. Nobody. Not one. I know no one who is not either vain or anxious. I have always been alone. And who troubles about a Grusinskaya who dances no more? Finished. No, I shall not parade about Monte Carlo, stiff and fat and old like the other famous women who have grown old. "You should have seen me in the days when the Grand Duke Sergei was still alive!" No, that is not for me. And where else am I to go? To Tremezzo to grow orchids, to keep two white peacocks, to have money troubles and to be alone, utterly alone, and to rusticate and die? That is what it comes to at last—to die. Nijinsky is in an asylum waiting to die. Poor Nijinsky! Poor Gru! I am not going to wait. The moment has come—now—now—now—now——

She stood still and listened as though she heard her name called. The veronal was already humming drowsily in her ears and its narcotic influence subdued her to a welcome indifference. Gaston, she thought as she went to the table. Dear Gaston, you were good to me once. How young you were! And how long ago it is! Now you are a minister, fat and bearded and sleek. *Adieu, Gaston. Adieu pour jamais, n'est-ce pas?* There is such an easy way of growing no older. . . .

Grusinskaya poured out another cup of tea. She was now posing a little, playing in sweet sadness a little tragic scene. There was a manner and a grace in her despairing resolve. With a rapid gesture she took the bottle of veronal tablets and emptied them all into her tea and then waited for them to melt. It took too long and she tapped them impatiently with the teaspoon. Then getting up she went once more to the looking-glass and began unconsciously powdering her face which was of a sudden beaded with cold sweat. Her lips ceased trembling and assumed the fixed stage smile. She put her hands in front of her face and whispered: God! God! God! Now too she noticed the funereal scent which rose from the basket of faded flowers and hung in the air of the room. She went over unsteadily to the table and tasted the cup of tea with the tip of the spoon. The taste was very bitter. She dropped in one lump of sugar after another with the sugar tongs and waited for them to melt. This took a minute or perhaps longer. In the stillness the clock and the watch raced each other breathlessly.

Grusinskaya got up and went to the door on to the balcony. Her breath came with difficulty and she had a longing to look at the sky. She drew back the lace curtain and collided with a shadowy figure.

"Please do not be alarmed, Madame," Gaigern said with a bow.

Grusinskaya's first movement was not one of alarm, but—oddly enough—of shame. She drew her kimono more closely round her and looked mutely at Gaigern as though deeply puzzled. What is this? she thought dreamily. Surely I have been through this before? Perhaps she even felt a certain relief at this postponement of the draught of veronal. She stood thus gazing at Gaigern for nearly a minute while her finely pencilled arched eyebrows met above the bridge of her nose. Her lips still trembled, and her breath was drawn sharply between them in little gasps.

Gaigern, too, felt his teeth beginning to chatter, but he controlled them perfectly. He had never been in such extreme danger as at this moment. All his previous enterprises—there had been only three or four of them—had been carefully prepared and so cautiously executed that not even the faintest suspicion had fallen on him. And now there he stood, caught red-handed in another person's bedroom with pearls worth 500,000 marks in his pocket and nothing lay between him and imprisonment but the little white bell-push surmounted by the enamelled tablet requesting you to ring twice for the valet. An access of sheer fury seized him, but he did not allow it to escape him. He kept it under, till it turned to strength and calm. It cost him a tremendous effort not to strike the woman to the ground. He was like a powerful locomotive under steam, fuelled and charged with atmospheric pressure causing it to vibrate from the centre through every part, and ready to launch itself with irresistible impetus.

Meanwhile he made his bow. He might have made a wild dash for the hotel façade. He might have struck Grusinskaya dead or silenced her with threats. It was the prompting of his good nature that chose a bow, an unpremeditated but courteous bow, instead of murder and violence. He did not know that he had gone a bluish-white under the eyes. Remotely he was aware even of danger as an enjoyment, like intoxication or the bottomless abyss of a dream.

"Who are you? How did you come here?" Grusinskaya asked in German. Her tone was almost polite.

"Pardon me, *gnädige Frau*, I stole into your room. I am— it is terrible that you should have found me here. You came

107

in earlier than usual. It is my bad luck. I can give you no explanation."

Grusinskaya stepped back a pace or two into the room, without taking her eyes off him, and turned on the cold light of the chandelier that hung from the ceiling. Very likely she might have called for help if it had been a rough and ugly man that she had discovered on her balcony. But this man, handsomest man she had ever seen in her life—as she now brought to mind through a cloud of veronal—caused her no alarm. Strangely enough, it was Gaigern's charming blue silk pyjamas that more than all filled her with confidence.

"But what did you want here?" she asked, and involuntarily she lapsed into the more familiar French.

"Nothing. Only to sit here. Only to be in your room," he said softly. He took a deep breath. There was nothing for it now but to tell the woman a fairy tale. He could see that, with a faint gleam of hope. The telltale socks over his shoes worried him; adroitly and surreptitiously he stepped on each in turn and pulled them off.

Grusinskaya shook her head. "In my room? *Mon Dieu!* What for?" she asked in her high-pitched bird-like Russian voice, while a strange look of expectancy shone in her face.

Gaigern, still on the balcony, replied: "I will tell you the truth, Madame. It's not the first time I have been in your room. Many a time I have sat in your room when you were at the theatre. I have breathed the air you breathe. I have left flowers for you. Forgive me——"

The tea with the veronal in it was cold. Grusinskaya smiled faintly, but she was no sooner conscious of doing so than she recovered herself and asked severely, "And who let you in? The chambermaid? Suzette? How did you get in?"

Gaigern resolved on a bold stroke. He pointed behind him into the night. "From there," he said, "from the balcony."

Again Grusinskaya had the feeling, as though in a dream, of having been through this before. Suddenly the memory came back. One evening at a castle in the south, down in Abas Tuman, where the Grand Duke Sergei used to take her, a young officer, a mere boy, had hidden himself in her room. It

108

was at the risk of his life, and indeed he died later through a mysterious accident while out shooting. It was thirty years ago at least. This forgotten incident suddenly came back to her as she stepped out on to the balcony, and looked out in the direction in which Gaigern had pointed. She saw the young officer's face. Pavel Jerylinkov was his name. She remembered his eyes and one or two kisses too. The air was cold and she felt at once that the man beside her on the little balcony radiated warmth. She gave a fleeting glance to the seven metres of the hotel front that parted her balcony from the next one.

"But that is very dangerous," she said aimlessly, thinking more of Jerylinkov than of the present moment.

"Not very," replied Gaigern.

"It is cold. Shut the door," said Grusinskaya curtly and went quickly past him into the room.

Gaigern obeyed. He followed her and closed the door behind him, drawing the curtains close. Then he waited with his hands hanging at his sides—a strikingly handsome, unassuming and rather foolish young man, who committed romantic follies in order to enter the bedroom of a celebrated dancer. He, too, after all, had a little talent for acting and his profession demanded it. And now life and death hung on the part he was to play. Grusinskaya bent to pick up her costume which lay where she had thrown it down, and took it into the bathroom. Her eye caught the glitter of the red cut glass which simulated the drop of blood. The sight cut her to the quick. No encore. No scandal when another danced in her place. Oh, the cruel public. Cruel Berlin. Cruel loneliness. She had got beyond those painful thoughts, but now they were back again and the anguish of them stabbed at her heart. For a few seconds she forgot the intruder who looked like young Jerylinkov. Then suddenly she went back and stood close in front of him, so close that she felt his warmth.

"Why do you do this?" she asked without looking at him. "Why do you take such a risk? Why do you sit secretly in my room? Do you want something of me?"

Gaigern took the plunge. Now for it, he thought. Without raising his eyes to her face, he said softly:

109

"You know why—because I love you."

He said it in French. It would have been too difficult in his native tongue. Having said it, he waited in silence to see how it worked. This is sheer madness, he thought meanwhile. He was bitterly ashamed of this humiliating farce. Such a breach of taste was an agony to him. Still—unless she rang—perhaps he was saved.

Grusinskaya drank in these few words of French with open mouth. They entered into her like medicine. In a few seconds she even ceased to shiver. Poor Grusinskaya! It was years since anyone had said anything of that kind to her. Her life rattled past like an empty express train. Rehearsal, work, contracts, sleeping-cars, hotel rooms, stage fright, agonies of stage fright, and then more work and more rehearsals. Successes, failures, critiques, interviews, official receptions, quarrels with managers. Three hours of work by herself, four hours' performance, each day like the last. Old Pimenov. Old Witte. Old Suzette and not a soul else, never any warmth. You held your hands to hotel radiators and that was all. And then when all was over and done with and life had come to the verge of the abyss, a man appeared in your room at night and spoke those long-forgotten words with which in other days the whole world had rung. Grusinskaya collapsed. She felt a sharp pang as of childbirth. But it was only two tears wrung at last and at last released from the stress of that night. She was conscious of these tears through her whole body, even in her toes and the tips of her fingers and then in her heart, and at last they reached her eyes and rolled off her long, thickly painted eyelashes to fall on the open palms of her hands.

Gaigern saw all this and it made him go hot. Poor creature, he thought, poor little woman. Now she is crying. This is really silly.

After the first two painful tears it was easier. They were followed by a light but copious shower, warm and cool at once like summer rain. Gaigern could not help thinking of the beds of hydrangea at Ried, though he could not tell why; then came a passionate downpour, a torrent that brought with it all the black paint from her eyelids, and finally Grusinskaya threw

herself on her bed and sobbed out words in Russian with her
hands clasped and pressed against her mouth. At the sight of
this, Gaigern changed from an hotel thief, who had been
within an ace of felling the woman to the ground, into a simple,
good-natured big-hearted man who could not see a woman
weep without wishing to come to her help. He lost all trace of
fear on his own account, and if his heart beat quickly it was
simply from pity. He went over to the bed and resting his
arms on either side of the little sobbing body he bent over her
and mingled his whispered consolations with her sobs. He had
nothing particular to say. He would have comforted a crying
child or a hurt animal in much the same words. "Poor little
woman," he said. "Poor little woman, poor little Grusinskaya,
she's crying. It does you good, doesn't it, to cry? Then cry,
poor little hurt creature. What have they done to you? Have
they ill-treated you? Are you glad I'm here? Shall I stay?—
Are you afraid of anything? Is that why you cry? Oh, you
poor little thing."

He raised one arm from the bed and took the clasped hands
from her mouth and kissed them; they were wet with tears
and black like the hands of a little girl; her face too was
stained with the trickles of black paint from her makeup. This
made Gaigern laugh. In spite of her tears Grusinskaya observed the hearty movement of the shoulders that a strong man
makes when he laughs. Gaigern left her bed and went into the
bathroom. He came back with a sponge and carefully wiped
her face. He had fetched a towel too. Now Grusinskaya lay
still. She had had her cry out and was content. Gaigern sat on
the edge of the bed and smiled at her.

"Well?" he asked.

Grusinskaya whispered something that he did not understand. "Say it again," he begged her. "You——man," Grusinskaya whispered. The word went home. It hit on his heart like
a tennis ball in fast play. It almost hurt him. The women with
whom he usually had to do had no great range of endearments.
They called him Schnurzi, Bubi, Darling or the 'Big Baron'.
He heard an echo in his soul as though from his childhood,
from a world he had left behind. He shut his ears to it. If only

I had a cigarette, he thought, feeling that he was getting tenderhearted. Grusinskaya had looked in his eyes for a moment with a strangely melting and almost happy expression. Now she got up and angled with her long toes for the slippers which had fallen from her feet. She recovered her self-possession.

"There, there," said she. "What a sentimental scene. Grusinskaya weeping. That is a sight worth seeing. It is many years since she did such a thing. Monsieur gave me a bad fright. It is he who is responsible for this painful scene."

She spoke in the third person, wishing to put a distance between them, but after what had passed it was not easy to do so. Gaigern had nothing to say in reply.

"It is frightful how the stage frays the nerves," she went on, in German, for she thought that he had perhaps not understood. "Discipline! Oh yes, we have plenty of that. But discipline is horribly exhausting. Discipline means always doing what you don't want to do and take no pleasure in doing. Have you experienced the weariness that comes of discipline?"

"I? Oh, no. I do only what I take pleasure in doing."

Grusinskaya raised a hand to which all its former grace had returned.

"I see, Monsieur. You take pleasure in coming into a lady's bedroom, and you come. You take pleasure in a dangerous climb on to a balcony, so you do it. And what is your pleasure now?"

"I should like to smoke," Gaigern said frankly. Grusinskaya had expected something else and the reply struck her as chivalrous and considerate. She went to the writing-table and held out her little cigarette box. She stood there in her much-worn, but genuine Chinese kimono and her trodden-down slippers, and all the charm and glitter and prestige which for twenty years had surrounded her on her travels throughout the Continent, surrounded her once more. She had forgotten apparently how tear-stained and utterly wretched she looked.

112

"We'll smoke the pipe of peace then," she said and lifting her long and much-creased eyelids she looked into Gaigern's face. "And then bid each other adieu."

Gaigern greedily inhaled the smoke of his cigarette. He already felt a great relief, though his situation was still an anxious one. For one thing, he could not possibly leave the room so long as the pearls were in his pocket. If, now that she knew him, he were to keep the pearls he would have to fly that night and in the morning he would have the police on his heels. This would not suit his book at all. Everything now depended on remaining in her room at all costs until the pearls were conjured back into their jewel case.

Grusinskaya had now sat down in front of the looking-glass and was intently powdering her face. She removed a line here and a mark there. She was beautiful once more.

Gaigern went up to her and interposed his body between her and the rifled suitcase. Over her shoulder he launched a sweet and seductive smile.

"Why do you smile?" she asked into the mirror.

"Because, dear, I see something in the mirror that you cannot see," said Gaigern. He said 'dear' without ceremony. The cigarette had restored him and now he felt in good form. Now for it, he thought, and spurred himself on. "I see in the mirror what I saw before when I was standing on the balcony," he said bending over her. "I see in the mirror the most beautiful woman I have ever seen. She is sad and she is naked. She is— no, I cannot say it or I shall go mad. I did not know it was so dangerous to look into a woman's bedroom while she undressed——"

And, indeed, as Gaigern strung together these gallantries in his school-taught French, he actually saw a vision of her in the mirror as she had been, and he felt again the warmth of admiration that he had felt on the balcony. Grusinskaya listened sceptically. How cold I have become, she thought sadly, when no tremor of response greeted these ardent words. She felt the deep shame of a cold woman. She turned to Gaigern with a consciously effective curve of her long neck. Gaigern took her shoulders in his warm and adroit hands and

113

then kissed her deliberately in the beautiful hollow between her shoulder blades.

This kiss, at first cool and remote, lasted long. It penetrated to her spine like a burning needle and her heart began to beat. Her blood became thick and sweet. Her frigid heart began to throb and flutter. Her eyes closed, and a tremor went through her. And Gaigern was trembling, too, when he released her and stood upright. A vein stood out blue on his forehead. Of a sudden his whole being was aware of her skin, of the sharp scent of her body, of her slowly awakening anticipation of delight. The Devil, he thought abruptly. He stretched out eager hands.

"I think you had better go now," Grusinskaya said weakly to his reflection in the glass. "The key is in the door."

Yes, the damned key was there now right enough, and now he could go when he chose. But now he didn't choose—for more reasons than one.

"No," he said with a sudden air of command to the woman, who trembled like a still vibrant violin. "I am not going. You know that I'm not going to go. Do you really think I should leave you alone here—I—you?—with a tea cup full of veronal? Do you think I don't know the state you are in? I am going to stay with you. *Basta!*"

"*Basta? Basta?* But I wish to be alone."

Gaigern quickly went up to her, took hold of her wrists and held them to his breast. "No," he said vehemently. "That is not the truth. You do not want to be alone. You are horribly afraid of being alone. I know well how afraid you are. You don't escape me. I know you, you strange little woman. It's no use play-acting with me. Your theatre is of glass and I see through it. You were desperate just now. If I go away now you will be more desperate than ever. Say I'm to stay with you. Say it."

He took her by the shoulders and shook her. He was wrought up, she knew. Otherwise he would not have hurt her. Jerylinkov had begged, she remembered. This man commanded. Weak and relieved she let her head fall on the breast of his blue silk pyjamas.

"Yes, stay a moment," she whispered. Gaigern looked away

over her head and let out a deep breath through his teeth. The crisis of fear began to relax while a whirl of pictures passed quickly before his eyes, as on the films. Grusinskaya dead in her bed with a fatal dose of veronal in her veins, and himself flying for his life, and a search of the house at Springe and then the prison cell. He had no idea what it was like in prison, but he saw it distinctly all the same. He saw his mother too. She died over again, although she had died long ago. When he came back to Room No 68 the menace of fear and danger changed to intoxication. He lifted Grusinskaya up in both arms and held her to his breast like a child.

"Come, come, come," he murmured in a low voice with his lips pressed to her temples. Grusinskaya had not been aware of her body for a long while. She was aware of it now. For years she had not been a woman. She was a woman now. A black, singing heaven began to revolve above her and she rushed up into it. A little bird-like cry came from her open mouth and drove Gaigern out of his make-believe into genuine passion and into a depth of joy such as he had never known. The tea cup on the table rattled lightly whenever a motor car went by below. At first the white light from the ceiling was reflected in the poisoned liquid, then only the red of the table lamp and then only the intermittent light from the electric sign shining through the curtains. Two hours raced by. From the passage came the click-clack of the lift. The distant church clock struck one amidst the hooting of the night traffic, and ten minutes later the electric lighting was once more in working order on the front of the Grand Hotel.

"Are you asleep?"

"No."

"Are you comfortable?"

"Yes."

"Your eyes are open, I can feel. I feel your eyelashes on my arms when you open and shut your eyes—a big man with eyelashes like a child's. Tell me, are you content?"

"I have never been so happy as now."

"What did you say?"

"No woman ever made me so happy."

"Say it again—say it."

"I have never been so happy."

Gaigern murmured into the cool softness of her arm where his head lay. It was the truth. The indescribable appeasement filled him with gratitude. He had never known this in his commonplace love affairs—this intoxication without disillusionment, this thrilling calm after the embrace, this deep intimacy of the body with another's body. His limbs lay relaxed and at peace beside hers, their senses shared a mutual secret. He experienced something that has no name, not even the name of love, a homecoming after long homesickness. He was still young, but in the arms of the ageing Grusinskaya he became still younger through the spell of her tender, experienced and thoughtful caresses.

"What a pity," he murmured into her arm; he pushed up his head a little higher and made a pillow of her shoulder, a little warm nest where there was the scent of a meadow. "I would know you anywhere in the world blindfold by your scent," he said, sniffing like a puppy. "Tell me what it is."

"Never mind. Tell me what is a pity? Never mind the scent, it has the name of a little flower that grows in the fields— *Neuwjada.* I don't know what you call it. Thyme? It is made for me in Paris. Tell me, what is a pity."

"That one always begins with the wrong woman. And so one goes on stupidly, night after night, believing that it must always be like that. What a pity that the first woman one sleeps with is not like you?"

"Oh, you're a spoilt child," whispered Grusinskaya. She buried her lips in his hair. It was warm and thick and strongly growing, with a masculine odour of cigarettes and hairwash. He passed his fingertips down her sides and felt her breath come and go.

"Do you know, you are so light. As light as anything. No more than a little foam on a glass of champagne," he said in tender admiration.

"Yes. I have to be light," Grusinskaya answered gravely.

"I should like to look at you. May I turn on the light?"

116

"No, don't," she cried and moved her shoulder away. He felt now that he had alarmed this woman whose real age nobody knew. And again he was moved to simple pity. He nestled up to her and they lay still, and thought. The light of the street was reflected on the ceiling and hovered to and fro. It was narrow and pointed like a sword, for it came through a gap between the curtains. Whenever a motor car went by below a swift passing shadow swept across this shaft of light.

The pearls, thought Gaigern, are for the moment with the Devil. If I have the luck and all goes well I can put them back in their case while she's asleep. There'll be an unholy row with my people when I return without them. If only the chauffeur doesn't commit some outrageous folly, if only the beast doesn't get drunk in his fury tonight and send us all to blazes. That business has failed completely. Where we are to get money from now, Lord knows. Perhaps this wealthy old boy from the provinces who groans every night next door in Room No 70 might be tapped. Oh well, the Devil take it, what's the good of thinking? Perhaps I can simply ask her to give me the pearls. Perhaps I can simply tell her early tomorrow all about it. If I play my cards well, she won't have me locked up in the morning, not she, the little crazy thing, as light as air. She leaves her pearls lying about unlocked! Funny little woman. I know her now. What does she care for pearls? She has done with everything, nothing matters to her. If I hadn't come, all would have been over for her by now. She shall give me the pearls. She is good, yes, as good as a mother, a little tiny mama whom one can sleep with.

Grusinskaya was thinking: The train for Prague leaves at 11.20. If only there's no hitch! I let go of everything today and tomorrow there will be a muddle. Pimenov is too weak and the girls twist him round their fingers. But whoever misses the train tomorrow shall get the sack, that's positive. If Pimenov hasn't troubled about the scenery tonight, it won't be packed by tomorrow. The scene-shifters ought to be working overtime tonight. If I don't see to everything myself, nothing gets done. Then there's Meyerheim's accounts. Good God, however did I come to run away like that? Witte, he'll leave

117

his own head behind in the hotel if no one looks after him. They all rely on me, and this evening I wasn't there. There will be a regular *débâcle*. Lucille has only been waiting for the chance to make a row. Their names are never in large enough type on the posters. They're never given a proper chance. But they never do a thing for themselves. If I don't hold the whip over them, they go to pieces. They have made me short-tempered and conceited and tired. Heavens, how tired I was yesterday. How little was needed to show them where they would be without Grusinskaya. But now I am not a bit tired. I could get up and dance the whole programme, or a new programme, or a new dance. I must talk to Pimenov about it. A dance of dread, oh, I could dance that for you now. At first on one spot only and only a tremor, and then three circles on the toes, or no, not on the toes perhaps, perhaps something quite different.

But I live, I live, she thought in a transport. I shall dance new dances and I shall have success. A woman who is loved always has success. You left me starving for ten years nearly now. That's what it was. To think that a foolish boy who comes climbing in over the balcony can give one such strength. A spoilt child who knows nothing of love but the silly talk of girls.

She pulled up the bedclothes and covered Gaigern up like a little child. He murmured gratefully and nestled against her. Their bodies were intimate, but in their thoughts they went their own ways like strangers. All the lovers in the world lie thus—so close together, and so far apart.

It was the woman who first began to grope after the mysteries of the other's soul. She took his head in her hands and held it as though it were a large and heavy fruit, gathered in the sun.

"I don't even know your name, my friend," she whispered in his ear.

"I am called Flix. In full Felix Amadei Benvenuto Freiherr von Gaigern. But you must christen me too. I want you to give me a name of your own."

Grusinskaya reflected a moment then she smiled softly.

"Your mother must have thought a lot of you when you came into the world to give you such beautiful names," she said. "The fortunate. The beloved of God. The welcome one. Did you cry when you were christened?"

"I don't remember."

"Do you know, I have a child too. A daughter. How old are you, Benvenuto?"

"Today I am seventeen, for this is my first love affair. In other respects, thirty" (he made himself out a little older than he was from a touching consideration for the woman who was afraid of her age and who would not have the light turned on). Nevertheless it hurt her. He might be the father of her eight-year-old grandson, Ponpon. She forced herself to think of something else.

"What were you like as a child? Very beautiful? Oh yes, I'm sure you were."

"Quite enchanting. Covered with freckles and bruises and scratches and scrubby and dirty. We had gipsies as grooms and stable boys, like most people on the border where our estate lies. The gipsy children were my friends. I got every sort of vermin and itch from them. When I think of my childhood I always smell stable manure. Then for a few years I was the terror of various schools. Then I was at the war for a bit. The war was fine. I felt at home in it. For all I cared it might have been a lot worse than it was. If there could only be another war I should be all right."

"Aren't you all right now, you fire-eater? What do you do? What kind of a person are you?"

"And you? What kind of a woman are you? I have never known a woman like you. But you make me inquisitive. I have a lot of questions to ask you. You are quite different."

"I am only old-fashioned. I am from another world, another century," Grusinskaya said and smiled in the darkness as she said it. Tears smarted in her eyes. "We dancers were brought up like little soldiers with iron discipline in the Imperial School of Ballet in Petersburg. We were little regiments of recruits for the beds of the Grand Dukes. It is said that those who grew too big when they were fifteen had steel rings

119

fixed round their chest to prevent them growing any bigger. I was small and lean, but as hard as a diamond. Ambitious too. I had ambition in my blood like pepper and salt. Duty made a machine of me. There was nothing but work, work, work. No rest, no leisure, never a pause. And then, fame always brings loneliness. Success is as ice-cold and as lonely as the north pole. And what it means to keep your grasp on success for three years, for five years, and twenty years, always on and on, but why do I tell you all this? Can you understand me? Listen. Often when you pass by a railway station waiting-room or motor in the evening through a small town, you see people sitting motionless in front of the door with stupid faces and their hands lying heavily on their knees. You, too, are tired and you wish you too could simply sit with your hands before you. Well, try it, when you are famous, disappear from the world and take your rest, let others dance, leave it to those ugly clumsy Germans and negresses, and all the other incompetents, let them dance and take your rest. No. You see, Benvenuto, it can't be done. It's impossible. Work is hateful, you curse it. But you can't exist without it. Three days' rest, and at once you are in a panic. I'm losing my form, I'm getting heavy, my technique is going to the Devil. You have to dance. It's an obsession. No drug, no morphine or cocaine and no vice in the world gets such a hold as work and success. I can assure you of that. You have to dance, you have to dance. Besides, it's important. If I give up dancing, believe me there will not be a single person left in the world who can really dance at all. All the rest are *dilettanti*. But this hectic and hideously practical world of yours cannot get on without someone who can dance and who knows what dancing means. I learned from celebrated dancers of my youth—Kchesinskaya, Trefilowa—and they in their turn had it handed down from the great dancers of forty and sixty years ago. Often I feel when I dance that I am dancing to defy the whole world. You all shout 'To-day, today,' and there you all sit, a theatreful of money-makers, motorists and war-service men and shareholders, and there am I—just little Grusinskaya, no longer young, a thing of yesterday, and all my steps have been known for two hundred years.

120

And all the same I carry you away, and then you shout and weep, and laugh and go crazy for joy. And why? Isn't it just for this old-fashioned ballet? So, you see, it has its importance. Certainly, for nothing can be a world-success unless it is important, unless the world needs it. But everything goes to pieces for it, nothing else remains whole. No man, no child, no feeling, nothing in life. You are a person no longer. Do you understand that? You are a woman no longer. You are nothing but an exhausted sense of responsibility hunted to and fro over the world. For one of us, life is over on the day when success comes to an end, on the day when we no longer believe in our own importance. Are you listening? Do you understand me?" Grusinskaya said beseechingly.

"Not all, but most of it. You speak French so fast," Gaigern answered. During the months of lying in wait for the pearls he had often been to Grusinskaya's performances and they had without exception bored him intensely. He was deeply astonished to find that Grusinskaya seemed to drag this ballet show round with her as a kind of martyrdom. She lay nestling so lightly against him and she had such a pretty and charmingly modulated chirruping voice, and at the same time she spoke such sombre words. What was he to say in reply? He sighed and reflected.

"That was good what you said just now about the people at evening with their stiff hands. You ought to dance that," he said at last with some embarrassment.

Grusinskaya only laughed at this.

"That? But one can't dance that, Monsieur. Do you think they'd want to see me as an old woman with a shawl over her head and gout in her fingers, sitting like a block of wood and resting."

She broke off in the middle of her sentence. Even while she spoke her body took hold of the idea and grew tense. She saw the scene and she knew a crazy young painter in Paris who could paint it. She saw the dance, she felt it in her hands and in the bent vertebræ of her neck. She lay silent with open mouth in the darkness. She was so wrought up that she did not breathe. The room was crowded with impersonations she had

121

never danced and still might dance. A hundred true and living figures rose before her eyes. A beggar woman stretched out trembling hands; an old peasant woman danced for the last time at her daughter's wedding. A haggard woman stood in front of a booth at a Fair and went through her poor tricks. A prostitute waited for men under a lantern. Here stood a servant girl who had broken a dish and was beaten for it, and here was a fifteen-year-old child forced to dance naked before a large, flashy man, and here stood the skinny caricature of a governess. There was one who ran as though pursued though no one followed her, one who wanted to sleep and dared not, one who was afraid of a looking-glass, and there was one who drank poison at last and died.

"Keep still, don't speak and don't move," Grusinskaya whispered and she stared up at the ceiling with its sword of light. The room had taken on that utterly strange and enchanted appearance often encountered in hotel bedrooms. Beneath the window a number of cars whirred and groaned like wild beasts, for the banquet of the League of Humanity was over and the departures from Entrance No II were in full swing. The night had grown cooler. Grusinskaya came back out of the whirl of her fancies with a start and a shudder. Pimenov—with his new butterfly ballet—will think I have gone out of my mind. Perhaps I have? The flight of her fancy had only lasted a minute, yet she returned from it to her bed as though from a long journey. Gaigern was still there. She was almost astonished to find this man still there against her shoulder and to feel his hair and his hands and his breathing.

"What kind of a man are you?" she asked again as she laid her face to his in the darkness. She was deeply conscious at this moment of her astonishment over such intimate closeness, when in so much they were strangers. "Yesterday I did not even know you. Tell me who you are," she asked with her lips close to his. Gaigern was about to fall asleep. Now he put his arms round her. She felt like his lean greyhound bitch at home.

"I? There's little to be said of me," he answered obediently, but without opening his eyes. "I am a prodigal son. I am the

122

black sheep of a good flock. I am a *mauvais sujet* and I shall end on the gallows."

"Yes?" she asked with a little gurgling laugh deep in her throat.

"Yes," said Gaigern with conviction. He had begun to recite the old phrases from the homilies of his school days in fun, but now the warm scent of thyme from the bed inspired in him a desire to confess and reform.

"I am uncontrolled," he went on into the darkness. "I am quite without character and unspeakably inquisitive. I can't live an orderly life and I am good for nothing. At home I learned to ride and play the gentleman. At school to say my prayers and lie. In the war to shoot and take cover. And beyond that I can do nothing. I am a gipsy, an outsider, an adventurer."

"Yes, and what else?"

"I am a gambler who is not above cheating. I have stolen too before now. Properly speaking I ought to be in prison. Meanwhile, I have a jolly good time and do as I please and live on the fat of the land. Now and again, too, I get drunk, and I ought to add that I have been work-shy since birth."

"Go on," whispered Grusinskaya in delight. Her throat quivered with suppressed laughter.

"Further, I am a criminal. A cat-burglar," Gaigern said sleepily.

"Nothing more? A murderer, perhaps?"

"Yes, of course. A murderer too. I was within an ace of killing you," Gaigern asserted.

Grusinskaya went on laughing a little at his face which she could feel but could not see. All the same she became suddenly serious. She clasped her fingers behind her neck, and whispered softly in his ear.

"If you had not come in yesterday I shouldn't be alive now!"

'Yesterday?' thought Gaigern. 'Now?' The night in Room No 68 lasted an eternity. It was years since he stood on the balcony and watched her. He gave a start. His arms gripped

123

her as tightly as a wrestler's, but her sinewy muscles held out against his pressure, as he felt with a strange joy.

"You must never do anything like that again. You must stay here. I shall never let you go. I need you," he said. He heard himself saying these astounding words in a husky voice that seemed to come directly from the depths of his heart.

"No, now it is different. Now it is all right again. You are with me now," Grusinskaya whispered. He could not understand, for she said it in Russian. But he heard the tone of her voice and this was enough to tune the night once more to rapture. Dream-birds started from the branches of the hotel wallpaper. He forgot the pearls in the pocket of his pyjamas, and she forgot her failure and the deadly dose of veronal in the tea cup.

Neither ventured on that fragile word—love. Together they glided into the vortex of their night of love. They went from an embrace to whispered talk, from whisperings to sleep and dreams, from dreams to more embraces. These two had come together from the ends of the world to meet for a few hours in the hotel bed of Room No 68 where so many had slept before them. . . .

Love had played no great part in Grusinskaya's life. All the passion of her body and soul went into dancing. She had had one or two lovers, because, like the pearls and a motor car and clothes from the best dressmakers of Paris and Vienna, they were part of the life of a celebrated dancer. Though she had been besieged, courted and pursued by numbers of men who had fallen in love with her, she did not in her heart believe in the existence of love. It seemed to her as unreal as the painted drop scenes, the temples of love and the banks of roses which formed the settings for her dances. But though she was cold and insensitive to love, she was esteemed a wonderful mistress. She herself practised love as a duty imposed by her profession, a part to be played that might sometimes please but always fatigued her and called for a high degree of art. To the nights she spent with her lovers she gave all the suppleness of her body, its hovering grace, its subtlety, its tenderness and its

124

sensibility, its impulse and its *élan*, its appeal and its delicacy, and in short all the qualities she had brought to perfection in her dancing. She could intoxicate but she could not be intoxicated. When she danced she could let herself go in self-oblivion, and often her partners heard her utter low cries or sing in low bird-like snatches to herself while she executed the most difficult and intricate figures. In love, however, she never lost her self-consciousness. She stood outside and watched herself. She did not believe in love and she did not need it, and yet, strange to say, she could not live without it.

For love, she knew, was an ingredient of success. As long as she was young, as long as flowers and notes poured into her dressing-room, as long as men stood rooted to the ground wherever she passed, as long as they were ready to ruin themselves or commit any folly and to sacrifice their families and fortunes for her sake she was conscious of success. It could be estimated in terms of declarations of love, threats of suicide, pursuits across the world and costly presents just as it could in terms of applause, critiques and the number of her curtains. She might not know it, but the lovers whom she bewitched and delighted were really to her only a public with whom she had a success. And the first time she realized with a shock of horror that success was deserting her was when Gaston left her and married an insignificant woman of good family. The atmosphere in which she lived began to cool off after being for so many years in a continual glow. The shadows lengthened to an inconceivable evening. It was a decline, though by steps so innumerable and so small that it was scarcely noticed. And yet the distance she had traversed was immense. Before the war, she had danced the whole world into an ecstasy of romantic delight. Now she begged her little applause from hostile and disillusioned cynics. And at the end of it all lay utter loneliness and a fatal dose of veronal.

Hence the man on the balcony was much more than just a man to Grusinskaya. He was a miracle. At the eleventh hour he had made his appearance in Room No 68 to rescue her. He was success coming to her in a simple shape; the world pressing eagerly to her; the proof that the years of romance when

125

a young Jerylinkov had been shot for her sake were not yet over. She had fallen, and there he had stood to catch her as she fell.

There was a dance in Grusinskaya's repertoire in which love and death danced a *pas de deux*. Youthful poets had occasionally sent her verses harping on the theme that love and death were brother and sister. Grusinskaya this night lived this lyrical commonplace in her own person. The dazed agony of the evening had changed to rapture. It had become an ecstasy of gratitude, a feverish grasping and taking and feeling and holding. The frozen years had thawed. The secret shame of her coldness, concealed all her life within herself, melted away. It was true of her no longer. She had been so wretched and lonely for years past that sometimes she had craved a pittance of warmth from the warm, young body of her partner, Michael. And now tonight in this ordinary hotel bedroom, in this bed of polished brass, she felt herself glow and pass into new being. Love in whose very existence she had disbelieved had been revealed to her.

Owing to the similarity between Rooms No 68 and No 69, Gaigern did not at once realize where he was when he awoke. Thinking that he was turning towards the wall in his own room, he encountered the sleeping, breathing form of Grusinskaya. Then he remembered. The deep and wonderful intimacy of their first sleep together weighed sweetly on his limbs. He slipped his cramped arm under her neck and thought with a tender solemnity of the events of the night. Without a doubt he was in love, in love in a sweet and utterly grateful fashion such as he had never known. Quite apart from the pearls, he thought, not without shame, quite apart from this ill-fated affair of the pearls, I am a rotter. I climb into a room and play an atrocious farce, and the woman believes in it. She positively likes it. Every man acts a part and every woman believes it. Every man is really a swindler and an intruder at the outset, but then later on—well, it has come true. I love you, little Mouna, dear little Neuwjada. Yes, I love you, *je t'aime, je t'aime*. You have made a fine conquest, little woman. . . .

It was cool in the room. Outside it must be nearly daylight.

The street was silent. A streak of pale dawning light came through the curtain. The pattern of the wallpaper began to steal out from the walls in the first glimmer of day. Grusinskaya was fast asleep with her chin pressed on her shoulder. Gaigern took her hand that hung over the edge of the bed and tenderly pressed its coolness and then put this limp little hand under the bedclothes as though Grusinskaya were an infant. He felt his way in the half light to the door of the balcony and slowly drew the curtains. Grusinskaya did not wake. Now, thought he, I must put this business of the pearls to rights again. He was surprised at himself for taking it so easily. A lost round, he thought without ill-humour. He often applied sporting terms like this to his adventurous undertakings. Next he groped about for his pyjamas, and, laughing softly as he collected his scattered articles of clothing, he went in the bathroom. The water made the wound on his right hand throb and begin to bleed again. He sucked it for a moment with indifference and then let it be. The bitter and faded scent of laurel was stronger than ever. Eager for fresh air he stepped out on to the balcony. His breast was still full of a new and sweet anxiety.

Outside a thin drifting mist of early morning hung over the street. Not a car nor a passer-by was to be seen. In the distance could be heard the noise of the trams starting off. The sun had not yet risen and the light was an unrelieved milky grey. Footsteps rang out at the corner of the street; then there was silence again. A piece of paper fluttered a moment over the asphalt like an ailing bird and then lay still. The tree that stood near Entrance No II stirred its branches in a dream. On this March morning, a sleepy bird high up on a budding twig tried its voice in the midst of the great city. A motor van laden with bottles of milk in cases careered noisily and self-consciously past. The drifting mist smelt of motor spirit. The balcony railing shone with moisture. Gaigern found his thief's socks on the balcony and stuffed them hurriedly into his pockets with the gloves and the torch and the pearls worth 500,000 marks, of which he had still to rid himself. Turning back into the room he drew back the curtains, and the light fell in a triangle on

127

the carpet and as far as the bed where Grusinskaya lay asleep.

She lay now stretched at full length, her head thrown back sideways on the pillow. The bed was far too large for her small slender form. Gaigern, for whom most hotel beds were too short, was amused and touched. He had a sudden tender inspiration. He took the tea cup full of veronal from the table and the empty glass tube too, and went with them into the bathroom. He emptied the cup, washed it as carefully as a nurse would do for a child, and dried it on his handkerchief. Childishly, he kissed the sleeves of Grusinskaya's bath gown which he found there. As there was nowhere else to put the empty glass tube, he put it in his pocket with the pearls. Grusinskaya sighed in her sleep when he returned. He bent over her attentively, but she was still asleep. It had grown lighter and he now saw her face quite clearly. Her hair had fallen smoothly back from her face and exposed the narrow temples with their shadowed hollows. Two deep wrinkles beneath the closed eyes showed the approach of age. Gaigern saw it, but it did not displease him. Her mouth over the delicate though faded chin was wonderful. There was a little powder still on her forehead with its indented line of hair. Gaigern remembered with a smile that she had pulled out a powder box from under the pillow before she allowed him to turn on the bedside lamp. I see you now, anyway, he thought with a primitive feeling of triumph in his conquest. He scrutinized her face, as though it were new country in which he went to seek adventure. He found two mysterious symmetrical lines descending from her temples past her ears to her neck as thin as threads, and lighter in colour than the rest of her skin. He passed his finger lightly over them. They were fine scars that framed her face as though they were the edges of a mask. Suddenly Gaigern realized what they were. They were vanity scars, incisions in the skin, with the object of stretching it and preserving its youth. He had read of such things. He shook his head with an incredulous smile. Involuntarily he grasped his own temples. They were smooth and braced by the strong and healthy beat of his pulse.

128

With an extreme tenderness he laid his face to hers as though he would infuse into her something of his own vitality. The strength, the softness and the pity that inspired his love for her at this moment filled him with astonishment. He felt clean and upright and a little ridiculous in the emotion he felt over this poor woman whom he had stripped of all her secrets.

He moved away from the bed and stood for a few minutes with contracted brow and open mouth before the looking-glass, plunged in reflection. He was wondering whether it was possible to keep the pearls in spite of all. No, it was not possible. For the moment, at least, he was still Baron von Gaigern, a somewhat easy-going fellow who kept bad company, in debt, certainly, but otherwise reputable. If he left the room with the pearls in his possession the police would hear of it within an hour or two, and his life as a man of leisure was over. He would be hunted down like any other criminal. And this would not suit him at all. To become the lover of Grusinskaya was not in keeping with his programme, but this was the fact, and it altered everything. He weighed the chances as he would have weighed the chances of a boxing or tennis match. Enterprises like this were a sport to him, and this time the game went against him. The change of circumstance made it impossible to steal the pearls. All he could hope was to be given them if he was patient. I must wait, thought Gaigern, and sighed deeply. His calculations so far were level-headed and perfectly clear. He did not go on to confess that a great deal more lay behind them. He did not wish to be ridiculous in his own eyes and he hated sentiment. He looked into the glass and pulled a face. The long and short of it is, he thought uneasily, I don't care to steal pearls from a woman I've slept with. I no longer even want to. It's against the grain—so that's that!

Neuwjada, he thought, remembering the bed on a wave of tenderness. Dear Mouna, I'd much rather give you a present, a big one, something pretty and costly, something to rejoice your heart, you poor dear. He pulled the pearl necklace out of his pocket, cautious not to make a sound. It did not please him now in the least. Perhaps after all they were false, in spite of all the newspapers' paragraphs. Perhaps they were not worth

129

half their reputed value. In any case, it cost him little to say goodbye to them now.

Grusinskaya tried to wake up, but she found her head swathed in sleep. The veronal, she thought, and closed her eyes. She had been afraid of waking lately. She dreaded the shock of facing the hard and naked facts of her life. She had a dim idea that something welcome and pleasant awaited her this morning, but at first she did not know what it was. She moistened her lips and found the sleepy parched taste of the night on them. She moved her fingers as a dog stirs in its sleep. Her body was utterly tired out, but she was profoundly happy, as she was after an evening of many encores when she had to expend her last ounce of energy. She felt the light of day beat on her closed eyelids, and for a moment she thought she was at Tremezzo, where the reflected light from the surface of the lake shone into her bedroom of rose and grey. She decided to open her eyes.

At first she saw an unfamiliar quilt over her knees that rose like a mountain before her eyes; then the hotel wallpaper with red tropical fruits on slender stems, a pattern calculated to fix the eyes in a feverish and senseless stare. The weariness of a life of incessant travel was bound up with such wallpapers. The corner of the writing-table was dim, for the curtain there was still drawn, and she could not see the time on the clock. The door on to the balcony was open and a cool air came in. Near the dressing-table her sleepy gaze discerned the broad black silhouette of a man outlined against the light from the balcony. He stood with his back turned to her and his legs apart. He was motionless and entirely unconcerned, and his bent head showed that he was occupied over something; but what it was she could not see. Surely, thought Grusinskaya, I was dreaming of this just now. She was still too dazed with sleep to be frightened. Surely I have lived this before, she thought next. Jerylinkov, she concluded at last. Suddenly her heart pulsed like an engine. She was wide awake and re-membered everything.

She breathed with closed lips, stealthily but deeply, and with each breath all the memories of the past night came rush-

130

ing back. She raised an arm from the bedclothes and found it as light as a bird.

She felt secretly for her powder box and began with earnest glances into its minute mirror to see to her appearance. The delicate scent of the powder delighted her. She was pleased with herself. She felt that she was in love with herself as for years she had not been. She encircled her small breasts with her hands. It was a habit of hers: but this morning it gave her peculiar pleasure to feel her own smooth cool and contented flesh. Benvenuto, she said to herself, and repeated it in Russian; *Zjellany*. He could not hear her say it, for she said it mutely within herself. He stood there, large-limbed and broad-shouldered—like one of Signorelli's executioners, Grusinskaya thought, delightedly—and his hands were busied with some object that lay on the dressing-table. She sat up with a smile to see what it was.

He was doing something with the case in which her pearls were kept. She distinctly heard one of the jewel cases snap as it shut. She could tell by the peculiar sound that it was the blue oblong velvet case which held the rope of fifty-two pearls. For a moment Grusinskaya could not understand why this sound stabbed her with such mortal fear. Her heart stood still and then gave three sudden heavy resounding beats, which she felt painfully all over her body. Her fingertips hurt and went numb. So did her lips. All the while she still smiled—she had forgotten to remove the smile from her lips and there it stayed, though her face was cold and as white as paper. So he's a thief—thought Grusinskaya in a flash. It was an extraordinary thought, mute and final like a cut straight through the heart. She thought she would faint and she longed to do so. But instead, for a second's space, her head was alert with a myriad thoughts that cut and crossed and collided, and flashed like a fight with daggers.

A crying feeling of having been cruelly ill-used, shame, fear, hate, rage, frightful agony—and at the same time an abyss of weakness that cried out not to see, not to understand, not to admit the truth, that cried out for the merciful refuge of a lie——

"*Que faites-vous?*" she whispered to the executioner's back. She meant to cry out, but only a whisper came from her stiffened lips. "What are you doing?"

Gaigern gave so violent a start, that his head spun right round. His fright spoke as clearly as a confession. Besides, he held in his hands the cube-shaped case of a ring; the suitcase was open, strings of pearls lay on the glass top of the dressing-table.

"What are you doing there?" Grusinskaya whispered again. That her blanched and distorted face smiled as she spoke, was piteous enough. Gaigern too understood her at once, and again his pity was so intense that he felt it beat in his temples. He held himself with an iron grip.

"Good morning, Mouna," he said affectionately. "I have come on a wonderful treasure while you were asleep."

"What are you doing with my pearls?" Grusinskaya asked hoarsely. Tell me a lie, tell me a lie, her distraught face implored him. Gaigern went to her and veiled her eyes with his hand. Poor creature, poor little woman.

"It was very rude of me to rummage about among your things," he said. "I was looking for some plaster, or a bandage of some kind, and I thought to myself there would be something of the sort in the little dressing case. But it was your treasures I found. I feel like Aladdin in the cave——"

Even her eyes had lost their colour and become leaden. Now their dark tint came back slowly. Gaigern, to convince her, showed her his right hand which was still bleeding a little. The tension was released and from sheer weakness Grusinskaya let her lips sink on his hand. Gaigern put his other hand on her hair and drew her to his breast. He could be fairly brutal and domineering with the women he usually had to do with. But this one, for some mysterious reason, called forth all his better instincts. She was so fragile, exposed to such dangers and so much in need of protection—and at the same time so strong. His own existence, always trembling on the edge of a precipice, taught him to understand hers.

"You silly——" he said tenderly, "did you think I had an eye on your pearls?"

132

"No," lied Grusinskaya.

These two untruths formed the bridge which united them again as lovers.

"Besides—I never wear them now," she added with a sigh of relief.

"No—but why not?"

"Well, you would not understand. It is a superstition. First they brought me good luck. Then they brought bad luck. And now as soon as I stop wearing them, they bring me luck again."

"Do they?" Gaigern asked thoughtfully. He still had a burden of uneasiness to get rid of. The pearls were safely back in their little bed of velvet. Adieu. *Au revoir,* he thought childishly. To prove it he put his hands in his pockets where he found his burglarious implements but no booty. This put him in a rollicking good humour. His spirits rose and he felt perfectly happy. He opened his mouth and uttered a shout of joy. Grusinskaya began to laugh, and at this he went over to her and playfully ended his shout on her breast; mouth and eyes and heart were all surrendered to her. She seized hold of his hands and kissed them. There was something genuine as well as playful in this submissive gratitude.

"There, it's bleeding," she said with her mouth on the little wound.

"You have lips like a horse's," Gaigern replied, "as soft as a little foal's, a black one of marvellous pedigree."

He kneeled down and embraced her bare ankles. Just as she was about to look down at him, there came a buzzing sound from the writing-table.

"The telephone," said Grusinskaya.

"The telephone?" replied Gaigern.

Grusinskaya sighed deeply. There was no help for it, her expression said, as she took up the receiver as though it weighed a hundredweight. It was Suzette.

"It is seven o'clock," she announced in her hoarse morning voice. "Madame must get up. There's the packing to be done. Will you have your tea now? And if Madame is to have her massage it is high time I began. And Herr Pimenov asks if

Madame will please call him on the phone as soon as Madame is up."

Madame considered for a moment.

"In ten minutes, Suzette—no, in a quarter of an hour you can bring in my tea, and then we'll make short work of the massage."

She put back the receiver but held it still in her hand, while she extended the other to Gaigern who stood in the middle of the room, lightly poised on the chrome-leather soles of his boxing shoes. After a moment she took up the receiver again. The Hall Porter replied with a dutiful promptitude, though he had not closed an eye all night, for his wife in hospital seemed to be in a bad way.

"Number, please?" he asked smartly.

"Wilhelm 7010. Herr Pimenov."

Pimenov was not staying in the hotel. He was in a second-class pension that a family of Russian emigrants had started in the fourth floor of a house in Charlottenburg. Nobody there was awake yet, apparently. While Grusinskaya waited she had a vision of old Pimenov hurrying to the telephone in his old silk dressing gown, with his narrow feet which were always turned out, as though for the fifth position. At last she heard his gentle, nervous old man's voice.

"Oh, Pimenov, is that you? Good morning, *dobroje utro,* my dear. Yes, thanks, I slept very well. No, not too much veronal, only two. Thank you, *tout va bien*—heart, head and all the rest. What? What is it? Michael has burst a blood-vessel in his knee? But, good heavens, why didn't you tell me this last night? This is awful. That will go on—well, we know how long that will take. And what have you done? What? Not yet? But you must wire to Tchernov, at once, do you hear? He must come to the rescue. Meyerheim must see to that. Where is Meyerheim? I'll ring him up at once. Too early? Pardon me, my dear, if it is not too early for us, it is not too early for Herr Meyerheim—please. And has the scenery gone to the station? But it must go, please, with the first shift—when does the first shift start work? At six? If it is not there I shall hold you responsible, Pimenov. I can take no excuse. You are the ballet-master. It is your business to see to the scenery, not mine. Yes, I shall expect to hear in half an hour at latest. Go to the station yourself. Adieu."

This time she kept the receiver in her hand and merely pressed down the hook with two fingers. She rang up Witte, whose wits were always astray in the mornings, and whose panic over travelling still put him into a fever in spite of all the years of touring and threw everything into confusion. She rang up Michael. He was staying in a small hotel. He was as piteous over his burst blood-vessel as a dog that had been trodden on. Grusinskaya shouted her strict injunctions and advice down the telephone. She was always in a rage and most unfair when any of the company fell sick. She rang up three doctors before she found one who was able to visit Michael at once and give him the requisite treatment and apply acetic bandages. She rang up Meyerheim and entered upon a dispute with him in French, finally commanding him to the hotel at half past eight to settle their accounts. She sent a telegram by telephone to Tchernov and a second in case of accidents to a young dancer in Paris, who could dance well and was disengaged. After that with the help of Senf, the Hall Porter, she ascertained the connection with the express from Paris which would enable the young man to reach Prague in time, and then sent a third telegram on the heels of the second.

"Please, *chéri*, turn on the bath," she said hurriedly to Gaigern in the midst of all this, and then drummed out a series of instructions in English to Berkeley on the telephone—for she was not taking the car and meanwhile it was to be thoroughly overhauled. Gaigern went and turned on the bath as he was told. He hung her bath wrap over the radiator to warm. He found the sponge with which the night before he had sponged her tear-stained face and took it into the bathroom—and still she telephoned on and on. He found bath-salts and threw in a handful. He would have loved to have done something more for her, but there was nothing more to do. Also Grusinskaya appeared to have done with the telephone for the time.

"That's how it is, and every day the same," she said. It was

135

meant to sound like a complaint, but her vitality and the pleasure she took in tackling things were irrepressible. "It has all got to be done. And then Michael says there's too much *chi chi* about Grusinskaya. That is what he calls *chi chi*, as though it were an amusement."

Gaigern stood in front of her, hungry for a little tenderness and intimacy. And indeed she held out both hands to him, but her thoughts were elsewhere. She was thinking of Michael's burst blood-vessel. And then she heard the race of the clock and the watch, and quickly seizing the telephone rang up Suzette once more. "Wait another ten minutes, Suzette," she begged her politely and rather guiltily. Her eyes fell on the table and last night's tea cup. There it stood washed and clean, looking utterly innocent and harmless, with the fantastic crest of the hotel in gleaming gold on its thick porcelain. What a mad night, she thought. Such things don't happen. And dances such as I imagined last night cannot be danced. It was my over-excited nerves. The Viennese would hiss me off the stage if I appeared in dances like that instead of the wounded dove and the butterflies. Vienna is different to Berlin. There they know what Ballet is.

Meanwhile she was staring into Gaigern's face, but she did not see him. This caused him a pain that was new to him, a vivid and peculiar pain in his chest. "Thyme—*Neuwjada*," he said softly, drawing the word from the deepest rapture of the night. Its scent came with it, the bitter and also the sweet and the unforgettable. And, indeed, at this invocation, Grusinskaya turned her eyes to him again and her face took on a tense look of suffering although she smiled. "I suppose we must part now——" she said in a voice loud and inflexible in case it broke.

"Yes——" Gaigern answered. He had forgotten the pearls. They were actually and utterly erased from his memory. He was conscious of nothing but the grip and stress of his feelings for this woman, and the infinite desire to be good to her, good, good, good. Helplessly he turned the signet ring with the Gaigern crest in lapis lazuli round his finger.

136

"Here," he said and held the ring out to her awkwardly like a schoolboy, "so that you shan't forget me."

But I shall not see you again, thought Grusinskaya, and at that her eyes became hot and Gaigern's beautiful face shone through her tears. It was one of those thoughts that cannot be spoken. She waited.

Let me stay with you. I will be good to you, thought Gaigern. But he held his mouth fast shut and not a sound escaped him.

"Suzette will be here any moment," Grusinskaya said quickly.

"You are going to Vienna?" he asked.

"First, for three days, to Prague. Then for fourteen days to Vienna. I shall be at the Bristol," she added.

Silence. The ticking of the clock. Motor horns below in front of the hotel. The smell of a funeral. The sound of breathing.

"Can't you come with me. I need you," Grusinskaya said at last.

"I—I can't come to Prague. I haven't any money. I must raise some more first."

"I'll give you some," she said quickly, and as quickly Gaigern answered, "I am not a *gigolo*."

A sudden overmastering impulse flung them into each other's arms and something greater than themselves held them fast bound together at the very moment when they had to part. "Thank you," they both said at once. "Thank you, thank you," in three languages, German, Russian, French, stammering, sobbing, whispering, weeping, jubilant. "Thank you, *merci, bolschoje spassibo*, thank you."

At this moment Suzette took the tray of tea out of the hands of the injured waiter. It was twenty-eight minutes past seven. The clock on the writing-table was racing breathlessly. The watch had given up in exhaustion. On—on—on it ticked reproachfully.

"In Vienna then?" Grusinskaya said with moist eyelids. "In three days? You will follow me. And after that you will come with me to Tremezzo. It will be beautiful, wonderful. I shall

137

give myself a holiday, six weeks or eight. We shall do nothing but live. We shall live. Everything else shall be left behind, all the nonsense, and we'll do nothing but live. We'll be perfectly silly from sheer idleness and happiness—and then you'll go with me to South America. Do you know Rio? I—no, enough. It is time. Go—go, and thank you."

"In three days at the latest," said Gaigern.

Grusinskaya quickly assumed something of the great lady.

"See that you don't compromise me too much in getting back to your room," she said as she shut the double doors behind him.

As Gaigern released his hand without a word from hers he felt it hurt him. It was bleeding again. The passage was deserted. The doors ran together in the long perspective and boots slept lop-eared at their thresholds. The lift was descending and someone in a hurry to catch a train was running along the passage on the third floor. One of the frosted-glass windows on the stairs was open to let out the cigar smoke of the night before. Gaigern stole in his boxing shoes over the pineapple carpet to Room No 69 and opened the door with a skeleton key. For the other was still hanging, for the purpose of his alibi, on the board above the Hall Porter's desk.

Grusinskaya had her bath and then gladly resigned herself to Suzette's hands for massage. She felt strong, elastic and full of energy. She had a boundless desire to dance and longed for her next appearance. She was sure that a success was in store for her. She was always a success in Vienna. She felt it already in her legs and hands, in her neck as she threw back her head; in her mouth that would not stop smiling. She dressed and went off like a top with the whip behind it. She plunged with irresistible energy into the morning's business, the dispute with Meyerheim, the subterranean battle with the disaffected members of the company and the patient management of Pimenov and Witte.

At ten o'clock, Pageboy No 18 brought a bouquet of roses. 'Au revoir, beloved lips,' was written on a scrap of paper torn from an hotel envelope. Grusinskaya kissed the signet ring with the Gaigern crest. "Porte bonheur," she whispered as though to an intimate friend. Now she had something to bring her luck again. Michael was right. I shall give away the pearls for poor children, she thought. Suzette in darned cotton gloves gripped the handle of the suitcase, while the luggage porter carried out the rest. Grusinskaya had no sentimental feelings over the parting from this eventful hotel bedroom with its wallpaper that always got on her nerves. Another was reserved for her at the Hotel Imperial in Prague, and also at the Bristol in Vienna, her usual room overlooking the court, Room No 184, with bathroom. And one, too, in Rio, Paris, London, Buenos Aires, Rome—an endless perspective of hotel bedrooms with double doors and water laid on and the indefinable odour of restlessness and homelessness. . . .

At ten minutes past nine, a drowsy chambermaid fleetingly swept up the dust in Room No 68, threw away the faded floral tributes, took out the tea tray and finally came back with fresh linen—still damp from the iron—for the next occupant. . . .

WITH THE treachery common to alarm clocks, General Director Preysing's failed to rouse him from sleep with the thoroughness and punctuality expected of it. At half past seven it emitted a brief raucous rattle, and that was all. Preysing, whose mouth was open and parched, moved a little in his sleep and the springs of his bed murmured in response. A gleam of sun showed behind the yellow curtains. Then at eight o'clock the Hall Porter duly aroused him by telephone, but by that time it was far too late. Preysing held his drowsy head under the shower bath, cursing his forgotten razor. It needed no more to deprive such a slave to routine of all joy in life. In spite of being late he wasted several minutes selecting a suit to put on. And when he had decided on his morning coat, he took it off again in a fit of impatience. He calculated—and perhaps with reason—that morning coat would put him at a disadvantage. His grey lounge suit, on the other hand, would show the Chemnitz people at once that the whole affair meant very little to him. He made unusual haste, but by the time he had put away all his cases and oddments, searched for, discovered and pocketed all his keys, looked once more through his papers and once more counted his money, it was after nine. He shot out of his room and at once collided with a man in the passage.

"Sorry," said Preysing and came to a stop in front of his door, partly to let the other pass and partly to get his second arm into his coat.

"Not at all," the man replied and went along the passage. It seemed to Preysing that he had seen that back before. When Preysing reached the lift, the man was just descending in it. He now presented his front and this too, Preysing thought, he had seen before, though he could not remember where. It was fairly clear, though, that he made a grimace at him as he went off with the lift under his very nose. Preysing, in nervous impatience, ran down the stairs and along the corridor and down

140

into the tiled basement where the hotel barber plied his trade in an odour of damp cellar and *peau d'espagne*. There, enveloped in white sheets like babies, sat several gentlemen waiting hopefully for the manipulations of the white-jacketed barbers. Preysing began to dance with impatience in his thick rubber-soled shoes.

"Shall I have long to wait?" he asked, rubbing his unshaven chin with his hand.

"Ten minutes at the most. There is only this gentleman in front of you," was the reply.

The gentleman who was in front of him was the gentleman of the lift, and Preysing looked at him with disfavour. He was a somewhat insignificant creature, thin and diffident, and he sat squinting into a newspaper with his pince-nez almost falling off his sharp nose. Preysing was distinctly aware that he had come across the man in the course of business, but he could not recall the occasion. He went up to him and, making him a perfunctory bow, said with all the amiability he could command:

"Would you be so very kind as to let me go first? I am in a great hurry."

Kringelein, hunched together behind his paper, collected all his forces. Emerging from behind the leading article and extending his lean neck, he blinked straight into the General Director's face and replied, "No."

"Excuse me, but I am in a great hurry," Preysing stammered reproachfully.

"So am I," returned Kringelein.

Preysing turned on his heels in a fury and left the barber's shop. And there sat Kringelein breathing heavily in an atmosphere of shaving soaps, utterly exhausted and done-up after his prodigious effort, but a hero in triumphant possession of the field. . . .

Behind time, unshaven, and with the tip of his tongue scalded by burning coffee, the General Director was the last to enter the conference room. The others had had time to emit plentiful clouds of blue cigar smoke into this room, which, with its green tablecloth and imitation damask wallpaper and its

141

portrait in oils of the founder of the Grand Hotel, presented an appearance of the highest solidity. Doctor Zinnowitz had his papers all ready to his hand, and old Gerstenkorn presided at the head of the superfluously long table. He acknowledged the new arrival by rising only slightly in his chair, for he belonged to the same close-fisted generation as Preysing's father-in-law. He had known Preysing as a young man and had no great opinion of him.

"Behind time, Preysing," he said. "Quarter of an hour's grace, eh? A late night? Yes, we all know Berlin!"

He laughed with a bronchitic wheeze and pointed to a chair at his side. Preysing sat down opposite Schweimann. He had the objectionable feeling of having got out of bed on the wrong side and his upper lip was moist under his moustache, even before the show began. Schweimann, who had red edges to his eyelids and the large protruding and flexible mouth of an ape, introduced a third gentleman.

"Our colleague, Doctor Waitz," he said.

Doctor Waitz was a young man who looked absentminded, but was far from being so. With his domineering and aggressive trumpet of a voice he could be a very ugly customer in a discussion. So the Chemnitz people had brought *him* along with them, thought Preysing.

"We've met before," he said without enthusiasm.

Schweimann offered the General Director a cigar across the table and Doctor Zinnowitz took a fountain pen from his breast pocket and laid it down on the table beside his papers. Farther down the table, on the far side of the water-bottle and the glasses which quivered on a black tray whenever a motor bus went by, there was still another person, a colourless individual, Flamm the First. She held her shorthand block in her hand. In appearance she was elderly and faded, with a thin white moth-like dust on her cheeks. She was silent and businesslike and by no means easily to be mistaken for Flamm the Second.

"That's a nice fountain pen," said Schweimann to Zinnowitz. "What make is that? Very nice."

"Do you like it? Got from London. Nice, isn't it?" said

Zinnowitz as he wrote his flowing signature on a memorandum block. Everybody watched him.

"How much was it, if I may ask?" inquired Preysing, and taking his own from his breast pocket, laid it on the table in front of him, whereupon everyone looked at it.

"A little over three pounds without the duty. A friend of mine brought it over," said Zinnowitz. "Rather a jolly thing, isn't it?"

They craned their heads over the table like schoolboys and gazed upon the malachite green fountain pen from London. It was an object well worthy to occupy the attention of these five grown-up business men for three minutes.

"Well, let's get on to business," said old Gerstenkorn at last, in his bronchitic voice, and Zinnowitz resting his white anæmic fingers on the green tablecloth began at once in a fluent and well-prepared speech to launch a statement upon the blue haze of the conference chamber.

Preysing permitted himself a slight release of tension. He was not much of a speaker and he was, therefore, devoutly thankful that Zinnowitz relieved him of this task and also that his periods flowed off his tongue with the smoothness and precision of a machine. This, however, was no more than a prelude. He said nothing, in fact, but what had long since been gone over again and again in preliminary negotiations. He was merely reviewing the state of affairs once more, and, in doing so, he fished out one document after another out of his portfolio, holding the long columns of figures close to his shortsighted eyes in order to read them off without hesitation.

Now this, to repeat, was the state of affairs: the Saxonia Cotton Company, which dealt chiefly in cotton stuffs, bed covers, and, as a means of utilizing waste products, in a very popular make of house flannel, was a medium-sized undertaking with plenty of capital. Its assets in land, buildings and machinery, in raw material and finished goods, in patents, etc., and particularly in debts outstanding, reached a very respectable figure. The annual turnover and the net profits maintained a sound average level. The dividend for the previous year was nine-and-a-half per cent.

Zinnowitz read out these, after all, very satisfactory figures, and Preysing listened to them with pleasure. Everything in the business was above board and in order, and the output from waste products, which alone brought in marks 300,000 gross, had been organized by himself. He glanced at Gerstenkorn. Gerstenkorn, in the meditative and rather simple fashion of the old and sly, was swaying his grey scrub of a head to and fro. Schweimann was fussing with his cigar and did not appear to listen. Waitz checked every figure that was quoted by some notes which he had in a small book bound in leather. Flamm the First, a model of a private secretary, strove to efface herself by staring at the reflections in the water-bottle, while she held her pencil like a small sharp fixed bayonet. Zinnowitz drew forth another lot of papers from the pile before him and passed on to consider the position of the Chemnitz Manufacturing Company. His long thin Chinese beard bobbed up and down as he spoke.

The Chemnitz Manufacturing Company—as the figures showed—was an appreciably smaller undertaking. It had scarcely half the assets and its balance sheet revealed an extremely shaky state of affairs. The least possible had been written off, but nevertheless an astonishing high dividend was shown. The annual turnover was high. The net receipts, however, were scarcely in proportion. For all that, the Chemnitz Company showed a surprisingly large balance. Zinnowitz's voice as he read the last figures implied that he begged leave to query them, and he looked at old Gerstenkorn.

"Rather more," said Gerstenkorn. "Rather more. You can put it at 250,000 marks in round figures if you like."

"You can't reckon in that fashion," said Preysing, who had got nervous. "You have to make allowance for the depreciation of the new machinery for the new process. You cannot simply write off the old machinery."

"Yes, we can. Yes, we can," said Gerstenkorn obstinately.

Doctor Waitz trumpeted: "Our figures are under-estimated, rather than over-estimated."

Doctor Zinnowitz handed a paper across to the General Director, who proceeded to study the figures on it with close attention. He was familiar already with the upshot. The Chemnitz Manufacturing Company was not by any means a sound enterprise. Floated at the outset with insufficient capital, its credit was stretched to the utmost. Nevertheless it had a big turnover; it paid; it obviously throve and it had the market on its side. Saxonia Cotton, on the other hand, hung fire. Sound and well capitalized as it was, it was all the same a somnolent concern. Cottons, bed coverings and house flannel. The world for the moment was not requiring bed coverings and house flannel. And the old man at Fredersdorf knew what he was about when he wanted to come in on the top of the market for knitted goods and turn it to the advantage of his own business.

"It doesn't matter. Let's get on," he said with the tolerant air of a man in the weaker position. Gerstenkorn took the balance sheet from Preysing's hand and tapped the paper. He laughed huskily.

Zinnowitz had meanwhile turned his eloquence to the state of shares, and here there was plainly a snag. Saxonia in actual fact issued twice as much stock as Chemnitz did. Accepting this as the basis, all the preliminary negotiations for the fusion of the two concerns had reckoned two shares of Chemnitz as the equivalent of one Saxonia. Now, however, the Chemnitz shares had gone up and the Saxonia shares had gone down. Hence the centre of balance had shifted and—as Doctor Zinnowitz admitted with a conciliatory movement of the hand—the basis of exchange, owing to the astonishing boom in the shares of the Chemnitz Manufacturing Company, was no longer the same. Preysing listened with irritation to the smooth legal voice as with pedantic exactitude it brought forward nothing but those unpleasant facts which he knew only too well. His cigar ceased to afford him any pleasure and after a strenuous pull he put it down. At a certain moment in Zinnowitz's exposition of the case, Doctor Waitz leapt forward like an actor at his cue. He made objection with rapid gesticulations of his hands over the green table; he read figures from his notebook without so much as glancing at it, new figures, different figures. Preysing contracted the muscles of his forehead till his eyes started from his head, so intense was his effort to retain it all

145

and to see through it all, to keep a clear view of the whole question. He took one or two hotel envelopes that were lying on the table and scribbled down notes on them secretly and agitatedly like a schoolboy in a fix.

Doctor Zinnowitz, for his part, threw the merest glance towards the trusty Flamm the First, and she duly took down the aggressive remarks in shorthand on her blue-lined block. Doctor Waitz summed up in his bellowing voice. No, it was not to be imagined that the shareholders in the Chemnitz Manufacturing Company were going to submit to an amalgamation that halved the value of their stock. There was no occasion whatever, in his opinion, to give the Saxonia priority over the Chemnitz Company, supposing an eventual (he mouthed the word 'eventual' like a strolling player) fusion between the two. Why should this flourishing concern be brought into submission, as it were, and shoved into a corner?

Zinnowitz looked at Preysing, and Preysing obediently began to speak. It was his habit to give utterance to matters of importance in a low and nasal voice and with a dreary lack of emphasis. He employed this method of showing an outward calm and superiority because inwardly he had no confidence in himself. The backs of his hands were moist as he threw himself into the battle. Schweimann's eyes crept like little grey mice out of the red cavities where they lived, and Gerstenkorn stuck his thumbs in his waistcoat with the air of a man who was enjoying himself. Such conferences took place every day in the Grand Hotel—here in this 'great pub' many a job was rigged which afterwards the shareholders had to make the best of. Sugar went dearer, silk stockings cheaper, coal short— these and a thousand other contingencies depended on the issue of battles fought out in the conference chamber of the Grand Hotel.

So Preysing spoke, and the longer he spoke in that voice of his that sounded as if it had been kept on ice, and the closer he came to grips with the business, the more ground he lost. Gerstenkorn's telling little interjections whistled in the air like bullets. There were moments when Preysing would gladly have turned tail and fled from the field, dropped the whole

146

rotten business of the amalgamation and gone home to Freders-dorf to Mulle and Popsy and Babs. But as he was the managing director, and as life was not all a bed of roses, and as this amalgamation meant a lot to the business and everything to his own personal standing, he stuck bravely to his post. He produced once more the statements of his assets and clung fast to this thoroughly sound demonstration of a thoroughly sound business. He wearied the Chemnitz people by falling into rambling details, and Zinnowitz had several times to get him afloat again like an unwieldy boat gone aground. He tied nooses and hanged himself in them. He made obstinate stands on mere side issues with the pig-headedness of sheer stupidity. He devastated them with the exact figures of the manufacture of house flannel from cotton waste, for this was his pet subject, and forgot to make the important points which he had scribbled on his envelopes. And at last he stuck in the middle of a sentence which had begun like a flourish of trumpets and ended like a blind alley. He took out his handkerchief and wiped his moustache and lit a cigar that tasted like hay. And suddenly it occurred to him that he was sitting at the table with hustlers, men of no principle; he felt the deep embitterment of a self-respecting man who is thought a fool for his pains.

Now, however, Gerstenkorn removed his fat common thumbs from the armholes of his waistcoat and began to state his opinion. This Gerstenkorn, with his scrubby square head and bronchitic voice, was a clear and ready speaker. He made use of every available dialect in order to say what he wished in the fewest words. His business talk was spiced with expressions from the dialects of Saxony, Berlin, Mecklenburg and from Yiddish.

"And now stop a bit and let the grown-ups talk," he said without taking his cigar from his mouth, and this had the desired effect of making his slovenly speech even more slovenly. "You've told us now what the Saxonia is good for and that we knew already. It don't go down, all the same. We've gone into all that with our principal shareholders and the upshot was to think twice and twice again before we went in for

147

the amalgamation. They don't see the fun of pulling the hot chestnuts out of the fire for your cotton business. So now you have it straight. Our position has improved appreciably since you first approached us. Yours has remained stationary, if I am not to be rude and say it has deteriorated. Under the circumstances—to speak plainly, my dear Preysing—the amalgamation has lost its attraction for us. We have come here this morning with instructions in our pockets under these circumstances to let the negotiations drop. At the time when you approached us, it was another story."

"We didn't approach you," Preysing said quickly.

"How can you say that, man? You did approach us. Doctor Waitz, please give me the correspondence. Here we are—on September 14th you approached us by letter."

"That's not correct," Preysing persisted obstinately, and he made a grab for the file of papers in front of Zinnowitz. "We did not approach you. Our letter of September 14th followed upon a personal exchange of views instigated by yourselves."

"If you talk of instigating, why, your old man sounded me in strict confidence as between old friends a good month before that."

"We did not approach you," said Preysing. He clung to this fact which was a mere side issue as though it were of vital importance. Zinnowitz sounded a warning note with his narrow feet under the table. Abruptly Gerstenkorn let the matter drop. He smoothed the green tablecloth with his square-shaped hands. "Right," he said. "*Bon!* Then you did not approach us, if that pleases you better. And whether you did or not, the circumstances were not the same as now. You will not deny that, Herr Generaldirektor?" (The change from the familiar to the official style sounded threatening.) "At that time we had reasons for wishing a close connection with the Saxonia Cotton Company. What reasons have we today?"

"You need more capital," said Preysing, quite rightly. Gerstenkorn swept this aside with two of his fingers.

"Capital! Capital! We have only to issue shares to have all the money we want chucked at us. Capital! There's one thing you forget. You had your time in the war. You were able to make a good thing then out of army cloth and blankets. Now it's our turn, eh? We don't need capital. We need cheap raw material so that we can profit to the full by our new process, and we need new outlets for export abroad. I'll tell you the views of the company quite frankly, Herr Generaldirektor. If the amalgamation were of any help to us in these directions, then we're for it. Otherwise not. Now, please, if you have anything to say?"

Poor Preysing! If he had anything to say! Now had come the point he had been afraid of ever since getting into the slow train at Fredersdorf. He threw a timid glance across at Zinnowitz, but Zinnowitz was examining his well-tended bloodless fingernails and made no reply.

"It is no secret that we have excellent connections abroad. To the Balkans alone we export house flannel to the annual value of 65,000 marks," he said. "It stands to reason that in the event of an amalgamation we should do everything in our power to open up a bigger foreign market for your products too."

"Are there any circumstances that would enable you to give this assurance a more definite form?" asked Doctor Waitz from lower down the table. He even rose half way from his seat as he said it. This was a habit contracted in his former activities as counsel for the defence in criminal proceedings. Wherever he might be he always looked as though he wore a barrister's gown and he had not lost the tone with which he used to browbeat nervous witnesses. The General Director allowed himself to be browbeaten.

"Can you tell me what circumstances you mean?" he answered with his pitiful habit of asking what he knew already.

Schweimann who sat opposite him had not so far opened his large flexible ape's mouth. He opened it now.

"The reference is to the proposed understanding with Burleigh & Son," he said without more ado. Gerstenkorn held a long cigar ash trembling on the end of his cigar in the keenest suspense.

"Unfortunately I am not in a position to make any statement on that question," Preysing answered at once. He had prepared this reply long beforehand and learnt it by heart.

"Pity," said old Gerstenkorn. Whereupon there was a general silence lasting several minutes.

The bottle of water rattled on the tray because a bus was going by outside, and the surface of the water catching a ray of sun threw trembling rings of light on to the frame of the portrait in oils of the founder of the Grand Hotel. Preysing's brain worked feverishly during these seconds. He did not know whether Zinnowitz had shown those ominous copies of the letters—now so entirely meaningless and unjustifiable—to the Chemnitz people. Once again he had that unclean and uncomfortable feeling in his hands. His unshaven chin began to itch in a ridiculous way. From the corners of his eyes he threw his legal adviser a questioning and imploring glance. Zinnowitz, as though to soothe him, closed the lids of his oblique and sagacious Chinese eyes. This was an extremely obscure gesture. It might mean yes. It might mean no. It might mean nothing whatever. Preysing pulled himself together. I must see it through, he thought—though it was more a sensation than a thought.

"Gentlemen," he said, standing up—for the velvet upholstered chair made him hot and uncomfortable behind. "But, gentlemen, we must after all stick to the main point. The basis of all negotiations between us so far was our credit balance and the standing of the Fredersdorf manufactory. You have had every opportunity to look into that matter. Herr Kommerzienrat Gerstenkorn has satisfied himself personally as to the state of our concerns, and I must draw the line at vague and incalculable elements being brought into the discussion today. We are not speculators. I certainly am not a speculator. I deal with facts not with rumours. It is no more than a stock exchange rumour that we meditated a business arrangement with Burleigh & Son. I have had to contradict it once already and I cannot admit that——"

"You can't take in an old stager like me with a tale like that. We all know what such contradictions are worth," Gerstenkorn threw in. Schweimann perked up. He sniffed with diluted nostrils and ape's mouth as though he already scented export possibilities with England. Preysing began to lose his temper.

"I refuse," he shouted, "I refuse to have this affair with England mixed up with the business before us. I am not going to reckon with castles in the air. I have never done it and with a business like ours, it is not necessary. I reckon with facts, with actualities, with figures. Our balance—here it is," he cried, and he smote three times with the flat of his hand on the file of papers before him. "This is what counts and nothing else has got to count. We offer what we offered from the first, and if your company suddenly finds that it is not enough, then I'm sorry."

He pulled himself up in alarm. He had galloped off like a runaway horse over a bog. I'll end by scaring them off with my noise, he thought in horror. I ought to keep them in hand and instead of that I'm bungling the business. He poured out a glass of water and took a drink. It was heavy, tepid and savourless and like castor oil. Justizrat Zinnowitz smiled faintly and tried to put things right.

"Herr Generaldirektor Preysing is conscientious to an exemplary degree," he said. "I don't know whether his scruples over allowing the affair with Manchester to be brought into discussion in any way are not unjustified, or at any rate exaggerated. Why should not a matter that looks so promising be thrown into the scales, even though it is not in black and white?"

"Why? Because I could not answer for it," interrupted Preysing.

Zinnowitz would gladly have trodden on his foot if he had been in a position to do so. As it was, he raised his voice and talked the General Director down. Preysing sat down again on the warm plush seat and said no more. He had been on the point of letting out the truth. Very well, he thought, if Zinnowitz would not let him have his say, then let this noted commercial lawyer see for himself where he got to. The affair was going badly. It had gone badly already. It was dead and buried. Negotiations finally broke off. Right. Good. He offered the honest terms that a sound concern and an honest man had to offer. But that was not what people wanted nowadays. They wanted their hypothetical arrangements, their wild rumours, their manipulated booms with nothing behind it all but hot air. Knitted goods, jumpers and sweaters and gaudy socks from Chemnitz, he thought bitterly. He could see them now at that very moment—all these many-coloured and frivolous articles of fashion which captivated the world on the persons of equally frivolous young girls.

Zinnowitz talked on. Flamm the First had sunk again into a professional lethargy. Gerstenkorn and Schweimann scarcely listened to a word he said. They were bending over to each other and whispering together in a very ill-mannered fashion.

"Our friend, Preysing," the Justizrat was saying, "perhaps carries his scruples too far. His company is said to be on the point of concluding a very favourable agreement with the excellent old firm of Burleigh & Son. And what has Preysing to say to it? He resists the imputation as though he was being called a bankrupt. Granted that it is actually no more than a rumour—all the same, there is no smoke without fire, as we all know. And an old business man like Kommerzienrat Gerstenkorn will agree that some rumours are worth more than many a signed agreement. But as legal adviser for many years past to the Fredersdorf business, I may be permitted to say that the rumour foreshadows perfectly definite arrangements. You must forgive me, my dear Preysing, if I don't maintain the same inflexible discretion as yourself. There is no object in denying that negotiations of a far-reaching kind have already proceeded a long way. It may not be possible to say today whether they will reach their desired conclusion. But they are in existence and every bit as much a fact as any in your balance sheet. In my opinion, it reflects the highest credit upon Herr Preysing that in this quixotic fashion he refuses to throw this affair into the scales as an asset of his company. Nothing could be more straightforward and gentlemanly. But it gets us no further. So you will pardon me if I take these gentlemen into our confidence in this matter."

Zinnowitz floundered on with his conciliatory discourse,

interspersing a number of 'thoughs' and 'seeing that's' and 'notwithstandings' and 'on the other hands'. Preysing had gone pale; he could tell from the prickling sensation as the blood flowed from his temples that he must be as white as a sheet. So, thought he, Zinnowitz has shown them the letters. Good God, but that's swindling. It is not far from actual fraud. 'Negotiations finally broken off. Brösemann,' he thought, and he saw the blue-black and blurred writing of the telegram. He put his hand into the breast pocket of his grey office suit, where he had stowed the telegram away, and pulled his hand out again as though from a hot oven. If I don't get up at once and say what's happened, there'll be no end of a muddle, he thought, and he stood up. And if I do say it, they will break off, there will be no more talk of the amalgamation and I can go back to Fredersdorf as the scapegoat, he thought, and sat down again. In the vain hope of accounting for this aimless and undecided movement, he poured out some more of the nauseating water and swallowed it down like medicine.

Schweimann and Gerstenkorn in the meanwhile had cheered up considerably. They were a couple of extremely *rusé* business men. Their attention was caught by the vehemence with which Preysing negatived the English affair and did his utmost to exclude it. Their keen noses scented something behind this—export, profits, competition perhaps. Gerstenkorn whispered what he thought into Schweimann's large right ear: "In the case of anyone else a contradiction like that would be as good as saying yes. But in the case of this blockhead Preysing it is even possible that he is simply telling the truth——" Gerstenkorn broke in roughly: "There's no object in our legal friend talking himself hoarse," he said leaning over the table. "Before we say any more, I must ask Herr Preysing to tell us plainly how far the negotiations with Burleigh & Son have gone."

"I refuse," said Preysing.

"I must insist on it, if I am to continue the discussion," said Gerstenkorn.

"Then," said Preysing, "I beg you in any further discussion to regard that matter as non-existent."

"Am I to conclude then that all prospects of an agreement with Burleigh & Son are over?" asked Gerstenkorn.

"Conclude what you like," said Preysing.

At this they were all silent for nearly a minute. Flamm the First discreetly turned the leaves of her block and the slight rustle of the paper broke the stillness of the conference chamber. Preysing looked like a sickly infant. It sometimes happened that from behind his managing director's face there peeped out the perplexed and obstinate look of a small boy. Zinnowitz, feeling that everything was over, was drawing little triangles on the cover of a file of papers with his malachite fountain pen.

"Then I suppose there's nothing further to be said for the present," Gerstenkorn said finally. "I suppose we may as well conclude our little discussion. We can always continue it in writing."

He got up, and his chair made grooves in the thick pile carpet of this very handsome conference chamber. Preysing, however, kept his seat. He took out a cigar with elaborate care, and with elaborate care cut off its end; then he lit it, took a pull and began to smoke with an abstracted and deeply meditative expression on his face. His cheeks were speckled with tiny red veins.

There is no doubt that General Director Preysing was a thoroughly respectable man, a man of principle, a good husband and father, a man who stood for organization and order and the strongholds of convention. His life went by programme. It lay open to inspection like a map, and the sight of it could not fail to please. It was a life of card indexes, of red tape, of many pigeonholes and much hard work. He had never yet committed the least irregularity. Nevertheless, there must have been a bad spot in him somewhere, a minute nucleus of moral disease which was destined to get a hold on him and bring him low. Yes, there must, in spite of all, have been just the merest trace of some inflammation, some microscopic speck on the irreproachable purity of his moral waistcoat. . . .

He uttered no cry for help at this fatal moment when the conference was broken off, though his plight was bad enough

154

now to justify a cry for help and succour. He stood up gripping his cigar between his teeth, as he felt for something in his waistcoat pocket with a sensation of complete drunkenness.

"Pity," he said casually, amazed at the careless tone of his voice, as it issued from his mouth past his cigar. "Great pity. What is deferred is done with. So that's the end of that. And now that you have broken off, I don't mind telling you that we put through the agreement with Burleigh & Son last night. I got the news early this morning."

He drew out his hand from beneath his coat, and in it was the folded telegram: *Negotiations finally broken off*. A sense of childish and triumphant roguery came over him as he stood there, after telling this thundering lie which bordered on downright fraud and with the telegram before him on the green table. He did not even know whether he wished to bluff them or merely to make an effective exit out of the mess into which he had got himself. Schweimann, the less controlled of the two Chemnitz people, made an instinctive grab for the telegram. Preysing, very quickly and with an almost ironical smile, raised his hand from the table, unfolded the telegram, folded it up again and put it back into his pocket with a deliberate air. Doctor Waitz, farther down the table, looked foolish. Zinnowitz whistled. The one thin piping note came very oddly from his sagacious Chinese lips.

Gerstenkorn began to laugh and wheeze at once. "My good fellow," he coughed. "My dear fellow! You're a deal smarter than you look. You've properly led us by the nose. Come on, now we must have another talk over this."

He sat down. The General Director remained standing for a few seconds with a sense of vacancy; all his joints had gone hollow and, as he felt a strange weakness taking hold of him and extending to his knees, he sat down too. He had swindled for the first time in his life and in a manner that was perfectly stupid and senseless and bound to be found out. At the same time, and, indeed, precisely because of it, he had at last got his head above water after many fruitless attempts. Suddenly he heard himself talking and now he talked well. A strange and until now quite unknown intoxication took possession of him,

155

and everything he now said had vigour and power and energy. The founder of the Grand Hotel stared down at him full of admiration. Flamm the First bent her old-maidish and down-covered face over her block and took it all down in shorthand —for now that a final settlement seemed to be approaching, every word was of importance.

Preysing's new and inspired condition was maintained till the end of the conference, which went on for three hours and twenty minutes longer. It was only when he grasped the fountain pen of malachite green to append his signature by the side of Gerstenkorn's to the draft agreement, that he observed that his hands were once more moist and singularly un-clean. . . .

"No 218 wants to be called at nine," said the Hall Porter to little Georgi.

"Is he leaving then?" asked little Georgi.

"Why should he be leaving? No, he's staying on."

"I only mean because he's never been called in the morning before."

"Well, you see to it, anyway," said the Hall Porter. And hence the telephone buzzed punctually at nine in Doctor Otternschlag's small and inexpensive room.

Otternschlag roused himself from his dreams as strenuously as any much-occupied man, and then he lay where he was and wondered at himself. "What's up?" he asked himself and the telephone. "What's up now?" Then for a minute or two he lay still and thought hard, with the disfigured side of his face pressed into the rough linen of the hotel pillow. Wait a bit, he thought—it's that Kringelein, poor fellow. We have to show him a bit of life. He's waiting for us. He's sitting waiting for us in the breakfast room.

"Shall we get up and dress?" he asked himself. "Yes, so we will," he replied after an effort, for he had a good sleeping draught of morphine in his veins. Nevertheless, there was a certain alacrity about him as he hurried here and there over his dressing. Somebody was waiting for him. Somebody was grateful to him. With one sock in his hand, he sat on the edge

156

of his bed and fell to considering plans. He made a programme for the day. He was as preoccupied as if he had a party of tourists to conduct. He was important and sought after. The chambermaid as she took a broom and pail out of a closet next door to Room No 218 was astonished to hear Doctor Otternschlag humming a song after a fashion while he brushed his teeth. . . .

Meanwhile, Kringelein was already seated in the breakfast room, still exhausted, excited and exultant after his exacting victory over General Director Preysing in the barber's saloon. Also, ten minutes before, he had made the acquaintance of the engaging and delightful Baron von Gaigern. Gaigern had been busy. After emerging minus the pearls from his night with Grusinskaya he had shot straight into an explanatory scene with the chauffeur, conducted in whispers, but none the less vehement. Immediately after that, when he had had his bath, done his exercises and rubbed himself over with toilet vinegar, he had run into the provincial gentleman of Room No 70, from whom in one way or another he hoped to raise the few thousand marks of which he now stood in immediate need. Inwardly he was filled with a radiantly blissful and devouring eagerness and impatience. Though it was only an hour since his parting with Grusinskaya he felt already an uncontrollable, yet tender, longing for her. Through his whole being he felt the desire to be with her again with all possible speed. Gaigern revelled in this hitherto unknown feeling with all the *joie de vivre* and all the alertness with which every fresh experience inspired him. He started upon his enterprise with Kringelein with enormous gusto. He went off like a rocket and in a quarter of an hour he had gone an immense way towards winning his confidence. Kringelein was captivated at once. He exposed his timid employee's soul with all its eagerness for life and all its acceptance of death, and what he did not say or could not express Gaigern guessed for himself. When at fourteen minutes past nine Kringelein had wiped the last traces of his egg from his vigorous moustache with the hotel napkin they were already friends.

"You must understand, Baron," said Kringelein, "that I

157

have come into a little money after living always in very restricted circumstances, oh yes, in very restricted circumstances. A man like you can have no idea of what that means. To be afraid of the coal bill, you know, to be unable to go to the dentist, until, after putting it off year after year, you find yourself minus most of your teeth—you don't know how. But I won't talk about it. The day before yesterday I ate caviare for the first time. You may well laugh, you eat caviare and so on every day, of course. When our General Director entertains people he has caviare sent by the pound from Dresden. Well, caviare, champagne and all the rest of it are not life, you may say. But what is life, Herr Baron? You see, Baron, I am no longer young, and besides I am not in good health, and then you suddenly feel afraid—so afraid—of missing life altogether. I don't want to miss life, if you understand?"

"You can't very well miss that. It's always there. You live—and that's all about it," said Gaigern.

Kringelein looked at him. He saw his good looks and his good spirits, and possibly, as he did so, his eyelids reddened a little behind his glasses.

"Yes, of course, for a man like you life is always there. But for a man like me——" he said in a low voice.

"Funny. You talk of life as though it was a train you have to catch. How long have you been after it, three days? And not got a glimpse of it yet, in spite of caviare and champagne? What did you do yesterday, for example? Kaiser Friedrich Museum, Potsdam, and at night the theatre. Well, and what pleased you most? Which picture? You don't know? Of course not. And the theatre? Grusinskaya? Yes, Grusinskaya," said Gaigern, and at the name his heart gave a bound like a silly boy's. "What do you say? It made you sad; it was so poetical. But all that has nothing to do with life, Herr Direktor" (he said 'Herr Direktor' from pure goodness of heart, because he was shocked by the plain plebeian name of Kringelein; and Kringelein blushed with pleasure). "Life is—look here, you know when you see those cauldrons of pitch boiling, bubbling and smoking in the street and making a stink for miles around. Well, now go and put your nose over those tar fumes. It's

158

beautiful. It's hot, and it has such a strong and pungent smell that it bowls you over, and the thick black drops glisten, and there's strength in it, nothing sweet and insipid. Caviare! You want to catch hold of life, and if I ask you what colour the trams are in Berlin you can't say because you haven't troubled to look. Now listen, Herr Direktor, with a tie like yours you'll never get even with life, and you'll never feel happy in a suit like that. I'm telling you this quite frankly, for there's no object in paying compliments. If you'll put yourself in my hands I promise you that we'll soon put some go into the business, and the first thing is to go to a tailor. Have you any money on you? A cheque book? No. Well, put some ready money in your pocket. Meanwhile I'll get my car out of the garage. I've given my chauffeur a few days off—to see his girl at Springe—so I drive myself."

Kringelein felt as if there was an east wind about his ears. The remark about his tie (bought in the Arcade for two marks fifty) and his good suit made a thoroughly painful impression on him. His hand went timidly to his over-big collar. "Quite so," said Gaigern, "it doesn't sit right and the stud shows all the time. Of course, you can't see life like that."

"I thought—I didn't want to lay out money on clothes," Kringelein murmured, and he saw figures capering giddily in his account book. "I'll gladly spend money on other things but not on clothes——"

"Why not for clothes? Clothes are half the battle."

"Because it isn't worth while now," Kringelein said in a low voice, and the soft, silly tears smarted in the corners of his eyes. He couldn't, confound it, think of his approaching end without emotion. Gaigern looked vexed. "It really is not worth while. I mean—I have not many more opportunities left for wearing new clothes. I thought—the old ones would be good enough to last me out," Kringelein whispered guiltily.

Good Lord, has everyone got a teacupful of veronal ready to his hand? thought Gaigern, whose sensibilities had been quickened by the tender scenes of the past night. "Don't reckon things up, Herr Kringelein. One's apt to reckon all wrong. You should not go on wearing old clothes. You should meet each moment as the moment requires. I am a man of the moment in this sense, and I'm all the better for it. Come along now, and put a few thousand marks in your pocket and then we'll see whether there isn't some fun in life. And now, let's be off."

Kringelein got up obediently, and as he did so he felt that danger compassed him on every side. A few thousand marks, he thought, with his mind in a fog. A good day. One day at a few thousand marks. As he followed Gaigern he was still putting up a resistance, and the walls of the breakfast room danced before his eyes. He felt uprooted. His will was gone. His feet in their blacking-leather boots took their own way with him along the hotel passages. He was afraid. He was uncontrollably afraid of Gaigern, of the threatened expenditure, of the smart tailor; he was afraid of the grey-blue motor car as he got into the front seat; he was afraid of life, although he was afraid of missing it, too. He clenched his dilapidated teeth together, pulled on his cotton gloves and began his good day.

As Doctor Otternschlag at ten minutes to ten coasted round the walls of the Lounge searching for Kringelein, he was handed a letter by the Hall Porter.

My Dear Doctor [it ran], I regret that I am unexpectedly prevented from keeping my engagement with you today. With respectful greetings, yours truly,

Otto Kringelein.

It was Kringelein's style but no longer altogether his handwriting. Hard, jagged strokes had crept into the smooth copperplate hand, and the dots of the i's had a tendency to fly away, like balloons cut adrift, to burst somewhere in the sky with a lonely and tragic little report that no one hears. . . .

Doctor Otternschlag held the letter out in front of him. The Lounge was a dreary waste of endless vacant hours. He pottered along past the newspaper stand, past the flower stall, past the lifts and past the pillars to his customary seat. Frightful, he thought. Ghastly. Hideous! His leaden cigarette-stained fingers hung down, and he stared with his blind eye at the charwoman who, contrary to all orders, was beginning in broad daylight to sweep out the Lounge with moist sawdust.

Kringelein's embarrassment as he stood in the fitting-room of the large tailor's shop was terrible. Three elegant gentlemen were busily occupied with him. Twelve very shabby Kringeleins were reflected in the mirrors set at acute angles to each other. One elegant gentleman brought in coats and suits, one elegant gentleman knelt on the floor and pulled down the bottoms of his trousers, one elegant gentleman merely stood by and surveyed Kringelein with a half closed professional eye and murmured unintelligible words. On a sofa, beneath pictures of impossibly beautiful film actresses, sat Baron Gaigern, flapping his stitched gloves on the palm of his hand and looking away from Kringelein as though he were ashamed of him.

Pitiful matters came to light, dread secrets of the book-keeper, Otto Kringelein, of Fredersdorf. His braces had given way and been mended, and then when they had given way again, they had been clumsily held together with string. His waistcoat, which had got much too big for him, Anna had taken in by stitching two thick tucks in the lining at the back. He wore his father's shirts, and they were too large for him. He wore indiarubber bands round the sleeves above his elbows to prevent their superfluous length overwhelming him. He possessed cuff-links as old as the hills, round and large as soup plates. There was a sphinx on them in red enamel in front of a blue enamel pyramid. The enormous shirt was made of wool, thick and discoloured, presenting in front only a small extent of linen front, like a little shop window on the street. There was still one more woollen garment beneath the woollen shirt, a washed-out and much-darned undervest. Below that came a dappled catskin, an approved preventive of stomach-ache and attacks of ague. The elegant gentlemen did not move a muscle. Kringelein would have found it easier if they had made a joke of it, or given him a word of consolation.

"I have never troubled myself much about being in the fashion. I'm one of the old school," he said, imploring the forgiveness of these icily professional gentlemen. No one made any reply to this. They stripped him off layer after layer as if they were peeling an onion. It is a little gruesome to think

161

what the defenceless Kringelein went through on this occasion. It was almost as bad as the operation theatre. There was the same glassy brightness over everything, and everything, he felt, came close up to him on all sides. Then the three gentlemen began to clothe him.

Gaigern cheered up and gave advice. "Have that," he said, or "Don't have that". No opposition apparently could be made to his decisions. Kringelein squinted at the tickets with the prices attached to each article. He thought of nothing but the prices, but he did not venture to ask. Finally, though, he asked, and then he received such an immeasurable shock that he wanted to run from the place. The fitting-room became a prison cell with four grim warders and looking-glass walls. He fell into a frightful perspiration in spite of having had his woollen coverings removed. They lay in a heap on a chair and looked utterly cast off and repellent. They had suddenly become strange to him. Those darned, fusty and discoloured articles of clothing nauseated him. And then something happened to him. He fell in love with the silk shirt he was being compelled to put on.

"Ah," said Kringelein, standing with his head on one side and his mouth open as though he were listening to a secret, "ah-ah." The tastefully patterned silk of the shirt caressed his skin. The collar fitted, it did not chafe nor scratch, it was neither too tight nor too loose, and a tie fell smoothly and softly over his breast, beneath which his heart beat in secret jubilation. It beat hard and somewhat painfully, but all the same with relief. Now socks and shoes were put before him, most obligingly, for Gaigern had explained in a few words that the gentleman was not very well and so all that a man of fashion required was collected from all four floors of the establishment. Kringelein was put to the last extremities of shame by his feet. It was as though all the misery and oppression of his life were to be seen in these feet with their swollen soles. And so he crept away with the new socks and shoes into a corner, and bending down with his back to the company he set to work clumsily tugging at the shoelaces. After this he was rigged up in a suit which the Baron had selected.

162

"The Herr Direktor has a wonderful figure," said one of the gentlemen, "it fits as though it had been made for him."

"Not the least alteration required," said the second.

"Astonishing. We haven't many such slim figures among our customers," said the third.

They led Kringelein to the mirror and turned him about on his axis like an unresisting wooden doll, and it was just then, at the very moment when Kringelein encountered himself in the glass, that he had the first inkling that he lived. He recognized himself with a strong convulsion as though by a flash of lightning. What occurred at this moment was that a well-dressed and most elegant stranger approached him with an air of embarrassment, a person who at the same time was appallingly familiar to him as the real Kringelein of Fredersdorf, and then the vision passed. A second later the sight was no longer new. The miracle of transformation was past.

Kringelein was now breathing deeply and with effort, for he was being menaced by an attack of acute pain.

"I think it suits me very well," he said like a child to Gaigern.

The Baron did the handsome thing. With his own large warm hands he smoothed the new coat down over Kringelein's shoulders.

"Yes, I think we'll have this suit," Kringelein said to the three gentlemen. He secretly felt the cloth between his finger and thumb, for he knew something about cloth. It was in the very air at Fredersdorf, even though you were employed only in the counting-house.

"Good material. I'm in the trade," he said with respect.

"Genuine English cloth. We get it direct from London, Parker Bros & Co.," replied the one with the pinched-up eyes. Preysing does not wear cloth like this, thought Kringelein. Preysing's suits were usually of that solid gray worsted which the factory had had in stock for years, and sold off cheap to its employees annually just before Christmas. Kringelein took possession of his suit as he dug his hands into its clean new pockets.

His fears were changed abruptly into the joy of buying and

possessing, and for the first time he experienced the giddy exhilaration that comes of spending money. He broke down the walls behind which he had lived for a lifetime. He bought and bought. He did not ask the price, but simply bought. He stroked stuffs and silks, felt the brim of hats, sampled waist-coats and belts, matched one colour against another and appreciated their harmonies with the relish of a connoisseur.

"The gentleman has wonderfully good taste," said one.

"Most distinguished," said another. "Most appropriate and correct."

Gaigern stood by, impatient to be off, and added his praises. From sheer boredom he looked at his hands. There was a cut on the right and the left looked naked after giving away his signet ring. Surreptitiously he passed them in front of his face to see whether any scent from the night clung to them, a bitter sweet scent of danger and calm, *neuwjada*, the little flower that grows among the fields.

Kringelein bought a brown lounge suit of rough English tweed, a pair of dark grey trousers with a fine white stripe to go with an elegant morning coat; he bought a dinner jacket and trousers, which only needed the position of a button or two altered; he bought underclothing, shirts, collars, socks, ties, a coat such as Gaigern wore, a soft and astonishingly light hat, bearing the trade mark in gold of a Florence firm, and finally, carrying in his hands a pair of wash-leather gloves just like Gaigern's, he repaired to the pay-desk. There things went smoothly. Kringelein was quickly at home when he encountered the familiar jargon of ledgers and the atmosphere of the count-ing-house. He paid a thousand marks down, the rest to follow in three instalments. "There we are then," said Gaigern with relief. An array of politely supple backs escorted the trans-formed and enchanted Kringelein to the mirrored door of the establishment. Outside, it was sunny but cold. The air was like iced wine, Kringelein observed in passing. Hitherto he had always crept about. Now he stepped out. He had three steps to go from the entrance of this fashionable emporium to the grey-blue four-seater and three times he raised his new-shod feet from the pavement with a vigorous and elastic step.

"Pleased?" asked Gaigern, laughing and with his hand already on the starter. "What does it feel like? More yourself?"

"Splendid. Tip-top. First class," Kringelein replied as he sat down beside him with a nonchalant air. He took off his pince-nez and rubbed his eyes with his finger and thumb. It was a habit of his when fatigued.

It had just occurred to him that he would no longer be there when the last instalment was due.

Gaigern's fingers were all impatience. At the street crossings there were red and green and yellow lights to direct the traffic and policemen stood there and laughingly held out warning arms. The car shot along past houses, trees, advertisement kiosks, blocks of pedestrians at street crossings, past fruit-barrows, hoardings and timid old ladies who went tripping across the street at the wrong moment with long black skirts in the middle of March. The sun threw a moist yellow gleam on the asphalt. Whenever a great clumsy bus was in the way the little four-seater gave two hoots. It sounded like the barking of excited dogs.

There were many people in Fredersdorf who had never been in a motor car. Anna, for example, had never been in a motor car. But Kringelein was in one now. His lips were tightly compressed, his elbows and shoulder joints were rigid, and the rush of air made his eyes water. Taking the corners made a severe demand on his nerves and his heart went up and down beneath his new silk shirt. It was the same fearful joy as when in his childhood the merry-go-round was erected on Mickenau Heath and you could have three rides for a penny.

Kringelein stared at Berlin as it flew past in streaks. He began to feel fairly familiar now with the great city. For example, he recognized the Brandenburg Gate from afar and also the Gedächtniskirche, which he greeted with a respectful glance.

"Where are we going?" he shouted into Gaigern's right ear, for the noise of the engine seemed deafening and he felt he was in the midst of an uproar of the elements.

"A little way out, to have lunch, along the Avus," Gaigern answered unconcernedly.

The street raced to meet the car with ever-increasing swiftness. They drew near the wireless tower, the Funkturm. Kringelein had been there the evening before with Doctor Otternschlag when night was closing in. He had been tired out by then and incapable of grasping anything. The remarkably smooth surfaces of the new and only half finished pavilions out in this neighbourhood had pursued him in his dreams and now reality and dream lay imposed one on the other, half menacing and half incomprehensible.

"Are they going to finish building that?" Kringelein shouted and pointed to the exhibition buildings.

"It is finished," was the answer. Kringelein marvelled. It was all bare like a manufactory, but it did not look ugly like the factory at Fredersdorf.

"An odd city," he said shaking his head and blinked the harder. He felt a shock that contracted the skin of his scalp, but it portended nothing. Gaigern had merely stopped at the north gate of the Avus and now he was already off again.

"Now we can let it rip," he said, and, before Kringelein understood what he meant, he had done so.

At first the wind grew colder and colder, and blew harder and harder, until at last it beat like a fist against his face. The engine sang on a rising note and at the same time something ghastly occurred to Kringelein's legs. They were filled with air. Bubbles rose in his joints as if they would burst. For several seconds, that seemed to last an incredible time, he could not breathe, and moment after moment he thought, Now I'm dying. This is what it's like then. I am dying.

His chest caved in and he gasped for breath. The car swallowed up one object after another before it could be recognized, streaks of red, green and blue. A patch of red just became a car before it vanished into nothingness behind, and all the while Kringelein could not breathe. He felt now an unimagined sensation in his diaphragm. He tried to turn his head towards Gaigern. Strange to say he succeeded without finding it torn from his shoulders. Gaigern sat a little forward

166

over the wheel and he was wearing his wash-leather gloves though they were not buttoned up. This for some reason was reassuring. Just as what was left of Kringelein's stomach strove to escape at his throat, Gaigern's closed lips began to smile. Without taking his eyes off the Avus road whirling past like an unwinding spool, he pointed somewhere with his chin, and Kringelein obediently followed the direction with his eyes. Having some intelligence he realized after a guess or two that the speedometer was before his eyes. The little pointer trembled slightly as it pointed to 110. Good Lord, thought Kringelein, and swallowing down his fears he bent forward and gave himself up to the rush of speed. Suddenly the new and appalling joy of danger overcame him. Faster! cried a frenzied Kringelein within him whom he had never known before. The car complied with 115. For a few moments it kept to 118, and Kringelein finally gave up all thought of breathing. He would have liked now to whirl on and on into darkness, on and on in the shock of explosion, and to get right beyond and out of time. No hospital bed, he thought, better a broken skull. Hoardings still whirled past the car, but the spaces between began to alter. Then the grey ragged streaks beside the road became pine woods. Kringelein saw trees eddying more slowly to meet the car and stepping back into the wood like people as the car went by. It was just as it was on the roundabout at Mickenau when it slowed down. Now he could read the names of oils, tyres and makes of cars on the placards. The rush of air relaxed and streamed in his throat. The speedometer sank to 60, trembled a little, then 50—45—and then they left the Avus by the south gate and drove along soberly between the villas of the Wannsee.

"There—now I feel better," said Gaigern and laughed all over his face. Kringelein took his hands from the leather cushion in which till now he had dug his fingers and carefully relaxed his jaws and shoulders and knees. He felt completely tired and completely happy.

"So do I," he answered truthfully. He spoke very little while they sat after this on the empty glass-roofed terrace of a restaurant looking over the Wannsee and watched the sailing-boats rock at their moorings. He had to think out the experience he had been through. What is speed? he thought. It can't be seen or taken hold of, and, if it can be measured, that too is probably only a trick. How is it then that it goes through and through you, and is even more beautiful than music? Everything was still revolving in circles around him, but this was just what pleased him. He had the bottle of Hundt's Elixir on him, but he did not take any of it.

"I must offer you my heartiest thanks for this wonderful drive," he said studiously, expressing himself in a manner he considered fitting to the circles in which he now moved. Gaigern—who had chosen very plain fare, an egg on spinach —made light of the obligation. "It amused me," he said. "It was your first experience and it's so seldom you find anyone who experiences something for the first time."

"But you do not give one the impression of being blasé yourself, if I may say so," Kringelein replied very aptly. He was quite at home in his new clothes and in his silk shirt. He sat and he ate in a different manner, and his thin hands emerging from the cuffs of his shirt gave him particular satisfaction. They had been manicured that morning by a pretty girl in the hotel basement.

"Good Lord! I, blasé!" Gaigern said delightedly. "No, certainly not. Only, a man like me has a full life." He had to smile. "Though you're right. There are things that even a man like me experiences for the first time—funny things," he added to himself. He clenched his fine teeth softly together and thought of Grusinskaya. He was devoured by impatience for the moment when he should have her in his arms again with all her tender need of him and hear again the sad twittering notes of her bird-like voice. The hours till then were a desert. He gave himself three days, inwardly fretting with impatience, in which to raise the few thousand marks that would keep his associates quiet and enable him to set off for Vienna. In the meanwhile he paid every attention to Kringelein and hoped that things would take a favourable turn.

"What is the next item on the programme?" asked Kringelein and blinked at him with a sincere and grateful look from his blue eyes. Gaigern took to this quiet fellow from the provinces, who sat like a child at a Christmas party. A human kindliness and warmth were so implicit in his nature that his victims always benefited by their due share of them.

"Now we are going to fly," he said in the soothing note of a children's nurse. "It's very jolly and not dangerous, not half so dangerous as a motor car on a fixed track."

"Was that very dangerous?" asked Kringelein with surprise. Now that he had overcome it he was conscious of his alarm only as a pleasure.

"Can't be otherwise," said Gaigern. "One hundred and eighteen kilometres is no trifle, and the road was wet. You never know when you may strike a slippery patch, and any moment the car may skid. Bill, please," he said amiably to the waiter, and he paid for his modest dish of spinach and poached eggs. There were still twenty-four marks left in his pocketbook. Kringelein paid too. He had only had a few spoonfuls of soup, for he suspected his stomach of rebellious and mischievous designs. As he put back his pocketbook—it was the old shabby one of his Fredersdorf days—he had a fleeting and now meaningless vision of his account book in black waxed cloth. Till that morning since his ninth year he had entered every penny he spent in such a little book. It was not worth while doing it now. The time for it was past. A thousand marks in one morning was altogether beyond entering. A part of Kringelein's world had fallen in noiselessly and without a sign. Kringelein, as he followed Gaigern down from the empty restaurant terrace to the car, moved his shoulders luxuriously in his new coat, new suit and new shirt. Now everyone stood with a bow to let him pass. I wish you good morning, Herr Generaldirektor, he thought, and saw himself flattened to the greenish-grey wall of the second floor of the counting-house at Fredersdorf. He put away his pince-nez when he had taken his seat beside Gaigern and exposed his naked eyes to the bright March sunshine. It was with a pleasant excitement and confidence that he felt the engine starting up.

"The road or the Avus again?"

"Oh, the Avus," replied Kringelein, "and at the same pace," he added lightly.

"Ah, you have pluck then?" said Gaigern and accelerated.

"Yes, I have," said Kringelein, leaning forward with taut muscles, ready with parted lips to enjoy life to the full.

Kringelein stood leaning against the white and red rails of the aerodrome, trying to get the hang of this astounding world which had come round him since the morning. Yesterday—it seemed a hundred years ago—yesterday he had ascended in the lift, stupidly as though in a dream, to the restaurant of the Funkturm; there had been no pleasure in it and Doctor Ottern-schlag's pessimistic comments made it all even more unreal and ghastly. The day before yesterday—and that seemed a thousand years ago—he was junior clerk in the counting-house of the Saxonia Cotton Company at Fredersdorf, a little miser-able employee among three hundred other miserable em-ployees, in a grey worsted suit, who had been given sick-leave on a mere pittance. Today, now and here, he was waiting for a pilot to take him up on a long special flight at a price corres-pondingly high. It was one of those thoughts that you could not see to the end of, though Kringelein's mind was alert and collected as it had never been before.

It was quite untrue that he had pluck. The pleasure that confronted him threw him into a perfect panic. He did not want to fly. He did not want to in the least. He would have liked to go home, home—not to Fredersdorf, but home all the same to his room, No 70, with the mahogany furniture and the down quilt of silk. He wanted to lie in bed and not to have to fly.

When Kringelein set out to seek life, something misty and formless hovered before his eyes, something at the same time well upholstered and filled out, with plenty of draperies and fringes and a profusion of ornaments, soft beds, heaped plates, voluptuous women, both in painted effigy and real life. Now that he was really seeing life, now that he began, as it seemed, to be in the middle of it, it had quite another aspect. It made demands upon him, and a keen wind whistled about his ears, and he had to break through walls of anguish and danger

170

before one small drop of its sweet and intoxicating experiences could reach his lips.

Flying, thought Kringelein. He knew it already in his dreams. His dream of flying was like this: Kringelein stood on the platform of Zickenmeyer's Hall with the members of the musical club round him, and he sang a solo. He heard his own fine tenor voice rising higher and higher and higher. It cost him not the least effort. It was a pure spontaneous pleasure that came of itself. Finally he ascended himself on the highest note and flew away upon it, accompanied by music of the clouds while the members of the club looked up at him. At first he hovered beneath the roof of Zickenmeyer's Hall, and then he flew quite alone and there was nothing whatever all around him. At last he realized that it was all a dream and that he must return to the bed where Anna was sleeping the frowsy sleep of slovenly and bad-tempered middle age. The anti-climax was frightful, and he cried out in horror as he woke to the dark stuffy room, the small window, the cupboards smelling of moth-powder and the little iron stove with a saucepan on the top.

Kringelein blinked. Flying, he thought, and shrank into himself as he stood on the Tempelhof aerodrome. Here, too, as outside round the Funkturm and along the Avus were the same glaring colours—yellow and blue and red and green. Mysterious towers rose into the air. Everything was attenuated and spare. The wind blew silvery clouds of dust fitfully over the expanse of asphalt beyond the rails and cloud shadows raced across the aerodrome. The little machine in which the ascent was to be made was already there. Three men were busy with it. The engine raced and the propeller revolved idly. Blocks were in position in front of the small wheels, and the ribbed silver wings vibrated to the throb of the engine. Others were landing, greeted by the hoarse note of a siren (like the one that was sounded at the Fredersdorf factory at seven in the morning, so perhaps all this was only a dream), others were taking off, heavily on the ground, lightly once they were in the air; silver ones with metal wings, golden ones with rigid wings of wood, and great white ones with four planes and three

171

whirling propellers. The aerodrome was so very large and so wonderfully still, and all the men there were slim and bronzed, happy and silent, and they wore white flying costumes with close-fitting caps. Only the machines had voices as they trundled over the ground barking hoarsely like great dogs.

Gaigern approached with the pilot, a decent fellow with the bow legs of an ex-cavalry officer. Gaigern appeared to be in his element out here. He was hail-fellow-well-met with every-body.

"We're getting off at once," Gaigern announced.

Kringelein, who had some experience of what Gaigern meant by 'getting off', was horribly alarmed. Help, he thought. Help! I'm not going to fly—but he would not for the world have said it aloud. "Oh, are we pushing off?" he asked, like a man of the world. He was proud of the expression 'pushing off', which he used for the first time in his life.

The next thing was that Otto Kringelein sat strapped in the little cockpit in a comfortable leather seat and 'pushed off' into the grey-blue of the March sky. Next to him sat Gaigern whistling softly and that was some consolation in a moment of utter prostration.

At first it was no more than a bumpy ride in a car and then the machine began to make a furious and appalling racket. Suddenly it shook off the earth beneath it and climbed. It did not by any means soar. It was not such a simple business as Kringelein's dream flights on his tenor notes. It sprang up into the air by jumps as though up steps—sprang and sank, sprang and sank. This time the sense of uneasiness was not in his legs as during the motor run at 120 kilometres an hour, but in his head. Kringelein's skull hummed. It became thin. It became quite glassy, and he had to shut his eyes for a moment.

"Air-sick?" asked Gaigern, shouting in his ear, and he wondered whether he could then and there prevail with Kringelein to give him 5000 marks—or only 3000—or even a miserable 1500, with which to pay his hotel bill and buy a ticket for Vienna. "Do you feel bad? Have you had enough?" he added kindly.

Kringelein pulled himself together manfully and courageously and replied with a cheery "No". He opened his eyes in his humming glassy head and fixed them first on the floor of the machine, which at least had its relative stability, and then raised them to the little oval of glass in front. Through this he saw again the figures and the trembling pointer. The pilot turned his keen profile and gave Kringelein a friendly smile. Kringelein was much relieved and highly honoured by this glance.

"Three hundred metres up at a hundred and eighty an hour," Gaigern shouted in his humming and deafened ears. Then all at once everything became gentle, light and smooth. The machine climbed no higher. It banked to the tune of its metallic engine voice and swept on above the city lying dwarfed beneath. Kringelein ventured to look out.

The first thing he saw was the sunlit, ribbed metal sheets of the wings, and they seemed to quiver with life; then—far below—Berlin chequered in tiny squares, with green cupolas and a ridiculous top railway station. A patch of green was the Tiergarten, a patch of blue-grey with four white specks of sails was the Wannsee. The edge of the little planet lay far beyond, arched in a gentle curve. Over there were mountains and forests and brown plough land. Kringelein relaxed his cramped lips and smiled like a child. He was flying. He had stuck it out. He felt fine. He had a new and vigorous sense of his own being. For the third time that day his fear left him and gave place to happiness.

He tapped Gaigern on the shoulder and in response to a questioning look said something that was swallowed up unheard in the noise of the engine.

"It is not so bad after all," Kringelein said. "There's nothing to be afraid of. It isn't so bad."

And with this Kringelein included not only the monstrous tailor's bill and not only the run on the Avus, and not only the flight in the aeroplane, but everything else as well and in particular the fact that he had soon to die, to die right out of this little world, leaving all its terrors behind and climbing perhaps even higher than aeroplanes can fly. . . .

The streets behind the Tempelhof aerodrome went to Kringelein's heart as they drove back. They were so like the dreary streets of Fredersdorf. Chimneys rose up behind railway embankments, and his distended nostrils were on the alert for the smell of size that in Fredersdorf always issued from the finishing shops. As he passed these poor streets, he was more than ever conscious that he wore a new suit and drove in a car. He tried to find a word for this curious mixture of feelings, but he failed. He did not recover his spirits till they reached the Hallescher Gate. There they were held up for half a minute. The flight still ran in his veins like a calm but powerful intoxication, and full of eagerness he asked with a politeness that came from his heart: "And what has the Baron in store for me now?"

"Now—speaking for myself I have to go back to the hotel. I have an engagement at five. But why not come too? I am only going to dance," he added, when he saw the forlorn and dejected look in Kringelein's eloquent eyes.

"Thank you very much, I'll come with pleasure. I can't dance though, unfortunately."

"Oh, rot. Everyone can dance," said Gaigern.

Kringelein reflected upon this remark until they were well into the Friedrichstrasse.

"And after that? What could we do after that?" he asked with importunate insatiability. Gaigern made no reply. He drove on fast till he had to pull up in front of the red traffic signal on the Leipsigerstrasse.

"Tell me, Herr Direktor," he asked while they were at a standstill, "are you married?"

Kringelein made so long a pause for reflection that the traffic signals turned to yellow and green and allowed them to proceed again before he replied.

"Have been. I have been married, Herr Baron. I have separated from my wife. Yes, I have taken my freedom, if I may put it so. There are marriages, Herr Baron, which are so irksome and sickening to both parties that one of the two can't see the other without getting into a rage. The husband can't see his wife's comb in the morning with the combed-out hair

174

in it without the whole day being spoiled for him. It's quite wrong, certainly, for how can a woman help it if her hair comes out? Or again when you want to read at night your wife keeps on talking, talking, talking, and if she doesn't talk, she sings in the kitchen. If a man is musical, singing of that kind makes him ill. And every evening when you are tired and want to sit down with a book, it is always, 'Come, chop up the firewood for tomorrow morning.' It costs a penny more to have the bundle of firewood chopped up, and that comes to a farthing a day, but no, that wouldn't do. 'You're a spendthrift,' your wife tells you, 'for all you care we shall end in the workhouse.' And then you see, there's my father-in-law's shop and she'll inherit it in time. She'll be all right. So I took my freedom. My wife never suited me, to tell you the truth, for I was always above the sordid cares of life, and that she never could forgive me. When my friend Kampmann gave me the old numbers of *Kosmos* for five years back, my wife went and sold them as waste paper; she got twopence for them. There you have the whole woman, Herr Baron. Now—we are separated. In any case she'll have to get on without me very soon, and a week or two sooner or later makes no odds. She'll go back to the shop and sell unmarried employees pickled herrings and sausage for their suppers. That's how I got to know her myself, so perhaps she'll get hold of another fool. And a fool I was, I can tell you, when I married, not a notion of life nor of women either. Since I've seen all these pretty girls in Berlin it begins to dawn on me by degrees. But there, it's too late for all that."

This speech, which Kringelein brought up out of his inmost soul, lasted from Leipsigerstrasse to Unter den Linden.

"Oh, things aren't so bad as all that," Gaigern replied absentmindedly, for he had the trying crossing near the Brandenburg Tor to negotiate and there was an incompetent owner-driver in front of him. The fumes of a sordid little kitchen rose from Kringelein's words. Those fumes depressed him and robbed him of the impulse he had had to demand a loan of three thousand marks.

And Kringelein, with his silk shirt, driving in a motor car, would also have been glad now to take back some of his un-premeditated confessions.

"So we are going to dance," he said all the more glibly. "I am most extremely obliged to the Herr Baron for taking me under his protection. And what could we do tonight?"

Secretly Kringelein expected a reply that would give expression to unexpressed wishes of his own. He had a hankering after something that was suggested by many pictures in the museum, but a little more tangible, something that the newspapers he read described as an 'orgy'. He supposed that men about town had the key to such things. The evening before Doctor Otternschlag had acceded to his obscurely expressed inclination for the fair sex by taking him to see the ballet and Grusinskaya. Well, that, so Kringelein thought, had been a mistake. Very pretty to look at, but too poetical. Very stirring and magnificent, but it sent you off in a doze and finally it brought on pains in the stomach. Today, however——

"The best thing you could go to tonight is the great boxing match in the Sporthalle," said Gaigern. "We'll see if the Hall Porter has a ticket left."

"Boxing does not interest me in the least," said Kringelein with the superior air of a reader of *Kosmos*.

"Doesn't interest you? Have you ever seen a fight? Well, just go and see one and you'll be interested quick enough," Gaigern promised him.

"Will you come too, Herr Baron?" Kringelein asked quickly. He felt in splendid form after the drive and the flight, alert and vigorous and ready for anything, but he knew he would collapse like a blown-up indiarubber doll the moment the Baron deserted him.

"I'd go like a shot," Gaigern answered, "but unfortunately I can't. I haven't any money."

Meanwhile they had passed the budding trees of the Tiergarten and the hotel front was already in view farther down the street. Gaigern slowed down to twelve kilometres to give Herr Kringelein time to express himself. Kringelein was utterly taken aback by Gaigern's laughing remark. They had stopped at Entrance No V. They had already got out. And still Kringelein had not digested his surprise.

"I'll take the car to the garage," Gaigern called out when Kringelein was once more on his rather stiff and tingling legs, and he disappeared round the corner. Kringelein walked thoughtfully on and passed through the revolving door whose mechanism had no longer any terrors for him. No money, he thought. He has no money. Something must be done about it.

Rohna and the Hall Porter and all the pageboys and even the one-armed lift attendant observed the transformation in Kringelein's appearance and then discreetly looked the other way. The Lounge was full of the odour of coffee and of people and talk. It was ten minutes to five. In his usual armchair sat Doctor Otternschlag with newspapers lying all round him. He surveyed Kringelein with an indefinable expression of scorn and sadness. Kringelein went up to him without any apparent concern and held out his hand.

"The new Adam," said Otternschlag without taking the hand, for his own was cold and moist and this embarrassed him. "The butterfly has emerged. And where have you been flitting about, if I may be allowed to ask."

"I've been shopping. Then a motor drive along the Avus; lunch on the Wannsee; and then I went up in an aeroplane." His tone towards Otternschlag had altered without his knowing it.

"Splendid," said Otternschlag. "And what now?"

"I have an engagement at five. I am going to dance."

"Ah—and after that?"

"After that I mean to go to a big boxing match in the Sporthalle."

"Indeed," said Otternschlag. That was all. He took up his paper and holding it in front of his face began to read with a feeling of mortification. In China there were earthquakes, but the paltry matter of forty thousand dead did not suffice to alleviate his boredom. . . .

When Gaigern reached the second floor with the intention of changing his clothes he found Kringelein waiting at his door.

"Well?" he asked with impatience. It began by degrees to

get on his nerves to have this odd little man tied round his neck.

"Was the Herr Baron playing a joke on me or is it true that the Herr Baron is embarrassed for money?" Kringelein asked hurriedly. It was one of the most difficult things he had ever had to say and he made a mess of it in spite of all his careful preparation.

"The absolute truth, Herr Direktor. I am down and out. The luck's against me, I have only twenty-two marks thirty in my pocket and tomorrow I shall have to hang myself in the Tiergarten," said Gaigern and laughed all over his handsome face. "But the worst is that within three days I have to be in Vienna. I have fallen in love, I may tell you. I am gone on a woman to a degree that no words can describe and it is an imperative necessity to follow her. And not a penny to bless myself with. If only somebody would tip me up enough to gamble with tonight———"

"I want to gamble too," said Kringelein quickly and from the bottom of his heart. The hundred and twenty kilometres an hour feeling and the flying feeling came over him again.

"*Tiens!* Then I'll pick you up at the Sporthalle and we'll go to a nice club I know of. You stake a thousand and I'll stake twenty-two," said Gaigern, and with that he shut his door and left Kringelein standing outside. For the moment he had had enough of him. He threw himself on his bed in his clothes and shut his eyes. He had a listless and bored feeling. He tried to recall the girl with the lock of blonde hair on her forehead, but without success. Something else always came between. Either it was Grusinskaya's bedside lamp, or the balcony railing, or a bit of the Avus, a bit of the aerodrome, or Kringelein's torn braces. Too little sleep last night, he thought, chafing and fretting. He fell into a three-minute sleep, an abyss of healing darkness, as he had learnt to do in the war. He was awakened by a chambermaid knocking at the door. She had a note for him, and it was from Kringelein.

My Dear Baron [wrote Kringelein]. Would you permit the undersigned to regard you as his guest, and at the same time accept the small sum enclosed as a loan? You would be doing him a favour by allowing him to be of any service to you and in his situation money is no longer of importance. With most respectful greetings,

Yours very truly,

Otto Kringelein.

Enclosures: Entrance ticket. Two hundred marks.

The stamped hotel envelope contained an orange-coloured ticket for the boxing match and two crisp hundred-mark notes, numbered in ink on the sides. The dots of the i's in Kringelein's signature were missing. He had finally said goodbye to them in the reckless exhilaration of this memorable day. . . .

PREYSING'S JOINTS felt hollow as he stood alone in the Lounge after the close of the conference, when the provisional agreement had been signed and Doctor Zinnowitz had taken his leave with all sorts of complimentary remarks. The feeling of a great success, the consciousness of having successfully bluffed the Chemnitz crowd, and the strain of talking and of triumphing under false pretences were all entirely new to the General Director and left him in a strange and not unpleasant tumult. He looked at the hotel clock—past three—and went mechanically to the telephone room to get a call put through to the works. Then he pottered about for a longish while in the gentlemen's lavatory and let hot water run over his hands while he stared at himself in the glass with an idiotic smile. Next he wandered into the dining-room, which was half empty, and ordered the lunch on the menu without a glance at it. He became impatient before the soup arrived and began to smoke a cigar. He had no idea it would taste so good. While he scanned the wine list he hummed a tune which he had picked up somewhere in Berlin. He felt a distinct desire for a sweet wine that would be warm to the tongue and he found a Wachenheimer Mandelgarten 1921 which seemed to promise well. Later he detected himself sipping his soup noisily—it sometimes happened in moments of distraction that his table manners betrayed his humble origin. The situation he was in appeared to him fortunate but extremely obscure. The swindle —so he forcibly described it to himself, and the word, very surprisingly, inspired him with a new kind of pride—the swindle he had perpetrated during the negotiations could be maintained at best only for three days. During these days something would have to happen if ruin was not to overwhelm him. The provisional agreement could be cancelled within fourteen days. Preysing had poured the first two glasses of the cold, heady and sun-sweet wine too fast down his parched

180

throat. His brain became slightly foggy, and through the fog he saw the main chimney of the works break in three pieces and explode. That meant nothing. It was merely a reminiscence of a dream that came to him at regular intervals. He had just reached the fish when a pageboy crowed his "trunk call for Herr Preysing" across the subdued murmur of the dining-room. He drank one more good mouthful of wine and marched off to box No 4. He forgot to turn on the switch. He stood in the darkness and, with the receiver to his ear, he put on that iron mask of the employer so notorious at Fredersdorf. Through a shrill buzzing caused by a disturbance on the wires he heard Fredersdorf speaking.

"I want Herr Brösemann," said the General Director with the unemphatic tone of command due to his position. Half a minute passed before the head clerk came to the telephone. Preysing resented the delay and drummed on the ground with his heels. "There you are at last," he said when Brösemann called through. Brösemann's respectful demeanour could be guessed through the telephone and was received as a fitting tribute. "Anything fresh, Brösemann, beyond your most unnecessary telegram of yesterday? No—not on the phone, we'll talk of that later. For the moment, I request that that business be regarded as not having happened, do you understand? I want to speak to the old gentleman now, Brösemann, do you hear? Asleep? I'm afraid he will have to be wakened. No. I am sorry. Yes, yes, at once, Brösemann. No, all further instructions by letter. I'm waiting, then——"

Preysing waited. He scratched the ledge with his fingernails. He took out his fountain pen and tapped with it on the walls. He cleared his throat, and his heart beat with a distinct triumphant insistence. The receiver in front of his mouth smelt of a disinfectant. A chip was broken off its rim, as he noticed while he impatiently handled it in the darkness. Then he heard the old man at Fredersdorf.

"Hallo. Good afternoon, papa. Forgive me, please, for disturbing you. The conference is only just over. Thought it would interest you to hear the result at once. The provisional agreement is signed. No. Signed, signed." (He had to shout now for the old man had a pig-headed way of making himself out deafer than he was.) "Hard work, you say? Well, we brought it off. Thanks, thanks, no ovations, please. But listen, papa. I must go to Manchester at once. Yes, it is imperative absolutely, absolutely imperative. Right. Right. I'll tell you in detail by letter. What's that? You are glad? So am I. (Yes, Fräulein, I've finished.) *Au revoir.*"

Preysing remained standing in the unlighted box, and it was only now that he thought of switching on the small light. What's this? he thought in astonishment. What's this about going to Manchester? What put that into my head? But it's true enough—I must go to Manchester. I've fixed the matter here, and I'll fix it there too. Quite simple, he thought, and a new self-confidence entered into him and blew him up like a balloon. This one little successful excursion into deceit had changed a solid, conscientious business man into an intoxicated gambler and speculator, whose jerry-built foundations threatened every moment to collapse.

"Nine marks twenty for the call," said the operator.

"Put it on the bill," replied Preysing. He was again lost in thought. "I ought to ring up Mulle," he said to himself; but he did nothing of the sort. He felt a strange disinclination to talk to Mulle. It was a little too warm there in the dining-room at home. Mulle liked over-heated rooms; it seemed to Preysing that he could smell the cauliflower in the dining-room at Fredersdorf; it seemed to him that he could see the folds of her cushion, printed in red on Mulle's round plump cheeks, as she woke from her afternoon nap to take hold of the telephone. He let it go. He did not ring her up. He left the telephone box and went back to the dining-room, where a well-trained waiter had, meanwhile, put his wine in fresh ice and now set freshly warmed plates before him.

Preysing ate, drank his bottle of wine, lit his cigar and then went with hot head and cold feet up to his room. He felt surprised at himself in a pleasant and nebulous way, but he was, at the same time, quite done up by the morning's transactions. The thought of a hot bath was tempting and he turned on the water. Just as he began to undress, it occurred to him that a hot bath was unwise on a full stomach. For a painful moment, he positively felt the heart attack that threatened him in the enamelled bath; and he let the comforting and steaming water run out again. The fatigue and discomfort he felt became concentrated in an itching of his face and when he scratched it he felt his unshaven cheeks. Taking up his hat and coat as though for an enterprise of great importance and avoiding the hotel barber, with whom he was still annoyed after the experience of the morning, he went to look for a reliable hairdresser in the neighbouring streets.

And now a strange thing happened to General Director Preysing, a man of principles, but without a razor, a man of sound views, who, none the less, had done something questionable; an unlucky man whose head was turned by success for the first time—it may seem a coincidence, and yet, for all that, it may have been the irrevocable decree of fate. This, in any case, is what happened.

The small barber's shop that Preysing entered was clean and inviting. There were four chairs and two of them were occupied. One customer was being attended by a young, curly-headed and amiable assistant, and the other by the proprietor himself, an elderly gentleman with the look and the demeanour of an official of the royal household. Preysing was ushered into the third chair and enveloped in sheet and bib. A moment's patience was politely requested—the senior assistant had just gone out to lunch—and then a bundle of illustrated papers was put into his hands to appease him. Preysing, too jaded to make any objection, leant his head back on the head-rest and, soothed by the perfume-laden air and the busy chatter of the scissors, turned over the pages of the papers.

He did this with indifference at first, and almost with distaste, for he thoroughly disliked this frivolous manner of passing the time. His choice was for sound and substantial reading. But after a while, he smiled all the same over this joke and that, emitting, as he did so, short puffs through his nose. Once, too, he turned the pages back to look more closely at a *decolleté* drawing, and it was then that he opened a page which remained open during the whole time that he sat in the barber's

183

chair. Yes, he became so deeply absorbed in the contemplation of this photograph in a magazine, that it quite upset him when the senior assistant returned from his meal and made ready to shave him.

Nevertheless, the photograph which so captivated him was nothing out of the common. Photographs of this description were to be found by the hundred in periodicals that were not in Preysing's line. The picture was of a naked girl standing on her toes and endeavouring to look over a screen that was too high for her to see over. Her arms were raised and, in this attitude, her extremely pretty breasts were shown to particular advantage. The muscles of her long and slender back were also visible. Her waist was incredibly slender and this slenderness was carried on in her hips until, widening, they swept in two long soft curves to her thighs. Here the body was given a slight turn to the front, so that you could just see her shadowy bosom, her thighs and knees as she stood straining upwards in eager curiosity. This exceptionally well-favoured and charming girl also had a face, and—here lay the extreme provocation of this particular picture—this face was known to the General Director. It was Flämmchen's short-nosed, gay and innocent kitten face, and the smile, too, was the confiding smile of Flamm the Second. It was the same lock of hair, with a high light cunningly thrown on it by the clever photographer, and above all it was her complete spontaneity and her matter-of-course unconcern, as she displayed her figure, stark naked before all the world, the figure that—as Preysing now remembered—she had accurately and modestly described as 'good'. Preysing went red as he held this picture before his eyes; a sudden hot flush sprang to his forehead and clouded his mind, as often occurred in those fits of rage at which the whole factory trembled. Then every vein in his body began to throb singly. He felt it; he felt his blood surge, and he had not felt this for years.

Preysing was fifty-four. Not an old man, but a man who had gone to sleep, the passive husband of a Mulle who had gone to seed, the amiable Pops of grown-up daughters. He had walked unmoved behind Flamm the Second along the hotel corridor and the soft tingling in his blood had subsided again of itself. Now as he sat and gazed at this photograph of the nude, it rose up again and took his breath away. "If you please——" said the barber, and, with a graceful flourish, he laid the razor on Preysing's cheek. Preysing kept hold of the magazine, lay back and closed his eyes. At first there was only red; then he saw Flämmchen. Not Flämmchen in her clothes at the type-writer and not the unclothed Flämmchen of the photograph in black and white, but a violently exciting mixture of both. A Flämmchen of golden brown flesh and red pulsing blood, naked, however, and on tiptoe, looking inquisitively over a screen.

General Director Preysing was not accustomed to the work-ings of his fancy. Now, however, it was at work. It had been in gear ever since he laid the telegram on the table that morn-ing and gone on to lie, without shame and without discrimina-tion. And it ran away with him entirely, and in a manner that was at once alarming and intoxicating. While the razor glided over his face with the lightness of a practised hand, Preysing passed through unexampled, incredible experiences with the naked Flämmchen and with himself too, experiences of which he would never have thought himself capable.

"Shall I trim the moustache?" asked the barber.

"No," said Preysing in a flurry. "Whatever for?"

"The tips are a little grey. That adds to your age. If I may advise—the gentleman would look ten years younger without a moustache," the barber whispered into the mirror with that cajoling smile common to all barbers.

But I can't go back to Mulle without a moustache, looking like a fool, thought Preysing as he looked at himself in the glass. True, his moustache was grey, and there was always perspiration beneath it on his upper lip. Oh, bother Mulle!— he thought. That settled it. His marriage vow was already broken.

"Yes, take it off. A moustache like that can always be grown again."

"Certainly, with no trouble at all," the barber agreed, and he made a fresh lather for the great undertaking. Preysing held

185

up the photograph again—but now it satisfied him no longer. He was done with looking. He wanted to grasp and feel. He wanted to feel Flämmchen burn. . . .

In the hotel, the absence of the moustache was spotted at once, without the least notice being taken of it. They were well accustomed enough, heaven knows, to the most strange transformations in provincial personages after a brief stay in a big hotel. Preysing, breathing hard, made a hasty inquiry for letters. One from Mulle was thrust into his hand. He put it, unread and unregarded, in his pocket and went straight across to the telephone boxes. I must ring up Mulle, he thought. But that will do later. He went into the local-calls box, and, ringing up the office of Justizrat Zinnowitz, had a brief conversation with Flamm the First.

He asked whether her sister happened to be at the office.

No, she had gone.

Where could she be found?

Flamm the First, after a moment's pause, said that perhaps she had got delayed. But she would certainly be at the hotel any moment now.

Preysing gaped like a fool into the telephone. At the hotel? Here? In the Grand Hotel? How was that?

Yes, said Flamm the First, discreetly choosing her words. So at least she had understood. Flämmchen was going to the hotel, and, as far as she knew, it was to take down some letter. But possibly, it may have been an engagement of another description. You could never be sure with Flämmchen. She had her ways and they were by no means the ways of Flamm the First, she inferred. But punctual she certainly was; when she undertook anything, she went through with it, and it was positive that she was going to the hotel.

Preysing thanked her and rang off in conclusion. He dashed back with a harassed air, straight across the Lounge to the porter's desk. The beat of the music could be heard clearly from the Yellow Pavilion.

"Has my secretary inquired for me?" he asked Herr Senf. The Hall Porter looked up at him. His care-worn face showed that he was at a loss.

"Who, please?"

"My secretary. The young lady to whom I was dictating letters yesterday," Preysing said irritably.

Little Georgi intervened.

"She did not inquire for you, but she was in the Lounge not ten minutes ago. The slim fair lady, you mean? I believe she is in the tea room now—in the Yellow Pavilion straight through the Lounge, second turn behind the lift, if you'll be so good— you will hear the music."

Can it possibly be any business of a General Director, in a grey worsted suit, to follow in the wake of the highly-seasoned strains of a jazz band, along unfamiliar corridors in search of a frivolous young typist, with whom he has, properly, not the slightest concern? But Preysing did it. He had left the rails. The crash was to follow. But he did not know it. He only knew that his blood circulated as it had not done for fifteen or twenty years, and that he must at any price keep hold of this sensation and follow it out to the end. His moustache was gone. He was not going to telephone to Mulle; and, as he opened the door into the Yellow Pavilion and stepped into his un-familiar atmosphere, he had almost forgotten Chemnitz and Manchester as well, with all the efforts they had cost him and the complications that had still to be cleared up.

At this hour, twenty minutes past five, the Yellow Pavilion is crowded with people, day after day. The yellow silk cur-tains are drawn. Yellow lights line the walls, and on every one of the small tables there is a light with a yellow shade. It is hot. Two electric fans are whirring. The air is a buzz of voices. People sit elbow to elbow, for the small tables have been crowded up together in order to leave the middle of the room free for dancing. The vaulted ceiling is painted with dancing figures in lilac and grey; sometimes it looks like a false mirror above the dancing crowd below. All that goes on here has a remarkably angular and jerky appearance. The dancers do not circle round, but zig-zag to and fro, and Preysing who had come here on the tide of his tumultuous blood in search of a particular person found himself at a loss. He saw no one at full length, for everyone was always cutting across everyone else, so that only a head or an arm or a leg was visible at one time—as in a certain kind of modern painting which Preysing detested for its perversity. But the chief and most remarkable features of the Yellow Pavilion was the music. It was produced with incredible gusto by seven gentlemen in white shirts and short trousers, the famous Eastman Jazz Band, and its vivacity was frantic. It drummed on the soles of the feet and tickled the muscles of the lips. There were two saxophones that could weep, and two others derisively mocking their tears. The music sawed, snapped, stood on its head, laid eggs of melody, cackled and proudly jumped on them—and whoever got within range of this music fell into the zig-zag rhythm of the room as if bewitched. Preysing, in any case, who—pushed to and fro by waiters with trays of ices—remained standing by the door, observed a certain springiness in his knee joints while at the same time he kept an impatient look-out for Flamm the Second. His shorn and rejuvenated upper lip was once more beaded with perspiration. He took out his handkerchief and wiped his face, and then put back his handkerchief in his outside breast pocket, usually reserved exclusively for his fountain pen. He even, with an embarrassed side glance, pulled up a corner of it to make a neat little white triangle in the approved style, as though he thereby established his right to be present in these gay regions of the Grand Hotel. In any case, no one bothered about him. He was at liberty to stand there as long as he liked, while he sought among the dancers for one slender young girl in particular, among the two hundred other slender young girls.

"When you weren't there at ten minutes past five, I thought He's let you down. You'll see he's let you down, I thought to myself," said Flämmchen, who was dancing with Gaigern an indolent variation of the Charleston, something new, with a syncopating jerk of the knees. Their two bodies moved like one.

"Out of the question. I've been thinking of you all day," said Gaigern. He said it as lightly and indolently and casually as he danced. He was only an inch or so taller than Flämmchen and he looked down into her kittenish eyes with a smile. She wore a thin blue silk dress, a cheap necklace of cut-glass and a neat little close-fitting hat bought at a sale for one mark ninety. She looked enchanting in this finery of a girl with her own way to make in the world.

"Is it true that you thought of me?" she asked.

"Half truth, half fib," answered Gaigern candidly. "I've had a frightfully boring day," he added with a sigh. "I've been taking an old fellow around. Enough to make you weep."

"Why do you do it, then?"

"I want something out of him."

"Oh, I see," said Flämmchen, quickly understanding.

"You must dance with him later on," said Gaigern drawing her a little closer.

"There's no 'must' about it."

"No. But I'm going to beg you to as nicely as I know how. He can't dance, you know, but he wants to so much. Just walk him about a bit along the wall—to please me."

"Well—I'll see," Flämmchen agreed.

They went on dancing in silence. A moment later he drew her body a little closer to his own. He felt her back yield to his hand. But instead of being pleased, he was vexed.

"Well. What's up?" asked Flämmchen, who was quick to notice it.

"Oh, nothing," answered Gaigern, who was annoyed now with himself.

"What do you want then?" Flämmchen asked, only eager to please. He was so handsome with that mouth of his and with the scar above his chin and his slightly oblique eyes. She was a little in love with him.

"I want to do something a bit mad. That's all. I want to bite you or play the fool with you or pull you about—well, I am going to see some boxing tonight. There'll be something doing there at least."

"I see," said Flämmchen. "You're going to see boxing this evening. I see."

"With the old fellow," said Gaigern.

"If you—Oh, that's the end," said Flämmchen, for the music had stopped, and she began at once to clap loudly and without stirring from the spot. Gaigern tried to get her away from the middle of the room to the table where he had left Kringelein. But the music began again as they were half way through the crowd. "Tango," Flämmchen cried in an ecstasy and she simply took possession of him. The way she stretched out her hands for his both beseeched and implied his consent. Without a pause they fell into the slow languishing tango-step and room was made for them on all sides when it was seen how beautifully they danced. "You dance very well," Flämmchen whispered. It was almost a declaration of love. Gaigern had nothing to say in reply.

"You were quite different yesterday," Flämmchen said a little later.

"Yes—yesterday," Gaigern answered. It sounded as though he said 'a hundred years ago'. "Something has happened to me between yesterday and today," he added. There was a sympathy between Flämmchen and him of the easiest and most spontaneous kind, and suddenly he obeyed his impulse to tell her all about it.

"I fell in love last night, really and utterly, I mean," he said in a low voice in the midst of the tango as it sobbed and sawed and sung, and filled the whole room. "That makes everything different. It goes through and through you. It is like——"

"But there is nothing extraordinary in that," said Flämmchen mockingly to conceal a stab of disappointment.

"Yes, yes, it *is* something extraordinary. You want to get out of your skin and become another person, you see. You find of a sudden that there's only one woman in the world and everything else is nothing. You find you can never sleep again except with this woman. You're carried off in a whirlwind— as though you had been rammed into a great gun and shot off up the moon or somewhere where nothing is the same."

"What does she look like?" asked Flämmchen, and every other woman in the world would have asked the same question.

"Ah—what does she look like? That's just it. She is very old, and so thin and so light that I could lift her up with one finger. She has wrinkles—here and there, and eyes tired with weeping, and she talks in a jargon like a clown till you have to

190

laugh and weep—and this is so utterly delightful that I cannot resist her. It is simply real love."

"Real love? There isn't such a thing," said Flämmchen. Her face stared with that astonished and capricious expression that you sometimes see in pansies.

"Yes, yes, there is such a thing," said Gaigern. This impressed Flämmchen so much that for a second she stood still in the middle of the tango and looked at Gaigern and shook her head. "How he talks!" she muttered at the same time.

This however was the moment when Preysing's searching eyes picked her up at last in the languorous maze of the tango. With reproachful and keen impatience he waited till the long dance came to an end, and then he proceeded to fight his way to the table where Flämmchen had taken a seat between two men both of whom Preysing already knew by sight. These unacknowledged acquaintanceships are always happening in hotel life. You brush against someone in the lift; you meet again in the dining-room, and in the cloakroom and in the bar; or you go in front of him or behind him through the revolving door— that door that never stops shovelling people in and shovelling them out.

"Good evening, Fräulein Flamm," said the General Director in his dry voice which embarrassment made even more unamiable; and then he planted himself beside her chair and hollowed his back to let the waiters get past. Flamm the Second screwed up her eyes in the effort to focus this unexpected apparition.

"Oh—the Herr Direktor," she said amiably when she had done so. "Are you dancing too?"

She gazed from one to the other of the three icy faces. She was used to this expression in her male companions. "Do you know each other?" she asked with an elegant wave of the hand which she had picked up from a film star. She could not proceed to introductions for she did not know her cavaliers' names. Preysing and Gaigern muttered something, and Preysing rested one hand on the table with the air of taking possession, just as a tray of orangeade swept dangerously past his head.

"Good afternoon, Herr Preysing," said Kringelein, all of a sudden, without stirring from his seat. Each single one of his vertebræ ached from the fearful exertion it cost him not to tremble and collapse into the pitiful Kringelein of the counting-house. He held his shoulders rigid, his lips and teeth too, and even his nostrils, and these in consequence dilated with a malicious and equine expression. But he sustained himself on the height of this great moment; his will-power tapped undreamt sources of strength in his well-cut black jacket, his linen, his tie and his manicured fingernails. What certainly went very near to throwing him off his balance was the fact that Preysing too was altered. He still wore his well-known Fredersdorf suit, but he had no longer a moustache.

"I am not sure—pardon me—have we met before?" Preysing asked as politely as his intense preoccupation over Flämmchen allowed.

"To be sure. I'm Kringelein," said Kringelein. "I am in the works."

"I see," said Preysing more coolly. "Kringelein, Kringelein. One of our representatives, are you?" he added with a glance at Kringelein's smart attire.

"No. Book-keeper. Junior book-keeper in the counting-house. Room 23. Block C. Third floor," said Kringelein conscientiously but without enthusiasm.

"I see—" said Preysing again and sank into reflection. He preferred to say no more for the present about the undesired and incomprehensible presence of a junior clerk from Fredersdorf in the Yellow Pavilion of the Grand Hotel. "I want to speak to you, Fräulein Flamm," he said, withdrawing his hand from the back of her chair. "It is about a new job of typing," he explained in his office tone, and this was particularly aimed at this fellow from Fredersdorf.

"Right," said Flämmchen. "What time would suit you, then? Seven, half past seven?"

"No. Immediately," Preysing said peremptorily, as he wiped his face. This personage from Fredersdorf also had a handkerchief in his breast pocket, a silk flag of mutiny and impertinence.

"I am sorry, I can't immediately," said Flämmchen amiably. "I am engaged—as you see. I cannot very well desert these gentlemen. I have promised Herr Kringelein a dance."

"Herr Kringelein will be so good as to forgo it," said Preysing stiffly. It was a command. Kringelein could feel his rigid lips expanding to the obsequious smile of twenty-five years of subordination. He forced it back. He appealed for help and strength to Gaigern. The Baron had a cigarette in the corner of his mouth. The smoke ascended past the eyelashes of his left eye and he screwed up this eye with a roguish and knowing wink.

"I have no intention of forgoing it," said Kringelein. No sooner had he got it out, than he stiffened like a hare squatting in a furrow. Suddenly this obstinate demeanour on Kringelein's part brought his case to Preysing's recollection. He had had it before him only a few days before.

"That is remarkable, indeed," he said with the dreaded nasal tone of the factory. "Very remarkable. Now I know where I am. You reported sick, isn't that so? Herr Kringelein, eh? Your wife is in receipt of support from the sick fund on account of your serious illness. We gave you six weeks' sick leave on full pay, and here you are amusing yourself in Berlin. You are indulging in a style of living quite out of keeping with your position and your income. Remarkable. Very remarkable, Herr Kringelein. Your books shall be very carefully examined. You may depend upon that. Your pay shall be stopped, since you are so well-off, Herr Kringelein. You shall——"

"Now, children, don't quarrel here. Keep that for your office," said Flämmchen with disarming good humour. "We are here to amuse ourselves, Come along, Herr Kringelein. We're going to dance now."

Kringelein got on to his feet. His knees felt like indiarubber, but they became noticeably firmer when Flämmchen laid her hand on his shoulder. The music was rattling off something pretty fast—something akin to the 115 kilometres an hour motor run and the aeroplane propeller. It inspired him with the strength to utter the remarks, for which twenty-five years of a subordinate's existence had prepared him. As Flämmchen dragged him away towards the middle of the room, he turned his head and exclaimed loudly: "Do you imagine you own the world, Herr Preysing? Are you different from me? Has a man like me no right to live?"

"Now, now, now," said Flämmchen. "This is not the place to squabble in. You're here to dance. And don't look at your feet, but at my face, and just walk, just walk straight ahead, and I'll guide you."

"If that's not a case of peculation——" Preysing blurted out, trembling with rage.

Gaigern continued to smoke. The word aroused in him an odd feeling of professional sympathy, and with it a strong and contemptuous dislike of the corpulent and perspiring director. You need a few leeches applied to you, my friend, he thought to himself.

"Let the poor devil have his fun," he said half aloud. "You can see he's not long for this world."

I didn't ask for your advice, thought Preysing; but he did not venture to say it, for he suspected that he would meet more than his match in the Baron. "Would you be so good as to inform Fräulein Flamm that I am waiting for her in the Lounge on a matter of urgent importance. If she does not come by six o'clock, I shall not require her services," he said, bowed stiffly and retired.

Alarmed by this ultimatum, Flämmchen appeared in the Lounge at three minutes to six. Preysing, who had been sitting on hot bricks, got up with a smile of heart-felt relief. He smiled so seldom, that it came as an engaging surprise.

"There you are——" he said foolishly.

For hours he had been possessed and tormented by one single thought—was Flämmchen to be had? His experiences with women had been few and long since closed. He had only the vaguest notions about the girls of the younger generation though at bachelor parties, and in the course of comfortable talks on his business journeys, he had often heard it said that they made very little of entering on temporary liaisons. He looked Flämmchen up and down from her crossed legs in silk stockings to her cut-glass beads and her painted mouth (she

was pursing her lips and touching them up at that moment)
and he was at a loss to know where in her whole unconcerned
person the answer to his thoughts was to be found.

Flämmchen snapped her powder box and asked: "Well,
what is it about?"

Preysing kept on with his cigar and said it all in one breath.

"It is that I have to go to England and I want to take a
secretary with me. In the first place for my correspondence,
but also for the sake of a little company. I am very nervous,
very nervous" (he said this by way of an unconscious bid
for her sympathy) "and need someone on the journey who
will take care of me. I don't know if you understand me.
I offer you a confidential post in which it—in which you—
in which——"

"I understand perfectly," Flämmchen said quietly, when he
got tied up.

"I think we could put up with each other very well on the
journey," said Preysing. The curious surging and throbbing
in his veins had been banished by the difficulty of this conversation, but as he looked at Flämmchen, he had the consoling impression that she could very quickly conjure it all up
again if she only would. "You told me that you had travelled
last year, too, with somebody and that made me think—I
think it might be very fine if you only would. Will you?"

Flämmchen thought it over for five long minutes.

"I must think it over first," she said, and then she sat lost
in reflection and puffed at her indispensable cigarette.

"To England?" she said at last. The golden brown of her
skin had become rather lighter, and this perhaps showed that
she had grown paler. "I have never been to England yet. And
for how long?"

"For—I can't say exactly at the moment. It depends. If the
business I have there goes off well I would possibly take a
fortnight's holiday afterwards. We could stay in London or go
to Paris."

"It will go off all right, I'm sure. I could tell that from the
letters," said Flämmchen with assurance. Optimism was the
element she lived in. Preysing was cheered by the fact that she

knew about the affair he had on hand and that she prophesied success.

"You must tell me, too, what salary you ask," he said in a flattering tone.

This time it took Flämmchen even longer to reply. She had to draw up a comprehensive balance sheet. The renunciation of the incipient affair with the handsome Baron figured on it, also Preysing's ponderous fifty years, his fat and his heavy breathing. Then there were one or two little bills, requirements in the way of new underclothing, pretty shoes—the blue ones were nearly done. The small capital that would be necessary to launch her on a career in the films, in revue or elsewhere. Flämmchen made a clear and unsentimental survey of the chances the job offered her. "A thousand marks," she said. It sounded a princely amount, and she was under no illusions as to the sums that were nowadays laid at the feet of pretty girls.

"Perhaps a little extra for clothes to travel in," she added, a little more timidly than was usual for her. "You want me to look my best, naturally."

"You need no clothes for that. On the contrary," Preysing said with warmth. He considered this a most apt rejoinder. Flämmchen greeted it with a melancholy smile which showed up strangely on her blooming pansy-like face.

"That's settled, then?" said Preysing. "There are one or two things to be seen to here tomorrow. We must have our passports in order. Then we could set off the day after. Are you glad to go to England?"

"Very," answered Flämmchen. "Then I'll bring my little portable here tomorrow and I could take down any letters right away."

"And tonight—if you'd like it, I thought we might go to the theatre. We must at any rate have a glass of wine to seal our contract."

"Tonight, too," said Flämmchen. "Very well, tonight, too." She blew her lock of hair aloft and dropped her extinguished cigarette end in the ashtray. She could hear the music from the Yellow Pavilion distinctly. One can't have everything, she thought. A thousand marks. New clothes. London, too, was not to be despised. "I must telephone to my sister," she said as she got up. Preysing felt a hot, impassioned wave of gratitude rise and overwhelm him. He went behind her and carefully took hold of her elbows. They were lightly pressed to her sides.

"Will you be kind to me?" he asked softly. And as softly with her eyes cast down to the raspberry-coloured carpet, Flämmchen answered: "If it's not forced on me——"

Kringelein, Motorist, Flier and Conqueror, went furiously on with the day on which he had begun to live. Perhaps he felt very like those stunt fliers who pass within an ace of death as they loop the loop. He had begun to throw himself head over heels and now he was whirled on in obedience to forces he could not control. To turn about would mean a crash, and so he had to go through with it—forwards, downwards, upwards, he could not tell whither, for his sense of direction was lost. He was a tiny hurtling comet that soon must burst into atoms. Once more the car hummed along the Kaiserdamm, once more they were at the nucleus of modern Berlin. The Funk-turm with traversing beams cut illuminated sections out of the city. In front of the Sporthalle there was a black and compact throng, like bees clotted about the entrance to a hive, motion-less and busily humming. Kringelein had never seen any-thing so immense as the interior of the hall and never such a mass of people in one spot. He made his way to his seat through an elbowing crowd, following Gaigern who went on before like a tower. It was well to the front, close to the bare and brilliantly illuminated square patch on which the eyes of fourteen thousand people were concentrated. Gaigern went into many explanations, but Kringelein did not understand a word. He was afraid this time, too; for he could not endure the sight of blood and fighting and barbarity. He was tortured at the moment by the memories of his duties as a ward orderly, which the war had imposed on him, since he had been unfit for anything else. He looked with alarmed amazement at the men of muscle as they stepped into the ring and took off their dressing gowns and exposed their hard flesh. He heard the stentorian voice of the announcer, and clapped whenever everybody else clapped. If it gets too bad, I shall look away, he thought in secret when the first round began. But, at first, it looked to him as if the two fine sinewy fellows up there with their broken noses, were only going to fool about. "They are playing like kittens," he said to himself and smiled with relief. Gaigern, on the other hand, was now so intense and excited that Kringelein wondered. The hall was still and so were the boxers. Sometimes they could be heard drawing in careful breaths through their nostrils and their quick feet in their boxing shoes were almost silent. Then, in the midst of the stillness, came the dull rounded thud of leather—and a thrill went through the hall from end to end and right up to the gallery, below the roof, where a thousand faces loomed through the haze. More, thought Kringelein, for the sound of the blow filled him with a sweet and feverish satisfaction that quickly turned to hunger. The gong went, and in no time men sprang over the ropes with jugs, chairs, sponges and towels. The boxers lay in their corners breathing hard. Their tongues hung out like the tongues of hunted animals. Water was sprinkled over them, but they were not allowed to drink even a mouthful. Some of the splashes even fell on Kringelein below, and he wiped the drops from his coat with awe and a wonderful sense of fellowship with the man in the corner nearest him. Gong. Immediately the square of light was cleared again for the fight.

The murmur of the spectators abruptly ceased and turned to rapt attention. Hit followed hit. Shouts from the gallery—then silence. Another hit. The first blood trickled down over the eyes of one of the two—and he laughed. Hit, hit and now and then a pant. Kringelein came upon his clenched fists in his coat pockets. They seemed to him like two hard inanimate objects he had found there. Gong. Again the corners of the ring were a turmoil of flapping handkerchiefs and tapping and massaging hands. The bodies of the two now shone with sweat. Below, every face showed cold and green in the hard light and men were standing up and engaging in excited debate.

"Now we're getting to work at last," said Gaigern just after the third round began. Kringelein shuddered slightly at this typically Gaigernian anticipation of stirring events. The boxers above—he could not distinguish one from the other, for both had broken noses and it was only between the rounds that he sided with the man in the corner nearest him—now went for each other wildly. When they clinched it sometimes looked like an enraged and misplaced tenderness. "Break away," shouted fourteen thousand throats. Kringelein shouted too. They ought to fight—those two up there, not reel locked together against the ropes. He wanted above all to hear once more the round full thud of the leather glove on flesh.

"Blynx is groggy. He can't hold out much longer," Gaigern muttered and he showed his strong teeth under his upper lip. Again and again the referee in his white silk shirt jumped in to part the two bleeding muscular bodies. Kringelein thought it very good-natured of them to let him. He fixed his eyes on the one who was 'groggy', a technical term which appeared to mean that, though he did not know it, he was coming to the end of his tether. This man Blynx now had a blue swelling that hung like a fruit over his right eye. His back and shoulders were smeared with blood, and sometimes too he spat out blood at the referee's feet. He held his head sunk low; this might be correct but it made an impression of great cowardice on the inexperienced Kringelein. Whenever this Blynx received a blow Kringelein felt a vivid and bestial joy rise from the depths of his being. He could not see enough of it. He greeted every hit that went home with a little cry of relief and then with mouth open and head extended he waited for the next. Gong. Interval. Round. Gong. Interval. Round. Interval. Round——

In the seventh round Blynx was knocked out. He reeled head first, fell to the ground, turned on his back, and lay there. The twenty-eight thousand hands thundered applause. Kringelein heard himself yelling hoarsely and saw his hands clapping like mad. He was not very clear about what was going on in the ring above. The man in the silk shirt was standing over the prostrate Blynx and making hammer-like counts with one arm. Once Blynx made a movement as horses do when they have fallen on the ice, but he did not get up. There was a fresh outburst of applause from the hall. People climbed over the ropes. There were embracings, kissings, roarings through the megaphone, and frenzy in the gallery. When Blynx had been carried out, Kringelein collapsed in utter exhaustion on his hard chair. He had overtaxed himself and his shoulders and arms hurt him.

"There, you are quite played out with enthusiasm," Gaigern said to him. "You get carried away with it, eh?"

Kringelein remembered an evening he had spent a thousand years before.

"It's something different to yesterday evening at Grusinskaya's ballet," he answered, and he thought with pity and distaste of the empty theatre, of the ghostly and sadly circling nymphs, of the wounded dove in the moonlight and of the feeble applause accompanied by Otternschlag's comments.

"Grusinskaya!" said Gaigern. "Well, yes, that's quite another affair." He began smiling to himself. "There's too much *chi chi* with Grusinskaya," he went on. He could see her at that moment. He could actually see her in her dressing-room at Prague, resting and thinking how tired the night before had made her, how tired, but how young, how full of courage!

"This fight was not up to much. The real event comes on now," he said to Kringelein. Kringelein was glad to hear it. He thought himself that there must be more to come—the thud of heavier blows, louder panting, and even more frenzied participation. More, he thought. More. More. On with it! On with it!

Two gigantic forms stepped into the ring, a white man and a nigger. The nigger was tall and slim with a velvety skin from which the light was reflected in gleams of silver. The white man was thick set. The muscles stood out in his shoulders and he had a square brutish face. Kringelein loved the nigger at once. The whole hall loved the nigger. The megaphone announced the fight and an incredible silence followed. And then it all began again as before. There was the same initial play and the nimble footwork, the jumps, the stealthy approach with lowered head and the elastic jump back. When they fought at close quarters the white body and the black were enlaced with the grim ardour of passion. Blow upon blow and nothing between but the gong for breathing space. Three minutes' fighting, one minute's breathing space, three minutes alternating with one minute fifteen times for an hour long. But this time the whole fight went faster and more furiously, with sudden onsets of the black man and wild outbreaks of the white, blazing up like a stubborn fire.

Kringelein melted like wax. Kringelein was cooped up no longer in his dilapidated body. Kringelein was one among fourteen thousand, one green distorted face among countless others, and his voice was indistinguishable in the one great roar that issued from every throat at once. He drew his breath when every breath was drawn, and he held it back when the whole hall gasped in sympathy with the boxers. His ears burned, his fists were clenched, his lips were dry, his stomach chilled and he swallowed the sweet spittle of excitement down his parched throat. On, on——

In the last two rounds the nigger, Kringelein's nigger, seemed to be having the best of it. Again and again repeated blows from his fist drummed in succession on the body of the white man, who twice was forced to lean on the ropes with outstretched arms. Each face wore a tranced smile. The breath was pumped from their bodies as though from machines. The last round was accompanied by an unbroken uproar and thunderous stamping throughout the hall. Kringelein roared and stamped too. Then the gong went, and it was over. Kringelein lay back in his chair covered with sweat. The megaphone made an announcement. It announced that the white man had won.

"What? What's that? Outrageous," roared Kringelein through fourteen thousand throats. He climbed on to his seat. All climbed on to their seats and roared against the decision. The hall went raving mad. Kringelein went raving mad. On with it, get on with it, fight it out! The gallery was in an uproar, whistling, screeching. The wooden tiers seemed likely to collapse in the dust and haze and tumult of a serried mass of indignant and outraged humanity. The boxers stood in the brilliant light between the ropes and shook hands awkwardly with their gloves on and smiled as though they were being photographed. The hall began to rain down boxes, cigarette packets, oranges, and finally glasses and bottles. The clean floor of the ring was covered with trampled wreckage. A continuous shrill whistling echoed round the roof. Towards the rear some were stamping and striking each other, and the confused tumult of the fourteen thousand presented a scene of panic. Kringelein got something very hard and heavy on the head, but he did not even feel it. Kringelein's fists were clenched. Kringelein wanted to be in the thick of the fray and to chastise the referee for his decision. He looked round for Gaigern. Gaigern was in front near the ring. He stood out alone above the rest, and he was laughing as one laughs when caught in a spring shower. Kringelein in his unbounded excitement was seized by a sudden and powerful attraction to this man who stood there laughing and looking like Life itself. Gaigern grabbed hold of him and led him out of the hall—now filled by a frantic mob. Kringelein walked out behind him as though protected by a warm and impenetrable shield.

On they went. Past the Gedächtniskirche, whose walls were white in the light of the thousand lights all round, and where the cars threw gleaming reflections on the oily asphalt. Everybody looked black in the brilliance of the illuminated shop windows of the Tautentzienstrasse. Then abruptly came the silence and darkness under the trees of the Bavarian quarter. Little squares started out of the darkness, with gravel and hedges and lamps. Still they went on, until finally they reached the gambling club.

It occupied the large rooms of an old-fashioned Berlin house which had been re-fitted as a club. Men in dinner jackets moved noiselessly about. There were many coats in the tiled cloakroom. Kringelein recognized a pale, lean figure, smartly clothed in black, who was smoothing his thin hair off his forehead, as himself. It came as a surprise to encounter himself in the glass. I can really stand a good deal, he thought. For the space of a second he thought of his friend, Kampmann, the solicitor. It seemed as though he had known him in a dream.

They made a short stay in a room with standard lamps and an open fire, where everyone talked and had drinks. In the next room there were a few tables of bridge. It was no better than nap, thought Kringelein, who was hungering for new sensations.

"We are going to the back," said Gaigern to a gentleman who was there. "Come with me, Herr Direktor, we'll go to the back."

The back was at the end of a narrow ugly corridor with many doors opening on to it. Through the last brown folding door they entered a smallish room, which was so completely veiled in a brown gloom that the walls were scarcely visible. All the light was concentrated on a table in the middle as it was on the ring in the Sporthalle. A few people were sitting and standing round the table, twelve or fourteen only. They had an intent and businesslike air and exchanged brief remarks that were quite unintelligible to Kringelein.

"How much do you want to stake?" asked Gaigern, who had gone aside to a desk where a lady in black, with the air of a governess, was sitting as though at a cash desk. "What do you think——?"

Kringelein had thought of ten marks. "I don't exactly know, Herr Baron," he said dubiously.

"Let's say five hundred marks for a start," Gaigern proposed. Kringelein, incapable of protest, took out his old pocket-book and produced five 100-mark notes. A handful of brightly coloured counters was thrust into his hand, green, blue and red. He heard others like them falling on to the table with little raps beneath the square green-shaded lamp. He waited impatiently for what was to follow.

"Now stake where you like," said Gaigern. "It's no use my explaining. Stake what and where you like. Those who play for the first time usually win."

How many times that day had Kringelein put himself in peril? He knew now that this was the only way with life. He knew now that fear and pleasure go together like the nut and the shell. He had an inkling that he might lose in an hour or two as much as he had earned in the forty-seven years of his dead-and-alive Fredersdorf existence. He knew that in this obscure room with the laconic men and the green table he could only let himself be whirled on as before and so gamble away the three or four weeks of vagabond life that remained. And Kringelein, in this new form of looping the loop, was almost curious to know what would happen next. On, then—on!

His ears and his lips had gone white as he stepped up to the table and began to play. His hands felt as though they were full of sand. He staked. A little shovel appeared and took up his green counter with the rest. Someone said something that he did not understand. He put down another, this time somewhere else. He lost. Another. He lost again. Gaigern across the table staked something, won once, then lost again. Kringelein threw a quick imploring glance across, but it was not observed. Here everyone was concerned with himself alone. Every eye was riveted on the green surface of the table. Each man bent all his force and will to draw the winnings to himself. "No luck," someone said somewhere. It was an ominous word to hear in this brown back room beneath the green billiard-room lamp. Kringelein, utterly preoccupied with himself alone, went to the lady in black and drew counters for another five hundred marks. He returned to the table. Another man was now shovelling up the counters. They made a gentle rattling sound. Restless fingers arranged them meticulously in little piles. Kringelein took his store in his left hand and staked with his right hand at random and almost unconsciously. He staked and lost. Staked and won. What a surprise when his green counter returned to him, accompanied by a red one! He staked and won. He put a few counters in his pocket because he did not know what else to do with them. He staked and lost thrice in succession. He left off for a few minutes. Gaigern, too, had ceased to play. He stood with his hands in his pockets and smoked. "Finished for today," he said. "My money's gone." "Allow me, Herr Baron," Kringelein whispered and thrust one of the two red counters he still possessed into Gaigern's hand, which trembled as he took it out of his pocket. "I'm too flat for play tonight," Gaigern muttered. He had a keen nose for luck. This was part of his questionable way of life, and at present the luck was against him, unless his love affair with Grusinskaya was to be called luck. Kringelein returned to the table and carried on.

A clock rasped out one o'clock as Kringelein with a little propeller whirling behind his forehead ceased to play and cashed his counters at the desk. He had won three thousand four hundred marks. He felt his wrists go limp and begin to quiver, but he controlled them bravely. Nobody troubled about him or his winnings. Kringelein had won all he would have earned in a year at Fredersdorf. He pushed it all into his torn leather pocketbook.

Gaigern stood by yawning and looked on. "I'm broke, Herr Direktor. You must take care of me. I haven't a farthing," he said in a tone of indifference. Kringelein with his pocketbook in his hands stood there not knowing what to do or what was expected of him.

"I shall have to come down on you for something substantial tomorrow," said Gaigern.

"Yes, please do," replied Kringelein with an air. "And now what happens next?"

"Good Lord. You're persevering. There's nothing now but drink or women," Gaigern replied. Kringelein turned a white and dissipated face from the mirror after putting on his hat to go. He put fifty pfennigs into the open palm of an undersized club servant who opened the street door for them. Again he put his hand in his pocket and this time it was a hundred-mark note he came upon and he shoved the tightly folded piece of paper into the pageboy's hand as they stepped out into the dark and silent street. He had quite lost his senses. He no longer knew what money was. In a world where in the morning you spent a thousand marks and won three thousand at night, Kringelein the Fredersdorf book-keeper wandered as though in a labyrinth, an enchanted forest where no path, no light directed his steps. The little four-seater was waiting under a lamp, dumb but alive. There was something of the patient devotion of a dog in its trusty vigil that stirred Kringelein to gratitude.

On and on. It was raining now. The screen-wiper made its half circular sweeps, and Kringelein watched it going to and fro, to and fro. The smell of the petrol now made him feel at home in a warm little home of his own. Long streaks of red and blue and yellow were reflected in the wet surface of the street. A glaring jet of flame burning on persistently in the dead of night threw up in black relief a gang of workmen soldering a rail. The car went much too slowly to please Kringelein. He gave Gaigern a side glance. Gaigern was smoking, his eyes on the road, his thoughts heaven knew where. The town at half past one at night looked as though some accident had occurred. It was completely alert and crowded with people, almost more crowded than by day. At the crossings, where now no police were on duty, there was a continuous warning hoot of cars. Above, a red and fiery sky rested like a portent of disaster, traversed at regular intervals by jerking shafts of light from the searchlights of the Funkturm. On they went.

A staircase filled with the noise of music from three floors. Flags and paper snakes below, half way up blind mirrors in gilt stucco frames, a medley of people, some drunk, some melancholy, cadaverous girls dark under the eyes. Kringelein forced his way upstairs past their powdered backs. The whole place was full of cigarette smoke. It hung in thick blue clouds round the paper shades that gave an up-to-date air to the electric light fittings on the staircase. Below the noise was loud and uproarious. On the first floor a less disorderly music issued from folding doors within which dancing was in progress. One floor up again and there was silence. A girl in virulent green stockings was sitting on the stairs with a glass in her hand and pretending to be asleep as they passed by. Her bare shoulders brushed Kringelein's new clothes and awoke him to expectancy. They entered a long, almost dark room. Only on the floor a few lanterns with paper shades that shone opaquely. There was music here too, but you could not see where it came from. Girls' legs were to be seen dancing in the light of the lanterns, distinctly seen as far as the knee but beyond all was swallowed in darkness. Kringelein wanted to keep tight hold of Gaigern's hand like a little boy. Everything here was obscured and indistinct. What went on beyond the painted partitions which separated the ottomans and low tables was left to the imagination. Kringelein observed that he was drinking iced champagne. He had visions of many forms. They crowded upon him with a strange and eerie sweetness. Kringelein sang a soft accompaniment in his high tenor to the melody of two invisible violins. Kringelein rocked to and fro. His head lay pressed in the cool hollow of a girl's arm.

"Another bottle?" a waiter asked him severely. Kringelein ordered another bottle. Kringelein was sorry for the waiter, who looked like a consumptive when he bent down to the light of the lantern to write down the order. Kringelein was in a soft-hearted condition. He was absurdly sorry for the waiter and for the girls who were so jolly and were all legs and had to dance so late, and he was absurdly sorry for himself. He drew the limp, warm, deathly-strange body of a girl across his knees which began to tremble as he sought her face. A drunken rapture of sadness came over him with the scent of powder from this unknown woman. He could be heard singing. Gaigern, lost in his reflections, was sitting bolt upright on a wicker chair near by. He heard the high tremulous voice singing, "Rejoice in life while the l-a-amp still burns." Fathead, thought Gaigern with malevolence. On the way back I'll get hold of his pocketbook and then for Vienna, he thought frowning, as he clung to the verge of his perilous existence. . . .

Kringelein was standing in a little stuffy cloakroom washing his face on which a chill sweat kept breaking out. He pulled out the little bottle of Hundt's Elixir and drank three mouthfuls and hoped for the best. I'm not tired, he said to himself, not a bit. Not a trace of tiredness. There was still a lot to be done that night. He savoured the cinnamon taste on his tongue and went back to the girl in the gloom among the ottomans. On—still on!

Kringelein alighted upon a mouth, as though upon some inconceivable island of adventure. With his lips there, he lay stranded a while. Little waves of drunkenness washed him away. "Be nice, Bubi," a voice was saying, meaning him. He became motionless, listening intently to himself. For one dreaming moment's space he had his hands full of ripe red juicy raspberries from Michenau Forest—and then something came swiftly nearer, something frightful, like a sword and a flash of lightning and a wing of flame.

Suddenly Gaigern heard him groan. It was a piercing and incredible sound, full of dread and tortured humanity.

"What's the matter?" Gaigern asked in the utmost alarm.

"Oh—pains," came the answer, wrung from the darkness near Kringelein's face. Gaigern picked up one of the lanterns and put it on the table. There sat Kringelein rigid and upright on the upholstered seat with his two hands clasped like the links of a chain. The lamp was blue and it made Kringelein's face blue, with a great round black mouth from which groans issued. Gaigern knew this mask of pain from severely wounded cases in the war. He quickly put an arm under Kringelein's head and, like a good comrade, supported his heaving shoulders.

"Dead drunk?" asked the girl. She was very young still and very common in her dress of black sequins.

"Be quiet," Gaigern answered.

Kringelein raised his eyes to him, tortured and torn with pain. He forced himself to a piteous and heroic attempt at good form. "Now it's I who am 'groggy'," he said with his blue lips, and he meant his dazed, almost unconscious, fought-out and collapsing condition. It was a lame but courageous joke that broke in the middle and ended in groans.

"But what's up with you?" asked Gaigern in alarm.

And Kringelein replied almost inaudibly: "I think—I've got —to die——"

IT IS quite a mistake to suppose that hotel chambermaids spy through keyholes. Hotel chambermaids feel no interest whatever in the people behind the keyholes. Hotel chambermaids have a lot to do and are tired out, and they are all a little disillusioned, and besides they are entirely occupied with their own concerns. Nobody bothers about anyone else in a big hotel. Everybody is alone with himself in this great pub that Doctor Otternschlag not inaptly compared with life in general. Everyone lives behind double doors and has no confidant but his reflection in the looking-glass or his shadow on the wall. People brush past one another in the passages, say good morning or good evening in the Lounge, sometimes even enter into a brief conversation painfully raked together out of the barren topics of the day. A glance that travels up does not reach the eyes. It stops at your clothes. Perhaps it happens that a dance in the Yellow Pavilion brings two bodies into contact. Perhaps someone steals out of his room into another's. That is all. Behind is an abyss of loneliness. Each in his own room is alone with his own Ego and is little concerned with another's. Even the honeymoon couple in Room No 134 are parted as they lie in bed by a vacancy of unspoken words. Many wedded couples of boots and shoes that stand outside the doors at night wear a distinct expression of mutual hatred on their leather visages, and many have a jaunty air though they are hopeless and lop-eared. The valet who collects them suffers terribly from chronic indigestion, but who cares? The chambermaid on the second floor has started an affair with the Baron Gaigern's good-looking chauffeur, and now he has gone off without a word, and she is in no end of a way over it, there is no question of her looking through keyholes. At night she tries to think, but she is too sleepy, and she cannot sleep because the chambermaid in the other bed is a consumptive and sits up and turns on the light and coughs. Everyone between his four

209

walls has his secrets; even the lady with the expressionless face in Room No 28, who is always humming, and the gentleman in Room No 154 who gargles so frantically and is only a commercial traveller. Even Pageboy No 10 has a secret of his own behind his sleekly brushed forehead—an oppressive and horrible secret lies on his conscience. For he has found a gold cigarette case that Baron Gaigern left in the Winter Gardens, and has not given it up. For fear that it would be found on him when he went off duty, he has left it, for the present, stuffed in between the seat and the back of an easy chair, and in his seventeen-year-old soul Morality and the Rights of the Proletariat wage a bitter war.

Senf, the Hall Porter, has his eye on the boy—Karl Nispe is his name when he is not merely a number—for he slouches about the entrances with a distracted air and black rings under his eyes. But Senf, too, has other things to think about. His wife has now been for days in the hospital. There can be no question now of a normal delivery. The pains have stopped and strange cramps have set in, but the baby's heart can still be heard beating, and they await the moment for expediting the birth by artificial means. Senf has been out at midday but he was not allowed to see her. She was lying in a drowsed state of exhaustion which the doctors termed sleep. This is how it is with the Hall Porter, Senf, as he carries on in his mahogany cage, occupied now with the board where the keys hang and now with the railway timetables. Rohna has offered him a few days off, but he does not want time off. He is glad to be in harness and not to have to think. As for Rohna himself, this highly competent Count Rohna, who puts in fourteen hours' work a day, he is a fine fellow, but a hopeless outcast from his own class, and what he thinks about it nobody knows. Perhaps he is proud of his position, perhaps he is ashamed whenever a man of his own class registers his name. His bright and narrow and fair-complexioned face betrays nothing. It has become nothing but a mask.

At two o'clock in the morning seven utterly exhausted, limp and dejected persons, carrying black cases, left the Grand Hotel by Entrance No II. They were the members of the

Eastman Jazz Band going home in their moist shirts, discontented with their play as all musicians are in every corner of the globe. In front of Entrance No V motor cars were driving off, and a little later the powerful lights of the hotel front were turned out. The Lounge was getting cooler, for the central heating had been damped down a little. Doctor Otternschlag, who sat on there almost alone, gave a shudder and yawned. Immediately after Rohna, too, yawned at his desk, closed a few drawers and retired to his five hours of sleep on the fifth floor. The night porter sorted the next day's morning papers, which had just been brought in by a messenger, who had got wet-through in the rain and now went out again with tired and muddy feet through the revolving door. Two loud-voiced American women went up to bed, and after that there was a profound silence in the Lounge. Half the lights were turned out. The telephone attendant drank black coffee to keep himself alert.

"Shall we go up now?" Doctor Otternschlag asked himself, as he drank up his brandy. "Yes, I think we might go up now," he replied to himself. He required about ten minutes to carry the decision into execution. Once on his patent-leather feet he was in better form and he embarked upon his customary circular tour of the Lounge till he reached the night porter. "Nothing for the Herr Doktor," the porter said unfeelingly and waved him off with his hand when he was still two or three yards distant. "If anyone happens to inquire for me, I have gone to bed," Otternschlag announced. He then picked up one of the moist morning papers and ran over the headlines. "Gone to bed," the porter repeated mechanically and made a chalk mark on the key-board. Through the revolving door there came a chill rush of air smelling of dust and rain. Otternschlag turned round.

"Aha," was all he said, after his one serviceable eye had taken in the sight that confronted it. He even opened his mouth in a wry smile. He saw Gaigern come in through the revolving door, large and strong and flourishing as ever, though now looking seriously preoccupied as he pushed the almost senseless Kringelein in front of him. Kringelein was groaning and moaning. Doctor Otternschlag was very well able to distinguish cases of drunkenness from cases of serious illness, in spite of the rather similar state of prostration that accompanies both. The night porter, less expert in these matters, threw a severe and watchful glance on the two arrivals.

"The keys of 69 and 70," Gaigern said in a low voice. "My friend is in a bad way. A doctor, the sooner the better." He supported Kringelein with one hand and took the keys in the other and then propelled Kringelein towards the lift.

"I am a doctor. Hot milk at once to No 70," Doctor Otternschlag said suddenly in a surprisingly alert tone of voice to the night porter, and then he followed the others without more ado.

"I'll look after Kringelein," he said to Gaigern as they were being taken up. "Don't worry, Herr Kringelein, it's over now."

Kringelein, who did not understand what he meant, stopped groaning and sank in a heap on the lift bench, clutching himself in agony. "Over already," he whispered with resignation. "So soon over? It's only just begun."

"You've gone at it too fast. Everything at once is too much," said Otternschlag. He bore Kringelein a grudge on many grounds, but he held his hand all the same and felt his pulse.

"Nonsense, Kringelein. It's not over yet! You've drunk too much iced champagne, that's all," Gaigern said to cheer him up. The lift stopped with a jerk and put an end to the misunderstanding. Kringelein's knees gave way when he stood in the corridor, greatly to the alarm of the dejected chambermaid. Gaigern picked him up and carried him to bed. While he got him out of his clothes and buttoned him in his new pyjamas, Otternschlag disappeared with a busied air.

"I'll be back in a moment," he said and went out with his stiff shanks galvanized by a new energy.

When he came back he found Kringelein lying rigidly in his bed with his hands pressed to his thighs like a soldier presenting arms. If he was not moaning that was due only to a supreme effort of will. When he had set out in search of life he had promised himself to die like a man and without making a fuss about it whenever the moment came. It was a debt he felt he owed to some unknown power for the extravagant licence of

212

his last days. To this vow he now clung in his brass bed, while pain and the fear of death wrung a cold sweat from his forehead and neck. Gaigern went and fetched his own silk pocket handkerchief from his overcoat pocket and wiped Kringelein's peaked and jaundiced face with it. He carefully removed the pince-nez from his thin nose, and this for the space of a second made Kringelein believe that he was already dead and that all was over. He waited for Gaigern's large warm hand to close his eyes. Instead of that, Gaigern left the bedside and made way for Otternschlag.

Otternschlag took a syringe out of a little black case. From somewhere he produced, like a magician, a glittering ampoule, broke off the end of it with a conjurer's dexterity and putting his thumb through the ring of the syringe, filled it with extraordinary dexterity with one hand and without so much as looking at it, while at the same moment with the other hand he took hold of Kringelein's bared arm and washed it over with sublimate.

"What's that?" asked Kringelein, though his experiences in hospital had already acquainted him with the beneficent drug.

"Something good. You'll like it," Otternschlag replied in a sing-song voice like a queer old nanny. Meanwhile he pinched up Kringelein's thin flesh between his finger and thumb and drove in the needle under the skin.

Gaigern looked on. "Lucky you had that at hand," he said.

Otternschlag held up the syringe against the light straight in front of his blind eye.

"Yes," he said. "It's my travelling trunk. Always packed up, you see. Readiness is all—that's the thing, as Shakespeare so finely puts it. Ready to move on, ready at any moment, do you see? That's the best of this little bit of luggage," he added, as he washed the syringe and put it back and snapped the case. Gaigern took the small black object from the table and felt the weight of it in his hand. An unexpected notion appeared to take him aback. How so? he thought.

"Are you feeling better?" asked Doctor Otternschlag, turning to the bed.

"Yes," Kringelein replied. He sat on a cloud with closed

213

eyes, and it bore him swiftly away. The pain relaxed, and he himself dissolved into a circling cloud. "There, you see——" he still heard the Doctor say, while everything became a matter of indifference and the fear of death retreated like a black beast.

"There we are," said Otternschlag, and after a moment he laid Kringelein's head down on the quilt. "He's at peace for the time."

Gaigern, who meanwhile had put Kringelein's new clothes in order, came up now to the brass bedstead and observed the short faint breathing beneath the bright blue pyjamas.

"For the time?" he asked in a whisper. "Will nothing—happen? Isn't it dangerous?"

"No, our friend will have to jog along for a bit yet. He has many a caper like this to go through before he is left in peace. His heart, you see, his heart's all there. It's still alive and kicking, and it won't shut up shop yet. It's a machine that's not been much used—Herr Kringelein's heart. A lot has gone to bits round about, but the heart itself insists on its rights. So the marionette must dance on while the last string holds. Cigarette?"

"Thanks," said Gaigern, and absentmindedly took one. Then he sat down beneath the still-life picture of pheasants and thought hard for a minute or two over what Otternschlag had said.

"And so he's really in a bad way? And can't die all the same? Seems a ghastly business," he concluded.

Otternschlag, who had nodded in reply to each question, replied: "Just so. That's it. That's why I value my little trunk so highly. You cannot really put up with all the pain that being on this earth entails unless you know that at any moment you can make an end of it. Life is a miserable sort of existence, believe me."

Gaigern smiled at this. "But—I enjoy life," he said innocently.

Otternschlag turned his surviving eye on him quickly. "Yes, you enjoy life. Your sort enjoys life. I know your sort and I know you——"

"Me?"

"Yes, you personally, you in particular."

Otternschlag extended his arm and pointed with his heavy, tobacco-stained finger at Gaigern's face. Gaigern drew back.

"I once took a nice shell splinter out of your face just there. That charming night you found so interesting; I stitched you up—you don't remember—at Fromelles? Your sort forgets everything. It is another story for me. I forget nothing, nothing."

"Fromelles! In that frightful dressing-station? No, I can't remember much. I wasn't conscious of much on that occasion. I was knocked out. I thought in those days you had to faint when you were wounded and so I fainted."

"I noticed you all the same. You were the youngest casualty to pass through my hands. 'Meeting death with a song on his lips' sort of thing. It's quite possible in any case that it wasn't you at all—only one of that sort, you know. And so now you enjoy life? Only to be expected. Glad to hear it. But, you'll grant me this, the revolving door must not be shut."

"What do you say?" asked Gaigern at a loss.

"The revolving door, I mean. Just sit in the Lounge and watch the revolving door for an hour. You'd think it was crazed. In and out. In and out. In and out. Droll thing, a door like that. Often it makes you quite seasick to look at it for long. But now listen to me: suppose you come in through the revolving door—well, you want to be sure you can get out again. You don't want to find it shut in your face, leaving you a prisoner in the Grand Hotel?"

Gaigern felt his blood run cold. The word 'prisoner' sounded like a concealed threat.

"Of course not," he hastened to say.

"Then we're agreed," Otternschlag went on. He had meanwhile taken the syringe out of its case again and he was playing lovingly with its smooth glass and nickel. "The revolving door must remain open. The exit must always be available. You must be able to die when it suits you, when you please."

"But who wants to die? Nobody," said Gaigern quickly and with conviction.

"Well——" said Otternschlag and swallowed something down. Kringelein was muttering unintelligibly under his drooping moustache. "Well—look at me for example," said Otternschlag. "I am a suicide, you must understand. As a rule you only see suicides after the event—when they have already turned on the gas or pulled the trigger. I, as I sit here, am a suicide before the event. To put it in one word, I am a living suicide—a rarity, you will agree. One of these days I shall take ten of these ampoules out of this box and inject them into my veins—and then I shall be a living suicide no longer. I shall march out through the revolving door, figuratively speaking; and you can sit on in the Lounge and wait."

Gaigern observed with surprise that this mad doctor Otternschlag appeared to cherish a kind of hatred of him.

"That may be a matter of taste," he said lightly. "I am not in such a hurry. I have no complaint to make of life. I find it splendid."

"Indeed? You find it splendid? And yet you were in the war. And then you came home, and then you find life splendid? And what, man, have you done about it all? Have you forgotten it all? There—we won't talk of what it was like out there. We all know that well enough. But how can you come back after that, and still say you're pleased with life? Where do you find it—this life of yours? I have looked for life, but I can't find it. I often think to myself: I'm dead already. A shell has torn my head from my shoulders, and I'm sitting as a corpse all the time buried in that dug-out at Rouge Croix. There you have the real and actual impression life makes on me ever since I got back."

Something in Otternschlag's impassioned words touched Gaigern. He got up and went over to the bed. Kringelein was asleep, though his eyes were not quite closed. Gaigern came back to Otternschlag on tiptoe.

"Yes, there's some truth in that," he said in a low voice. "It wasn't very easy coming back. When a man says 'out there', he means something like 'home'. Nowadays being in Germany is like being in clothes you've grown out of. We've become intractable and there's no place for us. What can any of us start to do with himself? Reichswehr? Drill? Electioneering scrimmages? Thanks! Flying? I've tried it. Toddling off twice daily according to timetable, Berlin—Cologne—Berlin. And as for voyages of discovery, that's all so stale and without danger. That's what it is, you see. Life ought to be a little dangerous, and then it would be all right. But you have to take it as it comes."

"No. That's not what I mean," Otternschlag said irritably. "But perhaps we only see things from a slightly different angle. Perhaps I should take as amiable a view of things as you do, if my face had been stitched up as well as I stitched yours. But when you look at the world through a glass eye, it has a remarkable appearance, I can assure you——— Well, Kringelein, what's up?"

Kringelein of a sudden was sitting bolt upright in bed. With a great effort he had got his drugged eyes open and he was looking for something. He was feeling about over the quilt with fingertips which the morphine had made insensitive.

"Where's my money?" he whispered. He had come straight from Fredersdorf and a quarrel with Anna, and it was with difficulty that he found his way back to the mahogany-furnished room of the Grand Hotel. "Where's my money?" he asked with parched throat. At first he saw the two men in the plush armchairs only as enormous moving shadows.

"He asks where his money is," Otternschlag repeated, as though Gaigern were hard of hearing.

"He deposited it with the Management," said Gaigern.

"You deposited it with the Management," Otternschlag repeated after him like an interpreter. Kringelein's dazed head tried to cope with this reply. "Are you still in pain?" Otternschlag asked.

"Pain? Why?" asked Kringelein from his cloud.

Otternschlag laughed with a wry mouth. "All forgotten," he said. "He's forgotten his pain already, and all I've done for him too. Tomorrow he's ready to start again, the—*bon viveur*," he said with undisguised contempt.

Kringelein did not understand a syllable. "Where's my

money?" he persisted obstinately. "All that money? The money I won?"

Gaigern lit a cigarette and inhaled the smoke into his lungs.

"Where is his money?" asked Otternschlag.

"In his pocketbook," said Gaigern.

"In your pocketbook," Otternschlag passed on. "Now go to sleep again. You mustn't get too lively, or it'll do you harm."

"I want my pocketbook here," Kringelein demanded with outspread fingers. He could not express himself clearly in his drugged condition. All that his obscured consciousness was aware of was that he had to pay for every minute of his life in ready money and pay dearly. In his dream he had seen both life and money escaping from him, running away in a rapid and strong stream, like the stream at Fredersdorf which was dry every summer.

Otternschlag sighed and got up. He felt in the pockets of Kringelein's coat which Gaigern had hung over the back of a chair, and found nothing. Gaigern stood at the window smoking with his back to the room and his face turned to the street —now silent in the white light of the arc lamps.

"There's no pocketbook there," said Otternschlag, and let his hands fall to his sides after this immense exertion.

In an instant Kringelein was out of bed, and there he stood in the middle of the room on his thin and tottering legs. His face was aghast and he was breathless.

"Where is my pocketbook?" he cried piteously. "Where is it? Where is all that money? Where, where is it? Where is my pocketbook? Where is my pocketbook?"

Gaigern, who had long ago taken possession of the pocketbook, tried to shut his ears to the plaintive clamour which arose shrilly in spite of the huskiness of sleep. Outside he heard the lift coming up. He heard steps come along the corridor and die away as doors closed upon them. He heard—or so he imagined—someone breathing in Room No 71. He heard his wrist-watch ticking. But he heard Kringelein's terror as well, and he hated Kringelein savagely at this moment; he would have liked nothing better than to murder him. He turned impetuously into the room, but the pitiful sight that Kringe-

lein presented disarmed him. Kringelein stood in the middle
of the room and wept. The tears fell from his dazed eyes and
down on to his new bright blue silk pyjamas. Kringelein was
crying like a child for his pocketbook. "There were six thousand two hundred marks in it," he sobbed. "You can live for
two years on that." For Kringelein without knowing it had
fallen back into the Fredersdorf scale of existence.

Otternschlag turned to Gaigern with a despairing gesture.
"Where can his pocketbook be, then, since the man's deter-
mined at any cost to live another two years?" he asked with an
attempt at a joke.

Gaigern, his hands in his pockets, smiled. "Perhaps the girls
at the Alhambra took it off him," he answered. It was the
answer he had long had ready.

Kringelein sank in a heap on the edge of the bed. "Oh no,"
he said, "Oh no, no, no, no."

Otternschlag looked from him to Gaigern and back again.
"So that's it," he said to himself. He took up his black case
and went over to Gaigern, stumping along by the wall in his
usual manner as though a little life and strength could come
to him from contact with walls and furniture, or as though he
had not yet learned to move without cover. He came to a stop
in front of Gaigern, and turning upon him the wounded half
of his face he fixed him with a stare from his glass eye.

"Kringelein must have his pocketbook restored to him," he
said quietly and politely.

Gaigern hesitated for one second and in this one second his
fate was decided. A rift opened in his being and his assurance
was gone.

Gaigern was not a man of honour. He had stolen and
swindled before now. And he was not a criminal, for the better
instincts of his nature and upbringing too often made havoc
of his evil designs. He was a *dilettante* among rogues. There
was strength in him, but not enough strength. He might have
felled the two sick men to the ground and gone off. He might
have pushed them aside and made his escape with his booty
over the façade of the hotel. He might have left the room with
a few jesting words, made a dash for the railway station and

disappeared. Everything in him drew to a crisis as he thought of Grusinskaya and felt her light form in his arms and carried her up the steps of her house at Tremezzo. He must go to her, he must, he must. But suddenly he was overcome by the unreasoning and irresistible pity that he had felt for Grusinskaya the day before; and he now felt it for Kringelein sitting there on the edge of the bed. He felt pity too for Otternschlag, for the war-wasted face fixed on his own, and pity, remote and unconscious, for himself, and this pity was his undoing.

He took two steps into the room and smiled. "Here is his pocketbook," he said. "I took charge of it earlier on in case Kringelein had it stolen at the night club."

"There we are then," said Otternschlag, relaxing again. He took the old worn and bulging pocketbook from Gaigern's hands. It gave him a peculiar forlorn feeling of tenderness to do so. It was so seldom he had occasion to touch the hands of another man. He turned his head and fixed the other eye on Gaigern with an expression that might have conveyed either gratitude or a secret understanding. But he started back at the same moment. Instead of Gaigern's particularly handsome and lively face he saw a mask so blanched, drawn, vacant and dead, that he was frightened. Are there nothing but ghosts in this world then? he thought with alarm as he made his way along the sofa to the bed and put down the pocketbook by Kringelein's side.

The whole scene had only taken a few seconds and during this time Kringelein had sat plunged in silent reflection.

Now that Otternschlag handed him the pocketbook over which he had made such a piteous lamentation he barely touched it. He let it fall on to the quilt without counting the money, all that money, the money he had won.

"Please, don't leave me," he said, and he said it, not to Otternschlag who had come to his help, but to Gaigern. He stretched out his arm to Gaigern who stood gloomily by the window smoking a fresh cigarette.

"There's nothing to be afraid of, Kringelein," Otternschlag said meanwhile to comfort him.

"I'm not afraid," replied Kringelein peevishly and with a

surprising alertness. "Do you think I'm afraid to die? I am not afraid. On the contrary. Indeed, I ought to be thankful that I have to die. I should never have found the courage to live if I hadn't known I had to die. When you know that you have to die, it's then you get courage—when it's always in your mind that you have to die, it makes you capable of anything—that's a secret——"

"Aha," said Otternschlag, "the revolving door. Kringelein is becoming a philosopher. Sickness brings wisdom. You've found that out, have you?"

Gaigern made no reply. What are you talking about, he thought. Life—death—how can one talk about them? They are not words after all. I live—well then, I live. I die—well then, good God, I die. As for thinking of death—no. And as for talking about it—still less. There is nothing but to die decently whenever the moment comes. If these two were to climb along the hotel front like monkeys, they would soon keep their mouths shut about life and death, he thought proudly. I am ready, too—and I need no help from a boxful of morphine. He yawned and drew in a deep breath of the early morning air that came in through the open window, and at the same time a faint chilliness gave a tremor to his athletic shoulders. "I am sleepy," he said. Then all at once he broke into hearty laughter. "I never got to bed at all last night, and now today again it's four o'clock. Come along, Herr Direktor, get under the bedclothes."

Kringelein obeyed at once. He lay down, with his heavy head and the pain, which, though dulled, had not left off, inside him, and folded his hands on the quilt.

"Stay with me. Please stay with me," he said beseechingly. He said it much too loud, because his ears were buzzing and half deafened. Otternschlag stood near and listened. Nobody cared about *him*. Nobody asked *him* to stay.

"Now you have the morphine inside you, you don't want me any longer, of course?" he asked Kringelein, but the scorn with which he said it escaped Kringelein.

"No, thank you," he said amiably. He was holding Gaigern's hand tightly like a little child. He clung to Gaigern. He loved

Gaigern. Perhaps he even had a dim notion that Gaigern had meant to rob him; nevertheless, he clung to him tightly.

"Please stay with me," he implored.

At this, Otternschlag in turn began to laugh. He lifted up his mangled face in the cold light of the electric lamp and began to laugh with his wry mouth, but it was not at all like Gaigern's laughter. It was noiseless at first, then with a sort of hissing sound, then louder and louder, more and more scornful and more and more malevolent. Next door in Room No 71, someone knocked three times on the wall. "I must really ask you to be quiet. The night is for sleep, not for playing the fool," was heard in the complaining, sleepy and injured voice of an unknown personage. It was General Director Preysing, who little dreamt that in the next room three lines of fate had met for a fleeting and decisive hour. . . .

IDEAS OF conventionality were elastic in the Grand Hotel. It was not permissible for General Director Preysing to receive his secretary in his room. But there was no objection to his engaging a room for her. He did so with a flushed forehead and stammered explanations after the decisive conversation with Flämmchen. Rohna, who knew his world, regretted that he had only a double-bedded room free, No 72, separated from Preysing's suite by the bathroom. Preysing murmured something that was meant for the sake of appearances to sound like an embarrassed objection, and then plunged feverishly into his adventure.

In the morning he had letters from Fredersdorf, several business letters, and one from Mulle, to which Babs had appended two scrawled lines. Preysing, however, who was now being carried along in midstream far from the shore, as occasionally happens to men of his age, this transformed Preysing read the letters coldly and without a pang of conscience during the breakfast which the charming and cheerful and entirely unconcerned Flämmchen shared with him in his room.

Kringelein, too, had letters from Fredersdorf. He sat up in bed free from pain, fortified by Hundt's Elixir and resolved at all costs to retain the hard-won and penetrating sense of life he had experienced the day before. Now that he had fought his way through the agonies of the night and left them behind, now that he had emerged from them alive, he felt that he was made of transparent substance as hard as steel. With his pince-nez on the thin nose that now was even thinner, he read the letter which Frau Kringelein had written him on a sheet of blue-lined paper torn from her recipe book.

Dear Otto [thus wrote this Frau Kringelein, who had never been near to him, and who now had vanished to an

223

unthinkable remoteness]. Dear Otto, I have had your letter and am quite sure you would ail nothing if you took care of yourself, and father thinks the same. He has made an application for me for support from the factory, but I have not heard yet how the matter stands. They only put me off with promises. I am writing to you, chiefly on account of the stove, for it can't go on like this any longer. Binder was here to look at it. The vent-pipe is blocked, he says, and in every house in the Settlement there is something or other wrong. If they put in stoves like this they ought to supply coals as well, for no one on earth can pay such coal bills as the stove runs up. Now I have talked it over with Binder. He says he cannot repair the pipe for less than fourteen or fifteen marks and that it would pay for doing by the saving of coal. Of course, that is a big expense and I should like to hear without delay what you think we ought to do about the stove. It can't go on as it is, but there is no good, either, in spending fourteen marks on a bad stove. I have talked with Kietzau too, on the sly. He knows something about these things. But he thinks it would cost rather more than less, and he won't guarantee that we should need less coal than before, he says. So I went to the factory and made a row. I got hold of Schriebes after a lot of bother and told him they ought to mend the stove, and it is only right since it is on their property. But they won't hear of it. Schriebes was uncivil, and he is only a common fellow who thinks of nothing but his own pocket. If I can get something now out of the sick fund —father thinks they might fork out thirty marks, but I don't, for Preysing, the old skinflint, lets nothing past him, and am I to have the stove mended, then, or not? Do you get sick pay extra when you are in the sanatorium, or do they take it all? People here are turning nasty and saying that you are shirking work and putting your pay in your pocket. I can't go outside the door, for they don't spare my feelings. Please, see to this business with the sick fund at once. Frau Prahm says that as long as you are sick, they can't deduct anything from your money. You must look into it, or you're a fool, she says. Bad weather here. How is it with you?

Your affectionate,
Anna.

Write to me at once about the stove, or shall I wait till you come? It smokes to such a degree that my eyes smart.

With this letter in his manicured hands, Kringelein sat lost in thought on the edge of his bed for about ten minutes, but he was not thinking of Fredersdorf, nor of his wife, nor of the stove, and not of the attack of pain or the fear of death during the night either. All the time he was thinking of the aeroplane and how he had not felt in the least air-sick. He was thinking of the thrill of pride and courage which came over him when on a sharp curve the world rose sheer up at him through the window of the machine without causing him a tremor.

I shall dress now and talk to Preysing, thought Kringelein, and with this resolve he got out of bed at once. He had to put things straight with Preysing, otherwise there was no sense or object in anything at all.

Kringelein had a bath and put on the new Kringelein, the one with a silk shirt, a well-cut coat and a sense of his own worth. His heart was as resolute as a clenched fist as he stood at the door of Room No 71. He opened the outer door and knocked on the white enamelled panel of the inner one.

"Come in," Preysing called out. He said it from habit and without thinking, for he had no wish at all that anybody should interrupt his cheerful breakfast with Flämmchen. But as he had called out 'Come in', the door opened and Kringelein made his appearance.

He appeared—and it seemed to Preysing as though an explosion had projected him into the Grand Hotel, on to the second floor, the floor of select visitors, and into Room No 71. He had put his handsome new felt hat from Florence on his head with the deliberate intention of keeping it on his head, and there he kept it. "Good morning, Herr Preysing," he said, and carelessly brushed the brim of it with two fingers. "I want a few words with you."

Preysing stared.

"What do you want? How did you get in here?" he asked.

The sight of Kringelein with his hat on his head, this junior clerk from his counting-house coming in with this resolute air, amazed him as much as if he had come to announce the end of the world.

"I knocked and you said 'Come in'," Kringelein replied

225

with astonishing coolness. "I want a word with you. May I sit down?"

"Please," said Preysing helplessly as Kringelein did so.

"The young lady will please forgive the intrusion," he said next to Flämmchen with address. Flämmchen, with lively amiability, replied:

"We know each other, Herr Kringelein, don't we? We danced a delightful foxtrot together."

"Quite so. We did," said Kringelein, clearing his throat of a slight huskiness. His throat was throbbing. After this there was a silence.

"Well, what is it? I have no time to lose. I have urgent letters to dictate to Fräulein Flämmchen," the General Director finally said in his General Director's tone.

Kringelein, however, showed no sign whatever of collapsing under it, though he did not quite know where to begin.

"It's a letter from my wife. The stove has gone wrong again and the firm refuses to have it repaired. Now that won't do. The settlement, where I live, belongs to the firm and we pay the rent punctually. It's deducted from our wages. Then the firm ought to see that everything is in good order in the houses on its property and none of us ought to suffocate because the stoves are bad." This was how he began. Preysing went a dull red between his eyebrows and had the greatest difficulty in keeping his temper.

"You know very well that these matters are no concern of mine. If you have any complaints to make you must make them to the estate office. It is absolutely unheard of to bother me with anything of this sort."

Full stop. And this might well have concluded what he had to say. But Preysing must needs add: "Instead of you people being thankful to have homes put up for you, you become impudent. It's intolerable."

Though Preysing stood up, Kringelein remained seated.

"Very well, we will leave it at that," he said carelessly. "You think that you can be as insulting as you like. I beg to differ. You think that you are something altogether superior, but you are quite a common man, Herr Preysing, though you may have

226

married money and built yourself a house in the country. You are quite common, and there was never worse said of anybody than is said of you in Fredersdorf. So now you know."

"That does not concern me. That does not concern me in the least. I advise you to leave this room."

But Kringelein found unsuspected reserves of strength within himself. He had twenty-seven years of drudgery of which to unburden his soul, and he was charged like a dynamo.

"Yes, it does concern you," he said, "it concerns you very much. Otherwise why should you have your spies and informers in the factory, your lick-spittles, like Herr Schriebes, like Herr Kuhlenkamp, creatures like that who tread on those below them and cringe to those above? If anyone is three minutes late, it is reported. They even get behind the servants. The whole factory knows that. But we can work the hearts out of our bodies and not a word is said. We're paid to do that. You don't bother to ask, Herr Preysing, whether it is possible to live as a human being on the salaries we get. You sit in your motor car and we can't even afford ourselves rubber heels. And when we're old and used up, we can go where we like. Nobody cares. Old Hannemann was thirty-three years with the firm and now he sits there with cataract and not a farthing of pension."

If Preysing had been as black a tyrant as he appeared in the imagination of a subordinate employee like Kringelein, he would have chucked Kringelein out of the room without another word. But as he was a self-respecting, well-meaning and vacillating man, he let himself be drawn into a discussion.

"You are paid according to the scale. And we have our Employees' Fund," he began in an embittered tone. "I know nothing of Hannemann. Who is Hannemann in any case?"

"A nice scale! A nice fund!" Kringelein cried. "I was in the paupers' ward in hospital. I was supposed to eat cheese and salami four days after the operation. My wife has made one application after another, but not a penny of extra allowance did I get. And I had to pay for the ambulance to Mickenau out of my own pocket. And I was supposed to eat cheese, with my stomach in the state it was! When I had been four weeks sick,

227

you wrote me a letter saying that I should receive notice if I was sick any longer. Is that so or not—yes or no, Herr Preysing?"

"I can't remember every letter I sign. But, in any case, a factory is not an almshouse, nor a hospital, nor a life insurance agency. You have now reported sick again and here you are living like a lord or an embezzler——"

"You shall withdraw that. You shall withdraw that at once in this lady's presence," Kringelein shouted. "Who are you to presume to insult me? Who do you think you are talking to? Do you think I am dirt? And if I am dirt you are a great deal dirtier, Herr Generaldirektor. So now you know. You are dirt, dirt!"

Both men now stood face to face glaring at each other in a frenzy of rage and slanging each other as hard as they could go. Preysing was flushed a dark red, almost blue, and big drops of perspiration stood on his shaven upper lip. Kringelein was completely yellow. His lips were utterly drained of blood, and his elbows, his shoulders and indeed every limb quivered. Flämmchen looked first at one and then at the other. Her head moved to and fro like a foolish kitten's after a swinging tangle of wool. All the same she understood pretty well what Kringelein had it on his mind to say, in spite of his distracted state, and it had her sympathy.

"What do you know or care how people like us have to exist?" he cried, white-lipped under his light, ruffled moustache. "But the way we live is enough to bring one to despair. It is like climbing up a bare wall. It is like being shut up in a cellar all your life. You wait on from year to year, and first you have a hundred and eighty marks, and, when you have waited five years, then you have two hundred, and then you crawl on and wait again. And then you think: It'll be better later on and later on you'll be able to afford to have a child—but it never gets to that—and then you even have to give up keeping a dog, because money doesn't run to it, and then you wait on in hopes of a rise, working like a nigger and putting in overtime without pay, and then another gets the rise with three hundred and twenty and family allowances, and you're left planted. And why? Because the Herr Generaldirektor doesn't know his business. Because the Herr Generaldirektor promotes the wrong men. Even Brösemann says that. Anything scurvier than my twentieth anniversary with the firm was never known in the history of the world. Did you even congratulate me? Did it enter anyone's head to make me a donation? There I sat bent over my desk and waited—but not a sign. Then I thought: It can't be possible. It's being kept as a great surprise, for it's impossible they would forget me after I've worked twenty years in their office—twenty years. And then midday came and then six o'clock, and I put on my best coat, and waited, but nothing whatever happened. And so I trudged off home, ashamed to be seen by my wife and ashamed to be seen by Kampmann. 'Well,' says Kampmann, 'did they celebrate the occasion in proper style?' 'Yes,' I say, 'my desk was covered with flowers, and they gave me five hundred marks, and the Generaldirektor himself spoke to me, oh yes, and he knew quite well that I was always the last to leave the office.' That is what I said to Kampmann, to hide the shame of it all. And seven weeks later Brösemann had me in and said, 'I hear you have been twenty years with us. It has been overlooked. Well, is there anything you would like?' And I said, 'I'd like to be dead and done with as soon as possible, that's what I'd like, for there's no pleasure in a dog's life like this.' And then Brösemann went to the old man, and he gave me a rise to four hundred and twenty from the end of May—but that didn't prevent it being a dog's life all the same. And that's when I swore that I'd tell old Preysing the truth one of these days."

Kringelein had begun in a loud voice, but while he spoke his voice sank and took on a note of sadness. Preysing, with his hands behind his back, walked to and fro in the small room. His boots creaked under his weight and the fact that Flämmchen was sitting there all the time listening as her eyes went from one to the other, made him furious. Suddenly he came to a stop in front of Kringelein, protruding his corpulent person menacingly towards Kringelein's new coat.

"What do you want of me exactly? I don't know anything whatever about you. You come in here," he said in a chilling nasal voice, "you have the impertinence to come in here and talk like a Bolshevist. What do I care for your twentieth anniversary? I don't bother myself with every single employee in our business. I have other things to think about. I don't sleep on a bed of roses myself, not by any means. Anyone who shows marked competence is paid accordingly and finds an opening. The rest don't concern me. You don't concern me. I know nothing about you. I have had enough of it——"

"You don't know me. Quite so. But I know you well enough. I knew you long ago when you first came to Fredersdorf and lodged in the bootmaker's back bedroom and owed money to my father-in-law for butter and sausage. I remember the day very well when you began to leave off being the first to say good morning, Herr Preysing, and when you began courting the old man's daughters. I have kept account of you, Herr Preysing, and don't you imagine that anything has been overlooked and omitted. And if any of us made such bloomers in little things as you have made in big ones he would have had the sack long ago. And the insufferable air you have as you go along the passage and look straight through anyone you meet as though he didn't exist. And when in 1912 there was an error in my books for the first and only time, and I was docked of three hundred and ten marks—the tone in which you reprimanded me was something I shall never forget. And the eight hundred workmen you dismissed, they curse you to this day, that's certain. And when you come along in your motor car and open the exhaust so that we get our bellyful of stink, then you think yourself somebody. But I tell you . . ."

Kringelein had got switched on to a side-track. He poured out all the experiences and all the hatred of twenty-seven years pell-mell. He mixed up the important with the trivial, the real with the imaginary, and office gossip with what he knew at first hand. This explosion in an hotel bedroom was nothing but the grievance of a sensitive and unsuccessful man against one who had simply made his way with a certain brutality—a genuine grievance, however unjustifiable and absurd. . . . Preysing, on his side, completely incapable of any sympathetic understanding, fell deeper and deeper into ungovernable rage.

When Kringelein mentioned the money he had owed in his earlier days to the greasy provision dealer, Sauerkatz, his head positively swam and he was afraid of a stroke. He heard himself gasp for breath. The tiny veins of his eyes were so charged with blood that his vision was red and turbid. In one stride he was on top of Kringelein. He seized him by the waistcoat and shook him like a rat. Kringelein's new hat fell off his head. Preysing deliberately trod it underfoot. Strangely enough, Kringelein felt a peculiar pleasure at this savagery. Yes, he thought with satisfaction, strike a defenceless man who is at death's door. That's just like you. Flämmchen, behind the breakfast tray, whispered to herself:

"Don't—don't do that."

Preysing threw Kringelein against the wall and tore open the door.

"Enough," he shouted. "Not another word. Outside. At once. You shall be dismissed. I dismiss you. You're dismissed, dismissed from this moment——"

Kringelein had picked up his hat and now, with a face as white as a sheet, he stood between the double doors of which the inner was open and the outer shut, and, as he leaned trembling and perspiring against the white enamelled wood, he began to laugh with his mouth wide open, he laughed in Preysing's furious face.

"You dismiss me? You threaten me? But you cannot dismiss me. You can do nothing to me at all, nothing at all. I am ill. Dangerously ill, I tell you. I have got to die. I can only live a week or two. No one can do anything to me. I shall be dead before you can dismiss me——" he cried, as he shook with laughter and at the same time tears smarted in his eyes. Flämmchen got up from the sofa and bent forward. Preysing, too, bent forward. First his clenched hands fell to his side, and then he put them in his trouser pockets.

"Man, are you crazy?" he said in a lowered voice. "I believe the man is still laughing. I believe he's glad to be dangerously ill. Are you drunk?"

At these words Kringelein became sober of a sudden and fell into reflection. He was also a little embarrassed. He stood where he was between the two doors a moment longer and his eyes took in the small hotel suite with a fleeting glance. He saw Flämmchen standing in a ray of sun at the window, the corpulent and sobered General Director with his hands in his pockets and the vista through the open bedroom and bathroom doors. It all trembled indistinctly through the involuntary tears that obscured his eyes and showed his emotional condition. He took up his trampled hat from the floor and made a bow.

"I hope the young lady will forgive the intrusion," he said to Flämmchen once again, in his high-pitched, pleasing voice.

Preysing, with a husband's bad conscience, felt this to be a vulgar and base insinuation. He took his hands from his pockets.

"Get out," was all he said.

But Kringelein had gone already.

Preysing with squeaking tread walked three times up and down the room. His temples throbbed and his forehead was flushed.

"Well?" asked Flämmchen.

Suddenly the General Director ran to the door, pulled it open, and, trumpeting like an angry elephant, shouted down the silent corridor.

"You won't escape. I'll have you watched. We'll see where you stole the money to idle about here on. You Communist— you swindler—you impudent cur. I'll have you locked up— locked up——"

But there was nothing more to be seen or heard of Kringelein.

"After all he was decent enough. He was actually crying at the end," Flämmchen said in conclusion.

That was her only comment on the whole scene. . . .

"Leave your stockings on, though. It looks so pretty," said Preysing. He was sitting on the sofa in Flämmchen's bedroom, in Room No 72.

"No," said Flämmchen, "I should feel horrid. I can't be in nothing but shoes and stockings."

Her body gleamed in the light of the table-lamp. There

232

were red shadows on its smooth gold. There were soft reflections on her rounded knees and shoulders where the skin was drawn tight. She sat down on the edge of the bed and first slipped off her blue shoes and then solemnly and carefully her new stockings. The light flowed into the tender hollow between her breasts as she bent down, and her spine rippled smoothly. These were phenomena that Preysing observed with drawn breath.

"You are sweet," he said, but he did not venture to move from where he was. Flämmchen nodded to him over · her shoulder with good-natured encouragement. She took her stockings to a chair where she had already laid her dress and underclothing as tidily as a schoolgirl. Preysing now got up and went to her on squeaking shoes. Cautiously he stretched out one forefinger, on which there was a tuft of light-coloured hair, and with it he lightly touched Flämmchen's back as though she were a strange, untamed and dangerous animal. Flämmchen smiled. "Well?" she said amiably. She was a little nervous and impatient. On her side there was nothing but willingness to carry out the unwritten agreement in every particular. After all, a self-respecting person could not take a thousand marks and a journey to England and a new costume and much else besides, and give nothing in return. But this General Director was so horribly clumsy. This was now the second evening that he had squirmed around (this at least was how Flämmchen described Preysing's embarrassed and constricted style of wooing). And it was more than unpleasant. It felt like having a tooth stopped by a singularly incompetent dentist. She wished the worst were already well over, but it went on and on, always on the tender spot; and it got on her nerves. She moved her back nearer Preysing's hand, but the timorous forefinger had already moved off and sought a refuge in his waistcoat pocket, where it now reposed itself after the bold adventure, beside his fountain pen. Flämmchen sighed and turned to face the General Director. Her complete nakedness at once enchanted and alarmed him.

"You see, now I see you. Now I can see you," he said stupidly. Her body exhaled so inviolable a freshness and cleanness that it affected him more with alarm than with intoxication. "Just as you are . . . In the picture in the magazine you looked quite different," he said, almost aggrieved.

"Different? How do you mean, different?"

"More coquettish. There was something so fetching about it, you know . . ."

Flämmchen understood. She was aware of the hidden disappointment over her cool unapproachability and of the repressions in Preysing's sluggish blood, the stagnation of his conventional nature, but she could do nothing to help him. I am as I am, she thought. "Yes," she said, "photographers always put one in some idiotic pose to be photographed. And then they touch it up as well. Did the photograph please you more than I do myself?"

"What do you think—you're sweet," Preysing replied. His vocabulary of endearment was limited. "But won't you say 'darling' to me? Please, do!"

Flämmchen shook her head emphatically.

"Oh, no," she said.

"No? But why not?"

"Just no. I can't do it. I can't really. You are a stranger to me, so how can I call you 'darling'? In every other way—in every other way, I'll do anything you like. But to call you 'darling' is impossible."

"You're an odd creature, Flämmchen," said Preysing, and he looked at her naked gleaming skin and her painted lips. "You take some knowing."

"Not odd in the least," said Flämmchen with an obstinate pout of the lips. She had her own variety of shyness. "One must think of the future," she tried to explain. "I can go with you to England and all that, but when it's over, it's over; and if I say 'darling', it isn't over. If I meet you in six months' time, I shall say, 'Good day, Herr Generaldirektor.' And you will say, 'That is the little typist I took with me to Manchester.' And that will be all right. But it wouldn't be very pleasant, would it, if I met you with your wife and said, 'Hallo, darling, how goes it?' "

The General Director positively shrivelled up at this. To be reminded at this moment of his Mulle at home was all that was needed to complete his discomfiture. Nevertheless, the sense of forbidden sin and of the taint of vice ran in a hot current through his veins, and added to this was the rather too high blood-pressure of a well-fed man threatened with sclerosis of the arteries. He sat down on the nearest chair and sighed. The chair sighed too. Boards creaked, furniture groaned and doors banged at every encounter with Preysing's heavy person. He stretched out his hands, and, in an access of courageous ardour, laid them on the fine curve of her body above the hips. He was surprised and disappointed, for instead of the expected softness he encountered a taut, elastic firmness. He drew Flämmchen on to his knees, and controlled their tendency to tremble.

"What muscles you all have. Like boys——" he murmured huskily.

"All of us? Who do you mean?"

"You—and the other girls I know," answered Preysing, who was thinking of his daughters, Babs and Popsy, in their bathing dresses. Flämmchen was beginning to feel chilly and the warmth of Preysing's body was comforting.

"There now," she said more familiarly, "he knows girls," and she stroked Preysing's hair to which the Berlin barber had given a stylish cut the day before and a pleasing fragrance. (Well, after all, it is not going so badly, Flämmchen was thinking.)

"Of course I know girls. What do you think? I am not made of pasteboard. I'm a match any day for the handsome young fellows you dance with at your *thés dansants*. Feel how strong I am," he said, and he doubled his arm. He felt that he was getting back the joyful intoxication and all the 'go' and pride in which he had emerged from the successful conference the day before, and had rushed on into this incredible adventure. "Just feel how strong I am," he repeated. He held his arm braced for Flämmchen to feel. Flämmchen gratified him by feeling it. And in truth she came upon an astonishingly firm and well-developed biceps under the worsted sleeve.

"Mm," said Flämmchen, impressed. "Iron." She got up from her uncomfortable perch on Preysing's knees and walked

235

back a step or two. She put her hands behind her neck and looked at him through half closed lids. There were the same light-coloured wisps of hair under her arms as there were over her forehead. Preysing suddenly felt a choking sensation.

"Will you be kind to me?" he whispered.

"Oh, yes. Gladly," answered Flämmchen, politely ready to oblige. The next moment the General Director threw himself upon her. In his face there was the expression of a man who had burst ropes, broken through walls and escaped from prison. He was running away from himself, this correct and conscientious and diffident Preysing. He discharged himself like a rocket and landed in Flämmchen's arms. There! thought Flämmchen, a little taken aback by the anxious and passionate surrender that Preysing's distracted state expressed. She put her arms round his neck and he felt her warmth break over him in waves in which he let himself drown, while telegraph forms, innumerable telegraph forms rioted in front of his closed eyes and became dark red and dark blue and disappeared, as soon as his mouth drank in the taste of violets from Flämmchen's painted lips.

It was late in the evening. An echo of dance music from the Yellow Pavilion vibrated in a quiver of melody through every wall of the Grand Hotel. The Hall Porter, Senf, had handed over his duties to the night porter more than an hour ago. Doctor Otternschlag had gone up to his room and lay with eyes shut and mouth open on his bed. He looked like a stupefied mummy. His small trunk was packed for departure, but now, as before, he had not yet summoned up the necessary resolution for this final formality.

In Room No 68 a typewriter rattled on without mercy. The representative of an American film company had taken up his quarters there, and on the brass bedstead, which had witnessed Grusinskaya's night of love, strips of celluloid lay in heaps. The American examined them while he cleared off his business letters. The bell of the machine could be heard in Room No 70, where Kringelein sat in his bath and watched the antics of a tablet of bath salts on the white enamel. He was sad, and

236

because he was sad he sang softly and shyly—to cheer himself up. He sang in his bath like a child in a wood. The day had been poor and disappointing. The explanation with Preysing had cost him much and left him prostrate and done-up. And, worst of all, Gaigern, the dynamo, this source of energy, this vitalizing and warm-blooded and untrammelled fellow with his hundred-and-twenty-miles-an-hour pace had vanished from his sight. Kringelein, as he lay in the pain-assuaging hot water, felt that he had read the last page of his life and turned it over, and that now there was no more to come, nothing, nothing more. . . .

Pageboy No 18, Karl Nispe, crept up the stairs and stopped, crept on, stopped and crept on again. The rings under his eyes were as black as if they had been painted. He swallowed his saliva—for he suffered from those nervous pangs of hunger that afflict most hotel employees. He came from a wretched slum, a backyard, to his duties in the hotel lounge with its pillars, its carpets, its Venetian fountain, and it was to this slum, with its drab poverty, that he disappeared when his time on duty was over. He was a callow youth of seventeen, but he had his girl and she made claims on him that his scanty earnings could not meet. And now he had the gold cigarette case which he had found in the Winter Garden. For four days he had left it buried and hidden away and that was very much the same as having stolen it. Now he had come to the point. He had screwed himself up. He was going to part with it and give it back as though he had just found it. There he stood in front of Room No 69, with beating heart. He took off his cap; and at this his face suddenly lost its uniformed air and became human. When he had stood there for some minutes, shaken by the beating of his own heart, he knocked.

Although he had seen Baron Gaigern take his key a quarter of an hour before and go up to his room, there was no reply from within. He hesitated and then ventured upon opening the outer door and knocked on the inner one. On the hooks however between the two doors, the Baron's dinner jacket was duly hanging for the valet to take away and brush. The pageboy knocked. Not a sound. He waited and knocked again. No reply.

237

He pressed down the handle of the inner door. It was open but the room was empty. The pageboy, Karl, who knew something of life, grinned, whistled once high and softly and put the cigarette case, warm from his hand, on the middle of the table. The room was exceedingly cheerful. The light was on and the air in it was so unusually fragrant and un-hotel-like with menthol, lavender water, cigarettes and the scent of lilac, that it was a pleasure merely to breathe it. One or two sprays of forced white lilac were in a vase. On the writing-table there was a photograph of a sheepdog. In the middle of the room Gaigern's patent-leather shoes were dreaming with a dutiful and self-contented expression. Karl was impressed. He sniffed this atmosphere of bachelor elegance, and grinned. Suddenly with a sharp throb of his heart he took possession of the cigarette case again, stowed it away inside his jacket and under his shirt and went silently out.

A chambermaid was sitting in her little office writing a letter as he passed by the open door. It was very quiet on the second floor. Down below, the miniature propeller of an electric fan was humming. In the Yellow Pavilion a tango was being played.

A faint echo of the music could be detected even in the expensive two-bedded room that General Director Preysing had engaged for his secretary. Preysing emerged from the violet fragrance of his first kiss and said, "Listen!"

"Yes. I heard it a long while. Music," said Flämmchen, "it's nice to hear it in the distance."

"Music? No. Didn't you hear anything else?" Preysing asked. He made a somewhat distraught impression as he sat upright on the edge of the bed and listened. His eyebrows were drawn up on the strain of attention, and his forehead was a complete network of wrinkles—the result of many years of intricate business cares. "I can hear something all the same," he said anxiously.

"What? Where?" Flämmchen murmured. She was getting sleepy and she put her hands impatiently on Preysing's head.

"I heard a knocking of some sort," Preysing pointed and

238

stared fixedly at the door into his bathroom which he had left open.

"I hear something too," said Flämmchen, as she put her hands on Preysing's waistcoat. "I hear your heart beating. I can hear it distinctly. Tac-tac-tac . . ."

Preysing's heart was indeed making an excessive noise in his capacious chest. It beat with a dull and heavy thud beneath his grey suit. He still kept a look-out on the open door on whose painted surface the shaded table-lamp cast a pink reflection in the dim room.

"Let me go. I must go and see——" he said. He pushed Flämmchen's hands away from his chest and got up. The bed wheezed as he rose from it. Flämmchen let him go with a shrug of her shoulders. Preysing disappeared with three creaking steps through the bathroom door.

This small white door ought, properly speaking, to have been shut. It separated the General Director's suite from his secretary's bedroom. The hotel management had done nothing whatever to do away with this barrier. On the contrary. The little door had no latch, and when it was shut there was no handle to open it by. Preysing, however, had employed a master-key, which he always had in his pocket at the factory and had brought with him. With this he had opened the door and forsaken his own tidy room with its boot-bags, collar-boxes, sponge-bags and all the other paraphernalia of a husband, and had stepped through the little door into the boundless and unimaginable realm of adventure. . . .

The bathroom was in darkness and he quickly passed through it. A tap dripped, pong—pong—pong, into the bath. Next to the bathroom was the small sitting-room, also in darkness and reassuringly silent. Preysing stood still for a moment and felt for the switch without success. He then felt his way on to the closed door of his bedroom and suddenly came to a stop, dazed and breathless in the middle of the room. He knew for a certainty that he had turned off the light, but now the light was on. It showed like a thread under the door. It quivered over the threshold at Preysing's feet, and then it was gone. Preysing stood riveted to the spot and stared at the place

239

where a moment since there had been a streak of light and which now was dark—as dark as the lighted hotel front and the arc lamps and electric signs allowed. As he stood there he was waiting for something extremely unpleasant to happen, though exactly what he did not know. He had a vague idea that that crazy clerk had forced his way in as he had in the morning and that he was in there now. He suspected that this revengeful Kruckelein or Kringelein, or whatever he was called, had caught him in a peccadillo and was now in a position to make himself highly unpleasant by denouncing him or blackmailing him or making a scandal in one way or another——

It was this that rushed in a dark stupor through Preysing's head as he seized the door handle and abruptly opened the door.

The room was in darkness. There was not a sound. There was nobody there. Nobody breathed. But neither did Preysing breathe.

He put a hand out behind him and switched on the light by the door. The next moment the room was dark again. There had been one spasmodic flash of electric light, so brief that he had seen nothing clearly. A second of the most extreme and eerie suspense followed. Preysing's brain worked like mad. There is another switch at the door into the passage, it told him of its own accord. A man is standing there and as soon as I switch on, he switches off.

"Is anyone there?" he said, in a voice unnecessarily loud and so hoarse that he himself was startled by it. No reply. Preysing made a dart forward and found the writing-table, knocking his shin against it most painfully. He turned on the table-lamp. Then he stared with all his eyes.

Near the wardrobe close to the door into the passage stood a man in silk pyjamas. It was not the clerk. It was—Preysing recognized his face in the light of the green-shaded lamp—it was the other fellow, the smart fellow he had seen in the Lounge, and in the Yellow Pavilion, dancing with Flämmchen. He stood there in another man's bedroom with a smile—a green grimace.

240

"What do you want here?" Preysing asked in a forced voice. He was afraid of the beating of his own heart. His knees tingled. His fingertips too.

"Sorry," said Baron Gaigern. "I seem to have mistaken the door——"

"What do you say? Mistaken the door? We shall see about that——" said Preysing hoarsely, and pushed his way round the writing-table. He held his head low like an animal, and though he saw everything in a haze of red, he came by a miracle on the one significant fact—that his pocketbook was no longer on the writing-table where he had placed it with particular care when he went to open the door into Flämmchen's room. "We shall see whether you mistook the room," he heard himself say, and he lurched forward from the table.

At the same moment the Baron extended his right arm and aimed at the middle of Preysing's face. "If you move a step I shall shoot," he said in a quiet voice. For one dizzy second Preysing saw the black mouth of a revolver barrel.

"You'll shoot, will you?" he roared. He made a grab for something and did something with it. He felt his arm swing something heavy through the air with the whole weight of his body behind it. The blow fell with a smashing sound on the man's head and came back like a shock through his own arm.

For a moment the Baron remained standing opposite him with an astonished expression. Then his knees gave under him and he fell against the trunk that stood on the stillage next the wardrobe and down on to the floor, and there he lay face downwards.

"Shoot, would you? Well, there you've got it," said Preysing, when the air streamed down into his throat and he came up out of his access of rage and terror as though out of deep water. "There you have it," he said again to the prostrate man at his feet. His voice already sounded much softer, half apologetic and half reproachful. The man made no reply. Preysing bent over him, but did not touch him. "What's up with you then?" he said, half aloud. Now he heard the music from the Yellow Pavilion. He heard his heart beat and his breath come

241

and go. He even heard the pong—pong—pong from the bathroom. The man on the ground, however, made no sound. Preysing looked about him. He now found in his hand the object with which he had dealt the blow. It was the inkstand, the bronze inkstand with the outspread eagle's wings. He discovered black ink marks on his fingers and on the lapels of his coat too. He took out his handkerchief and cleaned himself up after he had gently replaced the inkstand. Then he turned again to the man on the floor. "He's unconscious," he said aloud. He had a dazed and obscure feeling of suffocation as he knelt down beside him and heard the boards creak with a weirdly hissing and significant sound. I shall have him arrested, he thought, but he was still too distraught to ring. He did not like to see the man lie there like that on his face, with his neck that looked as if it was broken and his arms outspread. He looked about over the carpet for the revolver but he could not find it. An oppressive silence now prevailed in the room which a moment ago was full of the noise and the thud of a heavy fall. Preysing had to overcome something in himself before he could take the man by the shoulders and turn him so as to have a better look at him.

Then he saw Gaigern's open eyes, and saw, too, that he was no longer breathing.

"What's happened then?" he whispered. "What has happened? What has happened? What has happened?" He whispered it over innumerable times to himself, senselessly, without knowing what he said. He stayed there cowering on his knees beside the prostrate man and whispered, "What has happened? What has happened?" Gaigern listened with a polite smile on his lifeless face. He was already dead. He had already left that big hotel and vanished beyond recall. But his hands were still warm as he lay with open eyes on the floor of Room No 71. The green light from the writing-table lamp fell on his beautiful features, which still kept their look of astonishment.

Thus it was that Flämmchen found the two of them when she stole through the forbidden door to see where Preysing had got to. She came with bare feet and stood in the doorway

242

blinking her eyes. "What's the matter? Who were you talking to? Did you feel bad?" she asked, peering in the dim light to see what was going on.

Preysing made three attempts before he could reply.

"Something has happened," he whispered at last, in a voice no one in Fredersdorf would have recognized.

"Happened? Good Heavens, what has happened? It's so dark in here," Flämmchen said and turned on the ceiling light. It cast a hard white radiance over the room.

"Oh——" was all Flämmchen said when she saw Gaigern's face. It was a little short wailing cry. Preysing looked up at her.

"He tried to shoot me. I only struck him a blow——" he whispered. "Someone must call the police."

Flämmchen bent down over Gaigern.

"His eyes are still open——" she said in a low voice, that sounded consoling. Surely he's not died? I liked him so, she thought ingenuously from the bottom of her heart. She stretched out her hand.

"Nothing must be touched before the police come," said Preysing louder than he meant, and now alert. Then Flämmchen understood at last what had happened.

"Oh——" she said again as she fell back. Then everything began to turn round and the walls closed in upon her.

She ran from the room, through doors and doors, pulled herself together from the verge of a collapse and ran on stumbling. She saw doors, nothing but doors. "Help," she cried faintly. "Help." All the doors swayed before her eyes and all were shut. Only one was open. Flämmchen saw it and then she saw no more.

Often there is such a noise in the passages of the Grand Hotel that the visitors complain. The lift rumbles up and down, telephones ring, people pass along laughing loudly, somebody whistles, another bangs his door, at the end of the passage chambermaids quarrel vigorously in undertones and you are embarrassed by at least eight separate encounters on the way to the lavatory. Often, too, this same corridor will be completely silent and deserted. Anyone might reel stark naked

243

along its length of carpet crying help, help, help—and no one would hear. . . .

Kringelein, certainly, who could not sleep because he was on the alert for the threat of renewed pains in his stomach; Kringelein, whom suffering and the approach of death had made thin-skulled and acute of ear; Kringelein heard the low wail as Flämmchen ran by half unconscious outside his door. He did not turn a deaf ear, like the American film agent next door in Room No 68. He got quickly out of bed and opened his door.

The next moment the miracle entered his life to fill and complete it. . . .

The next moment, in fact, Kringelein saw to his astonishment Flämmchen's naked, perfect form. It staggered towards him, fell heavily into his outstretched arms and lay there.

Kringelein did not lose his head, nor did his strength fail him under the burden. She had fainted and although the helpless collapse of the warm and golden brown body in his arms filled him with a sweet enchanting terror, he did a number of perfectly sensible things. He put one arm under the limp neck, the other under her knees, and lifting her up with an effort, he laid her on his bed. Then he shut both doors on to the corridor and drew a deep breath, for the rush of blood from his heart was overpowering. And now something fell to the floor from Flämmchen's drooping hand. It was a blue and somewhat worn shoe with a high heel, which till now she had held pressed to her naked breast. She had snatched it up and taken it with her. She had rescued it as though from a fire or a collapsing house as the only article of clothing that a catastrophe had left her. Kringelein took hold of her hand and laid it carefully by her side. He looked round the room and found the bottle of Hundt's Elixir, and put a few drops to Flämmchen's lips. A quiver passed over her forehead, but she was too unconscious to drink. But she was breathing deeply and at every breath the tangle of her bright hair rose and sank again on the pillow with an indescribable softness. Kringelein ran into the bathroom and soaked a handkerchief in cold water. He sprinkled it with eau-de-Cologne (for since yesterday Kringelein was possessed of such refinements) and returned to

244

Flämmchen. He carefully wiped her face and her temples. Then he felt for the beating of her heart, and found it under her firm and rounded breast. He put the cool, wet handkerchief there and after this he stood beside the bed and waited.

He did not know that his face had taken on an expression of shy, unfathomable wonder while he stood there looking down upon her. He did not know that his smile was the smile of first love on the lips of a boy of seventeen. Perhaps he did not even know that at this moment he truly, actually and utterly lived. But this he did know—that the feeling which now penetrated him with an almost painful warmth of appeal, this buoyancy and moltenness and transparency and release was known to him only in dreams. He had never supposed that such a feeling could be experienced in real life. Under chloroform, something of the sort had occurred just before the blue, singing haze went black. And in secret, deep within, Kringelein had imagined it was like this to die, an unexampled solemnity, a completion that left nothing unresolved behind it. Certainly, though, Kringelein was far from the thought of death at this moment as he looked at this girl who had fled to him for protection.

It really exists, he thought, it really exists. Beauty like this really exists. It is not only painted in pictures and imagined in books and trumped up on the stage. It can really happen that a girl is naked and so wonderfully beautiful, so utterly beautiful, so utterly—he tried for another word but could not find one. Utterly beautiful, was all he could think, utterly beautiful.

Flämmchen frowned, parted her lips like a child waking up, and finally opened her eyes. The light was reflected as a round gleam of white in her pupils. She blinked, smiled politely, took a deep breath and whispered, "Thanks." Immediately after she shut her eyes again as though she wished to sleep. Kringelein picked up the quilt from the floor and spread it carefully over her. Then he pulled up a chair to the bedside and sat down and waited. "Thanks," Flämmchen whispered again after a long while.

She was now conscious, but she found it difficult to put her thoughts in order. A certain confusion was caused by the fact that at first she mixed up the puny Kringelein at the edge of the bed with another man, whom she had liked very much and given up with great sorrow. The bright blue pyjamas and an undefinable tender alertness in Kringelein's manner led her into this mistake.

"How did I get here?" asked Flämmchen. "What are you doing here, dearest?" She said 'dearest' and this gave him a shock of sweet surprise, but as he was already in the midst of wonders he took it as a matter of course.

"You fainted and came to me," he said simply.

Now Flämmchen recognized her mistake. Everything came back to her and she sat straight up in bed.

"Forgive me," she whispered. "But something so awful has happened."

She pulled the bedclothes up to her face and screwed them into her eyes and began to cry. At once Kringelein's eyes filled with tears too, and his lips, which still smiled, began to tremble.

"It is so frightful," Flämmchen whispered, "so frightful, frightful."

Her tears came in a flood that soothed and appeased her. She dabbed the sheet against her face and covered the edge of it with small red heart-shaped transfers of her painted mouth. Kringelein looked on, and the corners of his eyes smarted with the pain of his suppressed emotion. At last he put his hand on Flämmchen's neck. "There, there, there," he said, "there—there—there."

Flämmchen looked up at him with swimming eyes.

"Oh, it's you," she murmured with relief. Now at last she recognized in the spruce figure at the bedside the little man who had danced so timidly with her yesterday and who had been so courageous that day in his interview with Preysing. A confiding and pleased sense of security took hold of her now she found herself in his bed with his hand gently patting her neck.

"But we know each other," she said, and snuggled up to his fingers with the spontaneous gratitude of an animal. Kringelein ceased to pat her and collected his strength—an unexpectedly large resource of strength and aggressiveness.

246

"What has happened to you? Did Preysing do anything to you?" he asked.

"Not to me——" said Flämmchen, "not to me——"

"Shall I tell him off? I'm not afraid of Herr Preysing."

Flämmchen looked at Kringelein as he sat erect and collected, and fell into deep reflection. She tried to recall the frightful scene in Room No 71 to her memory; the two men on the floor in the green light, the one—dead and stretched out, the other—living and distraught and cowering. But already it was erased from her healthy and resilient soul. Only her lips grew rigid at the recollection and the muscles of her arms tightened with agitation.

"He has killed him," she whispered.

"Killed? Who has killed whom?"

"Preysing. He has killed the Baron."

Kringelein's head swam, but he pulled himself together and kept calm.

"But that's impossible. I can't believe it," he stammered. Without knowing it he put both hands round Flämmchen's neck and drew her face close to his. He stared into her eyes and she stared as fixedly into his. At last she nodded her head three times emphatically without saying a word. Oddly enough, it was only then that Kringelein believed this incredible thing. He let his hands fall.

"Dead?" he said. "But he—why, he was life itself. He was strength personified. How could a fellow like Preysing . . ."

He got up and walked to and fro noiselessly, with his thin feet in new bedroom slippers, blinking in extreme agitation. He saw Preysing going along the passage of Block C at Fredersdorf without deigning a word. He heard his frigid nasal voice discussing costs, and he felt the doors shake at one of the General Director's outbursts of rage before which everyone in the factory trembled. He came to a stop at the window in front of the drawn curtains, and looked through them to Fredersdorf.

"It had to be. It had to be," he said finally, and the sense of just retribution grew in the soul of one who had so long been kept under. "Now it is his turn," he added. "Have they

247

arrested him? How did you know about it? How did it happen?"

"Preysing was with me in my bedroom and the door was open. Suddenly he said he heard something and went out of the room. I may perhaps have dozed off for a moment. I was very sleepy. And then I heard voices, but not very loud and then a fall, and then Preysing didn't come back. And then I was frightened and went through, for the door was open, you know—and there he lay—with his eyes open." Flämmchen once more put the sheet to her blanched face and broke into a storm of weeping over the dead Gaigern. She felt, beyond her power of expression, that something of wonderful beauty had passed out of her ken, something she had missed and that could never now be recalled. "Yesterday I was dancing with him, and he was so nice, and now he has gone and will never come back," she sobbed into the warm darkness of the down quilt.

Kringelein left the window and the sight of the detested Fredersdorf as he saw it through the curtains. He sat down on the edge of the bed. He even put his arm round Flämmchen's shoulders and it seemed to him perfectly natural to be comforting and protecting the weeping girl. He, too, felt the sorrow of Gaigern's death, though he was silent and constrained and could not quite grasp yet that his friend of yesterday was dead.

Flämmchen, when her tears were over, returned to the unclouded sanity of her ordinary self.

"Perhaps," she said softly, "he was really a burglar. But it was not right to kill him for that."

Kringelein recalled the obscure affair over his own pocketbook the night before. He was in need of money, he reflected. Perhaps he had been in anxious search of money all day. He laughed and played the fine gentleman, but perhaps he was only a poor devil after all. Perhaps he had done something desperate. And then a fellow like Preysing had killed him. "No," he said loudly.

"You were quite right in what you said to Preysing early this morning," Flämmchen began, leaning against Kringelein's arm. She felt that he was an old friend and it came quite naturally to her. "I didn't like Preysing either," she added

248

naïvely. Kringelein thought for a moment or two over the in-delicate question that had been on his mind ever since the day before when Flämmchen left the dance hall to go to Preysing.

"Then why—why did you take up with him?" he asked at last all the same.

Flämmchen looked at him in full confidence. "For money, of course," she replied simply. Kringelein understood at once.

"For money———" he replied, not as a question, but merely in reply. His life had been a struggle over pennies, so how could he fail to understand her? And now he put his other arm round her and encircled her. Flämmchen nestled against him and leaned her head against his breast. She could feel each several rib under the thin silk of his pyjamas.

"They don't understand that at home," she said. "I have a rotten time of it at home. There's always trouble with my step-mother and stepsister. I haven't had a job now for over a year, and something had to be done. I'm too pretty for a business post. It's always the same story. The big firms don't like to have girls who are too good-looking, and they are quite right. Then I'm too big for a mannequin. They want forty-two figures or at most forty-four. And as for the films, I don't know what's the matter there. Perhaps I'm not coquettish enough. That doesn't matter later on—on the contrary; but at the start it does. However, I shall pull through somehow. Only I mustn't get old. I'm nineteen already and it's time to see about getting on. Lots of people would say that you shouldn't go with a man like Preysing for money. Just the opposite—it's only for money! I can't see anything wrong in it. I remain just as I was before. Nobody takes anything away from me, even though I am a little nice to him. When you've been a year without a job as I have, running round after film agents, and running round in answer to advertisements, and your clothes go to rags, and you look in the shop windows, I just can't help it—to be well-dressed is my dream. The joy a new dress gives me, no one could believe. Often I spend days thinking out the clothes I'll wear one day. And then travelling. I'm mad on travelling, getting right away and seeing new places. At home I have a thin time of it—you can take it from me. I'm not a

complaining person. I'm good-natured and can put up with a
lot. But often it's enough to make you run away—just to get
away, even if it was with the biggest blackguard on earth—
only to get away. For money—naturally for money. Money's
so important, and whoever says otherwise is talking bunkum.
Preysing was going to give me a thousand marks. That's a lot
of money. Enough to give one a start in life. But that's over
and done with. And now I'm where I was again. And at home
it's frightful——"

"I know that. I can imagine that. I understand that very
well," said Kringelein. "At home everything is always filthy.
Even the very air goes wrong when you haven't got money.
You can't open the window because the warm air has cost
money. You can't have a bath because hot water means coals.
Your razor blades are old and scrape your chin. You have to
save over the washing—no tablecloth, no serviette. You have
to be careful with the soap. Your hairbrush has lost all its
bristles, the coffee pot is broken and cemented together, the
spoons are black. The pillows are hard lumps of old, coarse
feathers. What's broken, stays broken. Nothing is mended.
Your life policy must be paid. And you can't see that your
life's all wrong. You imagine it has got to be like that."

He was resting his head on Flämmchen's, and thus they
went through the litany of the poor together, rocking to and
fro in time to the monotonous chant. They were both tired out
and over-excited and half asleep.

"Your hand-mirror is broken," Flämmchen went on, "and
you can't afford a new one. You have to sleep on the sofa
behind a screen. There's a perpetual smell of gas. The lodger
makes his daily row. The very food you eat and can't pay for
because you are out of a job is cast in your teeth. But they
shan't get me under—they shan't get me under," she said with
energy as she crept out of Kringelein's arms and sat up so
straight in the bed that the clothes fell over on to Kringelein's
knees, imparting to them the warmth of her young body.
Kringelein accepted this warmth as an overwhelming munifi-
cence. "I shall get through," said Flämmchen, and for the
first time she blew the hair off her forehead as a sign that her

gaiety and vitality had returned. "I can do without the General Director. I shall get through all right."

Kringelein had a string of difficult thoughts to master, and when he was through with them he tried to put them into words.

"As for money, I've seen in the last few days just what it means to have it," he explained with difficulty. "You become a different man altogether when you have money and can buy things. But I never could have imagined that you could buy anything like this."

"Anything like what?" Flämmchen asked smiling.

"Like this. Anything like you. Anything so utterly beautiful, so splendid. People like me don't know that such things exist. We know nothing and see nothing. We believe that everything, marriage and all the rest of it with women, has to be sordid and frayed and joyless or else as paltry as in the night clubs here. But when you were lying there unconscious a few moments ago, I could scarcely trust myself to look at you. How beautiful, how beautiful you are. How beautiful. And so a man like me thinks to himself—so it really exists, something so wonderful—so wonderful——"

Yes, that is just what Kringelein was thinking. He sat on the edge of the bed and talked, not like an assistant book-keeper of forty-seven, but like a lover. His secretive, sensitive and timid soul crept out of its cocoon and spread its small new wings. Flämmchen listened, her arms round her knees, with a wondering and incredulous smile. Now and then she gave a little sob, like a child that has been crying. Kringelein was not young, nor was he good-looking or smart, or healthy, or strong. He had not one single quality of the lover. If his awkward stammered words and the blinking of his fevered eyes and his shy caresses that always stopped short, made an impression on her all the same, the reason is not to be found on the surface. Perhaps more than all it was his acquaintance with suffering, his passionate desire to experience something of life and at the same time his silent readiness for death that made out of his little piece of ruined humanity something that was manly and worthy of love.

It was not to be expected, however, that Flämmchen would immediately fall in love with Kringelein. No, Life is very far from producing such delightful surprises. But in this hotel Room No 70 a sense of intimacy and security came over her and it seemed to her more reliable than the usual day-to-day experiences of her insect existence. Kringelein talked on and on. He opened his heart and told her the whole story of his life, and it seemed to him at this moment that all his life had been directing itself to one aim and one completion—this wonder that had befallen him, this perfection of beauty that lay in his bed, the girl who had come to him, who had left Preysing and come to him——

Flämmchen had no exaggerated opinion of herself. She knew her price. Twenty marks for a photograph in the nude. A hundred and forty marks for a month's office work. Two-pence per page for typing with carbon copy. A fur coat at two hundred and forty marks for a week as somebody's mistress. She had no reason, then, to set a high value on herself. But, as Kringelein went on talking, she discovered herself for the first time. She saw herself as though in a mirror. She saw the splendour of her golden skin and her pale gold hair. She saw her limbs, each one radiant with beauty. She was conscious of her freshness, of her untroubled existence always striving on into the future. She discovered herself, like a hidden treasure.

"But after all I'm nothing out of the way," she murmured in a glow of modesty. In the midst of Kringelein's torrent of rapture she started and shuddered when Preysing's name came up. In the last half hour they had both forgotten what had occurred in the green-lit Room No 71. Now of a sudden the whole horror came back.

"I am not going in there again," Flämmchen whispered. "They will have arrested him by now. They'd arrest me too. I am going to stay here in hiding."

Kringelein smiled nervously.

"Why should they arrest you?" he asked, but all the same he was afraid. He, too, had Gaigern clearly before his eyes, in the car, in the aeroplane, at the gambling table, in the white light of the boxing ring. He saw Gaigern as he bent over him, as he gave him back his pocketbook, and as he went through the revolving door.

"Why should they arrest you?" he asked.

Flämmchen gave an emphatic nod.

"As a witness," she said, out of the depth of her ignorance.

"Do you mean——?" asked Kringelein vaguely, looking straight through her with his eyes fixed still upon Gaigern. And suddenly he was once more keyed up to the whirling danger-pitch of the day before. "You needn't be afraid. I'll arrange it all for you," he said quickly. "Will you stay with me? You will, won't you? You shall have a good time with me. I only want to give you a good time. Will you? I have money. I have money enough. It will last us a long while. And I can easily win some more, gambling. We'll travel. We'll go to Paris. Where you like."

"My pass has a *visa* for England——"

"Good. England then. Where you like and what you like. You shall have clothes. One must have clothes and one must have money. We'll have a gay time of it. What do you say? I'll give you the money I won—three thousand four hundred marks. You can have more later on. Don't say anything, keep quiet and stay here. I'll go along now to the other room. I'll go along to Preysing. I'll see what's happened to him. I promise you you'll have a better time with me than with Preysing. Wouldn't you rather be with me than with Preysing? I'll go now and fetch your things. Trust to me, and don't be afraid."

Kringelein vanished into the bathroom and dressed with the utmost speed—black coat and the dark tie of thick silk. It gave him a strange feeling of fevered excitement to be dressing in the middle of the night while the street below became silent and the radiators cooled down. Flämmchen sat up in the bed, laid her cheek on her knee and breathed a sigh of relief. Her body now began to ache after her fainting fit and her throat was dry. She longed for an apple and a cigarette. She took the bottle of Hundt's Elixir from the bed-table and tried a sip, but she did not like its cinnamon taste. When Kringelein came back he looked quite the fine gentleman. Perhaps he really was

253

a fine gentleman, even though he had split firewood every day for his wife for twenty years.

"I'm going now. You keep quite still here," he said, and put on his pince-nez. His eyes blinked, but they were bright and gleaming and the pupils were large and black. At the door he suddenly turned back and going to the bed, knelt down. He put his face in his hands and murmured something Flämmchen did not catch. "Yes, yes, of course," she said. "Yes, gladly."

Kringelein got up, wiped his glasses on the corner of the handkerchief that hung from his breast pocket, and left the room. Flämmchen heard the outer door shut and his steps as he went along the passage. And then, in the distance, the music from the Yellow Pavilion, where the same people were still dancing as three hours before. . . .

Gaigern lay on the carpet in Room No 71. He was dead. Nothing more could happen to him. No one now could harass or pursue him. He would never now find himself in prison. And that was good. He would never now keep his appointment in Vienna with Grusinskaya. And that was sad. But he had lived his life to the full in all his outlawed beauty and strength. He had spent his childhood among the fields, his boyhood on horseback. He had been a soldier in the war. He had been fighter, hunter, gambler. He had been a lover and he had been loved. Now he was dead. His hair was moist and matted. There was an ink-stain on his dark blue pyjamas and an astonished smile on his lips. There were the thick woollen socks of a burglar drawn over his feet, and on his cold right hand the cut from his last adventure would never heal again. . . .

Preysing, too, heard the dance music, and it caused him inexpressible torture. Every thought that came into his head took on the syncopated rhythm which the Eastman Band in the Yellow Pavilion sent throbbing through the walls of the hotel. Nothing could have gone worse with the thoughts that were being thought up here all night long, than the music that all night long was being played down there.

It's all up with me, thought Preysing. Done. Finished. I

can't go to Manchester. The Chemnitz business will fall through. The police will arrest me. I shall be questioned and put on my trial. It was in self-defence. Nothing can happen to me. But there's the other thing. There's the girl. The girl, too, will be questioned. I was with her. The door was open. It's open now.

Preysing sat in the farthest corner of the room on a strange piece of furniture, a basket intended for dirty linen, which was further provided with an upholstered lid. He had turned on all the lights and in spite of this he did not dare turn round and look behind him. By some mysterious compulsion he was forced to keep his eyes fixed on the dead man. It was as though something frightful would occur the moment he turned away his head to look round at the open door.

"The door was open. I must not dare to shut it. Nothing must be touched till the police arrive. Tomorrow it will be in the papers that I had a woman with me in the hotel. Mulle will know about it. The children, too. Yes, the children, too. My God, what will happen to me? Where will it end? Mulle will divorce me. Such a thing will be utterly unintelligible to her—utterly. But she will be entirely in the right if she divorces me, entirely. It ought never to have happened, never. How could I touch the children with these hands?"

He looked at his numbed and ink-stained hands. He had an intense longing to go into the bathroom and wash them, but he dared not let the dead man out of his sight. An American jazz-song, 'Hallo, my Baby', came up from far, far below.

"I shall lose my children and I shall lose my wife. The old man will turn me out of the business for certain. He'd never keep me in the firm after a disgrace like this. And all because of that girl. Nothing else. Perhaps she was hand in glove with the man and enticed me into her room for him to carry out the theft meanwhile. That's it. That's what I shall say at the trial. It was self-defence anyway. He was going to shoot——"

Preysing bent forward, and for the thousandth time he stared at the hands of the dead Gaigern. They were empty— the right convulsively clenched, the left bent limply at the wrist; in neither was there a weapon. Preysing went down on

255

his knees, and in the full light looked all over the floor. Nothing. The revolver the man had threatened him with was nowhere to be seen—or else had never existed. Preysing stole back to his seat. He felt that he was going crazy. The solid basis of his conventional life had given way beneath his feet ever since the moment when he had flung the fatal telegram on the table at the conference, and since then he had been hurtling downwards from one adventure into another. He felt, as it were, the rush of air in his ears, as he fell from his well-regulated life down into bottomless darkness. He had known men such as he now was, men who had left the rails, who had done great things in the past and now in worn suits begged from one office to another for a job. He saw himself turned adrift to go the same round as they, unkempt, alone and in bad repute. His excessive blood-pressure gave him throbbing pains in the back of his head and made his ears ring. Preysing was so crushed that for minutes together he longed to die of a stroke, and expiate his sin. But nothing of the sort occurred. Gaigern remained dead, and he remained alive.

"My God," he groaned. "My God! Mulle, Babs, Popsy. Oh, God."

He would have liked to bury his face in his hands, but he did not dare. He dreaded the darkness in the hollow of his hands.

Thus Kringelein found him when shortly after two o'clock (the music had just stopped) he entered the room after a cautious knock on the door. Kringelein's lips that night were dead white, but there was a fevered patch of red in his cheeks. He was in a strange state of elation, dignified and aloof, and he was very conscious of his appearance in his smart, well-cut black coat, and also of his *savoir faire* in his conduct of the situation.

"I came on the lady's behalf," he said. "I gather that something has happened here. I shall be glad to do anything I can for you, Herr Generaldirektor."

It was not till he had finished speaking that he looked down at the dead Gaigern. The sight did not shock him. He was merely surprised. For on the way from Room No 70, the idea had come to him that all this was not true, that Gaigern still lived, that Preysing was no murderer, and that Flämmchen in his room was only dreaming, if indeed her being there at all was not itself a dream. But now he saw Gaigern actually lying there, as actually as Flämmchen was waiting for him in his room. He bent down over the dead man, touched by a familiar warmth of comradeship. He knelt beside him and the smell of lavender and scented Turkish cigarettes, in which he had passed so unforgettable and so illuminating a day, moved him profoundly. Thank you, he thought, as he caught his breath in a sob.

Preysing looked across with dazed and troubled eyes. "No one must touch him before the police come," he said unexpectedly, as Kringelein stretched out his hand to close his friend's eyes. Kringelein did not bother about Preysing in his corner, he performed the small solemn service. Flämmchen will do as much for me, he could not help thinking to himself. You look so happy. Is it so well with you? It is not so bad, is it? It won't be so very bad. And it won't be long, not long.

"Have you notified the police yet, Herr Generaldirektor?" he asked in a formal tone, when he was on his feet again. Preysing shook his head. "Would you like me to do so for you, Herr Generaldirektor? I am at your service," he went on. Oddly enough, Preysing felt an immense relief now that Kringelein was in the room, politely expressing his readiness to carry out his wishes.

"Yes. In a moment. Not now. Wait," he whispered. There was a semblance to the peremptory but confusing orders with which he harassed his subordinates at the factory.

"It will be imperative to let the old gentleman know of the occurrence. Would you like me to send a telegram to your esteemed family, Herr Generaldirektor?" Kringelein asked.

"No, no," Preysing answered in a quick, hoarse whisper, that sounded louder than a shout.

"Then I would suggest in any case that you put yourself in a solicitor's hands. It is late certainly, but in so exceptional a case one might be able to ring up a solicitor. You will undoubtedly be taken into custody at once on remand. I am very

257

willing to undertake this or anything else that may be necessary, Herr Generaldirektor, before leaving Berlin," Kringelein proceeded. He was deeply impressed by the consciousness of acting a part in important events, and the care with which he chose his words pleased him and seemed appropriate and adequate to the occasion. But the politeness of his manner towards the extinct and shattered General Director came from sources more worthy of remark. He stood there, small but erect, the conqueror in a battle of long standing of which Preysing till that day had known nothing. Nothing now was left of his rage and fear, exasperation and impotence. His Fredersdorf feelings were all dead. Perhaps, too, he felt a touch of that peculiar and inexplicable admiration that is felt for anyone who has committed an outrage, and in addition there was pity and a sense of superiority, and these two moved him to politeness.

"You cannot leave Berlin," Preysing said from his seat on the dirty-clothes basket. "Your presence will be required. I require you. There can be no question of your going away." It sounded exactly like a harsh refusal of leave. Kringelein could have smiled, but that it would have hurt him to do so while Gaigern lay outstretched and dead on the carpet with his head on the hard boards. "You will be required as a witness. You must be here when the police arrive," the General Director announced.

"My evidence will soon be given. In any case I am ill, and tomorrow I must leave for a cure," Kringelein replied with dignity.

"But you knew the man," said Preysing quickly, "and the girl as well."

"The Baron was a friend of mine. The lady sought my protection immediately after the murder," said Kringelein in good journalistic phraseology. His narrow chest swelled with pride. He was equal to the occasion, he felt with satisfaction.

"The man was a burglar. He stole my pocketbook. It must be on him now. I have not touched him."

Kringelein looked down at Gaigern. It seemed strange that he lay there without a word while they talked. And yet he

258

smiled in a vague, indefinable way. Kringelein shrugged his shoulders, encased in the horsehair padding of his faultless new coat. Possibly, he thought. Possibly he was a burglar. But is that so very important? What did a pocketbook matter in a world where thousands were earned, thousands spent and thousands won in play?

Suddenly Preysing woke from his absorption.

"What brought you here, anyway? Who sent you? Fräulein Flamm?" he asked sharply. This was how Kringelein learned Flämmchen's real name.

"Quite so. Fräulein Flamm," he replied. "She is in my room. She won't go back to her own. She sent me to fetch her things, so that she can be dressed when the police come. She had nothing on at all when she fainted."

Preysing considered this concise reply for some minutes.

"They will question Fräulein Flamm," he then said. It sounded like a cry of despair.

"No doubt," Kringelein said curtly. "It is to be hoped it will not take long. She is leaving with me tomorrow. I have offered her a post," he added, and a suffocating sense of triumph and victory made his cheeks go pale. But Preysing was a man no longer, and he was very far from fighting over a woman. What it meant to Kringelein that Flämmchen had passed from the one to the other never crossed his mind. He knew nothing of this indescribable miracle, this extreme and unsurpassable bliss.

"Fräulein Flamm's things are in her room. No 72. The next door on the left," he said. He tried to get up, but his knees failed him. His joints were numb and as though filled with sand. They had struck work. And still the dead man lay there on the floor. . . .

But when Kringelein had reached the door, Preysing realized that he was about to be left alone and struggled to his feet.

"Wait—wait a moment," he whispered in a hoarse suppressed cry. "Listen, Herr Kringelein. I have something more to say to you—before—before—the police arrive. The fact is —it is about the girl. You're going to take her with you when you go, you say. Couldn't it—she's in your room, you say—

259

would it not be possible to leave it like that? I mean—listen
to me, Kringelein, as one man to another. I can face what has
happened here. It was in self-defence—self-defence pure and
simple. It's bad enough, but I can face it all the same. But the
other business will finish me. It is utter ruin. Can't we—must
the police know of this affair with Fräulein Flamm? It would
be perfectly simple. I only need to lock the door into No 72
again. Fräulein Flamm spent the night with you. She knows
nothing about it at all. Nor you either, Herr Kringelein. Then
it is all in order. Everything will be all right. You won't need
to give evidence and Fräulein Flamm will not be called. Now,
Herr Kringelein, you can understand me. You know my wife.
You have known her almost as long as I have. And the old
man, you know our old man. After all, you are one of us.
There's no need to waste words. My whole life hangs by a
thread. I say it frankly. An idiotic affair like this over a woman
is nothing. Nothing at all. But it can mean ruin. Herr Kringelein, I love my wife. My life depends on her and the children," he said, as though he were imploring Mulle herself. "You
know the two girls, Herr Kringelein. If this business of Fräulein Flamm comes out at the trial I shall lose everything. I
shall have nothing left. I'm—I give you my word of honour
that nothing, nothing whatever passed between us," he whispered. It was only he remembered it. "Help me, Kringelein.
You're a man as I am. Take this affair on yourself. Pack up
and go away with the girl and say nothing. Leave all the rest
to me. You've nothing to do but hold your tongue, and get
Fräulein Flamm to do the same. Nothing else whatever. You
can go tomorrow, go right away where you like. I'll give you—
listen to me, Herr Kringelein. We had words together earlier
on today. There's nothing in that. You do me injustice, believe
me, you do. There are always misunderstandings between the
management and the staff, and there is no need to take it too
seriously. We stand and fall together after all. We're all in the
same boat, my dear Kringelein. I'll—I'll give you—you shall
have a cheque and go where you like. Now go into No 72
and shut that door. Fräulein Flamm will hold her tongue and
all will be well yet. If anybody asks her anything, she spent the

whole night with you and knows nothing. She saw nothing and heard nothing. Herr Kringelein, I beg you, I beg you——"

Kringelein looked at Preysing as he whispered rapidly and almost crazily. The white light from the seven bulbs of the chandelier cast black shadows on his face. It seemed to have fallen in and it was bathed in a cold sweat. His eyes were hollow, his newly shaven, unfamiliar upper lip quivered, his eyelids fluttered, his hair stuck to his forehead, lined by the cares of his business life. His hands gave the impression of a sick and ailing man as he rose to his feet and repeated: "I beg you, I beg you, I beg you——"

Poor devil, Kringelein thought suddenly. The thought was utterly without precedent. It burst chains and broke down walls.

"My fate hangs on you," Preysing whispered. He was begging for mercy and was not ashamed to use the melodramatic word 'fate'. And what about my fate, Kringelein thought meanwhile. But the thought passed, before it took shape.

"The General Director over-estimates my influence with the lady. If the General Director wishes to lie his way out, that is entirely his own affair," he said coldly. "But I would recommend him to notify the police without further delay. Otherwise a bad impression will be made. I will now remove Fräulein Flamm's things to my room. Number 70—if the General Director should require me. I will take leave of him for the moment."

Preysing stood up. He conquered the helpless state of his legs and got on to his feet, but he collapsed again at once. Kringelein sprang forward to support him. Poor devil, he thought again, poor devil. Preysing, resting his arm heavily upon Kringelein, still did not give up hope.

"Herr Kringelein, I will not say another word about your absence on sick leave. I will make no inquiries as to how you procured the means for this escapade of yours. I will—when you return, I will see if you can't be given a better post. I will do everything possible for you——"

But at this Kringelein merely smiled. He smiled without

261

concealment or constraint, and without a trace of gratitude, in an easy and perfunctory way. "Thank you," he said. "Many thanks for your kind intentions. There will be no occasion for them."

He leaned Preysing against the wall and there he left him— with his broad and sagging shoulders propped against the sprawling pattern of the wallpaper of Room No 71, looking like a man who had fallen into a crevasse. In the passage every second light was turned out. At the corner, however, 'Mind the Step' still shone out in illuminated letters. The grandfather clock struck three with its old-fashioned chime.

At half past three the night porter was rung up while he was nodding over the morning papers. "Hallo," he called down the black mouthpiece. "Hallo, hallo." At first not a sound issued from the telephone. Then somebody cleared his throat, and finally a voice said: "Send the manager to me at once. Preysing. No 71. And notify the police. Something has occurred. . . ."

The events that happen to people in a big hotel do not constitute entire human destinies, complete and rounded off. They are fragments merely, scraps, pieces. The people behind its doors may signify much or little. They may be rising or falling in the scale of life. Prosperity and disaster may be parted by no more than the thickness of a wall. The revolving door twirls around, and what passes between arrival and departure is nothing complete in itself. Perhaps there is no such thing as a completed destiny in the world, but only approximations, beginnings that come to no conclusion or conclusions that have no beginnings. Much that looks like Chance is really Fate. And much that goes on behind Life's doors is not fixed like the pillars of a building nor pre-conceived like the structure of a symphony, nor calculable like the orbit of a star. It is human, fleeting and more difficult to trace than cloud shadows that pass over a meadow. And anyone who attempts an account of what he sees behind those doors runs the risk of balancing himself precariously on a tightrope between falsehood and truth. . . .

For example, there was the odd affair of the trunk call from Prague shortly after twelve o'clock at night. A woman's voice asked to be put on to Baron Gaigern, Room No 69, and was duly put through. "Hallo," Grusinskaya called. She had just got into bed (the wretched bed of a famous, but antiquated hotel). "Hallo, hallo, *chéri*, are you there, dear one?"

And although Room No 69 was already empty at this moment, although at this very moment in Room No 71, two doors farther on, that unfortunate incident occurred, on account of which General Director Preysing was kept in prison for three months on remand and lost wife and children and all he had—in spite of this, Grusinskaya at her telephone heard quite distinctly, even though faintly, a beloved voice saying:

"Neuwjada? You? My darling!"

"Hallo," called Grusinskaya, "good evening, good evening, my dear. Aren't you surprised that I should ring up? You must please speak louder. There's something wrong with the line. I have just come from the theatre. It went well. It was splendid, an enormous success. They were crazy over me. I am very tired, but so, so happy. It is years since I danced as I did tonight. Oh, *comme je suis heureuse!* And you, do you think of me? I think of you every moment, only of you—I long for you. Tomorrow early we leave for Vienna. Will you be there? Speak—speak. Tell me. Hotel Bristol, tomorrow. Vienna. Can you hear? Why, Exchange. Exchange, I've been cut off. I can hear nothing. I want to know whether you will be in Vienna. I'm expecting you. I'm having everything prepared for us at Tremezzo. Are you glad? Only fourteen days' more work and then we shall be at Tremezzo. Do say one word, just one word. I can't hear you. What? Is that Exchange? What do you say? No reply from the Baron? Thank you. Then please give him a message. Say that he is expected tomorrow in Vienna. Good morning. Thank you."

Such was the conversation that passed between Grusinskaya and the empty Room No 69. She lay in bed in her hotel with her chin compressed in a rubber bandage, her eyes still hot with paint and her heart filled and glowing with tenderness. "But indeed I love you. *Je t'aime*," she murmured into the dumb telephone, when the Exchange at the Grand Hotel had already cut off the connection.

And then, just next door in Room No 70, there is that moment, between four and five in the morning, when the drawn curtains were becoming grey and Flämmchen for the first time took Kringelein in her arms. It was that first sweet moment of tenderness when she did not sell but freely gave. Then for the first time she learnt that it was not a mere pleasure, a meaningless gratification, that she had to give away, but something great—an ecstasy, a happiness, a complete fulfilment. She lay there like a very young mother and held the man in her arms like a child that might drink its fill. Her fingers rested in the hollow, between the sinews at the back of his neck, which illness and weakness had made. Everything is good now, thought Kringelein, no more pain. I am strong. Tired too, but I shall sleep. I have scarcely slept since I came here. It is a pity time is so short. I don't want to go off. I want to stay here. I don't want to have to stop now when everything is just beginning.

"Flämmchen," he whispered to her warm young body, "Flämmchen, don't let me die, please don't let me die."

Flämmchen at once held him closer, and began to comfort him.

"Die—what nonsense! I won't hear of it. It's not so bad as that by a long way. I'll soon look after you. I know a man in Wilmersdorfer Strasse who can work miracles. He has cured people who were far worse than you. He'll soon fix you up. We'll go to him first thing tomorrow. He'll give you a treatment of some kind, and then, you'll be all right again, you'll see. Then we'll set off at once for London, Paris, the South of France. It will be warm there. We'll lie in the sun all day and get sunburnt and be happy. And now you must go to sleep."

She let her unthinking health and strength stream into his exhausted being, and he believed her. He fell asleep blissfully in a blaze of gold that looked like Flämmchen's breast and was also a hill of broom in flower.

And then, two floors higher, there is Doctor Otternschlag dreaming the dream that comes to him every week. He is going through a dream-town which he knows very well and he enters a dream-house that he has forgotten. A dream-woman lives there and she has had a dream-child while he was a prisoner of war—a horrible child of whom he is not the father. It howls in its neat perambulator whenever it sees his mangled face. And then, as usual, he has to race breathlessly after his Persian cat, Gurba, all through the dream-town, and to fight on a roof with a stray tom cat with a human face, and finally he crashes down through a burning sky of bursting shells and arrives on his bed in the hotel. When the dream reached this point, Doctor Otternschlag woke up.

"It's enough," he said to himself. "That's done it. How long have I to put up with it? And what's the use? No, we'll make an end of it."

He got up, and fetched his little case. He washed the syringe and broke the tops of one glass tube after another. Ten of them—twelve. He filled the syringe, and washed his arm, which was covered with little inflamed wounds from the needle. Then he paused. He began to tremble. All the strength ran out of his hands. He emptied the syringe without using it, spurting all its precious and surreptitiously acquired contents into the air with the exception of a few harmless drops with which he appeased the craving of his nerves. Then he lay down again, fell asleep and heard nothing more.

Count Rohna emerged from his room just after half past three, after being called up by the night porter, noiseless and circumspect and smelling of toilet vinegar, just as though it were broad daylight. He proceeded to Room No 71, took it all in at a glance and gave the necessary directions. He ordered a cognac for the shattered Preysing and flicked away a winter fly that buzzed round the dead man's body. He stood for a quarter of a minute with folded hands and bowed head. It looked as though he was praying, and perhaps he did indeed pray for the dead man—his equal by birth, and, like him, an outcast. It can't have been easy for him either, perhaps he was thinking, and then he went into his little office and began to talk on the telephone with Police Commissioner Jädicke, whose special duty it was to keep an eye upon hotels.

A little later, when the first street-sweepers were at work on the streets, appeared four gentlemen in overcoats, who bore the corporate and unpleasant name of the 'Murder Commission'. Rohna himself took them up in the lift to the second floor. The mills of justice were beginning to grind. The hotel management begged the police to use discretion in order to avoid a scandal, to hush things up, if possible. . . .

But it was not possible. Soon even Fredersdorf will know what has happened. Soon Frau Generaldirektor Preysing will arrive in Berlin with her apoplectic father, in order to part for ever with her husband in a succession of frightful scenes. That he had killed a man she could get over, in spite of her horror. But the disgusting affair with that woman—and this Preysing, stammering and perspiring and to his own undoing, had to confess at the second inquiry by the magistrate—*that* was utterly incomprehensible to her, and utterly unpardonable.

As for the dead man, Freiherr Felix Benvenuto Amadei von Gaigern, opinions were divided about him, although friendly enough. Not a single person in the Grand Hotel had anything to say against him. There was no previous conviction against him. He lay under no suspicion. He was not known to the police. He had a few debts, and how he had come by his small car (pledged, in any case, as security for a loan) could not be ascertained. But that proved nothing against him. He was a gambler, fond of women, often drunk, but always a good fellow. Some of the hotel staff wept over the whispered news of his death. The pageboy, Karl Nispe, with the gold cigarette case in his pocket, wept. This boy was one of the first witnesses to be called and he was able to declare that the Baron was not in his room shortly before twelve o'clock. A lady on the first floor, in Room No 18, the room below No 71, heard the noise of a fall at about the same time. She noticed the time particularly, because the racket above annoyed her. But what had occurred between twelve and half past three, and why had not Herr Preysing notified the police at once? The story was carried on at this point by the clear, if reserved, answers of the witnesses Flamm and Kringelein—those very answers which were read in the midday papers and gave the final blow to

Preysing's moral existence. As for the weapon that Preysing talked about, there was no trace of it, no revolver was found, not even a little pistol such as considerate burglars sometimes employ merely to frighten people with. This told heavily against Preysing. If he lied on this point he was to be distrusted on all others. True, his pocketbook was discovered in the dead man's pyjama pocket. But, asked the examining magistrate, worming his way into the matter, may not Preysing himself have purposely placed the pocketbook on Gaigern's person in order to give colour to the fiction of self-defence against a burglar? There remained the fact that Gaigern wore socks over his light boxing shoes. There remained, too, a photograph which Baron Gaigern's chauffeur had given the second chambermaid of the second floor, and this photograph enabled the wideawake police officials to say that this chauffeur at least was a notorious thief and criminal. If they succeeded in laying hands on him, more light would perhaps be thrown on the matter. For the time, however, Herr Preysing remained in prison, under remand, suffering from terrible optical delusions. He was always seeing Baron Gaigern before his eyes, not however as he lay there dead on the floor, but alive and so close that he was seen with extreme distinctness—the scar above his chin, his long eyelashes, every single pore in his skin—just as he had seen him as they collided outside the telephone box. If ever he succeeded in chasing the picture away, it was immediately replaced by a red haze beneath his closed eyelids, and then Flämmchen appeared, Flamm the Second—or rather a part of her only—her hips, as they were shown in a magazine photograph that fell into the General Director's hands, when the moment came for Destiny to send him rolling down headlong into the abyss. . . .

It is an odd thing about the visitors in a big hotel. Not one as he goes out through the revolving door is the same as when he came in. Preysing, the pattern of propriety, went out as a prisoner and a broken man, under escort. Gaigern was silently and secretly carried out by four men down the steps by which tradesmen entered—Gaigern the Magnificent, who used to make the whole Lounge smile if he merely passed through in his blue overcoat and his wash-leather gloves, with his alert glance and the perfume of lavender and Turkish cigarettes. Kringelein, however, when he and Flämmchen had given their evidence, and they were free to depart, passed out of the hotel like a king. Every back was bent and every hand extended for a tip. In all probability his glory will not last long. Probably within a week or two his next attack of acute pain will end it.

But there is just a chance that this courageous 'moribundus' may develop fresh resources and remain alive in defiance of every diagnosis. That in any case is Flämmchen's belief. And Kringelein, borne aloft in ecstasy, wishes to believe it too. And, after all, it is not so very important how long Kringelein has to live. For, long or short, Life is what you put into it. Two full days may be longer than forty empty years. That was the wisdom Kringelein took away with him, when he stepped out of the Grand Hotel at Flämmchen's side and got into the taxi that took them to the station.

It was then ten o'clock in the morning. The hotel wore its customary aspect. The charwoman swept out the Lounge with damp sawdust while Rohna looked on in silent disapprobation. The fountain played. In the breakfast room men with despatch cases sat smoking black cigars and talking business. The staff whispered together in the passages, but so far nothing had reached the ears of the visitors. Room No 71 was locked by order of the police and both windows remained wide open for the whole of the chill March day. Next door in Room No 72 the beds were made up afresh and a moist cloth passed behind the wardrobe. At eight o'clock the Hall Porter, Senf, came on duty. His face was puffy, for he had spent the whole night sitting in the cold hospital corridor waiting to hear whether his wife would survive till morning. He scarcely heard all that little Georgi had to tell him, and he swayed unsteadily as he sorted the morning's post.

"My head's going round proper," he said in extenuation. "You'd never believe what a difference the lack of a little sleep makes. And you say Pilzheim spotted that chauffeur. Pilzheim's a smart fellow, and I've always said so. If we had put him on the track of that Baron, all this would never have arisen to mess up the reputation of the hotel. Breakfast for No 22," he shouted out meanwhile to the waiters' room, and then went on sorting the letters. "Here are some letters for him. What's to be done with them now? Hand them over to the police? Right. Good morning, Herr Doktor, I wish you good morning," he said to Doctor Otternschlag, who had fetched up at the mahogany desk, yellow, lean and glass-eyed, after making his usual perambulation round the Lounge.

"Any letters for me?" asked Otternschlag. The Hall Porter looked for one, partly from civility, but partly, too, because in the last day or two a note had been handed in for Otternschlag by Kringelein.

"I am afraid not. Nothing today, Herr Doktor," he said.

"Telegram?" asked Otternschlag.

"No, Herr Doktor."

"Anyone inquired for me?"

"No. No one so far."

Otternschlag steered himself round the Lounge to his usual seat. Pageboy No 7 flitted behind him, and the waiter brought him coffee. Otternschlag stared through his glass eye at the girl at the flower stand arranging her flowers, but he did not see her.

"Good morning, sir. Good morning, madam," the Hall Porter said to a married couple from the provinces, who had taken a seat in front of his desk. "A room? Certainly. No 70 is free, a very fine room, double bed and bath; then there is 72, with two beds, but unfortunately no bathroom. Possibly 71 will be free today or tomorrow. That has a bathroom, a charming suite. Perhaps you would accommodate yourselves next door meanwhile. What? Hallo? I don't catch you!" he called down the telephone. "What is it? Yes, I'll come. I must go to the telephone, on a private matter. From the hospital," he said to little Georgi and stumbled off through the Lounge and along Corridor 2 to the telephone room and into Box 4, as the telephonist directed.

Doctor Otternschlag got up, wooden as he was, and came across to the porter's desk.

"Is Herr Kringelein still in his room?" he asked.

269

"No, Herr Kringelein has left," Georgi answered.

"Left. I see. Did he leave nothing for me?" he asked, after a pause.

"No. Nothing, I am afraid," Georgi replied with a politeness copied from the Hall Porter.

Otternschlag turned about, and went back to his seat, this time in a bee-line straight across the Lounge—a most remarkable event in his case. The Hall Porter ran past him. His blond and trustworthy old-soldier's face was wet with perspiration as though after some gigantic exertion. He came to a stop behind his table, as though he had reached a haven.

"It is a little girl. There had to be an operation. But there she is and weighs five pounds. No danger at all now. None at all. Both of them alive and kicking," he panted, and took his cap off—thereby revealing the radiantly happy face of a purely private person, but he put it on again immediately as Rohna looked over his glass screen. The married couple from the provinces got into the lift, and were taken up to Room No 72, the room with two beds and without a bath. The scent of Flämmchen's violet powder still lingered there.

"Open the window," said the wife.

"Yes, and let in a fine draught," said the husband.

In the Lounge, Doctor Otternschlag sat and talked to himself. "It's dismal," he said. "Always the same. Nothing happens. One's always alone, dismally, alone. The earth is an extinct planet—no warmth left in it. At Rouge Croix ninety-two men were buried in a fall of earth and never seen again. Perhaps I'm one of them and sit there with the rest ever since the end of the war and am dead and don't know it. If only something worth while would happen in this great big pub. But no, not a thing. 'Left.' Adieu, Herr Kringelein. I could have given you a prescription against those pains of yours. But no, gone without a word. And so it goes on. In—out, in—out, in—out——"

Little Georgi, however, behind the mahogany table was revolving a few simple and extremely banal thoughts. Marvellous the life you see in a big hotel like this, he was thinking.

Marvellous. Always something going on. One man goes to prison, another gets killed. One leaves, another comes. They carry off one man on a stretcher by the back stairs, and at the same moment another man hears he has a baby. Interesting—if you like! But so is Life!

Doctor Otternschlag sat in the middle of the Lounge, a stone image of Loneliness and Death. He has his *en pension* terms, and so he stays on. His yellow hands hang down like lead, and with his glass eye he stares out into the street which is full of sunshine that he cannot see. . . .

The revolving door turns and turns—and swings . . . and swings . . . and swings. . . .

A SELECTION OF POPULAR PAN FICTION

IN THIS HOUSE OF BREDE	Rumer Godden	35p
THE GODFATHER	Mario Puzo	45p
THE FORTRESS	Hugh Walpole	30p
VANESSA	Hugh Walpole	30p
THE ITALIAN WOMAN	Jean Plaidy	30p
COME TO THE WAR	Leslie Thomas	30p
IMMORTAL QUEEN	Elizabeth Byrd	40p
SYLVESTER	Georgette Heyer	30p
FREDERICA	Georgette Heyer	30p
COUSIN KATE	Georgette Heyer	30p
HEIR TO FALCONHURST	Lance Horner	40p
YOUNG BESS	Margaret Irwin	35p
ELIZABETH, CAPTIVE PRINCESS	Margaret Irwin	35p
ELIZABETH AND THE PRINCE OF SPAIN	Margaret Irwin	35p
AIRPORT	Arthur Hailey	40p
HOTEL	Arthur Hailey	35p
SHOUT AT THE DEVIL	Wilbur Smith	40p
WHEN THE LION FEEDS	Wilbur Smith	35p
THE SOUND OF THUNDER	Wilbur Smith	35p
VENUS WITH PISTOL	Gavin Lyall	30p
ONE BULLET FOR THE GENERAL	Patrick Turnbull	25p
DEATH IS OUR PLAYMATE	Patrick Turnbull	25p

These and other PAN Books are obtainable from all booksellers and newsagents. If you have any difficulty please send purchase price plus 5p postage to P.O. Box 11, Falmouth, Cornwall. While every effort is made to keep prices low, it is sometimes necessary to increase prices at short notice. PAN Books reserve the right to show new retail prices on covers which may differ from those advertised in the text or elsewhere.